B.A.I.T.

Before Arousal ... Ignite Temptation

B.A.I.T.

Before Arousal ... Ignite Temptation

R. Jill Maxwell

MAX ICEBREAKER LLC

"The only way to get rid of a temptation is to yield to it. Resist it, and your soul grows sick with longing for the things it has forbidden to itself."

—Oscar Wilde

For the best man I know, love, and still lust after and our fabulous growing family.

TABLE OF CONTENTS

Chapter 55

HURRY TO WAIT

PARAMEDICS HURRIED TO the eerie, quiet scene only to have to wait. It had been one of the most bizarre and misplaced events in suburban U.S.A., let alone well-heeled Scottsdale, Arizona. The dispatcher was professional and calm, though shocked when he sent out the order. "Bomb detonated. Police station. Via Linda and 91 Street. Possible four casualties. Car overturned."

Seconds later, when the fire chief arrived on the scene, he didn't even reach for the sirens to turn them off. He'd been so shocked by the call, he hadn't turned them on. Hit by the out-ofplace burning, metallic stench, he immediately barked directives into his shoulder mic. "We need an EMS and an ambulance. Young, we have to wait for the bomb squad to clear the area, but stage triage as close as they'll let you near the overturned car."

"Yes, sir!"

"Ground control, block off and evacuate the surrounding three blocks, sidewalks, and streets. Reroute traffic. Keep any rubberneckers moving!"

Once the bomb squad's methodical efficiency cleared the area, firefighters and paramedics split up to make rapid initial assessments—casualties, survivors, injuries, severity, etc. Thankfully, officers on the scene suffered only mild injuries. "One civilian female dead near exploded vehicle. One civilian female still in overturned vehicle very close by. Condition unknown."

As paramedics carefully removed the woman from the car, they searched for her driver's license. "Julie Archer. A local resident," one read. They checked her vitals and sought to stop the bleeding. Finally, they loaded her into the ambulance. Another unit pulled up to care for the dead.

Julie had suffered a severe concussion when the explosion had thrown her hard against the driver's side window. Her first responders, however, had expected this, once they'd checked her vitals and began treatment while still at the accident scene. Because of their diligence and communication with the hospital, the ER team's frequent guesswork process had been removed. The ICU docs intubated Julie and put her in a drug-induced coma soon after she'd arrived at the ER. Swelling subsided shortly thereafter, and the medical team expected her to fully recover. Several days passed, and both paramedics followed up after the accident. Though Julie still hadn't awakened, she at least now breathed on her own. One of them returned regularly to check on her, speak to her, encourage her, touch her.

I'm trapped in my own mind! Shit! This sucks. I can hear everything, but I can't respond. I can't move ANYthing yet, either. This is BULLSHIT, God! I KNOW You can hear me! she shouted in her mind. *WHAT's the lesson I'm supposed to get from this? You open to a deal? How about let's make a deal? You KNOW what's in my heart, Lord.*

She waited for His response. Silence.

Okay. I've been lousy about taking care of myself. Clearly, I need to get better at it. How about physical therapy and recovery massage? That counts, right? That'll be my regular selfcare. I get that.

Still, no apparent response.

How about I focus more on my writing then? She heard the question asked in her mind and listened. *I know I'm not alone in my mind. I know You're in here with me.*

As she quieted her thoughts, she became aware of a sign—the commotion in her room, the flurry of activity, the air movement near her bed, the increased number of voices that surrounded her. She was aware, though only briefly, that she struggled to move her hands!

At first, her nurse thought she'd hallucinated. Julie hadn't awakened from the induced coma after the breathing mechanisms had been removed four days prior. She'd seen accidents like this before, and patients sometimes took weeks to awaken, not typically days.

What Julie heard was remarkable. *I'm that "poor woman"? Okay, Lord, how long has this been? What about my kids? My husband? Did they consider pulling the plug? That was my wish if I should ever end up a vegetable. Did You show them that there's been brain activity? That I'm still here? Was that why they hadn't pulled it? Did my mom know? Has she been here? My sister and brother? What about my dad? Thank you, God!*

That's when she felt it. It wasn't one she recognized, but she knew she'd been touched by it before. *Must be a hospital aide.* The hand felt strong and rugged. She brushed aside that thought and waited for another more familiar feel or sound. Instead, she felt the room's dynamics change—again. They were quieter. He whispered in her ear, "I knew you were still in there. I knew it when I first saw you at the accident scene. I could feel that you'd be back. If you can hear me, move your fingers, or even just one. *Please* ..." Then his voice stopped. She was stunned. She didn't recognize his voice. Though he encouraged her, she wasn't sure if she should move even a hair.

Guardian angel? She asked for guidance.

With that, she moved several fingers. She could feel him smile, hear him breathe. The room was so still, other than the rhythmic pulse from her heart monitor. She chose not to focus on that. His presence was unmistakable. Strong, firm, and kind, he willed her to move her fingers. She could feel him urge her through his touch. Remarkable. Then she was exhausted.

No! Please, God, not yet! I … okay, okay. I get it. Time to rest. They know I'm still in here. That's all that counts at this point. I understand that. When will I feel my children's touches? My husband's? Why isn't he here? Does he come often? Will they call him now? Okay, time to rest. Got it.

As she started to doze, she could hear the gentle stranger once more. "Ah … rest. I'll share this good news, but I'll also spread the news that you need to rest frequently. Minimal visitors. Would it be okay with you if I came back? Maybe I can sneak in some waffles. I know you like them," he whispered close to her ear.

How do you know that I like waffles? She moved her fingers once more and dozed off.

When she awoke again, she could hear her kids and her tears began to flow. *Thank you, Lord! Thank you! Please fill them with faith to know I'll be back! Please, speak to them. Speak loud and clear,* she begged in her thoughts.

Then she heard her husband and felt his tears mix with hers, his kisses on her face, his warm, strong, familiar touch. She was sensitive to each of them as they caressed and held onto different parts of her—her legs, her arms, and her hands. *This is wonderful! They bring such incredible energy. Do they know this?* She basked in it, even if only, for now, in her mind.

Gabe asked her, "Can you hear us? Is that why you're crying?" His pain was palpable. Her tears just flowed, though. Julie did something that even excited her. She nodded her head but realized she needed to make a greater effort, even if it was subtle. She'd sensed them all more than heard them. It must have been enough because her husband started to cry harder.

They're all crying! Even the hospital staff! I hear high fives and cheers! They're applauding me! She grew more determined. *God, please help me move my head more or squeeze Gabe's hand ... a sign to let him know that I'm on my way back to him and our kids.*

Julie moved all of her fingers and toes, so each of her kids knew she could hear them. As she continued to cry, Gabe gently urged her. "Come back to me, baby. Please come back to me. These are incredible signs that you're still in there. I love you. We all love and miss you so, so much."

The kids repeated the same things. "We miss you, Mom." "We love you so much, Mom." "Come home, Mommy." "We need you to hug us and hold our hands, Mommy."

During the last chorus of "we love you's," Julie started to drift off to sleep, exhausted but peaceful. She heard the nurses calm their fears. "Remember, this was a huge amount of activity for someone who's been asleep a long time."

She caught a few more of her kids' words. "You just wait! This is nothing! Our mom's the best! She'll come back from this better than she was when it happened!"

With Gabe still by her side, he whispered, "I love you, baby. I miss you next to me in our bed. The dogs and kids are great company, but they aren't you. Please get better soon. I miss you so much." He kissed her lips gently, and she ever so slightly started to respond. He kissed her again, then the nurse, as touched by the scene as she'd been, insisted with a clearing of her throat that he be on his way with the kids. She reminded him that this was incredible behavior for someone in Julie's condition, and that he had every reason to feel encouraged.

"But make no mistake—your wife's road to recovery is very likely a long and bumpy one. You will need to be patient, more so than you've ever been in your entire life."

Firmer words had never been spoken to him before. Gabe hoped he was up to the task.

RELEASED

JULIE'S RELEASE FROM the hospital came faster than most had anticipated. Her skull had done its job and protected her brain, which remained unharmed.

"Told you so!" The kids' singsong voices cheered on their mom.

Gabe was thrilled, too, but for more reasons than he'd shared with anyone. First, he had to move back in, even if just to care for the kids and ultimately his wife. Few were aware he and Julie had even separated, so the synergy felt right. Guilt haunted him, too. He didn't believe Julie when she'd shared concerns that someone had followed her. *I know she stopped talking about it because of me. What was she involved with that not one but two cars watched her? Did they follow the kids around, too? Me? Who wants to know our business—and why?*

His fear turned into great irrational desperation. Days post-hospital release hadn't returned his "wife" to him yet, either.

"It's a lot to take in, Gabe. I'm home, but I'm frustrated by how fast I fatigue. Alone, I try to process and analyze events. All logic remains disjointed and unclear, like I'm trapped, wading in murky thoughts."

"Honey, you just got out of the hospital." Julie shook her head, though, irritated she couldn't understand everything her husband shared. She handed him the whiteboard and marker from her lap. He scribbled. "You had a *brain* injury, not a paper cut. Ease up on yourself." He watched her as he scratched out, "Remember, it's gonna take time and rest to heal." *Summon patience, Pal. You can't yell hurry up 'cuz my right hand gets tired.* In spite of his feverish desire to make love to her and validate her warm existence, Gabe's conscience kept his libido on pause and he was thankful for all that Julie hadn't yet recalled.

She was faithful to physical as well as occupational therapy and worked insanely hard. Her hearing challenged her more than any other area. Her humor showed signs of recovery, too. Through diligence, she shared with her therapists and husband, "I seek to blast the concept of a long recovery."

He coached her to be patient, yet even he heard his hollow words. Julie sensed Gabe's overwhelm rebuilding. His plea for her patience may as well have been a commercial turned up louder than normal to "Hurry up! I can't do this alone much longer!" Little did he know he fueled her single-minded focus. She was often recognized for her recovery efforts and sensed Gabe felt left out. He hadn't put words to his emotions, though Julie knew instinctively that Gabe needed validation, too—from her, from the nurses, from anyone—that Julie would make it all the way back and that his support mattered.

Gabe soon realized that it was because he took his ex-girlfriend's call again that his wife had ended up in this place. *I should have ignored her first call for a job or money. I didn't see any harm at that time in a phone call, although, somehow it felt so wrong.* He willed himself to stay focused on his wife and children now.

Chapter 56

"ADVISE"

"WHAT HAVE YOU done?" Dane Michaels demanded with quiet, gritted teeth as he pressed END on his cell.

"At this point, the real question appears to be what have *you* done, doesn't it?" Tate Parker sneered at his legal counselor. "What has Mr. Bosko accused you of? I heard a very serious tone." Parker's caustic sarcasm was palpable.

"You apparently already know, so why don't you tell me what I've done."

Tate laughed and continued his torment. "Do you think I'm that easy? Surely, you *must* have figured out by now, as I 'pulled myself together' over the years, I've picked up a few skills. Patience is one of them."

"I'm sure 'Greed Control' was a lesson skipped," Dane shot back, patient as he searched for a crack in Tate's icy demeanor. *Why does he hate me so much after all this time? It's not over just sports*, Dane considered.

"If you must know, that lesson was, more or less, fine-tuned. 'How to Put Greed to Good Use,' I believe was the name of that one, and oh, I assure you, I've gotten quite savvy. You'll be hard-pressed to find my connection to any wrongdoing." Tate feigned an innocent tone. "If I were you, Counselor, I'd start to worry more about *your* wrongdoings against me, your client, as well as against your meal ticket, your firm." Tate's snide tone change gave Dane goose bumps. "You've been a very naughty, greedy lawyer. After all the hard hours you've worked, you've felt rather undercompensated and underappreciated. I doubt anyone blames you for such feelings, but there were more honest, noble ways to address these issues."

Dane listened, stone-faced, surrounded by the hum of the coffee shop patrons. To not appear as horrified as he was, he quipped, "So I gather Bob's not coming."

"I called Bob and told him that all further transaction paperwork needed to come to me directly, since I may change legal counsel."

"He just accepted that?"

"Did he have a choice if he wanted to be paid?"

"What is it you want from me at this point?"

"To file the paperwork I send you once I've looked it over from Bob. That's it."

"Why would I do that? You're about to fire me."

"Who said I was about to fire you?"

Dane knew he needed to contact his assistant … a.s.a.p.

NAUGHTY?

"OH MY," RACHEL Michaels fretted. "My ex-husband's done something naughty? I didn't know such a Dane existed. It wasn't an accounting department error or a cashed-in investment?"

"I don't know exactly what *has* happened, Rachel." Victor Bosko sighed. "Not yet, but I'm sure I'll get to the bottom of it rather efficiently."

"Meanwhile, what did you want me to do about the additional money in my account?"

"Please open a new investment account in your name

and mine, write a check for the overage, and deposit that overage check into that new account. This way, no one will accuse you of whatever because both of our names are on it. Okay? Give me a few days to get back to you on this."

"Victor, I need you to call me back today about this. I'll ring my divorce lawyer after I leave here. I have to protect my children and myself. You understand." Her eyes cool, she rose and left his office, her body language swift and decisive.

Victor shifted in his desk chair uncomfortably, as he'd just become aware of Rachel's involvement in the mishandled money, more than he'd even considered. He just hadn't a clue exactly how or why—yet.

Chapter 57

RECOVERY

THANKFUL TO BE safe at home on the mend, Julie sat in peace in the backyard. She couldn't remember the last time she'd taken a few minutes early in the morning and just stared into a rare, dark, desert cloud, orphaned raindrops chased from it by newly emerged sunbeams. Though the shock of the explosion wore off quickly, her peace turned into an emotional setback and a primal fear. *When will this end?*

Several weeks passed before Julie heard again. Remarkably, the physical damage wasn't permanent. Nevertheless, that period left her frightened and with so many questions unanswered. Swift, disjointed friction developed with Gabe.

At first, he was tender, supportive, and cooperative. Within days, though, he grew impatient and edgy. "What did you write that you were followed, and then … then *this* happened?" Gabe's hands signaled anger and frustration around his own ears. "You never thought about your kids or me, did you?" he shouted. As he stood in their kitchen, he ranted. "Don't look at me like that. I know the kids aren't home, thank God, and you can't hear me, but I wanna know what happened. *Normal* people don't get followed by multiple cars, then have *bombs* explode in front of them!"

Julie was thankful for her inability to hear at that moment, given Gabe's accusatory expression. *Whatever he just shouted, it couldn't have been good.*

Though he sat in on all of the police visits and detectives' interrogation sessions, Gabe's attitude didn't soften until the police revealed the identity of the woman who'd followed Julie and seemed intent on confronting her at the police station. The couple was shocked and understandably confused when they learned it was Gabe's ex-girlfriend, Jennifer Davis, from high school. The police had been able to identify her. Still, they had no answers as to what she'd been up to, for whom, or why. Neither did they know why she'd left her car and started to approach Julie's.

"Julie, we know you can't hear much," Detective Lightfield yelled, "but ..." He scratched out his question on the paper Julie handed him. Lightfield read it aloud so Gabe heard him, too. "Have you any ideas why Mrs. Davis followed you?"

Julie shook her head, despondent at her ineffectiveness in the investigation thus far.

"Gabe, have you and Julie had any discussions in the past about her being followed, by whom, or why?"

Gabe hesitated. "Not about by whom. More about that she believed it had happened. I figured she was paranoid."

"Perhaps it's good your wife can't hear much because I have to ask you tough, related questions." Gabe's shift in his seat was the stereotypical signal to the detective that he'd found a button to push. "Were you aware that your ex-girlfriend, a Mrs. Jennifer Davis, was here?"

"Yes, I was."

"Did you have any contact with her while she was

here?" The officer paused, though they'd been through many of these questions before.

Gabe knew the police would go to phone records, if they hadn't already, so he confessed, quiet but impatient. "Jennifer had reached out to me when she first arrived a few months ago." He glanced at Julie and wondered how much she understood or heard. She seemed to sit breathless, still. He wasn't sure what that meant, but he pushed on.

"She'd asked me for a job, but I knew there was no way I could or should hire her. First of all, she wasn't qualified for any position that was open. Secondly, she'd hinted that she'd kind of … run away from home and left her kids with her ex-husband. As a dad who loves his children, I take great exception to any parent who abandons theirs. Then she asked for a loan until she got on her feet. Again, I told her no. I also advised her to go home to her children on the East Coast."

"So you never asked her why she was here?"

"Not in that conversation."

"How many times did you speak with her?" The experienced detective grew agitated with Gabe. He became more aware that the whole truth hadn't yet emerged and wasn't about to without a serious prod. *Don't people realize that the truth will come out regardless, so they might as well quit the delaying?* Lightfield groaned internally.

Gabe's eyes darted toward Julie, who remained un-readable. As if he'd heard Lightfield's silent thoughts, Gabe threw it all out there. At least it would be off of his shoulders alone. "The conversation I referred to was the second one, and we'd had it in person." Ashamed and furious with himself, he looked down at his jittery hands as if they might power his courage.

"When she called me the first time, it was to say hi and 'get together for old times' sake.' Of course, I asked her if she'd come out on business or was here on vacation with her husband. She'd told me she'd explain all of it when we got together. I told her I'd check the calendar with my wife to find out her availability, too."

"Go on."

Gabe shuddered. "A dull alarm went off in the back of my mind, because she said she was right in front of my office … asked if she could run in. Of course, I said yes. So she came through the front entrance, where I met her, and I was embarrassed. She looked nothing like the girl I remember from high school. Anyway, I gave her a friend-like hug and quickly walked her back outside to her car. I had a packed calendar of appointments and didn't have time for drama or drop-ins. She told me she and her cop husband—no offense—had divorced recently because he was very verbally abusive. She admitted she'd gotten screwed up on drugs with several of his 'associates.' Not all of you law enforcement guys are on the up-and-up. I'm sure I don't have to tell you."

Lightfield nodded, thoughtful.

"At this point, I just wanted to run back into my office and pretend I'd never taken her call. I figured her unscheduled arrival at my office was not a positive sign. But, as Julie will tell you, sometimes I let my heart get in the way when it comes to old ties. Jennifer was clear that she was here for money or work and to start a new life. But she'd abandoned her old one, which meant she'd abandoned her kids. As an employer, I know what that means—clearinghouse paperwork, deadbeat parents, irresponsible adults. I'm so over that crap."

"So she told you she came here permanently?"

"She didn't say that, but what do you think she meant when she asked for work?"

"Did she say where she was staying?"

"Yeah. She said she'd crashed with some college friends for a few nights. I wasn't gonna pursue that issue."

"Did she tell you why she chose Arizona?"

"No."

"What could she have been up to in Arizona? She worked for someone who wants information on your wife. What else came up in your chats?"

"Listen, Detective, I don't appreciate your tone. I didn't tell Julie at the time this happened because I didn't want any more shit on our plates. We've had enough marital problems without my fucked-up, drug-addicted ex-girlfriend added to the list, who, again for the record, contacted me. I didn't call her. I just try to run my business and save my marriage." Gabe scowled, his tone salty, his volume rising.

"Pal, I'm not here to judge. I don't care what you did or didn't do with the deceased … yet. I'm here to gather information. Just give me the rest of the facts about your conversations, in person, on the phone, wherever."

"I didn't do—"

"Take a deep breath, Mr. Archer, and share just the facts to the best of your ability."

Gabe took several deep breaths, though his muscles remained taut and defensive, then spat out, "I told her I had appointments, it was nice to see her, good luck, and sent her off."

"That was it? Did she ask if she could stop by again?"

"I dismissed her, so there was nothing further for her to say. But the next day, she called me again. I didn't take her call. I was on a conference call. She left two more messages. She drove by, saw that I was in meetings, and left. In truth, it was creepy. It got worse when one of my managers saw her, stopped her, then asked her if she was lost, needed help. Of course, she told them she was my high school sweetheart. She was here to cause me trouble, so my loyalty disappeared at that moment."

Lightfield sat, impassive, and took notes, though he recorded Gabe's every word. Gabe wondered, *What's so fucking noteworthy at this moment?*

The detective looked up, straightened his spine. "Go on, please," he directed.

"She called me again, and I took her call. I thought maybe if I just got firmer with her, she'd go away." His annoyance flared. "So the final time we spoke, she made it clear that she had a problem. She sounded nervous and very testy. She said she'd tell Julie we'd spoken. Her blatant attempt to blackmail me for money, a job, or where she could get one pissed me off. I lied and told her Julie already knew. She was desperate to find my Achilles at that point. Her next move was to threaten to cause a scene for me. She knew that I've never been one for public tantrums. Of course, what she didn't know is that I've handled plenty worse than that. She didn't like that she couldn't scare me, so she broke down in tears and tried to pull the 'chick card.' It was ... I don't know ... pathetic." A wave of disgust nauseated him. "Normally, a guy might feel flattered that his ex came on to him. Not my ex, though. She was ridiculous—a total turnoff. I told her again to go home, or I'd call her family and ask them to come and get her. She begged me not to tell them that she was out here. I told her to leave me alone, to leave my family alone. She got in her car, drove away, and the next time I heard her name was when you'd ID'd her body.

Damn this is weird."

Despite the cool room, sweat dripped down Gabe's back, his shiver involuntary. House fans circulated a perceived oppressive airlessness.

"We need to figure out who this college friend was that she stayed with. Mrs. Davis was bound to have left some belongings there. Her phone will prove useful. Glad you came clean with me before I had to ask you. Your number would have turned up on it from what you've told me."

"Lightfield, do you think she'd intended to hurt Julie or blackmail her? It feels like we've missed some detail, doesn't it? Like why Jennifer had followed her to start with?"

"Mr. Archer, that's just the tip of the iceberg of our questions. Clearly, she hadn't wanted Julie to know for weeks that she followed her. She wore her hair up under a baseball cap and wanted her identity hidden until she'd decided to approach Julie in the police lot. She kept a regular eye on her, knew Julie's every movement. It was also clear that Mrs. Davis worked with somebody who didn't trust her. I've assumed the second tail watched her, but who and why?"

"Don't the police have any more leads?"

"Frankly, until your wife can hear our questions, we have quite a game of 'fill in the blanks.' Your wife told dispatch that night she was never able to see whether there were one or two people in each of the cars behind her. She only determined that she was followed—pretty remarkable for a suburban mom ... um ... I mean, an untrained eye. They're usually the worst to pay attention beyond themselves, their kids, and their husband's whereabouts." The officer let the last option sit unanswered for a moment, then he looked Gabe in the eye before he continued.

"There's zero doubt about that now. The police had sounded skeptical when she had first called that day. Julie detected it in the dispatcher's voice. Mr. Archer, you're married to a sharp lady. Saved her own life. I'm not sure you realize how lucky you are. Anyway, Dispatcher Johnson's a professional. She'd later admitted she, too, figured it was a crazy Scottsdale housewife. The events of that afternoon blew up all assumptions. No pun intended. The second car that had turned around near the station was never stopped. The explosion distracted us. I'm sure that was part of the plan."

"Now I guess I need to take Jennifer's family's calls. You told them how she died?" Gabe almost didn't want to know.

"Bizarrely, the bomb was not what had killed Mrs. Davis directly. As she turned to speak with police, the bomb detonated and threw her against the fender of Julie's car. She hit her head directly on the temple, never knew what hit her."

"Crazy as this sounds, that's a relief to know."

"Why? You feelin' guilty about it?"

Gabe's spontaneous snarl caught the cop off guard. "Why the hell would I feel guilty? I'm glad she didn't suffer."

"You've a motive to make her go away. Blackmail is a pretty good one."

"Okay, seriously? If you're gonna go down that road, I'm gonna need a lawyer. I haven't done a damn thing. I wouldn't know how to make a bomb or who to call to have one made and ... NO! I DON'T have a reason—"

"There's no reason to yell, sir." Lightfield was aware

the insinuation was unfair, but then again, so was life, he reasoned. *Is it fair a woman's dead? Hell, it's out there. Let's just see how this plays out.*

Controlled rage boiled through Gabe's veins. "Yes, there is. I have an alibi. I have witnesses. I know I didn't cause any harm to anybody. I just go to work and try my damnedest to provide for my family and keep people employed. You know what I do in this town, so come on now." Sweat under his arms appeared.

SHAKEN, NOT STIRRED

WHO WANTED TO hurt Julie, and why? The question weighed heavily on the Archers throughout the entire recovery process. The police had only started to see a genuine threat just prior to the bomb explosion, which stunned them and validated Julie's fears.

Whoever this Jennifer Davis had become, at some point, she'd been a mom to her children. I can't imagine what had happened in her life that had been so horrible she'd left them behind. Now they were forever without her. Julie felt bad for Davis in spite of the angst she'd caused for weeks. *She must've been desperate to come all the way across the country to tail her ex-boyfriend's wife. I wonder if she'd felt her life spiral to its end.* Questions nagged like a leaky faucet. *Eventually, I need a conversation with Gabe about Jennifer, when I can hear again. Like, why was Jennifer followed? Who did she work for? How long had Gabe known she'd been in town? Had they spoken to or seen each other?*

The weeks she spent unable to hear left her to her own thoughts. *Silence. Plenty of it for me right now. Silence sits like a sharp knife in its block as it awaits purpose. It deafens but heals. A strange contradiction. I'm so tired of only my own thoughts and voice. How do deaf people cope, especially those who'd been part of the hearing world once upon a time?* Her temporary loss offered peacefulness at times from the "noise" of daily life until chaotic thoughts shouted in her restless mind. *The police had their suspect cornered but clearly hadn't expected a bomb to go off in the suspect's car. Who would've expected it? That's a very bizarre twist to this already strange affair.*

Julie's mind froze. *Affair. No. That couldn't have happened. Could it?* Julie brushed away the thought. *There's no way Gabe had an affair with his ex. No way he'd had anything to do with a bomb. No way. The last time Gabe had seen Jennifer, at least as far as I know, had been years ago, and it wasn't a positive encounter. So he couldn't have been aware of her recent in-state presence, right?*

Unless Jennifer had reached out to him, in need, maybe, and his kind-to-a-fault heart got enmeshed—unintentionally. Even if she had, he would've told me. For certain, he would've known that I wouldn't have been happy about it, but he would've shared this with me. He'd seemed distraught when the police revealed her name to us during one of our "interviews." When we saw her name written down it was a shock to both of us, but I'd brushed it off as us caught off guard about someone he once knew. Nevertheless, we all do that ... feel sadness when someone we know has been injured, lost, or terminally ill. She decided to ask Gabe about her wild thoughts. Julie was confident her imagination and skewed reflections were in overdrive now. *I'm in desperate need to hear something—anything—outside of my own mind ... and soon.*

Mercifully, her wishes were met. Each day, she was able to catch more sounds. As she heard her kids laugh and dogs bark, she let out a sigh. *Thank you, God!* She hadn't realized that she'd almost held her breath while she waited to hear again.

She decided to surprise Gabe with her progress early one morning and wandered toward his office. Though he was on the phone, he still assumed she couldn't hear and seemed almost annoyed at her presence. In order to communicate, he had to yell or write his thoughts down. They'd decided not to learn sign language, since the audiologist had expected a full recovery. He urged the couple to be patient and kind with one another. He'd sounded more like their former marital counselor than a medical doctor.

When Gabe finished his business call, he yelled good morning to her. She started to laugh, and he just stared at her, puzzled.

"What?"

"Why are you yelling?" Julie frowned at first. She waited for Gabe to pick up on what she implied. When a look of comprehension washed over his face, Julie beamed.

"You can hear me?" He still spoke loudly, but his eyes grew wide. His wife nodded. Gabe jumped up from his chair and reached for her to give her a relieved hug. Julie was so touched by his excitement—until his hardcore requests began. He expected her to take back some of the responsibilities he'd been saddled with since the incident.

Julie's face fell. *Was that why he was so happy? So I could relieve him? Not because I'd regained my hearing?* She must've worn her thoughts on her face and in her embrace because Gabe felt her go cold.

"What? What's the matter?"

Julie just shook her head with a small smile as her spirits fell and walked away. An acute awareness clenched her heart. *There's more to my recovery than I'd realized.* It would be a few days before she could and would attempt to explain to Gabe what tormented her mind that morning.

Neither comprehended what price the ordeal had cost the other.

Chapter 58

TOUCH BASE

DANE HEARD ABOUT the bomb explosion just moments after it happened. He knew Julie was injured but alive and safe. His contacts kept an eye on both her and her shadows. While he'd "cancelled" his tails in front of her, he'd left the message on his contact's voice mail. His contact would know that meant Julie was too aware of their presence and needed to back off.

Ever since some invoicing discrepancies with one of his accounts were brought to his attention, Dane wondered where they'd come from. He traced how they'd been discovered in the law firm's billing department through one of Isabella's reluctant counterparts. The embarrassed assistant hadn't wanted to tell Isabella that her boss might have stolen money. But as her friend, she hadn't wanted Isabella to be wrongfully accused again. Once by Dane Michaels' jealous now-ex-wife was enough.

While it seemed to be a simple case of greediness by the staff accountants, he knew they rarely acted on their own. A little friendly bribery and whispered confession confirmed that Victor turned Tate's mining company account over to Dane as part of that "greed." He just didn't know who had directed these inconsistencies—or why. *Was money kicked back to Tate? Does he call the shots? Or did Victor feel Tate wasn't honest in some way and wanted a piece for the continued legal "protection?" Was there someone else involved?* Dane hadn't figured that out yet.

He'd been shadowed for weeks, locally in Zurich as well as while he traveled overseas. Dane thought he'd get at least a small reprieve in the U.S. It turned out to be quite the opposite. There seemed to be multiple shadows on him and shadows on his shadows. *Shadows on the shadows.* Dane chuckled to himself. *What a bizarre notion. I know several of my clients run intricate businesses. I can only imagine how 'intricate' they must be if I'm so obviously watched.* He hadn't cared enough to know. Now he needed to care. "Plausible deniability is no longer an option for me. Rare are the moments in law when less information is better," he'd once shared with Isabella.

"I've never believed I'd be hurt if I just did my job and didn't ask 'unimportant' questions." *I've never even considered someone I know but outside of my business a potential target. Perhaps I've been presumptuous as much as Julie had thought she'd sounded paranoid. Her paranoia saved her life that night. Even so, my arrogance may have endangered her.* He decided to check in with Julie, but he had to do so without too much attention as to why he asked beyond her safety.

"Julie?"

"Dane?"

"Hey!" His heart leaped at her voice. "Yeah, it's me. I just wanted to touch base with you. I know we said that we'd give each other some space, but I'd heard about your horrendous incident. Are you okay?"

Dane Michaels entered Julie's thoughts more often of late, triggered by the recent discovery of Gabe's *high school ex's explosion involvement. "How did you hear? Couldn't possibly be that big of a deal in your neck of the woods. I mean, after all, you guys go through all sorts of crazy scenes over there, don't you?"

"You'd be surprised what makes news over here. We have a department that just listens for explosive issues, shall we say, around the world. Bombs, riots, rebellions, and so on. I know that sounds kind of outrageous, but in our business, we can't be too careful with any of our clients. We've a number of high-powered clients with conflicts, etc., so we rely on that special office to keep us abreast of world events. Because we never know where we'll travel at any given time, 'preparation is key to success,' as Alexander Graham Bell once said. Perhaps survival contributes to that equation as well."

"Yes, I suppose that makes a great amount of sense, particularly if you represent some less-than-classy clients." Julie chuckled.

"That's in all businesses, my dear. Money is money, and as long as we can make and process it legally, then it's all the same, isn't it?"

"Good point," Julie conceded. "So kind of you to think of me. Thank you." She was a mix of emotions.

"Of course I think of you. I think of you more often than you know." He softened. "And you're welcome." He almost felt the warmth of her face as it flushed, the sensual shade of pink it had always turned when she was just a little touched or embarrassed, a soft glow. "Well, I'm relieved to know that you're okay." He returned to a more businesslike tone. She heard someone interrupt their call. "I have to run for an appointment now, but I'll be in touch. Stay safe." The line went dead.

Julie just stood there and held the phone as if Dane was still on it. She wondered what he'd been up to since she'd last seen him at Starbucks and expected he'd be wildly successful, in spite of some of his scurrilous clientele.

Flattered and humbled he'd made the effort, she was concerned somebody in his office took the time to monitor such activities around the world. *Could that be true?* She'd many friends who were lawyers and thought it was a good idea to just ask a few questions. Although she trusted Dane, still an old Russian proverb jumped into her head—*"Trust but verify."* She continued to wonder how all the different and strange occurrences of the last few months, since her return from the reunion, since she ran into Dane at the Phoenix airport, were related to him. *That was when all the madness began. Hmm ... after more than twenty years, a bizarre coincidence or someone's impeccable preparation? How cynical.* She mocked herself.

Then she stared at the phone. *Preparation.* The problem was simple. Julie didn't believe in coincidences.

COFFEE?

"IT'S TOO BAD I employ you." She accepted the proffered cup of steamy coffee from her naked partner.

"Why is that?" He opted to tower over her and stand at attention bedside.

"You fuck like a porn star." She saw him twitch in her peripheral vision as she sipped her wake-up joe.

He stared down between his blatant arousal and her hardened, rosy tips. "So vulgar for such a refined lady."

"Oh, now I'm a lady? That's not what you called me last night." Her phony pout puffed a bit more by her still-swollen lips from the previous night's shag session.

A baritone chuckle at her pseudo little-girl lip further hardened him. "Given how that mouth of yours worked me, could you blame me?" He rocked his hips. Slow, provocative, then a growl emitted, low and deep. Like a call to mate, she turned her head to look at his impressive manhood and raised her cup to her lips. Always the gentleman, he reached for the cup and waited for her to submit. A fractional movement signaled the gift of her consent. They both accepted that Elena Bosko's only submission came in the bedroom.

Chapter 59

DIRECTIONS

"HOLY *SHIT*, JULIE! I didn't realize that was you who was part of that bomb explosion issue. I haven't seen all of the details that included the names of the people involved yet. There's only one name that surfaced recently, and it wasn't yours. I'm not at liberty to divulge who the other names are, but once I'm up to speed and can share more information with you, I will. So, my friend, give me a few days, and we'll speak again. Meanwhile, you have my direct number as well as my cell. If, however, you're truly worried or upset, please do *not* wait to call me right away, okay?" Aubrey hated to lie to her longtime friend, but she had a protocol to follow. Everyone's a suspect in an investigation.

"Thank you. Seriously. I feel some weight off my shoulders. I'm glad somebody else knows and cares. I started to feel like I was on an island here by myself, except for one person. Dane called the other day, said he'd heard what happened, and had been worried about me. It was sweet. I certainly appreciate your support, too, Aubrey."

The FBI Special Agent winced but followed along as she'd been directed. "That's what friends are for. Keep your head down, your eyes open, and give a big hug to your family for me. I'll talk to you in a few." As Aubrey hung up, Julie breathed a sigh of relief but felt her heart palpitate. She knew that conversation was intended to remain private. She also had a sense there was one person who needed to know what had taken place … a just-in-case measure. As Aubrey had taught her in college, backup was best, always safer.

Julie decided right then to trust that person, knowing he wouldn't be endangered by any information. *Now to find my keys, leave the house, and locate a "clean" phone—one that even if sourced, the tracers wouldn't understand why. Either I've gotten crazy paranoid, or my guardian angel smacked me over the head with intuition*, she speculated.

"Keys, cell phone, purse, water bottle. Okay, let's go," Julie spoke out loud to herself.

ISABELLA SHARES

R u alone? Dane texted Isabella, despite how late it was at home.

No. How fast do u need me 2 b? she replied.

Impressive response time given the hour. Now

Give me 2 sec

Ok hurry

Ok

Just seconds later …

There

This isn't normal. Isabella fretted.

Call me

"Hey, Boss. You know what time it is here, right? You okay?" Dane had never called Isabella at a late hour in all the years she'd worked for him. Her stomach lurched.

"No, I'm not okay. Our phones may be bugged, so we've got to be careful. I may need your help." *Oh, please remember this code.* Dane urged his young assistant with his thoughts.

"Stand by, Boss."

Dane heard some movement. *Is she dressing? Ugh. I interrupted who knows what.* He thought he heard her whisper. Then his cell disconnected. It rang right away from a strange number.

"Hello?" he answered, tentatively.

"Boss, it's me. Someone else's number. I know, Miss Obvious here. Your turn," and Isabella disconnected. *What the hell? OH!*

Dane turned to the young couple cozied up on the coffee shop couch next to his chair. "I'm so sorry to interrupt," he said in his most formal voice. He presumed his only slightly different accent would gain him approval. "I'm a lawyer. My cell phone has been bugged, and I need to call my assistant back in Europe. I wouldn't ask if this wasn't an emergency." He opted for the truth and crossed his fingers.

The couple looked at each other, then the young woman shrugged and said, "No problem," and handed Dane her phone. Dane looked at her and started to offer her money to cover the bill she'd receive. She stopped him. "Please, don't worry. I've an international calling card with unlimited calls to Europe. My parents insisted while I traveled over there the last few weeks. Help yourself."

What were the odds? "Awesome. Thank you."

He looked at his phone and dialed the number from which Isabella had last called him. He turned away from the pair. "Hey, it's Dane."

"Impressive, Boss, though I doubt we have long before they figure out what we've done."

"Listen. Tate and Victor have some sort of 'other' deal together. I can't guarantee who calls those shots, but I think it's Tate. Victor had been prodded to make a call to me yesterday here in the States at a specific time. He claims it was Rachel who came to him. I haven't pieced together her part in this yet—if there is one."

"We know your ex, Boss, and I'm sure she's involved. Sorry."

"Apology accepted, though not necessary. You're likely right, sad as that may be. After all, why would any woman, especially a single mom, report extra money deposited into her bank account? Why would she want anyone to know?"

"She did that? Is that what Victor said?"

"Yes."

"What a bitch! Oops, um …"

"Agreed." He heard Isabella catch her breath in relief. "Sorry it took me so long to say it."

She laughed. "Apology accepted. So what do you need from me?"

Chapter 60

UPDATE

THE COOL, CLIPPED voice on the other end of the phone sounded like a metronome on a piano. She spoke in exact, measured, and deliberate stern words. "What. Exactly. Happened?"

"She was a liability, Boss. Her drug issue got expensive. When she started with us back East, she was eager to do just about anything to escape her abusive ex and whiny brats. Once she got to Arizona, though, she became unfocused, shall we say. Turns out her mission and our mission weren't the same. I think she was so depressed that her ole high school flame wouldn't give her the time of day that her drug need skyrocketed. She thought she could blackmail me and had planned to go to the cops in Arizona that night. That's where the bomb detonated—in the cop lot."

Silence.

"Boss?"

"Excellent preparation, Tate. She never knew she drove a genuine time bomb. What clues do the feds have about her or us?"

"Almost none. Now before you wet your pretty, lacy panties in excitement, let me tell you what they DO know. They're aware that she hadn't worked alone, since Mrs. Archer spotted the second tail. We had to oversee our druggie. Anyway, Mrs. Archer communicated the secondary tail's existence to the police dispatcher. We were able to tap into that call to know this tidbit. The bomb explosion created an unexpected diversion, which allowed the second car to get away almost unnoticed." Tate paused and waited for her usual agitated sigh. *Hmm … none. Cool.*

"Officials here know she stayed with some old college friends until she landed on her feet. They know this because Mr. Archer picked up one of Jennifer's phone calls by accident. That's when she told him of her basic whereabouts in the Valley. Because she was never specific with him, he's not been of any further help to the authorities on that issue."

More silence.

"An autopsy will take weeks, but I'm certain they'll find drugs in her system. At that point, the whole event may be dismissed as an East Coast divorcee who turned to drugs to cope with abusive ex-husband cop, ran away to where her old flame lives in the Wild West, and hoped to win him back, or at least guilt him out of money. Her addiction ran into financial trouble with her supplier, who tailed her, and they blew her up before she could squeal. Her connection to Mrs. Archer will likely be seen as an attempt to upset the husband/disinterested ex-boyfriend, even possibly hurt, more like 'remove,' her. That's my belief to date."

"Admirable loose-end maintenance. What about the second car?"

"Chalked up to the drug dealer who confirmed problem managed. Even when they track it down, all rental ID was fake."

"Fine. Let's move on. Is the next car body en route to

Mr. Couvey?"

"Yes. The installation has been completed at the warehouse, and it's been en route for several days. U.S. Customs always takes longer than necessary to process any incoming shipments. Couvey will likely have it by week's end."

"Very good. Process this one as we have the others, and I'll be in touch with the next one's altered instructions."

ANSWERED PRAYERS

SO MY PRAYERS have started to be answered ... at last. She breathed, reassured for now for the first time in weeks. *I started to think Tate's learned patience had dried up. Dodged a bullet. Next—what to do with my dear Mr. Michaels. I'd press on any betting action that he's redirected his curious mind and knows bombs happen for reasons. Wonder how long before he figures this one out.* "Let's go for a run, pups."

Chapter 61

WAFFLES

SINCE HE'D BEEN called to assist at the bomb scene months ago, "Waffles" had complete access to all of the investigation records. His skill set went beyond that of the usual fireman. His extensive explosives education with the ATF, coupled with his engineering degree, uniquely qualified him for most urban fire departments. For those departments in the midst of a complicated transition from a privately held company to a municipally run one, he was the ideal, all-purpose hire.

His role for this case as the lead investigator was to determine all the usual bomb details. Basics like where the bomb was placed, how it was made, what it was made of, what kind of explosion it was, and how it was triggered would help the feds track down the responsible parties and determine their why. Though a firefighter, he still needed to make clear why his expertise was required to look at all of the facts to speed up his part of the investigative process. His reasons weren't all professional, however. He knew the survivor.

Once upon a time, as a young fireman who put himself through college, he worked hard to separate his emotions about those he rescued from his own. Early in his training, he'd witnessed an almost career-ending loss of a classmate. He'd also been in love with her. His chief had been through a similar tragedy and coached the young "probie" through his initial trial period enough to consistently compartmentalize.

For the first time in decades, he struggled once more.

Rarely was it celebratory when police and fire chiefs, crime scene specialists, FBI agents, and varied other unit detectives gathered. "This isn't your standard car bomb hole in the ground," he explained to the audience of crime scene investigators. "The pros who planted it wanted to make sure their target was eliminated. You've shared only basic information on the car, and that all came from the video cameras surrounding the station—make, model, color, year. The few tips received about plate information turned up that the exploded car was a rental. No surprise. Has anyone looked to see who rented the car? How it was paid for? A driver's license must have been shown at the time the rental papers were processed. Do we have a copy of it? An address? This is all you have?"

A few head nods and a couple of grunts, otherwise blank stares. "Let's check the video surveillance at the car rental place, surrounding businesses, even DOT's highway videos, etc., depending on which routes these drivers took. Also, we want to get a search warrant to request a cell tower dump of all cell users at this scene, as well as at the car rental place, once we zero in on the rental time frame."

He wondered if any witnesses had seen the second car and opted to broaden his scope of research. He started with where the deceased last lived. She'd left a clue in the cell phone found in her pocket.

When he'd arrived at the apartment complex, he looked around, thankful, even in his single status, to live in a well-kept facility. After his wife died, "Waffles" sold their home and moved into a dog-friendly community. A young neighbor, eager to make a few extra dollars, often apartment and dog sat when he travelled.

The building's frayed hallway edges betrayed the turnstile of tenants. Permanent stains and walls in desperate need of fresh paint held captive smokers' and alcoholics' habits. His forceful knock on the door left no one on that apartment complex floor with any doubt about his authority.

"Excuse me," he said to the woman on the other side of the closed door when she asked who was there. "Are you Jennifer Davis's college friend? She's been in an accident." No response. "I'd appreciate a few minutes of your time. I'm not a cop." With that disclosure, the locks on the door began to be undone.

A plain but polished-looking woman in her sixties opened the door as much as the chain lock allowed. She bore a paint smudge on her cheek, donned a bandanna, kerchief style, and appeared to be a seasoned artist. "Is she okay?" came the wide-eyed, affected reply.

"She's dead." *I could've delivered that line with a little more finesse, but then again, she's opened the door pretty fast now.* Waffles glanced at the woman's face as she scrambled to get the locks undone, looked down for a moment at his feet, and opted for a more gentle tone. "I'm sorry." *Not really.* "I could have said that with a touch more tact."

"Please, come in. If you're not a cop, and you're clear-ly not one of the bad guys, who are you then? Do you have ID?" She was quite matter of fact in her demeanor. He couldn't read if she was businesslike in the same engineer way he was, or if it was her preoccupied-artist-still-in-her-project whom he'd interrupted.

"I'm an explosives engineer assisting in the investiga-

37

tion—"

"You said you weren't a cop."

"I'm not. You trusted me enough to open this door and let me in. Please trust me enough to provide the information, and then feel free to ask me what you want. Okay?"

She nodded without another word.

"Did you hear about the explosion in the Scottsdale Police Station lot?" Another affirmative nod. "You also heard, then, that an unidentified woman died and another survived, etc.?"

"Yes."

"Jennifer is the one who died."

"Holy shit! You don't want me to ID her body, do you?"

"No, I don't. Haven't the cops been here yet? They're the ones who would have wanted you to do that." She shook her head no. "She wasn't blown up, though. Thankfully, it wasn't gruesome like that. She died as a result of a head injury. She got out of the car she drove to confront someone when the bomb detonated. The explosion's impact threw her down. Her head slammed the car bumper on its way to slamming the ground."

"Damn. No. No cops here yet, just a creepy dude with a ponytail who claimed to be an absent-minded detective who'd left his badge at home. I remember the *Columbo* TV show days, so I let that slide. When I realized, by his questions, he couldn't be a cop, I claimed to be sick with the runs so he'd leave." Her tiny smile approved of her clever exit strategy. "He did without any issues."

"What kinds of questions did he ask that turned you off?"

"At first, he knocked to ask if I'd heard about the

explosion. I told him I hadn't a clue. He asked if my roommate was home, was she okay. I told him she wasn't home and wasn't my roommate, just a visitor from out of state. That seemed to intrigue him because he commented that she claimed to be my roommate when he sold her an ounce. I asked him, 'An ounce of what? I thought you said you're a detective.' He chuckled, breezed past me into the apartment, and asked if I partied. Then I asked his name. He pretended to be a neighbor, just moved in down the hall, so 'no card necessary as a neighbor.' He smirked, then checked me out like I was some stupid broad who needed to get laid. Well, first of all, I know all of my neighbors and he isn't one of them. Second, a detective AND neighbor? Guess he figured I don't pay attention. And third, getting laid wouldn't be with him if in need. I decided that was my cue to get him out as fast as he came in and before I said another word."

"So other than the explosion and implication of a drug sale, he shared no other information."

"Right."

"Do you remember what day and time that was when he'd stopped over?"

"Hmm ... let me grab my agenda. It may sound strange, but I wrote it down after he left. That's how freaked out I was."

Waffles looked around the apartment. How odd for an artist to have an agenda. Whiffs of discontent stifled the immediate space, almost stale with complacency. He opted to call her out on his observations, figuring he'd been off in his tone from the start anyway. "Artists I know don't keep agendas."

"How many artists do you know?"

"Enough to know they could give a shit about their

calendars, unless they have an appointment to sell their art. The appointment's typically written on a body part then."

"You pride yourself on your observations, don't you, Mr.—Oh, I've not caught your name, either."

"And I've not asked for yours, for that matter. Let's keep this simple. Here's my investigator badge." He flashed it at her just long enough for some level of acceptance. "You can know me as the explosives engineer in case asked, and I'll keep your identity to just 'Jennifer's local college friend,' okay? I'd guess you were more like one of her instructors, though, than classmate, but I'm not here to judge." Waffles turned to leave. "Before I forget, did he leave a card in case you wanted to share anything? His number?"

The older woman shook her head.

"Thanks for your time.

This minor opening in the investigation is farfetched. He also knew that with this "off" information, Julie was in way over her head.

Chapter 62

POST-BOMB SOCIAL

WEEKS AFTER THE bomb went off in the Scottsdale PD lot, Julie recognized that, once again, she was followed or watched. She accepted that her intuition hadn't let her down before and couldn't imagine that it would let her down now. Nor could she understand why the police continued to come by to ask questions about Gabe's ex-girlfriend from over twenty-five years ago, especially why she'd followed his wife.

Julie grew more anxious and decided that since the cops weren't clear about what they sought, she'd check out some of their concerns herself. *Could their suspicions be more obvious? I'm confused about what, though. Might as well do what I do best—ask questions. Ask questions of friends, family, fellow business owners, even random strangers in line wherever I might be, the usual places I've turned up information, whether I've wanted it or not, couldn't hurt.* But most of the answers were the same. They knew zero out of the norm. Occasional replies were gossip about kids on drugs, spousal infidelity, teen pregnancy scares, etc. She learned nothing new or helpful … yet.

Julie didn't like to hear any of the local gossip. She kept at least an arm's length away from it all whenever possible, so she didn't take on any of that negative energy. She didn't like the way it sounded, nor did she care for how she felt when she heard about other people's lives. Idle talk always bore an impressive resemblance to invasion or even mean-spiritedness. It didn't matter that it wasn't her life. She knew so many of the characters in the chatter.

Though it didn't hurt to ask questions of this nature, Julie recognized she needed to be cautious. She had to be precise and consider who she asked what and how she asked them. Awareness was imperative. Such questions would get around to the person or persons who caused the trouble. She opted to make phone calls outside of her community to family and friends in other parts of the country with great expectations to drum up information. It worked.

One of Gabe's closest buddies was in town for an event that Gabe had a major role in running. Poker events turn up the most entertaining fans as well as competitors. They all have stories. Many are false, but a scarier number are true. One of the tournament competitors had been Gabe's high school and college classmate. Joe's sister had gotten horribly sick and recently died of liver disease. (That was true.) Another was that same sister had given birth to a child whose father was unknown. (That was false.) After a rapid round of catch-up over cocktails one night, Julie was on a mission to keep the beer and "boy talk" fluid. When gregarious but tightlipped Joe drank too much, he loosened up with regard to family updates, humor, and "guy" gossip.

"Hey Julie, do we have any more cold ones in the fridge? Can't believe I'm already out. Must be a hole in the can." He chortled, thought he was funny. Julie ignored the comment, since she'd heard it from him too many times to count that night alone.

"Of course, Joe, and while I'm out there, I'll put a few more in the fridge. I'll be a minute, though. Good idea, guys?" Julie could tell from his tone that Joe hadn't finished his beer and was simply anxious to gossip with Gabe. So she hung around the corner and waited.

"Gabe, listen, before Julie gets back, have you heard any of the gossip about Jennifer? There was shit-talk in the air at home that she came here, or was headed here, to 'talk' to you. I think I know the last time you two spoke. Wasn't it years ago at our high school reunion? You didn't part friends, right? She was pretty messed up. So I thought it was really weird when I heard that crap. Any truth to it?"

Julie covered her mouth to keep her gasp to herself.

"Yeah, there was truth to it. Before I tell you about it, though, what'd you hear about *why* she'd want to talk to me?"

"She supposedly wanted you back. Yeah, don't look at me like that. I find her pathetic, too. I felt, though, it had less to do with wanting you back and more like needing money. She got into some bad shit."

"What are you talking about? I heard she got divorced and had kids. I'd also heard that she worked, though."

Joe hesitated and looked down at his hand clenched around the beer can.

"What?" Gabe pushed.

Self-critical, Joe's words slurred in hushed tones. "As if I would've made such a different choice given your situation."

Gabe sat there and turned red and irritable. "What situation? What are you talking about?"

"She said weird shit. I can't even imagine why any guys, 'cept maybe her husband, the prick cop, would wanna be with her. I wouldn't touch her with a ten-foot pole, let alone meet with her."

Gabe fumed as he lied. "I didn't meet her, Joe, but I did speak with her on the phone. She said she wanted to meet me, but I said to get together I had to check with my wife and her schedule first. I told her that I'm happily married. When she got pushy, I felt uncomfortable and reminded her we had zero left to say. She cried and spewed her story that at least one of us was happy, she was a divorcee loser, and what a deadbeat dad her ex was with their kids. I said that it was too bad to hear and good luck. As I started to hang up, she did ask me to loan her money, but I started to get pissed, said I couldn't. She sobbed and insisted we meet. She wanted to apologize in person for the way she'd acted at that high school reunion. I said thanks, that she'd just apologized, no need to do so in person. I confirmed that a personal visit wouldn't change my mind about the money loan, and I hung up. That was it!" He finished his partial truth in muted but emphatic tones.

As Julie weighed Gabe's reactions, they troubled her. *Why'd he just lie to his longtime friend? I know the truth from his confession to the police detective. He'd always had a big heart, literally often to a fault. He just isn't the type to cheat.* Though she'd considered him in that light only once before, she wouldn't wrap her head around such a skewed concept with Gabe. *Am I naïve?*

After a brief recollection of a challenged, lonely time in their marriage, Julie decided then that his tremendous indignation was her fault, at least in part, for false accusations. As other events in their marriage unfolded in less complimentary ways, the couple chose to trust each other. Instances to cause Gabe, the boss, trouble, even attempted blackmail, arose due to other people's jealousy or greed, and the lure to make a quick buck tempted even a few of the faithful. Since her spirits fell with every strike, she chose instead to not feed that green-eyed beast and to think highly of her husband and their marriage. *Solid expectations usually yield solid outcomes, right? He knows better than to get caught up in seedy choices. Not our style,* she reminded herself. Unfortunately, as a human, one is often left with too many options and perhaps too much room for error.

Have I only lied to myself all these years? Is it time to open my eyes? I know if he's lied to his best friend, he might lie about other details. It's his journey, and I know it's not for me to judge. Guess I have to ask him some questions.

DATE NIGHT

GABE AND JULIE recognized they struggled on professional as well as personal levels. Their lives, overscheduled and in perpetual motion, moved in varied directions between their four kids, careers, events, and travel.

"You know, what we really need is to remember why we enjoy each other's company."

"Uh-huh."

"Have a little fun."

"Yup."

"When we do that, we're able to reconnect easily, right?"

Gabe's nod was almost imperceptible.

"Solve problems, *love* each other. Let's just go back to the basics." Julie breathed patience into her last sentence. "The K.I.S.S. method? Always effective. Keep it simple, silly."

They picked a night, reminded the kids to call only in

case of an emergency, and to be good to each other. Of course, there were always the typical last-minute safety reminders.

"Don't open the door to strangers."

"We aren't expecting any deliveries or people."

"No friends over unless we talk first."

"Turn off the oven after baking."

The kids' unison-droned response, "Yes, Mom," made Julie and Gabe either wince or laugh. "We're just up the street, so we can be home in three minutes, but ONLY if necessary ... as in an extreme reason." They kissed each child, doled out specific instructions, then headed to The Office, their neighborhood bar and restaurant.

Just after they'd ordered dinner, a group of their friends walked in. "Oh boy," Julie simply stated. "We knew before we got here this might not be the best place to stop for a datenight dinner and private discussion."

"I know," Gabe chimed in. "Still, we wanted to see the Cardinals-Eagles game ... supposed to be one of the best matchups of the early season."

Julie nodded. *Often, our tougher talks seem easier to sort through, to find common ground faster, if our focal point isn't the conversation.*

"We may get sucked into this, you know."

"Why can't we just tell them we'll join them shortly?"

"We can try, but you know how they get. This is usually a fun group."

"I know, but we've got to take at least a few minutes for us. How about we join them after we eat?"

Gabe agreed, especially since they'd placed their order right after they were seated.

However, this particular group of friends had the art of distraction perfected. "HEEEEYY!" Shouts of familiarity rang through the restaurant. The Archers wouldn't get off the hook easily. After all, everyone knew this as a place to gather, not a place to get down to "serious" business!

Dinner with friends at a local sports bar was fun, but it wasn't conducive to overcoming relationship challenges. In fact, at times it created more.

"Shit," was all Gabe muttered to Julie, who hadn't decided if this was a better idea than what they'd planned.

"All the goofy energy makes it nearly impossible to focus on even remotely serious topics." Gabe's point was valid, and his inclination to avoid a heavy discussion was obvious. "We're also intensely private people, baby, who detest any possibility of others in on our personal business."

"True. So what do you suggest?" The brief respite from all their serious stuff felt well timed. They agreed to join their friends and talk the next day.

While the four couples gathered in a darker area over by the restrooms, the Archers' food order followed them, drinks were ordered, and the energy and laughter were lively. The group's goal was almost always to poke fun at themselves, but not each other. Talk of crazy occurrences in their kids' schools cruised through conversations. Otherwise, most matters about children were avoided. As the norm, the vibrant, talkative gang kept adult time strictly adult time. So when their corner of the room went silent, all eyes dialed in on the same sight.

"Oh shit," Gabe mouthed to his wife who sat across from him equally stunned.

A couple emerged from the same bathroom, and they weren't married to each other. What had transpired was quite plain. This wasn't supposed to happen … not within their friend group.

Arnie and Rose were married—just not to each other. Yet they emerged from the men's room together, a bit flustered, the stereotypical lipstick on the side of his mouth and neck, her mascara smeared suggestively under her eyes. They hadn't anticipated a stunned and silent crowd to welcome them from their obvious tryst. No one had been seated in that area when they had disappeared at that end of the bar. Arnie looked completely guilty while Rose appeared only flushed, clearly a seasoned swinger.

Shock and shame broadcast across the group's faces. Rose, though completely caught off guard by the presence of familiar faces, immediately tried to lighten up the surprised looks.

"No applause? Guess I've slipped as entrances go," she quipped. "I'd stay, but I've got to pick up at gymnastics. See ya, kids!" She scurried after the already-disappeared Arnie.

Guilt spread, as they knew they wouldn't share with Arnie's or Rose's spouse what they'd just seen.

One couple voiced what everyone else likely thought. "Okay, did that just happen? Is it possible I just had a bad dream, and we're all in it? All of you realize that we're now part of their cover-up, right ... which we choose to keep quiet?"

"Crap," came another reply.

All wished somehow the now "outed" couple would stop any future hookups or that their spouses would somehow find out—just not from one of them. Each had heard stories of infidelity, but not within their crowd. Theirs had been one of respect, family, laughs, and friendships.

Julie's flesh prickled. "I can't speak for anybody here,

but I'm confused and pissed and … well … what you do behind closed doors is a private choice. Bring it public, like that"—her palm outstretched toward the bathroom door—"then it's no longer private, is it? I mean, don't shove it in front of friends in a place frequented by them as well as neighbors. Clearly, they wanted to be caught. We could have been their spouses."

"So their choice was about as illogical as … say … trying to have a private, serious talk in a neighborhood bar, right?" The gentle tease thawed the frozen faces, drinking resumed, and stunned whispers gave way to laughter. It took a while for the heavy atmosphere to lift. Of course, the "ugly exposure," as someone called it, was a heated topic of conversation for Gabe and Julie, however, once they got home.

"Well, we went from awkward to fun, back to awkward, then back to just some level of fun, and well, here we are at awkward again," Julie summarized.

"Okay, what does all that mean? Well, at least the last part of it. I get the rest." Gabe grilled Julie with a bewildered and aggravated tone. "What did I do?"

"More like what we *didn't* do, except drink too much."

"What the fuck? We had fun! You drank, too."

"That's what I said. But I could still drive, honey."

"Pleasantly tipsy does *not* make me drunk. You took my keys, which was like permission. Your choice. Jesus F. Christ. Don't act like some righteous prude."

"Whoa! That's extreme."

"Is that what's so awkward? A little alcohol?"

"No. What's awkward is that we didn't get to discuss what we needed to discuss. We succumbed to peer pressure by our usual cohorts, which kinda meant neither one of us placed a priority on our relationship. Then we faced one of the ugliest moments of our entire time here by two people whom we know and thought were quasi-happily married—at least I thought one of the couples was. Evidently, the ole saying that goes, 'you don't know what happens behind closed doors' is truer than we sometimes care to realize."

Gabe's abrupt, almost vacant, expression snapped Julie to attention. "All true."

"I know that if"—she hesitated—"*you* had been un-happy enough to be involved elsewhere, I'd want you to talk with me. At the very least, I'd want somebody to care enough about me to tell me. Wouldn't you?" Again, Julie paused. "And yet, I can't even imagine how or which one of that crew would be brave enough to share with either of us." Gabe's demeanor cooled. "Maybe that's the point. Does anybody care enough to talk about what happened?" She puzzled over this, conflicted. "No one has the guts, decency, or perhaps personal interest to stand up for the truth," she lamented. "I suppose that includes us."

Indignant to an extreme, Gabe about-faced and seethed. "What are you saying?" The horrified expression on Julie's face made Gabe pause, regroup, and calm his tone a tiny bit. "Julie, stay out of it. Please. We do *not* need to get any more involved than we already are," he cautioned, defensive, borderline aggressive.

"I know." Guilt flooded her. Her eyes lingered, hurt at his tone, unsure. "I agree. This is awful. Neither of us is close enough to say a word, yet neither are we far enough to be disconnected from it. Must be what purgatory feels like. Limbo torments."

"Just stay out of it, okay?" Another extreme emotional swing as his vacant expression returned.

"Fire then ice. Aggressive then passive. Sheez. You've

already said that. So insistent." Julie teased and chuckled, but then frowned as her husband's reaction to her silly tone morphed from haunted to soured.

Whoa. What the hell's happened?

Chapter 63

AIRPORT, TAKE TWO

"I LOVE YOU. Call me as soon as you land, okay?"

"Of course. I love you, too." Julie smiled as she kissed her husband good-bye just before she headed through airport security. "Thanks for walking me in. You didn't have to."

"I know, but we had some extra time, and we've needed to take advantage of every minute, right?"

Months had passed since the Arnie-Rose debacle, and the couple reevaluated their issues. Gabe focused more on greater balance and harmony between home and work, understood that Julie needed her own career again, and began to share in her excitement ... a little. He wasn't always thrilled because it meant she traveled alone more, while he had more "kid duties." Julie, in turn, recognized Gabe's support and efforts. As their appreciation for each other grew, their attraction reignited, too.

A little time and distance apart won't hurt us, that's for sure. She was amazed at how her love for Gabe had grown more than she'd ever imagined it could. "Wow. I'm so impressed that you feel that way."

"Ah ... so you thought I didn't pay attention in our conversations?" He grinned. "We chose to make our marriage work." Gabe slid his hand around Julie's waist and kissed her deeper. "Safe travels. You look so beautiful, you make my heart ache, and you haven't even left yet."

"You're so sweet."

"Nope. I'm *not* sweet, just honest. You're beautiful, and I *do* need to tell you more often."

"Thank you." She blushed and looked down. "Okay, I better go. I love you. I'll call when we land."

"I love you, too."

As she left him at security, she glanced back once more to catch his eye. Instead, she saw him check his cell phone. A wistful sigh escaped. "You grumble about how much you work." She teased him.

"We're busy gettin' our asses kicked already today."

Julie chuckled. "Hmm ... if the opposite were true, slow to no business, you'd 'cry me a river,' right? First-world problems. Thank God for them! I have faith in you."

As she stood in the security line, she said to herself, "Oh, crap. We spaced about our imminent travel plans for Katie's basketball tournament." After she fumbled to reach her cell, she shot a text to Gabe, who'd already left her line of sight. She excused Gabe's sudden disconnect— again. *He's busy.* "This is good, right?" she stated aloud to no one in particular. *This bittersweet sensation must come from the fact we're in a better place.* An introspective smile crossed her lips. *Focus on you right now*, she reminded herself. *This is your time to zero in on what's important to you. Don't walk! Run to it!!*

She made her way through the scanners, gathered her property, and beelined to the coffee shop counter. "Some proper fortification for flights, right?" she asked the mom with the sleepy stroller baby ahead of her in line. Typical new parent chitchat while they waited for their drinks. As she turned to walk away from the cashier with her hot venti latte, she never expected to look up and see someone she knew, though almost every time she was in any airport she did. Typical "It's a Small World" moment. But this time, *who* she saw nearly caused her to drop her hot coffee.

"What the … oh, shoot. I'm sorry!" *This is too weird.* "This man's entirely unexpected, anywhere," she mumbled aloud, mopping up what spilled on the young mom's diaper bag.

"Thankfully, just the bag. Have a better day."

The women chuckled, but Julie was preoccupied. *Here he is … again … in Phoenix?*

Over the years, she half-assumed she'd run into him. As she contemplated his reappearance, she speculated probability was low such a reoccurrence would happen, let alone in the same airport. She felt her face flush and the buried warmth resurface, as she recalled her deep attraction to him.

Yet, here he was—again.

LISTEN

ISABELLA PAID ATTENTION. Discreet attention. "Good thing I love my job and my boss," she cooed to the bamboo plants in her shower. "Otherwise, I might believe those 'poor single mom' bullshit stories from his ex. She gives single moms a bad rap. She wants for nada, other than her ex-husband's attention, despite her knowledge that one, he's not interested, never was, and two, his clear messages confirm that no chances exist, either."

She reached for her fresh towel from their newly wall-mounted towel warmer and sighed. "And, weirdly, according to the break room gossip queen, Rachel's confession to Victor about extra money is meant to stir up trouble between partner and partner-to-be, even innuendo that she'd had an affair with Victor. What is that woman up to now?"

DIVINE OR DESIGN

HE SEEMED TOO preoccupied to notice her, so she pretended she hadn't seen him, either. She fidgeted with another napkin, dabbing spilled latte from the cup's side. *Better to play it safe until I have my thoughts gathered and feel more ... prepared.*

She made her way to her gate and settled into a seat as well as a moment of clarity. His repeat appearance was no coincidence. *What the hell.* She decided not to miss an opportunity to answer an obvious question. *Hmm ... perhaps I'll gain the closure I still want. I also wonder why Dane would have met with Tate Parker? They're no longer friends, if I remember correctly.*

As she re-gathered her belongings, her skin prickled with goose bumps. Her sixth sense detected a presence. Slow and deliberate, she lifted her head on an angle, just enough to catch the point-blank observer almost toe-to-toe with her.

Dane looked down at Julie and smiled.

She smiled back and said, "I *just* began to gather my stuff to come find you. I didn't want to miss the opportunity to say hi and have closure."

He confessed the same. "In fact, I'd done a double take, hopeful you'd run away, just as you did. That way, I didn't have to feel the pain of our last, premature goodbye. Didn't matter. Still felt it. This is your gate, too?" He ignored Julie's closure statement.

Of course. She chuckled and nodded in agreement.

"It's mine as well. We're on the same flight, as fate would have it."

Julie didn't believe in coincidences. *Fate? Meant to be's? Maybe. A reason behind why the stars align this way? Whatever the reason,* she decided, *I'm gonna take advantage of this opportunity.* A weird sensation of mistrust crept over her as she wondered why he was here. *Legitimate? Contrived?*

"This is like an out-of-body experience. In the airport on the way to complete some research, about to be interviewed for my brand-new sequel, and run into an ex-boyfriend ... seems sort of soap-opera-ish. Is this real life?" She giggled because she remembered her youngest daughter had asked the same question throughout her early teen years. *I finally understand this phrase!* She laughed aloud.

"Are you laughing at me?" Dane cringed, his self-consciousness a rarity.

Julie clasped her hand across her mouth, eyes as big as saucers. "Oops, didn't realize I'd laughed out loud! Sorry."

"I thought the very same thing as it came out of your mouth!" he continued.

"How many times have my teens said that to me, and I thought they were ridiculous. But right now? I'm so relieved to hear you thought the same."

They laughed easily for another moment. "Where are you off to, and why not in one of the company jets?"

"I'm headed to Chicago for a few days to finish a deal. There's a buyout in process, and the company I represent wants me to go and check on them—a kind of unan-nounced spot check. You?"

"I'm also headed to Chicago for some"—she hesitat-ed—"research on a story. Wouldn't you normally come from back East? Why through Phoenix?" *Again?*

"Normally. This will sound obnoxious, but there have continued to be ... well ... challenges with the fleet. They're grounded until the issues are resolved. All company trips, which are well planned out, are now more of a challenge than usual. I was supposed to fly through Dallas, but the weather events there caused us to be rerouted through Phoenix—again. And you? What story? Why Chicago?"

"I've been working on an auto exposé." Julie paused for effect, her mouth dry. "Chicago and Detroit are ... um ... car cities." She watched Dane's reaction.

Dane felt his world shift. He didn't understand why, but he suspected this day would come. *This is too weird. Company jet out of order, weather problems, reroute through Phoenix—again—where she lives ... and she writes about cars? Why does that worry me?* His insides lurched, and a chill ran through him.

He tried to appear unaffected and replied, "Such spontaneity between us is clearly meant to be. I mean, funny how things work out, wouldn't you agree? We run into each other here in Phoenix. Again. At *this* airport, headed to the same city." *She blushed?*

Just then, an announcement came over the loud speaker in its usual garbled, airport tone. "Ladies and gentlemen, Delta flight 1492 will be delayed another twenty to thirty minutes. The weather pattern headed at us makes takeoff too dangerous, so the tower is holding all flights on the ground until it passes. They've assured us that it seems to be a swift storm front. Please stay in the vicinity of the gate for further announcements. Thank you."

Dane and Julie resettled into seats after the announcement and watched the sunset as the storm loomed over Sky Harbor. The subsequent colors of the sky, typical for the desert, amazed airport onlookers. The collective breath held, anxious over the imminent delays. Even within the crowded gate area, the atmosphere felt intimate. They were just two people who'd known each other, well, years ago and now lived very different lives.

He decided, for the moment, he'd keep the tone very professional and even tried very hard to just imagine her as one of his client's acquisitions. But he found, as he sat there next to her, he was overwhelmed by his conflicted thoughts and emotions. *Stop it. Stop with the self-torture about our last kiss. It shouldn't have happened. She's married, Pal. Get over it. Tate's early arrival at our last meeting spoiled any further chances anyway.*

He was drawn to her, almost ensnared. *And I thought I'd been over her all these years,* he reasoned with himself. *SHIT! I knew one day I'd run into her, but I never expected that I'd be more fucking attracted to her. Who the hell would've thought she'd be more beautiful each time I saw her?* He snarled at his own denial and recalled a long-ago warning from his mother. "To let Julie go for long would prove the worst choice you could make, Son." *How right she'd been. She'd warned me that Julie would age magnificently in many ways.* He thought he rolled his eyes at himself inwardly, but Julie observed him.

"Wow."

"Wow what?"

"You'd think that you'd been forced to sit here with that look of disgust on your face, or you're so spoiled and aggravated that you're not on your private mode of transportation. Welcome to the real world." She sounded put off as she teased him. She'd picked up on his mood, as she always had.

Oh boy. Time to backpedal a little with her, he cautioned his thoughts.

Look shocked and contrite. He stuttered. "Oh … um … was I … was it that obvious? I'm sorry. I guess I *am* more spoiled than I realized. Fly the way I do, yes, it does spoil people. As far as the company is concerned, I couldn't have chosen better. I'm terribly sorry if I offended you. Sincerely, I am."

She smirked. "You're good. You certainly haven't lost that off-color, charm-and-avoid technique."

"Wait, what? That was a genuine apology. Seriously."

Julie continued as if Dane hadn't spoken. "I know about the way you fly. You've forgotten my dad used to have a plane? Albeit not a big jet, but private nonetheless." She chuckled. "It's a great way to travel. Very indulgent, as you know. My husband and I have had the privilege to fly privately on a few business trips. Very nice." She thought if she mentioned her husband, the troublesome guilt might be alleviated.

This is absurd. Do I think I need to have a chaperone present? Seriously? What's with me? I'm a grown-ass woman who can talk with whomever I choose! She failed to notice Dane's slight cringe at the mention of Gabe.

His legal wit supported a quick recovery. "So"—he couldn't help but smirk—"what have you been up to this last year, besides playing with bombs?" *What a line.*

She laughed a peculiar laugh that left him to wonder exactly what she'd been doing. She turned the conversation to him instead. "I'll ask you the same question." With a mischievous look in her eyes, she continued. "You met with Tate Parker, went back to Zurich, and then?"

He sparred back. "Well, I went back to my usual legal world—unlike you, apparently. Have you figured out why that happened?"

"You *follow* that sort of event. You don't know?"

Dane chuckled with a little, playful grin. "Touché, and no, I don't."

Julie knew he wasn't on the level and hadn't a clue why. She toned down her gut reaction, however. "I'm surprised." She still dug a little. *Dane's amused. That's clear. Why do I feel a twinge of disappointment?*

"What do you mean?"

"You called fairly quickly after I'd left the hospital. You'd had me followed and—"

"If you'll recall"—he interrupted Julie, then paused as he often did with clients who needed to be humbled—"*you* had me cancel that tail. *Explosions* are *news.*"

She didn't appreciate his tone. "Oh, I remember. Forgive me. If I recall, you cancelled your associates, and then I found myself double-teamed within days again. I'd planned to follow up with you, but then life sort of … well … blew up."

The dismayed look on Dane's face stopped Julie's edgy banter. He shifted subjects.

"So you work from home?"

"Nice change of subject."

He opened his mouth to make a comment but snapped it shut. *Called out.* He took a calm, deep breath instead and nodded. "That was fair. I'd still like your take on the work from home concept."

Julie sensed his edginess with a bit of chauvinism versus Dane's proclaimed curiosity and opted to challenge him. "Before I answer that, let me ask you how involved you truly are with your kids, their activities, their schedules, etc. as a *single* dad. I certainly don't hear you speak of them often."

As a shrewd lawyer, Dane knew this type of counter was a setup. As a divorced father, he knew he'd wandered into dangerous territory. *Rachel hung me by my short ones to win the decision as resolutely as she had.* He realized he'd let her down most of their marriage.

"Okay, hold on. I love my kids. Easy, killer. I merely asked a question. A bit sensitive, are we?" He tried to turn the focus on her.

"Ah ... got it. So you weren't all that involved. That's how your wife won the divorce big. Now you've had to step up your game with the kids so they don't call her new partner 'Daddy,' right? Did I miss anything?"

"Ouch. How did you ... I thought I was good," he conceded with his hands held up, as if Julie held him at gunpoint.

"Well, you'd definitely not be the first chauvinist I've had the pleasure to chat with on this subject, including the one I'm married to. A great way to reconnect with an old ... friend," she mumbled. There was a brief pause when Julie made a snap decision to be bold. "I figured you to be different after I saw you at the reunion. I guess that old European background has you more walled in than open than you care to own, huh?"

"Double ouch. Apparently," he reticently admitted, though not sure to which comment.

She sighed but continued, as she had many times before. "Listen, Dane, kids, like marriage, take work. It's obviously best when that effort comes from both parents. From a strictly logical perspective, all parties benefit. Once lopsided, everyone suffers, and I mean the entire world."

"Isn't that a little dramatic? Emotional?" he questioned with a more gentle approach.

"It's not. Think about it, again from a non-emotional

business perspective, which is how I got my husband on board with this team child-rearing concept. This will make sense. Let's say you have a client who wants to start a new company, an offshoot of what exists now."

"Okay."

"That client does the research, or jumps right in, to get the wheels in motion. Doesn't really matter HOW it happens, it just does. Okay?"

Julie's wink made Dane smile.

"The business shifts into first gear, but the 'going gets tough,' as the old adage goes. There are recruitment challenges, employee problems, growth concerns, product development postponements, parts issues, paperwork delays, and so much more, right? This happens all the time. The construction industry has typical setbacks with budget overruns, for example. Legal cases take much longer to resolve when new evidence or jury interference happens, right? BUT—and this is big—if the owners of this young business talk with each other regularly to sort out the issues, hear the concerns, listen to their employees, attend to the parts supply-and-demand problems, for example, then they're able to game plan together, and that operation stands a chance of survival. Makes sense, right?"

"Yes, this makes sense, but you talk about a business and products, not people or kids."

"Sheez, for a smart guy, you're clueless," she put it bluntly. "You're obtuse, except where your world is concerned. Sorry, but I went through this with my husband for years. When I experienced complications after our second child was born, he had to step up to handle so much more than just his world. He felt lost and overwhelmed, and that was AFTER I'd covered with him what he needed to know. I'd gone so far as to write it all down in case he forgot something, or I wasn't able to answer!"

They both smiled, took deep breaths, and then Julie continued.

"Products or kids? Company or family? Same difference! Raising healthy, thriving kids *is* a business. Consider this. Marriage is not just a sacrament or institution. It's a business proposal. At a basic level, it's a deal between two people to come together, have, hopefully, great sex, share DNA in the production of kids, and combine their lives, homes, finances, and, with any luck, more sex"—her eyes twinkled—"and fun, etc. Sounds like a pretty intense business arrangement to me. Why else would people commit to each other?"

Trick question. I got this one. "Because they love each other."

Tickled, Julie softened. "I'm impressed. Still a soft side to you, after all the years of hardcore legal crap. Yes, that's the usual and hopeful intended reason. Much like business partners, an initial attraction creates common ground." *That sudden emotion again.* Her skin tingled. "Couples come together"—Julie's breath caught—"due to love and attraction. We have kids because that's what we're pre-programmed to do—procreate to assist the survival of our species. How come we don't stay together then?" *This ought to be good.*

"We grow apart, make less-than-honorable choices, lose respect for each other or the ability to communicate, or"—he took a deep breath—"we should never have been together to begin with." He darkened and looked out at the airport activity.

Julie paused and witnessed Dane in his pain. When he realized she'd stopped speaking, he slow-turned back to look at her. The hurt in his eyes was undeniable. He started to shut down this vulnerable place she'd brought him to, but she gently placed her hand on his forearm and lingered there … a moment too long.

"I'm sorry, Dane. I didn't mean for … I mean … I didn't realize. …" She stuttered and removed her hand.

"It's okay." He was closed off again. "It's been three, four years already since we finalized the divorce. I pretty much gave her everything, except my future wages. I had to have some way to sustain myself and support her and the kids, of course. She didn't need it, but she deserved it. As you've already said, child development takes a great amount of work. To be fair, she worked outside of the kids quite a bit as well. I know that now. How long have you been married?"

"Over twenty-five years. They've not all been hearts and rainbows and butterflies and unicorns, I assure you. But I'm still here. He's still here. Poor bastard," she joked. *So far.*

Dane laughed cynically. "More like lucky bastard, if you ask me."

"You're kind."

"I'm truthful, not kind. Just ask my ex-wife."

They were interrupted by another gate area announcement.

"Attention passengers of Delta flight 1492 to Chicago O'Hare. We have both good news and bad news. The bad news is that we are delayed here a bit longer due to events beyond our control once again. Please turn to the television monitors for the latest development at LAX International Airport. This event has delayed flights across the nation as well as here. We do not expect to be further delayed once the situation is under control there. The good news is that the storm here has passed, and the winds have died down enough to allow takeoffs once again. We're sorry for the aggravation this may have caused many of you. We've all been challenged. Thanks for your continued patience."

"Guess we're here for a while yet. If you need to work, I understand."

"I will shortly. Why? Don't you want to talk with me anymore?" he teased.

"I just gave *you* an out in case *you* needed one." Again, they sat in amiable silence for a moment. "Your ex-wife didn't know you well then. You've always been kind. Intense, honest, determined but always kind."

"You didn't know me after we graduated from high school." Dane half-smiled, but Julie saw a sort of darkness pass over his face. Motionless, she waited. "I had a great time in college. In the beginning, I attended the rare class, spent time instead almost always on the water, until a call from my parents served to yank me out of my complacency. I'd decided to try for a spot on the Olympic team, I told them. 'Fine, but first, however,' they said, 'get your degree.' I just about flunked out my first year. Water ski bum." He stopped, all of a sudden, and watched Julie. She was patient, though. "Then there was a car accident. It was pretty bad." His speech slowed. Pain gripped his chest.

Heavy weight settled in her heart. *There's the darkness I saw before. What haunts him?*

"While I recovered, my competitiveness in the water disappeared. I took the accident as a sign and went to law school sooner than I'd originally considered ... at the urging of my parents and grandparents. I found an apartment in New York City, graduated with honors, and was relocated in Switzerland by the firm that hired me. I became pretty focused, even obsessed, after college. My family, of course, was thrilled. I passed all bars I needed to practice law domestically in two countries, since I have dual citizenship, as well as internationally. That was brutal for a beach bum, eh?" They both laughed.

"An exceedingly smart beach bum. So what happened after that?" She knew not to pry about the accident—yet. She smiled and nudged him. She wanted the attention to stay on Dane, happy to keep the focus off of her.

"I helped one of the firm's partners with a Swiss client here in the U.S. on a merger in the lingerie industry." He glanced at Julie, skeptical, and waited for her reaction. He was accustomed to them from those who'd asked over the years how he and Rachel met. Julie simply nodded her head, curious, and raised her eyebrows as she waited for Dane to continue.

"And that's how you met your now ex?"

Why am I flustered? A little embarrassed? "Yes." He peeked over at Julie again as confusion weaved through him, an emotion unfamiliar to him.

"So? What? What's the matter? Is that the end of the story?"

"I'm blown away," Dane admitted to her. "Every time I tell that story, I get the worst looks, the sarcastic comments, but you—"

"But I what?"

"You want to hear the rest of the story! Is this real life?" They both smiled.

"Who am I to judge? Who you meet and where you meet them is to be judged? Not by me. I'm always fascinated about the inner transitions of people, how they come together, why they make the choices they make, etc."

"Wow." He shook his head. *I'd undoubtedly been married to the wrong person. Superficial versus super real.* "Mom was right about you all these years," he blurted. "She said it after we broke up after graduation. 'Dane, do not let her go, at least not for good. You'll regret it for the rest of your life. You may intimidate her now, but *you* will be in awe of *her* later. She will age beautifully in all ways.' That's what she said." He glanced over at Julie, who sat wide-eyed and speechless. "Oh, shit. Why the hell did I just tell you that? I'm … I'm sorry. I just seem to be able to tell you whatever, and I—"

"If you'll excuse me, I need to use the ladies' room. Will you hang on to my bag while I go? Please?" She didn't wait for an answer. She fought the urge to throw up, grabbed her purse without even a glance at Dane, and scrambled off to the ladies' room.

What the hell just happened? Did I hear what I thought I just heard, or did I imagine that? One minute he tells me about events post-high school graduation, then how he and his ex had met, and, if I'd heard him right, how he should never have let me go. Julie muttered all the way to the bathroom line and looked at the lady in front of her. "Interesting world we live in, isn't it?" The stranger half-smiled and moved up.

This is crazy. She locked herself in a stall and stood there in disbelief. *You've got the most ridiculous ego.* Julie scolded herself. *Get ahold of yourself! Okay, what are my options? Hide in this stall? He's got your bag, remember? Emerge from this stall when they make the actual boarding announcement? That would be the ultimate wimp move—avoidance. Since when are you a wimp? Okay, okay. I know what I have to do.*

After she pulled herself together, Julie approached Dane, who made a most gentlemanly move. He stood at once to apologize to her.

"Julie, I'm so sorry. Even I can't believe what I told you. It's true. All of it. But you're a happily married woman, and I put you ... me ... us ... again in such an awkward position. Complete selfishness. You do look terrific. Sincerely. I shouldn't be surprised. I'm thankful for this time to catch up with you. I—"

Julie cut Dane off mid-backpedal. *My turn to shock you.* "I need you to tell me the truth." Dane's chest tightened as he floundered for air.

"Why didn't you ever call me when you came home from college? I can't imagine that you never saw your family, even in the bum stage. I'm sorry, but I have to ask—again."

Dane was so shocked, he felt the air knocked out of him. *It's not often that I'm unprepared for questions or challenges.* He prided himself on his preparation skills. *But this interaction? I thought I'd prepared for this since the reunion, but apparently not as well as necessary.*

"What's the matter? Lawyer got your tongue?" She blinked, alert and watchful, but her lips parted in anxious anticipation.

He stalled, licked his dry lips, and breathed to regather his wits. "I was so sideways when you initiated the 'when to break-up' conversation that night so, so long ago. I totally lied to you ... out of pride. When I told you I agreed with you?"

Julie eyed Dane. *Bullshit alert.*

"That I, too, thought that since we were headed off to college, we ought to go our separate ways? The truth? I'd heard a rumor that you'd lied to me and that you planned to break up with me over some superficial reason. I was so hurt and embarrassed, I wasn't going to call you, of course."

"Superficial reason? What are you talking about?"

"I know this is absurd, and it'll sound even more so now that we're so many years beyond high school. You apparently planned to break up with me because I was too short and my ears were too big. Jesus, that just sounds ridiculous now, but I was truly hurt then."

"Why didn't you ever ask me about it? I would've told you if I'd said that. Haven't I always been honest with you?"

"I expected a complete denial."

"To be honest, I did say one part, so I could justify why I walked away from—and now I quote—'a wonderful, brilliant, and charming young man whose mom and grandmother love you.' My mom told me the same as yours."

"She did? Wait, which part do you admit you said?"

"Since I loved to wear heels, I lied to Mom when one of my girlfriends was over. I joked that I couldn't be serious about a guy I couldn't wear heels with. She called me horribly superficial. She was right and wrong. I *was* superficial, but not because of the height comment. I rarely wear heels." She laughed at the irony. "I couldn't admit to anyone, especially myself, that I was nervous about the magnitude of your depth. It far exceeded mine."

Julie inhaled, slow and deep. *Might as well go for it. I wanted closure.* She deliberately closed and opened her eyes. An acute awareness of her surroundings settled into her body. Her slowed breath set her world on half speed. *This is insane.* She shifted in her chair and didn't want to acknowledge a warmth and dampness where there hadn't been one before, but did so anyway.

"I'm sure you see *my* uneasiness now, right?"

"Can't miss it. I'm just not sure if it's good or bad."

"I assure you, I'm not gonna share that." Julie took a deep breath and held it.

Dane swallowed and sat back. *Not sure if I want to hear what she has to say.*

"I felt immature and silly when I was with you. I believed one hundred percent that you'd lose interest in me in the snap of your fingers and the bat of some female's eyes because of it. The thought that you'd eventually reject me, once we were both away at college or had even graduated with all the choices you'd have in front of you, made me sick. I knew it'd be better for self-preservation— for us both—if we'd had the space to grow while away."

Julie paused and positioned her hand on Dane's forearm to signal she'd not finished.

"The few times I asked about you through mutual friends, you were still in California or Mexico, waterskiing. I knew if I'd asked too often, it might get back to you. I didn't want you to call me to tell me to stop, so I decided to leave you alone. I hoped that one day I'd get the chance at closure, to explain. We started to get there at the reunion, then you grabbed me outside of the elevator and distracted me." She smirked. "Then Tate Parker interrupted. I guess this was the next chance, unexpected as it's been. Had you ever asked me about the comments, I would've readily admitted to what I'd specifically said, then tracked down the idiot who'd made up the rest. I don't appreciate nasty rumors. Never have. Never will. Once upon a time, you didn't either."

Dane was once again rendered speechless. *Her admission is remarkable, incredulous. Julie felt immature with me? My turn to gather thoughts.*

"My turn for the restroom prior to boarding." As she

looked up, she noticed he'd taken his bags with him. When the announcement finally came, Dane hadn't returned to the seat next to her. Saddened by their revelations, Julie retrieved her boarding pass from her purse and checked her seat assignment. She wondered if he planned to change his flight, or if he'd gone to make those calls he'd mentioned earlier.

She didn't want to appear anxious, so Julie opted not to look around for him. Her attempt to distract herself with her phone and look unaffected by their conversation didn't work. Truth was, she was hardly able to concentrate on any one task and elected to stare at the planes until her time to board was announced.

When it finally came, Julie handed her pass to the ticket agent to scan and headed down the jetway. She'd decided to save money and sit in coach this time and thus likely miss Dane. Though she longed to look in first class for him, such desperation would be pathetic even to Julie herself. Her vision blurred as she settled in.

To her surprise, she fell asleep mid-flight, thankful the passenger next to her was a sullen teenager. *Headphones on and mom oblivious. Perfect. No temptation this time to converse.* She'd planned to stay awake to work, but sleep always made a flight go faster. *Too bad it didn't diminish the butterflies in my stomach.* As she gathered herself together, she spotted Dane as he left the forward cabin, just as she'd suspected. He didn't turn to look for her, either.

Chapter 64

NOT SO CLEAN

THEY MARVELED AT the warehouse space. Ballroom dancers might have waltzed an entire lap around the facility's interior to Strauss' "Blue Danube" prior to the installation of the modular units, the control room, overhead office space, etc. They'd concealed their intentions from law enforcement through the purchase of automotive paint booths but confounded them when it all disappeared one night without a trace.

"Turning them into three self-contained cleanrooms was genius and idiotic simultaneously."

"Now what do you expect me to do with that statement?"

"The brilliance? Watch the process in three stages combined. The foolish part? Triple the headaches to keep it all secure. For the last eighteen months, we've been without a hitch. Why all of a sudden? What or who changed?"

"We're in the process of analyzing all videos, samples, pretty much whatever we have. We'll figure it out and manage the situation." They exchanged glances.

As the couple continued to huddle in the corner of the control room, they watched a team unload another car body from its trailer onto sticky, aluminum tracks on the floor in front of each bay. The sticky strips had what appeared to be inconsequential soil stuck to them. "That's a new process since the original installation."

"It is."

"Why is it necessary?"

"So glad you asked." His eyes glimmered in appreciation of the rare upper hand.

She rolled her eyes, exacerbated. "Enjoy your brief moment."

He smirked with satisfaction but drew a deep breath to slow his thoughts. "The purpose of a cleanroom is to eliminate—our preference—or, at the minimum, limit air particles such as dust contamination during the gold's insertion process. The more contamination we remove means the less opportunities for us to be traced."

Her impatience flared. "I know this. Tell me what I don't know."

"Any dirt that might have been missed at the start before the strips is now captured. Each one of the new sticky strips is removed from every track. Then, each strip's dirt is tested for its properties, like what type of dirt's on it, nutrient contents, pH levels, strength, etc. The computer determines the place the trucks likely came from. Every frame and strip of dirt is categorized for future reference. Car bodies, tacticians, and even the gold are simultaneously prepped for the implantation process. The bay and chase setups allow for any further soil, hair, and debris of any size and/or significance to be captured as well without the entire process jeopardized."

"Impressive." Her head nodded.

"Thank you. As you see, we're able to watch all of it from here, too."

As cleanrooms went, this setup was state-of-the-art. From TSI precision monitoring systems to the highly reliable Cleanpak modules, cleanroom standards weren't met but exceeded. Those in charge took zero for granted, however. Regardless of the high security, humans were still responsible.

Chapter 65

HEADS UP

THE FLAT-ROOF, ADOBE-STYLE home sat nestled in a quiet neighborhood at the base of the McDowell Mountain Range. Homes varied widely in architecture from contemporary, Frank Lloyd Wright's unobtrusive ranches to two-story eyesores and most styles in between. Cloaked in warm, desert tones and drought-tolerant xeriscape, this community was typical for well-heeled Scottsdale, Arizona.

All homes in this neighborhood, however, possessed two crucial qualities for their inhabitants—they were removed enough from the busy city hubbub, private in an ordinary sort of way, and none had lavish gates, grand signage that announced its existence, a guardhouse, or extensive safety camera setups, at least not to the untrained eye.

Of course, this was exactly the way Bob Couvey liked it. Easy enough for his clients to find, but private in that unwarranted attention couldn't just happen. Bob was most often thankful for the discretion his property offered his varied business transactions. Mixed reactions existed where Tate Parker was concerned, however. "It's the rare client like Parker that makes me wish we lived in a gated, guarded community," he'd once shared with his wife.

At times, when he knew Tate Parker was scheduled to

arrive, he adjusted the surveillance cameras, checked the recording systems, and even had his shop assistants clean up areas most likely to be touched by the young industrialist. Other times, he didn't care and hoped shop grime would keep him away. Without fail, though, Bob made sure at least one assistant was visible on property with him, and his wife was in the house with the housekeeper, contractor, or a girlfriend.

He didn't trust Tate Parker. At all.

When Tate showed up unannounced early after breakfast in the middle of the week, Bob was alone. His assistant was late, and his wife had just left for the grocery store. Fortunately, he'd just finished another car for the brash, young capitalist.

"Looks like you're ready for the next one."

At his age, he no longer easily startled, but he still found that Tate's tone unsettled him. Regardless, he needed to hold his ground. "I don't do impromptu visits, Mr. Parker." Bob kept his head down under the car's hood. Tate didn't move. A last turn of a bolt, and with an innate sense of how close his head was to the hood's sharp edge, he stepped back, precise with each foot, stood methodic and deliberate to stack each vertebrae, and turned to his uninvited guest.

"Damn, Bob. If looks could kill—"

Bob wielded his wrench, stood his aged frame as straight up as possible, looked Tate square in the eyes, and repeated, "I don't do impromptu visits, Mr. Parker. There's a reason." Bob moved toward Tate with a snarled lip, like a provoked animal. "I. Am. Focused. I do not like to be interrupted when I'm focused. My assistants know this. Even my wife knows this."

"Well, I'm not—"

"I don't care who you are or who you *think* you are. I've been hired to do a job. I must focus to do the job for which I was hired and for which I am well paid. I value my reputation, my work, and my clients." He took another step closer to Tate, who took a step backward.

"Hey, Boss, sorry for my late … ooh, dang."

As Bob turned away from both men, he barked, "Hope you had your Wheaties."

Tate stopped the young apprentice. "He doesn't like unplanned visitors?"

"Ooh. You interrupted him? No wonder he looked like he was about to eat you alive."

"Let him know the new body on its way has slightly different instructions."

"Cool."

Chapter 66

TAKE THREE

JULIE CONSTANTLY SCRAMBLED. The rush to Chicago O'Hare Airport was just another absurd example. Her pulse crashed through her veins. *Just never enough hours in the day. Shit. I sound like a statistic. Not cool on such a sophisticated trip.*

"*I'm* run *by* my life instead of *me* running *it*," she muttered, as she mindlessly watched the home developments cruise past on the expressway. She wasn't sure all the hustle and chaos were ever worth the loneliness acquired. All too often, Julie considered a fugitive's life. *Change my name, start all over again ... like a Witness Protection Program participant.* She grinned at the silly thought.

I've only myself to blame. I need to question my choices, do some serious soul evaluation. I've often wondered that if I might ever disappear, would anybody even notice? Do all moms think this way? Just as she processed that thought, the middle-aged cabbie delivered her safely to the terminal.

"That'll be forty dollars, ma'am." He waited. His patient, kind smile and tone guided her out of her own mind and back to reality. "Miss? You all right?"

"I'm sorry? Oh." Julie looked around and realized they'd arrived at O'Hare. "Yes! Thank you." She handed him a fifty. "Here you go."

Julie looked puzzled at the driver.

"Your change, miss." He again spoke with such gentleness.

"Thank you." She shook him off, genuinely touched. "Please, keep the change." *God, You always make sure I know that I'm wanted, needed, and loved.*

"This is too much, ma'am," he offered in his heavy, Polish accent.

"No, it's not. Your kindness alone is worth that and more. Thank you." *God, You've always made that clear in the most wondrous ways.*

"No, miss. Thank *you*."

She looked him in the eye as she smiled, swiftly collected her bags as she got out of the taxi, and turned to double-check that she'd gathered it all. He dashed out of his seat and asked if she needed any help. Instead of rushing off to his next fare, he waited for Julie to close the door. *Remarkable. Chivalry isn't dead.*

Chivalry. Gallantry. A gentleman. Of course, I think about my husband. I can't help but wonder how much he understands about gallantry, about the courage and boldness our life together requires. We've been through such challenges and made such strides. Our tender goodbye was a new treat. Are Gabe and I forever? Maybe.

As she stood in the airport security line, she muttered, "Life guarantees zip, nada, nothin', except for death, taxes, changes, and compounded effects. Oh, and lines." Those within earshot snorted their humored agreement. *However, as savvy as I am to question what it takes, I grasp it takes us both to dance.* "I'd be naive to believe I could make it happen unassisted." More chuckles, though the double message was Julie's alone.

Julie didn't appreciate the second fiddle position. She recalled dates with her then boyfriend. Gabe was attentive, watched her with eyes of a hunter, interested in all that mattered to her. *Now? Too often, I make excuses for him. Then my patience thins or evaporates, testy with his negligence, which I've allowed. I either withdraw, pissed at myself, or lash out.* "If you had a girlfriend, you'd *find* time for her," she'd grumble. "I want to be your girlfriend." To blame Gabe was easy, but in reality, she was aware she only had herself to blame.

"Think the grass is greener elsewhere? That's a lie. It's not. We all have the same issues. The grass has *got* to be greener at another security checkpoint, though, right?" she asked no one in particular as she stood in the longer-than-usual security line. She was thankful for the chuckles, which acknowledged more frustrations than those around her knew. *Take responsibility for my own actions. I'm accountable for my choices. No one's got a gun to my head. Grow up, my dear,* she lectured herself. "This trip is crucial, people. At least we're almost there." *I needed to be unavailable to Gabe and the kids, only focused and available to my own needs and goals. Time to fill up my own well … myself.*

Once through security, Julie found an open seat in the crowded gate area, knew she was early for a change, and opened her computer. *I might as well get some work done while I wait*, she decided, and opened up a Word document. She started to type but what came out read like gibberish. *Ah! Never mind.* She turned the device off and put it away.

She opted to check out the newspaper, an instant regret. One of her favorite authors had recently died. Tom Clancy's copious research on military topics and thoughtful approach to craft clever story lines marked him as a hard worker. She recalled his businesslike thoughts about writing from a few years back. "Writing isn't divinely inspired—it's hard work." His other wellknown opinion made her smile. "Writers' block is just an official term for being lazy, and the way to get through it is work."

Permission granted to stop the guilt about time I invest in this "new" career. I've been a writer all my life. I chose to put our children first. I own those choices. I chose to help my husband start the business. Come on, be honest with yourself. She taunted her own mind. *Make no apologies. There's no right or wrong. No need to forgive yourself for NOT writing all these years.* She just neither anticipated that she'd write "real" stuff, nor that what she wrote might affect any part of her life, too.

Deep in thought, Julie stared at the newspaper headline when a gentleman interrupted gently. "Excuse me for the intrusion, ma'am, but is this seat available?" Startled that she may have mistakenly heard his voice but felt his strong presence in her core, Julie dragged her gaze up into Dane's warm, brown eyes. "Mind if I join you ... again?"

Smooth. Wordless for the moment, she moved her purse and work bag from the otherwise empty chair next to her and kept an impassive expression on her face. *Hmm. Swap some crazy honesty. Seek closure. Get blown off. Nice.*

Finally, he broke the awkward silence between them in the midst of the bustling airport terminal. Deciding to use sports tactics, he knew the best offense was a good defense. "I thought maybe you'd run away again if you saw me approach just now. Thanks for—"

"I'm sorry?" She surprised herself with her reserve, her tone indifferent.

"You boarded the plane in Phoenix before I returned from the men's room, so I took that as a cue to leave you alone." *Uh-oh, here it comes.* He squirmed. *The inevitable fallout.*

"You did, did you?" Julie hadn't looked at him since he'd taken the seat next to her.

Can't be good. "That was why you boarded, wasn't it?" He pushed a little more. *Beg to be reprimanded much?*

"Dane, I'm neither a gun-toting, idiot client nor a legal or illegal, for that matter, game player. I've never been one, as you know. Once upon a time, a long, *long* time ago, you weren't, either. You knew exactly what you were doing in Phoenix when you took all of your shit to the bathroom with you. You didn't need to set off any flares to punctuate your message. I'm not stupid, nor will I allow you to play me as such." Julie's quiet but eloquent delivery had Dane on his heels.

"Julie—"

"Attention passengers. Please be advised that Delta flight 1707 will be delayed due to storms on the East Coast. We are very sorry for any inconveniences this delay may cause. Mother Nature operates on her own timetable. Please check back here with us in about an hour for an update. Thank you."

Julie gathered herself and muttered, "Here we go again."

"Julie, I'm sorry. You're right. I was a coward. Let's talk over a drink. May I buy you one? Sounds like we'll be here for a while. Might as well enjoy it."

"Sounds fine to me."

"Uh-oh. There's that word—fine. It's like—nice."

"Let's talk over a drink." She dismissed his word objection.

Why did that sound like I was dismissed? He considered.

With no interest in distant pasts, their impromptu get-together required them to be present in the moment. With cell phones secured in their bags, conversation between the former companions was easy.

"Just to sit here and talk with you makes me wonder why we don't allow this sort of connection to happen more often in our lives."

"Feels ... decadent, like I'm playing hooky," Julie shared.

Dane laughed. "I haven't heard that word in years—hooky."

"Well, seriously, when was the last time you paid such rapt attention to whomever spoke, *and* it wasn't about business? Go ahead. I challenge you to remember." She strained to maintain a straight face, licked her lips instead, and sipped her drink.

Dane thought for a minute as he watched her lips glisten.

"You have to think hard, right?" Julie wryly noted. "How sad."

"You mock me. Are you calling me pathetic? I object."

"Don't bother to object, Counselor. Fact is fact. Sad. Pathetic. Whatever. Legalese won't change that, regardless." Julie parted champagne-damp lips, breathed deep and languid, then dragged her heavy lids to stare right into his soul-stirring intensity. She heard herself gasp. *Fuck. He stole my breath. STOLE it.* She forced herself to swallow as she struggled to reclaim what was hers and strained to speak coherently. "I think I need some water." *What the hell was that? WHAT is wrong with me?*

Dane's eyes glimmered. *If she only knew she enchanted me.* He called the server over as he remained dialed in on Julie. "We'd like two more of the same plus two waters, please." Julie studied him, sought what was behind his eyes. She put her elbows on the table, interlaced her fingers, and nervously touched her lower lip. *Warning, Will Robinson!* She cautioned herself.

One cocktail each and a shared appetizer led to another ... a slow, almost calculated dance. Neither seemed to notice at first. They took deliberate, methodical turns. Picked up a chip, dipped it, raised it to their lips. Repeated. They memorized each other's movements, not wanting to forget even the slightest one. To an observer, they were lost in each other. At times, they sat in companionable silence, taking in the presence of the other. Measured sips allowed delayed answers to questions asked. Neither seemed anxious to head to the departure gate area.

"Which seat did you say you had?"

"I didn't, but it's 14A. Last-minute reservation yielded economy. Why?"

"I'll be right back. I'll leave my briefcase with you, okay?" Dane needed some way to keep them both there, suddenly pained at the thought she might bolt—as she had from the coffee counter, as he had in Phoenix.

"I'll be here," Julie guaranteed. "What are you up to? Should I be worried about this ticking or …?" She smirked, intent to conceal what she felt but didn't understand. *What is with me? I'm married. I've no rights to this man, even as a friend.* She trusted her playfulness would keep him at arm's length.

Humored, he chuckled then feigned hurt. "Ticking? After all these years? Bathroom run. Be right back."

He asked me where my seat was, then said bathroom run? Oh, well. Julie decided she'd ask him when he got back. She took the moment to herself to check her cell phone. *Gabe called. Shoot. A text, too, for a safe flight and a reminder to call upon landing.* As she looked up from her phone, Dane approached the table from the gate area, not the bathroom.

He saw her confused expression and explained. "I hope it was okay, but I took the liberty to have your seat moved next to mine. There was an empty one. We're about to board, and I know we haven't finished our conversation. We're likely to be busy once we touch down. Okay?"

"Dane, you're seated in business class."

"I know. I took care of everything. Don't worry." He saw the concern rise in her flushed cheeks and defended his actions. "There were no seats near you, or I would've switched. Besides, you told me you enjoy business class when you travel long distances."

"New York is not a long distance from here. You of all people know that." She tried to stay cranky with him but just couldn't. His look questioned her. She attempted to stifle a smile but opted to be gracious instead. "Thank you, sounds great. So much for getting any work done. You're very distracting." She gently scolded him.

Pleased, he lowered his head slightly, looked almost shy, and broke into a timid smile. "As I'd hoped."

VARIATION

"HOW DIFFERENT?" BOB asked his math wizard apprentice.

"He didn't say. Why?"

"You know how I feel about surprises."

"If it makes you feel a little better, he didn't say surprise. He said different."

"You can play semantics with me, but it's all the same. Ask my youngest daughter, who despised change. Different with notice is change. Different without notice is surprise. Change I can live with. Surprises? Well, let's say I've had enough of those in my lifetime."

"That's all he shared."

Bob shook his head and pursed his lips, annoyed, but

otherwise remained focused.

"Has the scheduler called with the scale tech's arrival time yet?"

"Not yet. Find another body that seems heavy?"

"Either we've missed another engine piece to remove, or the scales have to be recalibrated. I believe we've been thorough, but we're human."

"I'll let you know what he finds when you're in next time."

CONSOLATION

VICTOR HATED THAT he and Dane were both mixed up in Rachel's vindictive web. He wasn't sure in what role he'd been cast yet and guessed that Dane had been sideswiped by their last phone call. He looked for the account Rachel was supposed to open in their names together. "Hopefully, I won't need to alert Elena about this shit," he muttered.

Once he'd ended their sexual affair and she'd remarried, she'd come around crying poor less frequently. Ever since she filed for divorce from her second husband, a nice looking but dull man, she'd claimed financial challenge only a few times. "I don't know why you think I believe your wallet's tighter than a frog's ass, my dear, when you still dress like royalty and have quite the retainer set up here."

"Oh, Victor, I just don't know what he'll do once he's out of the house." She sighed.

"Rachel, he signed your prenup. He's a bore, but an honorable bore ... not that I ever understood why you married him."

"Because you weren't available."

Victor laughed and shook his head. "You're good, sweetheart. You'll be fine." Then he handed her a check for five grand. "A little consolation shopping money."

"Something you'd like to see me in perhaps?"

Victor felt a twitch and bulge but didn't dare move until she left the room. He knew precisely what the lingerie model meant. "Very thoughtful, but off you go. I've work to do." *Uhoh.*

His former mistress stood up, slow enough to ensure Victor noticed the sleek, suggestive way her dress fit, and circled around to his side of the desk to share a proper Swiss parting. As she bent over and brushed his cheeks with hers, she looked down between his legs and couldn't help herself. "Nice try."

"You're welcome."

She waved the check shoulder height as she cat-walked out.

Chapter 67

DEEP BREATH

THE LOUD SPEAKERS announced the start of Julie and Dane's boarding process. They gathered their bags, made their way to the gate, and headed down the jetway.

"Nice to see you again, Mr. Michaels." The pretty flight attendant smiled warmly, a little surprised.

"Thank you, Faye. You, too. By the way, Faye, this is an old friend, Julie Archer. Julie, meet Faye Donazio. Faye's been in charge of business class for years. I used to see her more before our firm began to fly me on their private jets, which are currently undergoing some significant maintenance. How about a couple of glasses of champagne? We've a little celebrating to do"—he turned and smiled at Julie—"don't we?"

"Yes, we do. Nice to meet you, Faye." She got herself situated in the window seat, laughed at the absurdity of this entire scene, and started to relax a little.

Faye returned with the two glasses in hand and over-heard Dane and Julie's toast. "To old friends, happenstance, and re-acquaintance."

Faye turned to another flight attendant. "This is going to be a fun flight after all. The stern, all-business Dane Michaels broke a smile! Shock!" Fresh energy buoyed the senior flight attendant and her cohorts. "Perfect pick-me-up after all the storm delays today." *Hmm ... I can't help but wonder about one minor detail. Where's the missus? She's more uptight and proper than Mr. Michaels.* "Whoever the lady is next to him has brought a sense of fun and lightness to the high-pressured lawyer, which he needed—desperately."

SPELLS

THEY CHATTED THE entire flight. "Thick as thieves." Faye gossiped with her coworker. Both travelers appeared calm and relaxed, an ease between them.

What a great change from my normal business trips, Dane realized. *I could get used to this—fast.*

Julie unbuckled her seat belt as they awaited the New York ground crew's expectant knock on the cabin door, and she turned to fully face Dane. She gently placed her hand on his bare forearm, his shirtsleeve still rolled up to his elbow. A skin-to-skin current snapped his attention to her wedding ring-clad hand, then to teal-green eyes that shimmered at him like a Fijian adventure as she spoke. She waited for him to track her gaze. "Thank you for the seat upgrade and the champagne. They were unexpected treats on this trip." Her smile was soft, genuine. His breath hitched.

Shameless, he reached over with his free hand and caressed hers. He wanted more of their connection. His flesh tingled. As their eyes locked, the pull intense, he rasped, "The pleasure was all mine. Completely the opposite of my normal business trips." The flight attendant's voice interrupted them as she brought overcoats to fellow passengers. Dane straightened up a little, hesitant but mindful he may have overstepped boundaries with his married friend. Pain shot through him as their spell broke. *What the hell just happened? I nearly kissed her. Shit!* he screamed in his head.

Julie hid her disappointment as she felt him pull back. She'd truly enjoyed their almost magical time. *WHAT am I doing? Too much champagne.*

"Unfortunate, but back to reality." Dane continued. "Ask Faye. She's been on many of the same commercial flights I've taken," Dane intoned. *I suck at fake casual.*

They thanked Faye, made excuses to stop in the restrooms on their way through the terminal, and promised to stay in touch. Neither were clear about what had happened between them. What *had* been clear, though, left them winded but energized, turned on but calm, the effects visible in their eyes.

A spell cast.

Chapter 68

CLEVER

AFTER HER BOSS texted her so late at night, Isabella knew Dane's ex-wife, Rachel, wasn't just a "part" of her boss's troubles—she was likely the leader of them. *Still, the question is why is she after him? What's her motivation?*

"That woman's been trouble ever since I've known Dane Michaels," the petite legal assistant vented to her partner of two years.

An aeronautical engineering analyst, Olivia Noyer most often kept "banker's" hours. Olivia wasn't asked often to work more. Legal offices were a different breed of business, however. So she was always amazed at Isabella's boss's restraint. His expectations for his assistants to work more hours were limited. Though Swiss-born, Dane's American upbringing, education, and lifestyle influenced his relentless, self-imposed workaholism.

"I'm sure she's highly involved with, if not in charge of, whatever attack on him is happening. I just can't figure out why, yet, but I will."

"Isabella, you know how we women are when we've been cast aside as unwanted."

"True. However, how might you feel if I made it clear *you* were still desirable *and* wanted, and I had a problem— *and* I gave you *everything*, because, as a lawyer, I *knew* it *was* my problem? I couldn't disagree with your accusations. I conceded."

"I'd feel like you were trying to buy me off, and—"

"And what?"

"And, like maybe you had something, or someone, to hide."

Isabella searched her lover's eyes for hints. "Couldn't I have found out intel that mattered to me and just wanted out of the marriage?"

"Sure, but you've heard the phrase 'a scorned woman wants revenge, a strong woman moves on,' right? The problem is Rachel is both strong and scorned."

"Rachel's more scorned than strong, though, because she's still in love with my boss. From the way I described her in the course of their divorce, she'd experienced a near psychotic episode." Isabella paused and considered multiple options. "When you deal with a huge ego, especially one who's depended on her beauty to fund her life, this ego must be handled with great thought and consideration ... like a chess match. Had Dane Michaels already wanted out of the marriage and knew his wife would likely lose it—hence his generosity—or had he, in fact, something to hide? And still does?"

Chapter 69

WHOSE SIDE

AFTER HIS LAST meeting with Rachel, Victor shook his head. He mentally confirmed what his gut suggested. He decided to call home to have lunch with his wife for the first time in years.

"Hey, honey. How are you?"

"I'm busy as usual. You?"

"I've got the customary madness on my plate, but I need to get out of the office for a while. You too busy for lunch?"

"Wow! You must be substantially off-balance to ask me to lunch."

"Ouch. Fair point, though."

"Dane can take over for you while you escape for a little?"

"He's out of the country for another day or so, but the girls can handle it for a couple of hours. I hoped your schedule permitted and you'd be willing to grab a bite and check out the newest roadster for our upcoming group excursion. Care to join me?"

"I'd love it. Are you picking me up, or am I meeting you?"

"Uh … I'll come to you."

"Victor, this isn't about your excitement in a car. You sound very distracted. What's the matter?"

"You know me too well." He chuckled. "Though it's been several years since Dane and Rachel divorced, something's been stirred up between them. I'm sure Rachel's instigated it, since Dane seems ... well ... happier lately."

"Victor, my dear, sweet husband, the bottom line comes down to whose side you're on and why. I await your imminent arrival."

Chapter 70

ENHANCE

WHEN SHE'D DISCONNECTED from Julie, Aubrey buzzed the department's intern.

"Lilly, please grab me all files on the recent bomb detonation in Scottsdale, Arizona. Thanks."

Firm, brief knocks on her office door told Aubrey without eye contact who awaited her enter signal. Her supervisory special agent had uncanny timing.

"Just got off the phone with her, sir, and Lilly's hunting down the other files for me now."

"Good work. Next challenge. Close your eyes."

Aubrey looked dismayed.

"Close them, please," her boss confirmed with his controlled monotone. "Aubrey, to be cerebral with facts is one technique. You'll have those shortly. We already know you're excellent at acquisition and assembly of them. You wouldn't have gotten this far so fast without such an advanced talent. Now, however, we have to connect the dots. We have to consider all of the possibilities—expand and enhance possibilities—rationally, sanely, unemotionally, and even insanely, especially when a former classmate's involved."

"We discussed this when you first brought me here, sir. I haven't forgotten." She opened her eyes to make direct contact with her superior. Aubrey's stomach churned. Her boss wasn't aware of all there was to know about her relationship with this "former classmate," a.k.a. one of the main persons of interest, a loving Fed term for those who may be subject to further investigation and follow-on surveillance.

He signaled for her to close her eyes again. "Special Agent Pulaski, as you consider each and every fact, reflect also on possibilities, real and imagined, likelihoods, based on those possibilities, outcomes in each scenario, and predictions. We'll cover this again once we have the information you've requested. Meanwhile, take a few moments and let your mind wander through the facts, as you know them right now, with those reflections I just shared. Your instincts are excellent. Time to enhance them."

"Yes, sir." She opened her eyes. He was already gone.

Chapter 71

RESEARCH

RITA KARLSEN PARADED her new author around. From publisher to publisher, she upped the demand for Julie's fiction novel about grand larceny in the auto industry. A new author's presence served as physical evidence of a promotional work ethic, especially since she'd come from the other side of the country. Julie was exhilarated but exhausted as they finally returned to the senior agent's office.

Rita's cozy office was stuffed with five-foot-high stacks of books she'd read, was soon to read, or had just received by unsolicited authors who'd hoped theirs would be read. When she "disappeared" daily, she merely hid amongst them, as they walled off a corner and created an unexpected quiet, peaceful, and private space. A small, rolled-arm love seat and elegant, contemporary floor lamp permitted Rita to "get lost" or be in "the eye of my daily storm." Julie wondered when the successful but harried agent ever had time to read a word.

Visions of a long soak in a hot bubble bath with a cold glass of champagne danced through Julie's head like sugar plum fairies in a little girl's Christmas dreams. She just wanted to head back to the hotel. Rita had other plans for her, though. She'd insisted during their planning of this trip that Julie visit a particular nightclub while she was in town. "One of your characters seems straight out of it. What a great way to further develop her," Rita had asserted.

So tonight was the night. Rita said there was an incredible DJ mixing. "Besides"—Rita winked at her—"not only will the music help you through your struggle to describe her more vividly, but the eye candy will stimulate your imagination. Trust me on that one." Their conversation was briefly interrupted when a cell phone rang. "Sorry, Jules. I've been waiting for this one. Excuse me for a moment." Rita left Julie to her own thoughts, as she consulted with someone about an author's whereabouts. *Now to figure out what to wear.* "Okay, so where were we? Yes, the nightclub. I warn you—there's so much to watch, it may be better to go when you have someone with you, a spare set of eyes."

"I don't understand," Julie said with confusion. "You spent so much time trying to convince me *how* much I needed to go, now you're warning me off? Which is it? To quote The Clash, 'Should I stay or should I go?'"

Rita tried to repress her Cheshire cat grin. "People go there with one intention, and let's just say it's unavoidable." Julie's scowl pressed Rita to clarify. "They find whatever they look for. My girlfriend's husband runs the place, so I'll have her put your name on the list at the door. You won't have to stand in a horrid line. Gives you the option to go. I need to get you on it before you change your mind, okay? Listen, I gotta run. I've another author to visit with today. Stay here in my office as long as you'd like. Let me know tomorrow if you went, what you thought, etc., but be careful." Rita warned her with a strong hug, then dashed out of the office.

Julie stood there frozen, total confusion riddled

through her. "Why do I feel embarrassed and suddenly very naïve?"

She returned to Rita's computer to see if she could throw some of what she and her agent had just spoken about into the story, but jotted only a few thoughts down instead. Annoyed with herself and her preoccupied state, Julie grabbed her jacket and headed back to her hotel. She left a message for Gabe and relaxed in a lavender bath. *My plans for the night will formulate themselves.* She exhaled. *Spontaneity seems to be more than a fun idea. It's critical.*

CALIBRATED

AS HE'D SUSPECTED, all scales were fine.

"Bob, you know we were just out here a few weeks ago, right?"

"Yes, Tom."

"I hate to waste your time and money."

"I appreciate that. Then check the damn thing and move on with your day."

The unflappable technician had just one more question. "Bob, now don't get upset with me. How often have you used it since we were out here last?"

"If you're concerned that I'm losing it, just ask that, for Pete's sake, and to answer that, I'm not. Satisfied?"

"Well, actually, I do have another question. Then why another call?"

"What do you care? You get paid."

Must have had a fight with the wife. "Because if this equipment isn't performing to standards, we need to know."

Bob drew in a long, deep breath. "Tom, I'm sorry to snap. I hadn't planned to share, but I consider you a safe, neutral source. Probably a good idea that someone other than my apprentice and wife are aware."

"Damn, Bob, that sounds kind of ominous."

"It sure as heck is a bit of a predicament. I've got some car bodies and engines coming to me much heavier than they ought to be. I've been in this business long enough to know better. I don't dare discuss this with my client because I believe he's part of the issue. Havin' a dickens of a time diagnosing the cause."

"I'll check all possibilities. No charge. I'll make note that it was a repair call, so neither one of us runs into a receivables department issue. Will that work for you?"

"One more thing. After you document it, please make sure it's in the system, too. We'll keep this weirdness between us until I figure out the next step. Oh, and my wife plans to take me to the doctor ... just in case."

Bob's wink verified Tom's earlier assumption regarding the wife. *At least I know why now.*

EDGE

THE CAR RIDE over was uneventful. Still, as anticipation and nervousness simmered just below her composed surface, an energy of anticipation and excitement mimicked the stop-and-go traffic of New York City nightlife. She felt like this was almost an out-of-body experience, as if she watched an actress in a movie role. *Why do I feel reluctant, almost hedonistic? Is it because I'm alone?*

"I'm going for research purposes," Julie explained to her husband. She realized the concern in Gabe's voice just reflected her own and felt the angst in his body all the way across the country. She knew what happened to him when he was like this. He'd called her at least twice while she'd been out with Rita, then freaked out when they'd finally connected.

"What happened? I couldn't get ahold of you!" Though such a rarity when Gabe showed any level of jealousy or insecurity, it was rough when he did. He became an overzealous micromanager, called her dozens of times in a day, and questioned her mercilessly when they did connect. "How you have the time to call me that often is beyond me! You're ridiculously busy with work."

"I always have time for you!" he roared.

"Stop it. You only have time to roar and stomp when I'm out of reach. I'm fine. I'll take care of me and focus on my work. You focus on your work."

Julie struggled but knew how to keep her husband from the clutches of quicksand-like possessiveness. Gabe's reaction was like a caveman who'd just discovered fire after he rubbed two pieces of flint together—volatile, unusual, and sudden when it sparked. His backlash was triggered by the harsh combination of his loss of control fueled by her loss in a delicious daydream. When she'd first seen this side of him, she thought it was almost humorous, but she quickly grasped his anxiety and worry for her welfare, or so he'd claim.

He trusted her. She'd given him no reason to do otherwise. She was baffled over his reactions, though, because they reflected those of a man who'd deceived his wife or was severely ill. Julie was certain Gabe could be described with many adjectives, but deceptive wasn't one of them. He either seemed completely disinterested and detached, or he was furious and passionate, with little in between. "Maybe we need to make our annual physical appointments," she suggested. He belittled her idea as "trivial, a time waste."

"I can't believe my great fortune sometimes ... you're the best thing that's ever happened to me, followed closely by our children," he'd whisper in a manic change of direction. His bizarre outbursts had become cyclical.

Right before she left for Chicago and New York, Gabe, once again, was so distracted with business, he was barely aware of her presence. *That's why he'd made such an effort at the airport. He was so dialed in at that moment, so I know he'd been paying me "lip service" for years up until that point. Time to fill my own well. Some space is crucial, not only for my sanity but for the passion in our marriage.*

As Rita's driver pulled in front of the nightclub, Julie's disdainful look mirrored back at her in the darkness of the black sedan's windows. Gabe all but begged her not to go tonight before he snarled about how selfish she was.

"There's nothing I can do from here if you need help!" he yelled, decidedly unhinged.

"So this is all about you now? *You* can't help if I'm in need, so I should sit on my hands in my hotel room? NOT make a completely different choice outside of my usual box to help *me*?" she growled back at him. "Well, I won't put my drink down and pick it back up, Dad. I'll watch the bartender's every move, Dad. I won't go anywhere with any strangers, Dad ... blah, blah, blah. Okay, Dad?" She had to laugh out loud at that moment on the phone. "I sound as if I'm talking with our daughter!"

Even Gabe backed off at that moment and conceded. "Please be careful. The nightclub scene has changed so much since you and I were in it."

"How would you know?"

A strange silence came over the phone. Julie shivered ... and not from a chill. "Gabe?"

"Sorry. Distracted." He covered. "Hasn't most of

what we knew when we were club age changed in the last twenty plus years? Anyway, be careful. We've read shit in the paper and watched it on the news. Left us both worried for our kids, right?"

"Fair point. Just remember, I'm after some sensory input that's very different from where I've been writing. It'll be helpful. You'll see." Julie appreciated she'd deflected a long-distance fight, but she didn't like how much her mood had sunk from that strange silence they'd shared. *Shake that bullshit now or go home*, she willed.

As she stepped out of the sedan, heads turned. *Heads always turn to see who's stepped out of an unmarked sedan. Enjoy the fleeting attention, even if it isn't for me specifically.* She knew she looked good, especially for such short notice regarding clothes. She hadn't come prepared for this experience, though she knew it had been a possibility. *Women in line with their dates are either snarling at me or working hard to redirect their dates' attention. This clear observation is at least some validation that I look good. I don't stand out like the proverbial sore thumb. Phew. My clothes don't scream, "MOM! BEWARE!"* She'd been acutely self-conscious about how not to stick out too much, period. She didn't want to be hit on, but she also didn't want to feel frumpy. *Mission accomplished.* Bouncers nodded approval as they asked her name, found it on the list, and escorted her in.

"Let the research begin."

Chapter 72

RACHEL

PROVOKED BY UNIDENTIFIED fear after her talk with Victor, Rachel reflected on her life's path thus far. She sought to recall any overlooked detail in her then-new romance with Dane.

There comes a time in every Swiss child's school life when they're sorted based upon their interests and abilities. Rachel Bieri accepted that regular academic high school wasn't for her. She and her parents opted for an extensive apprenticeship as an aesthetician, hoping the additional practical education might assist Rachel in a career path decision. When certain teachers met her, though, they soon realized she was far more intelligent than she'd allowed the system, or her parents, to believe. Not long after, through family friends, Rachel began a dreamlike modeling career.

As grueling as it was, Rachel managed her own schedule and finances. Her social life also took on a life of its own. She and her fashion friends flocked to the big cities for club scenes while on assignments. That's when she met Tate Parker.

He offered that "bad boy" fun element absent from her proper life, and he knew his way around the New York and Toronto club scenes. Tall, good-looking, smooth, and clearly bright, her parents didn't care much for the spirited playboy. They tried to warn her about his less-thanstellar background and highlighted when he landed in juvenile court in his more formative years in the States.

Rachel was shrewd, too, though. "Mutti (Swiss German for *Mom*), he's fun ... for now. I go with Tate more for his varied business connections, quite a basic level of interest. I care about him, but I'm not in love with him."

"Does he know this?" she wondered.

"I seriously doubt he even thinks about anyone that way." She smirked. "I'm one of several models he hangs around with, so there's zero for either of you to worry about."

She didn't share Tate's stories he'd told her in confidence about his early teen years, why he'd made some poor choices, and how he'd turned his life around. Tate's business successes spoke for themselves. His scrupulous finances so impressed Rachel and her parents, they changed accountants to Tate's. Through those accountants, the family established a relationship with the law firm Kasen, Blenz & Bosko, LLC to manage all of their legal affairs, especially Rachel's expanded investments with her thriving modeling career.

When it was time to meet their new lawyer, Rachel tagged along with her parents. Dane Michaels was young, handsome, athletic, and easily passed their parental tests. "Quite the opposite of your playboy," they noted. Again, concern grew for their daughter when she and Dane began to date. Dane drove himself with such determined focus to become established in the firm. Rachel continued to model. However, she managed to find spare time for Dane. The reverse was rare, her parents had noted. As the young professionals dated for several years, it was clear

Rachel was far more invested in the relationship.

"Rachel, schätzchen (*baby*), we despise the need to risk such blunt talk with you about this, but better to hear us now rather than later. We don't want you to be furious with us later and ask why we hadn't warned you. You've fallen harder for the young corporate attorney on the rise than he has for you. You must be aware of his true feelings for you."

Unfazed and determined to hold herself in check, her mouth dried as the truth of their words fueled her resolution. "I know what I've undertaken with him. Do you think I'm oblivious to his being so distracted? I'm sure it's his working obscene hours at the firm. All young lawyers are like this," she challenged. "Once he's more established, he'll be much more connected and, well, charming." She winked at them and hoped her phony confidence masked deep insecurities she stuffed further.

Dane's proposal startled her parents despite Rachel's hints to expect it. To them, he proposed more out of respect, duty, and apparent compatibility than because he felt passion for their youngest daughter. Nevertheless, they gave their approval to him when he asked for their permission to propose to Rachel. Their normally astute daughter ignored all parental concerns.

"Have you ever seen me fail when I use my femininity to win over the opposite sex?" She laughed easily with them and tried to appear more confident. Her big hand gestures flashed a beautiful engagement ring.

"Of course not, angel, but you sound like Dane was more a conquest to be had rather than a man to adore. Unlike you, we just don't see him as distractible or invested as you'd like to believe he is. Perhaps you're too much alike. Perhaps work goals aren't the reason, either.

As a man, I know too many reasons for lack of connection. When I met your mother, however, the world stopped for me. Your mother and I pray we're wrong. Divorce is a tricky and unfortunate process here." Her dad tried to reason with her.

Rachel wasn't interested in why she and Dane may *not* work out. She only wanted assurances about why they would, unrealistic or not. She was crazy in love with him and was convinced she would win him over.

Too bad I still am.

Chapter 73

WANTED—INFO

THE MUSIC DIDN'T coerce Julie. No force was used. It lured her. She understood immediately what her editor tried to explain to her. "Just go. You'll understand faster than I could explain. Trust me."

Bodies bumped into Julie with apologies as they passed hand in hand with their dates. As her eyes adjusted to the darkness, she almost couldn't believe them. *Is that—? It can't be. Is he standing there, or am I seeing things? What's he doing here? Is he alone?* She looked away, hoping he hadn't seen her. She didn't want him to think she'd followed him as he appeared to have been there first.

She lowered her head and ducked to the end of the bar. Screened by a tall, young couple from his vantage point, she needed a cocktail to blend in but also a minute to gather her thoughts.

Before she could get a bartender's attention, though, Dane was at her elbow and handed her a glass of champagne. She looked at him curiously. He leaned in close to her and said, "I've been waiting for you." His delicious, smooth voice vibrated in her ear, and she shivered in response. Dane knew why but kept his face relaxed and silently marveled at her responsiveness to him.

"Me?" she asked, as she looked around for his date.

"Yes. Why? Are you expecting someone else?" he

asked casually.

"No, I'm just looking for your date."

"I've already told you. I was waiting for you."

She looked at him uncertainly. "How can that be? We've not spoken since we left the airport."

"I checked information for your agent's name. You spoke so highly of her during our in-flight chat, after all."

"And?"

"And I called her to ask for her advice. I asked her about you, of course, and since she was also a little concerned about you being here alone—I think she felt guilty she couldn't come with you—she was only too happy to share that you might be here tonight. She sounded relieved I might join you." He looked at her, hoping he'd removed further suspicion of an additional woman who might enter the scene.

"I don't know whether to be mad at Rita for thinking I needed a babysitter and then giving out information as to my whereabouts to a stranger—"

Dane mocked offense. "I'm a stranger?"

Julie ignored him, "—or mad at you for pulling the information out of her, or—"

"Or what?"

She debated mentally, afraid she'd definitely give him the wrong impression if she shared her thoughts. *Should I be flattered he'd not only remembered my agent's name but also then made the effort to track me down? Hmm. That is, after all, what I've wanted from my husband and haven't gotten, isn't it? To be desired enough for efforts to be made?* Julie made a mental note to call Rita again to explain *Dane's* call. *Sheez, this visit to New York has become complicated.*

"Julie. You okay? Did I say something wrong?" he yelled over throbbing music.

"Should I be flattered or frightened?"

He laughed. "I've never known you to be so skeptical." She watched him with an unchanged expression and waited for his reply. He looked away for a moment at the glass of bubbles in his hand, then square into her eyes. "Flattered."

"What were you planning to do with my glass of champagne had I not arrived?"

"What *anyone* would do with a flute of this very special champagne ... drink it, of course." He smiled, searching for a small crack in her guarded composure.

Keep calm. Smile. "Nice you remembered. What are we celebrating?"

"Nice? *Not* my adjective. You know this. I'm sure you've got a better one to describe me. There've been plenty of them used to describe me over time," he said darkly. "Using the adjective 'nice' is much like using the adjective 'fine.' It's very milquetoast, run-of-the-mill, humdrum—a quality neither you nor I have ever possessed."

"Don't sell the word 'nice' short." Julie taunted him. "I'm sure you've used it to describe a pleasantry, right?"

"Only if I struggle to identify said pleasantry."

"See? It has a use—to fill the need to be positive." Her smug smile beguiled but challenged him.

Dane's heart pounded at her obvious challenge. "Even then I'll rack my brain for a more impactful word. I hate to waste words, and I refuse to be seen as ... average. Therefore, my word choice must always be the best it can be."

"Such a pompous reply for club banter."

He sputtered and paused for her further reaction, saw none, and continued. *Why do I feel the need to share with this woman?* He turned up his lip to show his nonchalance. "Pompous? Hmm. Some people, when they first meet me, think I'm perhaps not too quick. I'm often deliberate with what I have to say." He shouted to be heard over the loud music. "Or, I've been told I'm arrogant, and I sound like I need to impress myself with a conceited vocabulary. Pompous is a new one for me." He nodded his head in acceptance and smirked. Without apology, he leaned in closer, his cheek grazing hers, his lips inches from her ear as he spoke softer. "I also seem soft-spoken, as you know. It takes most people a while to figure out that, in reality, I'm E. none of the above."

Flushed, Julie's easy laugh concealed her increased heart rate. *He knows exactly what he's doing to me, damn it.*

Finally, a reaction I understand. He breathed. "I just have to walk softly to carry a very large, strong stick with discretion. This way, they never see me coming." Her nod and perceptive smile encouraged him to continue. "Then once I 'hit them over the head,' if you know what I mean, they usually have to look at me twice, think extra hard if what they just felt was real, and by then, it's all over." He smiled as if to say "ta-da!"

"But then you've established yourself. You've shown your hand, right? What's your tactic after you've 'walked softly with a big stick' and whacked them over the head?" As she propped her elbow up on the bar, she brushed his arm. *That current! His skin.* She steadied her chin on her fist and inclined her head toward him, anxious to catch his every word, yet grateful to not look in his eyes.

"They still never know quite what to expect when they see me because of my naturally soft approach," Dane explained in what sounded like a whisper in the midst of the club's noise. "I usually can use the same approach multiple times, even with the same clients. They simply don't expect the same tactic twice in a row, or they tend to think that maybe it was a mistake, a fluke. It's very rare they figure me out after the second time … or even the third, to be candid."

Conspiratorial in her body language, she placed her hand on his arm, as she had on the plane, and tilted her lips to his ear now. Without a missed beat, she teased him. "You're humble, too." She leaned back and raised her glass to toast him.

His warm laugh broke whatever ice remained between them. He raised his glass, too. "But you've always known. Even after so many years. Remarkable indeed."

"Why do you look at me like that?" Puzzled, Julie studied Dane's eyes and waited.

"Do you have enough information? Did you get whatever it was you needed here?" bellowed Dane, louder than he preferred.

"No, why?" she yelled back.

"It's so hard to communicate over this volume. What else do you need? Can I help you at all?"

She thought about it and grinned. "Yes. You can help, if you really want to, that is." She dipped her head down but taunted him with her eyes on his.

Uncertain about what he'd gotten himself into, but not about to leave without her, he hesitated. "Okay. Challenge accepted. What do you need?"

They finished their champagne and left their glasses on the bar. Julie led Dane to the dance floor, where the beat beckoned and the base seduced. She wanted to be out on the floor to watch those around her. The interactions, the facial expressions, "the vibe," as her daughter had once educated her. Julie was there to take notes, get ideas, and unclog her mind so she could finish her novel. *Perfect.*

Now I don't have to ask a stranger to dance, she confessed internally.

She was also thankful to be on the dance floor with him. Deeply aware of how nervous she felt about too much alone-time with Dane, she needed a little space and levity between them. *I hadn't expected that familiar pull to return. Damn, it's powerful. The same one that brought us together in high school and has kept him often on my mind since I saw him in Phoenix that first time. I'd guess he feels the same way—after all he tracked me down—but I don't dare ask. I don't want to mislead him or be misled.*

She looked up as they'd maneuvered through the crowd on the dance floor to see him watching her. *I'm here for a reason, "on a mission,"* as she'd told her family. With raised eyebrows, a small smile escaped her lips as the music invited and ignited all onlookers to the floor.

FRESH IDEA

HISTORY PLUS INSTINCTS revealed Dane Michaels to be an honest man. History may set precedence, but instincts don't hold up in court. Work in a law firm, and that message is drilled into every employee's brain. Facts win cases. Even twisted facts.

However, instincts do lead to questions that lead to facts.

One irrefutable fact was her boss's attention to details with his cases. Because he despised time and/or money waste, both his and his clients', Dane was efficient and expected his assistants to follow suit. Such a "fresh idea" in the firm was scoffed at by his freshmen colleagues, not to mention the partner under whom he billed. Dane defended himself when Victor questioned the frugal approach as a way to set himself apart from the time wasters.

"When I'm efficient with my time, you'll share more cases in quantity as well as quality, and I'll make partner sooner." Victor couldn't argue with such an admirable approach, since he'd be pushed to senior partner faster, too—until recently.

As Isabella delivered files to Victor's assistant's office, she thanked God for her light footsteps and open ears. "How much do you think has vanished? Surely, there's been an error. I'd trust Michaels with my life."

I'll walk files over later. She opted to scramble back to her desk and text her boss.

WATCH YOUR BACK! Overheard V. Talk soon.

NEEDED—FRESH AIR

AS THRONGS THICKENED on the dance floor, people pushed and pressed against each other, sometimes unaware, often quite deliberate. A Major Lazer song that featured Ellie Goulding called "Powerful" evoked its own lyrics. When Julie felt an energy surge from behind, sweaty bodies drove her flush against Dane's. She caught herself from falling as she grabbed his jacket lapels. *Oh damn, "powerful" is right!* Her knees weakened as she took in the musk of his cologne, lavished the hardness of his body. Afraid her arousal was exposed like honey on warm toast, she cast her eyes down and focused on the floor. *Research. This is why I'm here.* She licked her lips, dry from a swift flash of self-conscience fear. Her heart pounded in rhythm with music she no longer even heard.

Always the gentleman, Dane's poise and manners

rushed to their rescue. *Finally. I can hardly keep my hands off of her. At least it's not like I grabbed her or reached out for her.* He held her protectively but glared over her shoulder at the unknown offenders. He took his time as he assisted her back to her feet to regain her balance. He propped her upright by her shoulders and ducked a little to meet her gaze, checked in, and made sure she wasn't hurt. Her nod and easy laugh reassured him. "Can't have your agent upset with me."

They danced to several songs without any further issues. When a slow dance gave the crowd an opportunity to breathe, Dane didn't miss his chance to hold Julie. "Now you can observe what you need without concern."

She nodded and winked at him. *Clever but transparent excuse.* As soon as the rhythm picked up, they were reluctant to separate but did so.

She didn't want to yell, so she leaned back in close enough to be heard. Now her lips grazed his cheek. *Oh damn.* "Ready to go whenever you are." She pointed to her feet with a little shrug and smile to calm the increased sensuous charge between them. "I need some fresh air anyway." *More than my feet ache. My body lit up when I was pushed into his. Holy frenetic shit. His scent's an aphrodisiac. Heady, erotic. Talk about my feet. Perfect. A total turnoff ... for both of us. Good idea.* With her feet sensitive from the years she hadn't danced, she finally relented.

Dane smiled, grabbed Julie's hand, and immediately led them off the dance floor. *Thank God. Mess with fire, it's gonna burn. I must remain a gentleman. She. Is. Still. Married.* He cautioned himself. *She's technically working right now, too. But damn! I almost kissed her when she fell into me and then again when she leaned in.*

She excused herself and signaled a need for a ladies' room pit stop. *Ladies' room then fresh air. Yes. That's what I need.*

As Julie met back up with Dane, she caught a glimpse of a familiar person. *I've seen that ponytailed guy before, but where? He's out of place, I'm sure.* Dane caught her perplexed expression and followed it, cautious, hesitant.

She tried to distract him with talk of her weary feet, aware she risked the loss of the dynamics established between them on the dance floor. However, clearly in control of their exit, Dane put his arm around her waist and whisked her through the entrance. They walked out of the club and right into his waiting car. "I took the liberty we'd leave together and called my driver while you were in the ladies' room." He saw her emotions mix as if she were a world-class bartender in the club. Straight up, over ice, on the rocks, shaken, and stirred. *I know how you feel.* His heart thudded so loud in his ears, he wondered if Julie could hear it, too.

She merely nodded her comprehension. Though she'd assumed they'd head out together, Julie found herself off-balance again and worked to regain her composure. "I don't know exactly where we're headed, but—" She caught herself.

"But?"

Fuck. Headed anywhere with Dane will either be a great catch-up session and bring the closure I need, or a foolish, even dangerous, ruse to which neither of us is privy. He's so selfassured, so collected, regardless of topic. I'm scared if I grumble another word about my feet, he'll flick off my shoes, pull my legs across his lap, and massage wherever his hands land. God knows any physical tenderness right now between us would be bad, inadvisable, and one hundred percent erotic. She smiled and chose not to answer.

They left the nightclub, preoccupied. They'd also been followed.

Chapter 74

SEEK CLOSURE

DANE'S LIMO DRIVER wasn't in his usual position. He'd normally have been in front of the valet desk after Dane called. No matter where he was, Dane's drivers knew to meet him there. In fact, he was on the opposite side of the pick-up/drop-off driveway. Once Dane helped Julie into the warm limo, he said, "I need to give Paul a few instructions. I'll be right back, okay?"

Wide-eyed, she merely nodded.

Out of Julie's earshot, Dane asked, "Paul, why weren't you parked in the usual spot? What's happened?"

Ever the calm, experienced driver, Paul replied, "I had no choice. The cops directed me here. I thought it was an odd request, too, but they didn't elaborate. Given their tones, it didn't seem like the right time to question them. They pulled away just moments before you both emerged from the club."

His driver was unable to answer Dane's unspoken question about the police presence. "What about the tail?"

"He followed you out. I've got an eye on him."

Dane knew not to turn around. Instead, he nodded, drew in a big breath, released it, and climbed in next to his former high school girlfriend. "Sorry about that. You ready?" He turned to see Julie's warm smile, though her eyes were laced with concern.

She'd agreed to dinner with Dane prior to her return to the hotel. She doubted she'd get another opportunity for the closure she still sought. Since they'd run into each other en route to their high school reunion, unexpected events had happened between them—words had been spoken, sparks had flown. When he'd disappeared in the midst of their second unanticipated runin, she believed her opportunity had come and gone. But here they were again, and they were headed to dinner.

"I am." She'd seen Dane compose himself before he reentered the car, so she calmed her own nerves, prepared to tackle what had been left unsaid between them and quite unaware of any newly arisen issues.

Her request to leave, and Dane's suggestion to talk, offered the couple relief. Personal questions yelled in a loud dance club were no way to communicate. She was afraid at first, though, hence her need to stay to "complete her research." *A little more time to complete my mission, as well as to get my emotions, thoughts, and hormones in order, was a wise game plan,* Julie surmised.

I must've said too much, or he's a lot like my husband and needs time to think and process what's both happened and been said between us. Well, either I'm to completely close this chapter of my life now, or we'll be superficial and he'll turn up at some other point in some other way. I've waited all these years for this opportunity. He shared thoughts I'd never imagined he'd say. I said things, too. There can be no regrets. Life's too short for those.

After the limo had pulled away from the club, Dane pressed the privacy button. The glass rose silently between the passengers and the driver. *What is she thinking over there?*

"Your gears are turning so loudly, I almost can't hear *myself* think." He teased her. "What's going on? Where are you?"

Julie looked down at her hands just briefly enough for Dane to catch her hesitation. He froze. *Uh-oh.*

She knew she wanted to reassure him but couldn't—yet.

"Did you have fun?" She glanced over at Dane.

"Started with the easy questions first." He chuckled to her profile. "More than I'd expected. More than I've had in years, if we're being candid. Did—"

Julie cut him off and blurted out, "'Running' into you at this nightclub was completely unexpected—for me—not to mention a little unnerving. We hadn't exchanged information about where we were going to be or when. So how did you know? Why did you make this effort?" She waited and turned just her resolute chin and anxious eyes toward him.

"As I mentioned to you when you first arrived at the bar, I remembered the name of your agent and tracked her down."

"Dane."

"I haven't answered the second question." He patiently waited for her posture to relax. "While I'd tried to put you out of my mind throughout my college years, my law school years, *and* my apprenticeship years, I've never been able to do so, regardless of the massive amount of hours I worked. I've dated plenty of gorgeous, bright women. I even married one and had children with her. She ought to have expelled you from my memory, or, at the very least, put you in the 'historical data' section of it. Instead, the opposite happened.

"Rachel, however, grew to accept, not specifically about you, just accept I wasn't fully present for her. I'd been 'distracted' and disconnected from the start. She thought her guiles and femininity would prevail. To be fair, I wanted them to, needed them to, so I married her. Years passed before she figured out I wasn't ever going to engage the way she wanted me to, and she cut me loose. Until our reunion, I hadn't any idea I'd been unreachable ... because of you." He paused to sip some water. "You wanted closure. Genuine closure begins with honesty."

"Dane." Julie tried to interrupt again, but Dane silenced her when he grasped her gesturing hand and rested them together on the empty seat between them.

They locked eyes as he continued, neither his body language nor his tone impassive. "I know we shared this information at the airport. Then I ran out after our second impromptu reunion—don't bother to call it anything else—and couldn't bear to look for you. I'd exposed my heart about a married woman *to that* married woman. Quite frankly, I felt humiliated, like I did when I'd first learned you were about to break up with me in high school. Total regression. Juvenile cowardice, mind you, but take that at face value. Barefaced honesty froze my emotions, manners. I went on autopilot and focused on work, my safe, go-to choice. After our last flight, which I enjoyed more than any flight I've taken in decades, I knew I'd be a damned fool to let you go once again without even another word. Time to be a grown-up about what I want. So I tracked down your agent, promised I wasn't a stalker, and here we are."

"Wow." She panted, immobilized to even glance away.

"I know," he admitted, quiet, resigned to bare his soul to her.

"Thank you for such raw candor. I need to catch my breath after that admission."

"Tell me about it," he mumbled.

"You risked candor, so I'll risk gullible." She broke their eye contact to study their clasped hands. His nails were manicured, clean, and short. As she rotated his hand to be on top, she noted soft skin on his strong grip and reveled in the powerful control a simple pen stroke from it emitted. She returned to gaze at him and silently called upon his soul within to communicate. Julie turned their hands again, hers on top, a shadow of amusement behind her gaze. *Strategic.* She shifted her knees toward them. "In essence, you tell me I was the cause of your divorce, even though I've neither laid eyes on you in over two decades nor did you ever come for me. This makes no sense. Why now?" She searched for relevance, yearned for belief, looked past him through the window, confused.

The hired car prowled at first, almost catlike, through the busy city streets. Outside of it, onlookers could only see their own reflections. Inside, privacy was at a premium. The music's deep pulse, almost a tormented, raw rhythm with a haunted beauty to it, entranced its two listeners. Each note ached for the successive one to come. The pair released their hands and shifted their positions.

Julie held her breath as she realized how wet her panties had become and re-crossed her legs, tight. *Shit. That's not supposed to happen.* She caught Dane as he observed her movements. She noticed his casual readjustment of his pants. Their shifts, observable in the dark windows, reflected the same dramatic musical movements. Each one mesmerized and enticed them to physically inch closer to the other. Though they remained deliberate, reserved, off-limits on the surface, the atmospheric charge between them penetrated and betrayed their palpable energy.

A dramatic, abrupt finale allowed a brief break of the musical spell, long enough for the couple to catch their breaths, collect their thoughts, and put a moment of space between them. Another spell startled them as it began its magical assault with a deep bass and an electronic keyboard sound. An almost eerie tenor followed. Intense, rich beats pulsed with a deep level of intimacy in the small confines of the limo.

Steamy lyrics reflected Dane's thoughts with startling accuracy. Julie felt Dane almost stiffen in recognition of how he felt. The rush at her thighs' apex confirmed her own. Dane cautiously reached for Julie's hand. *Great question. I can only reply with one, though.* "Why not?" he whispered, and then hoped she hadn't heard him. *Isn't this supposed to be just a car ride, a simple transfer from the club to the restaurant and then our respective stops?* Dane knew he shouldn't reach for this closeness, this connection with her, but he just couldn't muster his well-known reserve any longer. To touch her made it all clear for him. She didn't push him away, either.

Neither expected a musical force to quicken, even throb their pulses. The power of the music, however, coupled with the Bose sound system, made them both feel as if they were in a movie. *This is nuts. I need to get out of here before something happens we'll both regret. Well, at least I will.*

"Your world, Dane, is merciless, complicated, so time with me seems, maybe, like an oasis in the midst of it all … like the proverbial life preserver thrown to a drowning man." Dane pulled her closer to him, gentle but firm. "Your world is also complicated, but—"

"You could make them both more so." *I can't believe what a soap opera I sound like.*

"This is beyond unwise," he whispered. His hand

found the back of her head, his fingers weaved under her soft hair. "Completely stupid." Like super-charged magnets in slow motion, he drew their lips close and hesitated long enough to look into Julie's eyes. As he was about to kiss her, the drive came to a bizarre stop. Julie used the opportunity.

"Dane, I'm sorry." She panted, her breath husky, vulnerable. "I've waited a long time to talk with you, but I'm not sure I'll make it to the restaurant ... like this. I ... I need to get out ... here. Please." She looked down at her hand in his, gently pulled it away, and reached for the door handle. Before she could pull it open, however, Paul explained through a speaker he thought they had a flat tire.

"We've stopped three blocks from the restaurant, and we must've driven over a nail. I'll check it out. Be right back." The vehicle door opened and closed unobtrusively to its passengers.

"Wait, before you leave—I'm sorry. I overstepped my bounds. I'm thankful for your companionship." Dane turned back to Julie to try to continue their conversation when a strange but close series of small explosions sounded. Dane quickly grabbed Julie, pushed her down onto the car floor, and covered her head with his body.

Though she didn't want to believe it, she whispered, "Is that what I think it is?"

"Please, don't say a word. I've no idea. But whether it's just around the corner or random, I don't think now is the time to pop my head up to find out—yet. Do you?" He smiled slightly, trying to keep the situation light. Then, just as fast as the fear-provoking sounds began, they ended. Silence was soon replaced with sirens and Julie's chattering teeth. She shook, cold with instant fear.

"I better check on Paul." He didn't get far, though. Julie clutched on to him.

"I don't th-th-think," she stuttered, "it's a go-go-go-good idea for you to go anywhere yy-y-yet like you s-s-said"—Julie slowly raised her eyes, ghostly pale, having no idea tears rolled down her cheeks as she tried to speak steadily—"until the police c-c-c-come and knock on the door or the windows and show their identification."

"I'll only be a moment."

"I don't believe it's a good idea for either of us to go anywhere this split second. You don't want to be accused of anything, nor do we want any further confrontations with whoever may s-s-s-still be out there. What if they're just waiting for us? What if it's the police, and we've been caught in the crossfire? When they get here, they're gonna be skittish as it is—won't know what's happening inside here versus outside there."

Julie looked calm and thoughtful in spite of her uncontrollable shaking. Her cool logic and collected demeanor kicked in. Her only thought was to keep them both safe. She fought her secondary instinct to scream, cry, and have a complete meltdown, but she knew that had to wait. *The time to melt down is not mid-crisis but after it. I'll process this later.* She'd learned this with children. *Holy crap! My kids …* she thought at that moment, her jaws clenched tight. Her eyes widened, big as saucers. She wept as her hands clasped together so hard, they turned white against her mouth in an attempt to be as quiet as possible.

Dane saw the fear and panic in her eyes but heard the logic of her words and tone. "You make good sense. I'll stay put. Besides, you're shaking. You're cold. I don't have a blanket to keep us warm. Afraid we're going to have to use body heat to help keep each other warm until we know what's happened. Hope you won't think me too forward." He hoped she'd hear his light tone and waited for her approval.

Julie barely nodded. "No, I won't. Please."

Dane's swift movement came with internal sighs and aches. *Thank Christ she said yes. Even right now, I'm desperate to hold her. I'm so fucking selfish.*

"Thank you." She robotically recalled her manners.

Dane knew Julie wasn't cold. The limo had been plenty warm, almost too warm, and Julie wore an extra layer. He just didn't want to push her too much about what she thought or felt. His instincts screamed to him that she wore a delicate balance somewhere between selfcontrol and emotional collapse. Her usual warm facial expressions had been highjacked by measured breaths to quell pure fear as it raged through her body. He took her in his arms with a deep inhale of her hair, grateful for any reason to hold her. He let it out slow and steady, hoping to send a calm signal to her, one he barely felt.

Simultaneously, it felt like forever since the shots rang out, yet as if only seconds passed while he held her. Mere minutes had elapsed, though, when police yelled for them to come out of the car with their hands up and showed their identification badges. Police and paramedic lights illuminated the immediate neighborhood as if a carnival had come to town. The aftermath of the attack began to unfold.

Dane called out just before he and Julie emerged, slowly, with their hands up as instructed by the police. "WE'RE UNARMED! JUST TWO OF US IN THE CAR!"

Nevertheless, police approached the vehicle from all sides with speed and caution in low, crouched stances.

They yelled team signals as per police communication procedures and confirmed the absence of any suspects or additional survivors elsewhere in the limo with great caution, their guns fixed on the inside. Once the couple had been extracted from the car and searched, the "ALL CLEAR!" made it obvious to the police that these were victims and not perpetrators of any crime. Julie started to collapse to the ground in front of them, but Dane caught her before she hit her head. Paramedics rushed in to assist them.

"I'm ... I'm ... I'm all right, really. I'm all right," she said, as her teeth chattered otherwise. Dane helped her get to her feet. "Easy, tiger, take it nice and easy." The medics threw silver blankets used by marathoners after a race over each of them to help warm their traumatized bodies. Julie looked up to thank them and Dane when she spotted the carnage. Dane wrapped his arms around her again, assumed the previous permission still existed, and turned her away from the bloody scene, her eyes wide with disbelief.

"Holy shit," she murmured. Not trusting her eyes, she squeezed them shut tight and buried them into Dane's shoulder as she clung to him and the silver cover. The limo driver, Paul, was dead next to the driver's side front, flat tire. Julie was shocked he had a gun in his hand and asked Dane about it.

"All of my drivers are either ex-cops or off-duty agents to protect me to some extent. For them to carry is quite commonplace today," Dane stated to Julie via the explanation he gave the officer who asked him similar questions. She shook uncontrollably from the fear-based adrenaline rush, though she worked so hard to find any level of composure. She watched Dane for affirmation of her own sanity, their connection as trauma survivors. What was clear, however, was less that they'd come through alive together and more that this hadn't been Dane's first encounter with such an event. While he was openly unhappy about it, he wasn't as shaken as Julie.

She receded into her thoughts and searched for the familiar, the calm. "Grandfather had been an undertaker, but I've never seen a bloodbath before. All evidence of bloodshed had been cleaned up, groomed, coifed even, and ready for burial. This is a small, fucking war zone. Oh my God—a third one," she rambled aloud. Next to Paul's corpse was another body, and several feet away was a third. Blood pooled next to each of them. Without realization, she spoke aloud again. "I hope they didn't suffer." She settled down a little. Logic attempted to return. She whispered in his shoulder, "I can't help but wonder what you're involved with to need armed protection." She felt his body stiffen, ever so slight an adjustment as it was.

Police shared that there'd been quite a bit of drug activity in the area in the last several months. It was unclear if Paul had been an unfortunate victim of mistaken identity or involved in events that went very wrong. In either case, he'd been prepared to protect himself and Dane, they observed. Unfortunately, only one of them survived, no doubt due to Paul's preparation. The police were able to immediately identify one of the other two bodies. It belonged to a known local drug dealer. The newest cop on the scene eagerly accepted the detectives' order to ID the third corpse.

The police interrogated Dane alone. They moved away from Julie since her loud teeth chatter challenged her to respond. Dane's brisk professionalism regained control of the interview and he explained. "I'd hired a driver, as usual when here on business, and Mrs. Archer was simply my guest."

"Who is Mrs. Archer to you?" the senior detective asked.

Respectful but quite cool, Dane remarked, "She's an old high school friend whom I unexpectedly ran into this evening." He knew better than to offer any information unless asked for it.

"Where were you headed, Mr. Michaels?"

"We were headed for dinner when this unfortunate turn of events occurred."

"Unfortunate turn of events? Mr. Michaels, are you aware of the fact that three men have been murdered? Gunned down in the street? One of them the driver you hired?"

"Detective … Handley, is it not? To point out the obvious is unnecessary given the terrified state of my companion. Quite insensitive, don't you think? I *am fully* aware of what's happened. In fact, I'm not only aware, I'm nervous and anxious, whether you think so or not, because I know—knew—this man had family. I'm trying to remain a calm, *adult* presence considering the trauma we've both faced. Wouldn't you agree that to intensify it with more emotion right now would be counterproductive?"

"Mr. Michaels, your tone—"

"I don't approve of *your* tone. It not only sounds like the borderline panic *we're* feeling, it's rather accusatory and completely unprofessional," glared Dane.

"Very well then, sir." The detective took a deep breath, clearly aware of how Dane acted more the professional he was supposed to be. "What are you able to share right now that could help us understand at least a little of what's happened here?"

Dane recognized he was very much in control of this interview now. He also accepted that he needed to give these officers just enough information to satisfy their immediate concerns. He'd thus be able to still use the trauma of the events as an excuse later on for what he wouldn't provide immediately. He used his thoughtful speech pattern to his advantage. He appeared to work hard at composure and knew he needed time to get and review facts. "I do know"—Dane took a deep breath and began with caution in his deliberate lawyer pace—"that I'd called Paul while we were still inside of the club, Club Nu, where Julie and I ran into each other. Paul wasn't parked out front where he normally would've been. I found this very odd. When I asked him about it, he'd said police had directed him to move. He never told me why the police had been there. He didn't seem to know."

The police detective listened to Dane without interruption. He didn't scribble even a single letter, though his pad and pen were in hand.

"As we proceeded to the restaurant, Paul slammed on the brakes and pulled over. He explained to us that he thought we had a flat tire. He parked the car on the side of the road, where it is now, and told me what he planned to do. I didn't get out of the car to go and assist him because I was enjoying the company of my guest. I knew he'd had it under control. He was highly capable and competent. I trusted him without reservation. Period."

"Where were you headed to dinner?"

"To an Italian restaurant in the Village."

"Name?" The detective was curt with his questions.

"Probably a place you don't know." Dane tired of the

cop's attitude.

"Try me, Michaels."

"Olio e Piú on Greenwich Avenue." The pen was now in motion.

"Did you have a reservation?"

"No."

"What were you doing in the limo while your driver attended to the flat?"

"I've already told you."

"Run it past me again."

"Enjoying my former classmate's company. It's been about thirty years since we've seen each other. We have a lot to catch up on." Dane's tone cooled the detective's blistered attitude.

The cop glanced at Julie's frightened, pale expression, and his stance shifted enough for Dane to adjust his own. "Continue, please."

Dane drew in the evening's cool air. "He was only outside of the car for a few seconds when the popping noises began again. Instantly, I knew it hadn't been a blown tire to start. I knew it was far more sinister." Dane paused for a moment, making it clear he needed a deep, slow inhale and exhale to calm his own nerves. "I instinctively grabbed Julie, Mrs. Archer, and pushed her down onto the floor of the car. I've heard such sounds where I'm based in Europe, and they always provoke fear, to say the least." Dane's morose stare caught Julie's attention. "When what I assumed to be shots fired was over, I was going to get out of the car to find Paul, make sure he was okay. I didn't recall hearing him get back in the car, let alone say he was fine. Julie, Mrs. Archer, however, requested that I not get out of the car. She was frightened and concerned we didn't know who was or wasn't still outside of it. We didn't want to get caught as innocent bystanders in the middle of some bad situation going down, whether between good guys and bad guys or just bad guys, whichever. Very soon after it was all over, though it felt like hours, we heard your sirens, your shouts through the windows."

Dane looked down at his hands on his thighs. He recalled how warm Julie's felt, how close her lips were to his, before the shots parted them. He caught himself disconnected from the bloody reality and jerked his eyes up from his legs to see her watching him. He held the gaze of her blue-green eyes, lined in crimson from soundless cries she'd shed. Her face strained to remain calm, professional even. Dane was impressed by her courage and strength, so he pressed on a little bit more, encouraged by the confidence she seemed to have in him.

"Detective, I don't know why this happened, but I do know that whenever I was in town, I called Paul directly for hire. I paid the company, for whom he usually drives, a flat fee to have unlimited and direct access to his services as I needed them when in town. We had a very beneficial relationship established. Again, I refer to my relationship with the company as well as with Paul."

"Mr. Michaels, how long had you known Paul?"

"He'd driven me for about the last six years."

"And you had no reason to doubt his loyalty, his abilities, his competency?"

"None. Ever. As I mentioned earlier, I trusted him implicitly."

"That'll be all the questions for now. Please stay available. Here's my card. If you think of any further details, please call me. We'll look for and question all other witnesses, bystanders, etc. after we wrap things up here.

We'll most likely be in touch with more questions for you after we gather additional information."

Dane accepted the business card, nodded curtly to the two officers, as well as the detective who'd said nothing during the entire interview, and turned back to Julie and the paramedics who attended to her. Her face continued to grow pale while her hands grew clammy and colder. He caught one of the medic's eyes.

"What are you doing for her profuse perspiration?" he murmured. "She's going into shock, man. *Help* her," he urged an apparent new team member. At that very moment, Julie became so confused.

"Dane, what time do we leave for the airport?" were her last words as she started to fall into him. She'd no idea she'd even uttered them.

Dane quickly shifted her into his arms to help her onto the nearby stretcher. She rallied enough to argue that she was fine, somehow had the presence of mind to lean away from the men who helped her, and then promptly threw up.

CHANGE ORDER

"BOSS, WE CAN'T hide much more without getting red-carded, unless we change our approach."

Tate deplored the words "can't" and "impossible" almost as much as he deplored Dane Michaels. "What's the problem?"

The chief of the transfer team, in turn, hated confrontations with Tate Parker almost as much as he hated Siberia. He and his teammates had been on the "freezer assignment" when Parker needed experience and meticulous execution. The subarctic temperatures of the

Yukon were a few degrees more reasonable that year. "The car bodies weigh too much with the increases as you'd requested, sir."

"I assume you and the team have spread it out, etc, etc, yada, yada."

"Of course, sir. We do have another idea, though, if you're open to suggestions."

"Always." *Well, at least I try to be.*

"The engine blocks are eventually painted. What if we liquify the gold, paint certain removable areas with it, such as the timing cover and the intake manifold to give a detailed appearance, then paint the rest of the engine, block and heads, together another color? Hide in plain sight."

"What about the older models 'whose engines were painted already assembled?"

"We'll stick to our current method but back off the quantity."

"Do it."

Chapter 75

SHAKEN AND STIRRED

SHE OPENED HER eyes to find herself in a hospital room, hooked up to all sorts of strange equipment in her right arm. Her tears immediately flowed, though she tried to stifle them with her left hand. Soft, classical music played, and room lights dimmed so the space glowed, felt less sterile. She knew someone here had known it would soothe her. She already knew this was not standard hospital procedure. So despite her tears, she began to smile when she felt the warmth of his hands.

Slowly, she followed that warmth to its source as her gaze sought his. "I'm so cold. Will you please help me feel warm again?" her whispered request raw, authentic. Her shakes had returned. He was more than grateful to oblige, since he couldn't bear to see her upset.

"Thank you." Julie breathlessly took in his warmth.

"No, thank *you*."

"Why do you thank me?"

"Because I accept such an incredible invitation to assist selfishly. There is indeed not one shred of moral decency in me as I climb into this bed to comfort you." Dane whispered his confession.

Julie froze. "What do you mean? I don't understand."

"You're going to make me spell this out?"

She didn't move. She tried not to breathe.

He took her silence exactly as she'd meant it. "Apparently you are." Unspoken words eclipsed by the beeps and whistles of hospital devices begged for relief between them. "This is a terrible time to bring it all up, especially because I'd take dreadful advantage of your … condition. Your husband will likely call any moment—"

"You called Gabe?" Dane felt her heart flutter and body tense.

"Yes, of course. You'd asked me to as they wheeled you in here last night." Julie had zero recall of her apparent request.

Dane explained. "You didn't want him to wonder where you were when you didn't answer your phone. Naturally, he sounded strained when I called, but at least he knew you were okay, not doing anything he might have been—"

"Wait, what? What do you mean?"

"Well, when men sound suspicious of their spouses, it's usually because they themselves have perhaps made less than honorable choices for which they're less than proud. When—"

"And you say he sounded … suspicious? Gabe?"

"Well, perhaps not suspicious, but … well … more guarded than concerned. I'm sure when another man who's not a cop calls about one's wife, one might … um … be guarded. Am I being unfair here? This is rather awkward."

"I'm sure anything's possible, but yes, I believe you're being unfair here. After all, how would you know about the way a less honorable man may behave? Since you're not exactly a good judge of how to read people in *human* circumstances versus business ones, I'm not sure—"

Oh damn. She's tough even in a compromised space. "Julie, I didn't mean to upset you. You've been upset enough. I merely did as you'd asked of me ... as I do now, too. Forgive me if I've passed some sort of judgment on the man. Completely unfair of me. After all, I've only barely even met him. He deserves at least the benefit of the doubt, since you've been married to him all this time."

"For all the physical warmth you provide right now, you've gone cold, formal lawyerspeak on me. Curious way to avoid explaining to me what you meant before."

Dane froze. In an attempt to push her back off that track, he kept quiet. He became aware of his body language and summoned his humanity. *She's far sharper than I'd recalled. Far more perceptive than I'd have expected after such trauma, too. Oh, fuck it.*

He let his shoulders drop an inch and felt fear, even a dash of disappointment, as it coursed through her toned figure. He indulged and lingered in the experience of their bodies pressed together. "You're far more perceptive than I'd remembered, I mean ... um ... than I'd expect after such a terrible ordeal. I tried to—" *Oh crap, did that just come straight out of my mouth?*

"Dane, what is it you need to say to me? If I'm to be shocked anymore today, this is the time and place. At least they can help me here, right?"

"And you still have a sense of humor!" *This woman is maddening.* "Let's leave it all alone for now. I'm just jealous that he's married to you and I'm not. There. I said it. Further talk will only find trouble—"

"You're *about* to find trouble, Mr. Michaels, for being in bed with this patient. First from me, and secondly, from her husband, who's headed down the hallway," quietly spat the night nurse as she warned them both. "*I'll* question the patient later," she decided as she glared at them.

Just as Dane had straightened out the bed and himself, then tucked behind the room's door, Gabe entered the room, winded, flustered. Julie immediately began to shake again. If Dane hadn't seen her shake from the trauma just moments ago, he'd have been concerned about why she did so in this man's presence.

"Oh God, baby, are you all right?" Gabe was by her side, kissed her head, and touched her face when Julie realized she was rude and looked to reintroduce the two men. The only other person in the room, however, was the night nurse, who shook her head "no" as she scowled at Julie. The nurse put her finger to her lip, a signal to Julie to keep quiet. Julie didn't want the nurse to have the wrong impression, nonetheless, and pressed her.

"Where did Dane disappear to? I wanted to thank him again."

"Yes," Gabe said warmly. "I need to thank him for calling me and for watching over you until I got here."

"Julie, honey." The nurse's shrewd answer paused her patient's uneasiness. "Mr. Michaels left when you last fell asleep hours ago, when he knew your husband had landed. He didn't want to intrude on your reunion."

"Well, that gratitude will have to wait until another time then. We just need to focus on you getting back on your feet. Holy crap, you look amazing considering what went down. Dane explained the whole thing to me. Sounded scary! All those years I commuted in and out of this city for work, and I never experienced any incident like that. Guess I was just lucky. At least you're safe. I love you, baby." Gabe spoke with such relief. In fact, overwhelmed relief. To Julie, it seemed over the top, especially for Gabe.

Chapter 76

COVER

WHAT A STUDY in mindfucks. From behind the door, her initial little girl voice portrayed innocence with a demure appeal. Once the door opened, however, a vivacious adult woman betrayed a dignity and strength to be respected. "Little Girl" kept "Adult" tucked away until challenged. Attractive cover. "Damn sure that's an act, cuz shit, there's an energy there. Couldn't miss it. I know she thinks she hid it. Her fundamental power oozed, hidden, like she's waiting for unsuspicious prey to stray into her crosshairs. That's fucked up. I've got to warn Julie, but about what? I'm just gonna call her and say, 'Hey, Julie, watch out for some sixtyish-year-old weird artist.' Right."

Waffles shook his head as he drove around the apartment complex's block a couple of times, attempting to clear his muddled thoughts. *No one ever told me that to talk to an artist could jumble your own thoughts. I feel like a box of colored crayons strewn across a table badly in need of sorting and organizing. An organized artist. That's bullshit. She may have me at arm's length just now, but it's temporary. Who's she connected to? Someone at least somewhat important because I've had the same dumb-asses follow me since I left her. Do they seriously believe I don't know they're there? One with an unmistakable ponytail, too. Nothing better for the law than a stupid criminal.*

He headed back to the firehouse for dinner ... and then it hit him.

Chapter 77

DOWNWARD TREND

SIMPLE TASKS IN Julie's life commingled levels of awareness both remarkable and mundane. Humor could always be found amidst these uncomplicated nibbles of time, especially after the harrowing experience in New York. After a brief reprieve, though, her every move seemed fraught with paranoia again. She wondered who followed her now. *Will this ever end?* She lamented. *I've been connected to God knows what. If I had a clue—people, place, or object, animal, mineral, or vegetable—that would help. But I've no idea to what. Tensions compound daily, often hourly, with Gabe over this, too.*

"Just stop writing about the auto industry!" he barked. "The articles must stir up trouble because of the questions you ask, and the press about the novel release must be setting nerves on edge. Concerned? I'm more than concerned about our safety. What the hell are you writing?"

"What?" *Deep breathe.* "What is *with* you and the *drama?* The anger and the snapping? You've *read* them yourself, so you *know* there's nothing provocative in them! Get a grip, because your losing it doesn't help us, me, the kids, yourself, for God's sake!" Julie lashed back. "You're stressed about work, so you take my head off. Please. Just stop it. People are weird."

"Yes, I'm stressed about work. I try to keep a roof over our heads, and you seem almost ... well ... *determined* to let someone blow it up!" Gabe just spat hurtful words at this point.

"Your world, which seemed clear and obvious, Gabe, has blurred. Yes, some scary and even creepy challenges exist here, which I'm puzzled about, but you've been more distressed and anxious than I am. I need to take time to reason and talk through possibilities, sort through options, and process via elimination what the fuck I'm onto. Just conversations with you *about* your work, or mine, for that matter, seem to provoke even more stress. They're meant to be expansive and forthcoming, open, but instead, they cause more communication failures between us, like bad games of telephone. I'm damned if I show concern and ask because I'm accused of interrogation, and I'm damned if I don't because then I must not care. These are your assumptions either way. 'Houston, we have a problem!' How do you want me to go forward here? Please, tell me what you want from me." Julie bit her lip. She didn't want to exacerbate the already escalated tension between them but was aware she probably had. *Screw it.*

After New York, Julie noted that all the gains they'd made in their marriage disappeared. Strains multiplied like viruses. However, this conversation appeared more extreme than usual. Gabe paced, drove his frantic hand through his thick hair, and stopped to grab a handful of it at one point. "You think you're so smart, don't you? That I'm just stupid, unaware? Well, I just don't get how you miss this real live nightmare we're in. It's not fucking complicated! What you write wreaks havoc. Bam. Fucking simple, my dear. Instead, you want to play the victim now? Poor you! Misunderstood bullshit!" Gabe stomped out of the room but pivoted and returned a dozen footsteps away, finger pointed at his wife, teeth gritted, combative, angry. "And it IS bullshit!"

"Gabe, you're right. No victims here. Never said I was one, honey." She zigzagged their tenuous emotional landscape. "Just frustrated, as you are, by the tailspin we're in. Yes, there are other factors—for us both—we can't finger, yet. Why not just share yours with me so I can help, or, at the very least, be compassionate? Then I'll share with you."

Gabe's belligerent denial wasn't new. It was more extreme and animated. Then a sudden energy shift, not a pendulum swing in the opposite direction, more like tectonic plates, his tone defeated, chilled. "There's nothing else to it. The stress of work and the pressures of growing a business."

Her blood cooled. Fear edged to the forefront of her brain. "Gabe, a while back, you claimed I was critical of you. You said I'd cite your inadequacies, which exemplified my lack of support. Now you've about-faced and my novel is contentious. Instead of pointing fingers, how about we be honest with our feelings?"

"You're one to talk about honest feelings," he stabbed, jaws clenched again. His hostility simmered. "Go ahead. Share."

Crap. Here goes. "Okay. I don't understand why I have to get information from others and not from you about me. It hurts me when you don't share directly with me, other than angry words."

"What does that have to do with this conversation?"

"You said share. I shared."

"Stalled, more like. What are you talking about?"

"My random conversations with managers yield very

unexpected information. I've heard grumbles about the company's overextended, generous schedule. Threw up a red flag for me. Why not share your frustrations with me? I'm a safe person to vent with. You know this. I know your generous heart. I'm not here to judge. I might even offer a little balance to what you think? Maybe? I'd like the same balance with my thoughts. Reciprocation."

Gabe, smug and combative, startled his wife with bitterness. He narrowed his stare and bore into her confusion. His lips drew back from sneer to snarl. "So it's now about *you?*" He stalked toward her. "YOU want to matter? YOU want to be heard. YOU!" Julie didn't back away. Instead, she lifted her chin, discreet, regal, defiant. "The drain on company resources, combined with your gratuitous auto industry articles, seem to be a sleazy Catch-22 for us, like rubberneckers as they pass a grisly accident. They want to see but regret it immediately. Then there's the car auction, maddeningly at almost the center of it ..." His irrationality yielded to an empty gaze as his voice trailed off, disturbed and sadly disconnected.

Gentle. "Why focus so much to any one event? Makes zero sense to me. Some of the most ordinary but fabulously wealthy people in the world attend that auction. For reasons I'd love to learn, it's one event to which you can rarely seem to say 'no.'" Julie took the chance, dangled the disguised question as a concern, and waited. *What nags me about it? Is Gabe's philanthropic kindness somehow connected to my shadow ... or vice versa?*

Just as the idea jumped into her mind, she defended her husband in her own thoughts. *Remember—my shadows started to appear just after I'd returned from my high school reunion. Dane's likely connected.* She lowered her eyes a moment, saddened by her deduction. *He, too, is involved in the auto industry as Bob's and Tate's lawyer as well as Bob's client. Bob, my neighbor,* she considered. *Perhaps if I spoke with Bob, figured out who else of Dane's auto industry clients were also Bob's and what they were involved with, I might figure out who's got me under surveillance and why. I hope it's not drugs. That just wouldn't make any sense to me. Dane's not into that scene at all ... is he? Time to get neighborly.*

Rather than answer his wife at all, Gabe served her a heaping portion of irrelevance, glowered, and fumed out.

DIGGING

MID-BREAK, BOB WARNED his apprentice, "Don't talk with anybody who doesn't have the respect to call ahead." But as he finished his sentence, Julie walked in. "Except a good neighbor. Well, hello, good neighbor."

"Hey." She raised her chin to the apprentice. "Hey, Bob. How goes it? I'm sorry I didn't call first." She'd overheard.

"I'll forgive you this time." He winked. "Tighten those wires and give her another try. We can weigh her afterward. I'll be right back." Bob walked to where Julie stood in the doorway. "What can I do for you, young lady?"

"I'm in the midst of some research, need a few details for my story, and hoped you might fill in some blanks."

"I'll help if I can."

"Thanks. Often, the cars you renovate end up at the Barrett-Jackson Auction. Whether you bought, redid, and sold them yourself, or clients hired you for your genius, many end up there, right?"

"Right."

"What percentage of your work is sold at that auction

do you think versus privately?"

"Curious question. Why do you ask?"

"Well, in this high-tech age of instant gratification and heavy competition, I wondered how many consignors and members are independent versus work with a team?"

"And that's an interesting question."

"You work mostly alone, right?"

"Except for a couple of assistants." His head nodded toward the young guy in the shop.

"Unless all the input from the varied contributors is on the same page, discrepancies might impact the end result, right?"

"Absolutely."

"For example, how might those discrepancies affect, say, a classic look?"

"Too many variations to consider." Bob laughed, but his watchful eyes bore into hers.

"Color choice? Interior materials? Matte or bright chrome trim?"

"What are you after, Julie?"

"I seek to understand collaboration within this tight-knit but cutthroat community."

"What do colors and materials have to do with this?"

"I don't know. I don't understand how group dynamics might be an issue, what spurs the cutthroat part. Well, anyway, back to an earlier question. What percentage of your work is sold at the Barrett-Jackson?"

"I'd have to look up the exact numbers, but more than seventy-five percent of my work ends up at auction. Work on my own stuff takes much longer because it's just a hobby, for fun, for me."

"What percentage is just yours versus with a team?"

"Most of that percentage, clients hire me."

"Are you part of a team that works for those clients, or are you the only one?"

"Both. Mostly I'm part of teams, though. Like any industry, there are specialties and subspecialties."

Her playful smile and bright eyes softened the barrage of questions. "What's your favorite area to work on?"

"The engine rebuilds."

"Is that the area of expertise for which you're most called on?"

"Yes." Bob grew uneasy out of the blue.

"So the bodies, or frames, come to you with a messed up engine?"

"Usually."

She saw him shut down. "Bob, what just happened?"

"I got uneasy about your questions."

"I noticed. Why? I'm just trying to understand the general process, gauge what's happening industry-wide, and share that." Julie saw Bob breathe and lower his shoulders.

"Okay, sorry. I had a strange start this day. What was your question?"

Julie continued as if nothing had transpired, but she knew she'd stumbled on a touchy topic. *What was it? My neighbor appears very off, and he doesn't ruffle easily.* "Sure. I asked about the condition of the engines when they come to you."

"Frankly, I prefer the whole vehicle comes to me. BUT, when it's just the engines, I inspect them quite carefully. What irregularities have they suffered prior? What are their idiosyncrasies? They all have them. Just like people." He smiled at Julie.

She smiled back and placed her hand on his arm. "Are you always busy? It sure seems like it!"

"Busier than I ever intended to be. Certainly, busier than my wife would like me to be."

"So to take on clients is—"

"I'm not." Bob cut her off.

"What happens if one of your current clients insists?"

"I have no problem telling them 'no.'"

"When was the last new one?"

"Julie, there's no delicate way to ask, so I'll just be blunt. What does that have to do with this story?"

"Fair enough. Based on when you last took on a new client, plus an assessment of how busy you are in comparison to others locally, I'm able to hypothesize what's happened regarding industry-wide growth. Make sense?"

"Understood. I took on my last client, at least for a while, a few months ago. Didn't want him. Sorry I took him, too."

"Why is that?"

"He's a young upstart and a bit of a bully. Thinks he can be gruff and get his way."

"Oh. You okay, though? I gather he was the one here earlier then."

"You gather too well. Never mind him. Where were we?"

"Who are your clients in general? Business owners, the independently wealthy, collectors, fellow renovators, young upstarts?" She winked and smiled.

Bob stared at Julie.

"Bob, I would guess that this is a rich man's game, especially because of all the glamour that swirls around the auction—the opening gala, the VIP areas, the furs, the jewelry, etc. With that said, I've also seen some rather inconspicuous folks, even downright destitute-looking, spend unthinkable amounts of money. See why I ask? What's the scoop?"

Bob nodded his head. "Yes to all of those options. My assistant, for example, graduated from college with a math degree. Planned to teach, like his parents. He wanted to make some extra cash several summers back tinkering with cars, a hobby to enjoy but get paid for. He just loves what we do and never left. He's paid far more than a teacher. I know he's made a small fortune, some from helping me (I pay him well), some from translating his knack with numbers into an ability to run this business. He apprentices in the shop with me part of the day. We dive into the books in the office the other part."

"How do your clients find you?"

"Word of mouth."

"But you just said you weren't taking—"

"I know what I said, and that's true. Normally, though, it's through word of mouth. This newest client, acquired by word of mouth, keeps me busier than normal."

"Again, I hear the aggravation. You said you're sorry you took him?"

Realizing he'd said too much, Bob tried to reverse the course of this conversation with the simplest proven method—a coughing fit. "Young people get uncomfortable when an old person sounds like they're about to kick the bucket," Bob once shared with his wife. Within minutes, Julie helped him to a stool in his workshop, thanked him for his time, and left him with his assistant.

"Works every time."

Chapter 78

CONCERNS

FROM THE FIRST day he met Tate Parker, Bob Couvey's instincts urged him to turn this one away. He and Victor had been friends for so long, though, that he'd decided to ignore his gut. Months after the initial request, Bob chalked up his reservations to an old man's foolishness and took on this new client.

His skepticism continued, however, while he worked with Parker. Though it had only been for a few months, he knew a problem existed with this most recent English import. *AustinHealey's just don't weigh that much.* He'd looked it up to be certain. *The '62 3000 Mark II Roadster is a solid, powerful car, but a ton and a half just seems to be a giveaway that an issue exists. It's way off.*

Bob checked his scales three times. He had his wife look over his shoulder while he weighed the body a third time. They had the scales recalibrated, confirmed there wasn't a random part in the car they'd forgotten to remove, and even had his wife take his temperature to make sure he wasn't coming down with some bug.

He was perfectly fine.

Chapter 79

REFLECTION

DANE KNEW THAT night in New York City. He knew he and Julie had been followed. As he stood at the bar and ordered a bottle of Veuve Clicquot La Grande Dame Champagne with two glasses, Paul's text warned Dane. Shortly after he'd arrived at the nightclub and waited for Julie, somebody had followed him in. A second, unidentified person followed Paul in the valet lot. *Who the hell was it?* Dane couldn't be certain yet.

"The one thing I *am* certain about is not wanting Julie involved any further than she already appears to be, albeit unintentionally. I wonder if I can dissuade her from writing about the auto industry." He hadn't yet warned her local police department about any of his suspicions, because he wasn't certain they were equipped for what may be ahead. *Sometimes it's just better for a community not to know. It can lead to hysteria.* Even more importantly, he didn't want Julie's good name or her safety to be compromised. At all costs, he'd keep her safe.

Chapter 80

SCHEMING

RACHEL KNEW SHE needed to play Victor just right. *He's far too smart to be easily manipulated,* Rachel acknowledged to herself. *Yet he seems to be falling for my "maiden in distress" act. Maybe he's playing me?* She considered her options when Tate walked in early for their lunch appointment.

The Widder Hotel, located in the middle of Zurich, was a perfect location to conduct quiet business. A courtyard table in the restaurant allowed for an undisturbed exchange between the part-time lovers. Tate leaned down for a traditional Swiss greeting but, on the third pass, grazed his cheek slowly against Rachel's and inhaled her perfume. She smiled as he began his premeditated seduction.

"So you'll be my dessert, and now to figure out lunch." He grinned. He knew Rachel could handle his presumptuousness.

"I know you say that to all the girls, so I won't be terribly flattered," she countered with their typical flirtatious banter.

"But former Mrs. Michaels, as a married woman, albeit to a different man, I'd think you'd be scandalously turned on by my advances, even after all these years we've known each other."

"Mr. Parker, you shock me by how uninformed you

are. I've just separated from husband number two and am propositioned too often to count by more established men than yourself."

"More established? Posh. Separated? Well"—he shifted his now uncomfortable pants—"how about I make *you* my meal instead of waiting until dessert? I know who manages this hotel." He pushed and took his cell phone out of his jacket pocket.

She placed her open palm over his phone. "Why don't we talk first? I know you've not gotten laid in, what, hours? If you're still so turned on after we chat, then—"

"So crass for such a well-bred woman. To be as frank, but not as tactless, it's been weeks, truly."

"Lost your touch?"

"Hardly. I, too, am in the midst of a breakup, if you must know, plus this complicated nonsense with your ex. Eh. Travesty." He smirked at Rachel.

"Isn't it?"

"But if I don't get in your delectable panties immediately, Im afraid I may be woefully disagreeable to whatever you choose to share." He hardened in two ways.

"Tate." Rachel leaned in to eye him, their noses skimming conspiratorially. "That sounds too much like—blackmail."

"Don't tell me you're not aroused. I know you, remember?" He murmured, licked his bottom lip, ready to send the approaching waiter away, when Dane Michaels walked in with a client and made eye contact. "Need to kiss me right now." Before Rachel could turn around to see what had pushed Tate, he took his arm from the top of her chair and pulled her in for the most passionate kiss she'd experienced since their last kiss so many months ago. She succumbed, completely unable to resist or even think through it to stop herself.

When Dane left the terrace, Tate withdrew from Rachel, though he kept but a breath's distance between them. "Thank you for trusting me. Now, where were we? Yes, more of this." He couldn't be discreet enough for Rachel in public, so he reached for her hand to touch his leg and made clear his intentions.

Smart to Tate's ways, she shook her brain free of the natural dopamine shot and whispered, stern with a smile. "I'll give you what you want when we've finished here, *and* you share what just happened."

"I'll *take* what I want when we've finished here, and share what just happened after I get what I want," he coyly negotiated.

"Deal." She kissed him to seal it, pleased with the outcome. Then, just to make sure she walked away satisfied from their lunch, she taunted Tate. "I need to address an issue you brought up earlier. Just for the record, and to make sure I have your rapt attention, I don't have on delectable panties."

"You don't? Please don't burst my bubble intentionally and tell me you've moved to granny's."

Got him. Poker-faced, she touched her bottom lip and demurred, "I'd like to think what I have on aren't granny's yet."

Tate waited, shifted away from her slightly, and fully checked out her glove-like dress. His eager eyes travelled her body and grew wider as he caught his breath.

"That's right, Mr. Parker, I wear nothing today. Now who's been presumptuous?"

"Let's get on with why we appear to be here before I bend you over my lap right at this table." *She's got my attention all right, and now I've got hers.*

She smiled and knew they were both smug with satisfaction and purred cotton candy, phony sweet. "It's this awful drivel about Dane. It would appear he's stolen money from his firm."

Tate sat back enough to give them both room to think and scheme. "Oh?" he said with mock concern. "And I thought he was a scrupulous fellow."

"Apparently not."

Chapter 81

SPIRAL

AFTER GABE'S IRATE outburst about her writing, he winced as he admitted to Julie how much he just missed her and was afraid for her safety and the safety of their family. "My frustration and fear took over." He begged her forgiveness with his eyes, self-conscious in his desire to hold her and feel her physically safe in his arms. His forceful stride across the room caused Julie to reflexively shrink back an inch as he sat beside her on the couch and laid his head in her lap, a passivity she'd not seen since they'd dated. His justification was supposed to explain away his outlandish fury. "I'm a man, Julie, and real men protect their families. I feel out of control, like I can't protect you from these fucking, weird events. You don't understand because you're not a man."

As he turned his head toward her body to hide his face, a little ashamed, he breathed deep to resettle himself. Julie felt his body tension both skyrocket then calm with only his head in her lap. Uncertain, she placed her hands, tender to his admission, on his face. He felt her warm hands stroke his hair and neck. His near-rabid breaths steadied as he sought her naked skin, reassurance of her presence. He unbuttoned her jeans, unzipped them to expose a pale lavender, lacy band, and pushed her untucked shirt up enough to nuzzle her bare lower abs.

His exhales slowed and deepened. Julie leaned over her husband's buried head in her own small, protective gesture. "Oh, honey." She oozed concern. *What is happening with you? I'm not sure whether to be terrified or mollified.*

Her scent is hypnotic. Gabe burrowed his erratic nose and heightened senses farther into her skin without even the slightest glance up for her approval, each inhale slower, more erotic than the last. He reached his hands under her legs and behind her. As he grasped her jeans-clad ass, now his captive audience, he thumbed where the cheeky seam of her jeans came together. *I need to be in her.*

Julie turned her husband's face up to hers and begged with her eyes for an answer to her unasked question. Gabe's softened, apologetic gaze appeared drugged with lust as he answered hers and rose up, like a man reborn, powerful on his elbow, and skimmed her sex with his fingers along the way. She froze, confused and turned on. *His messages are so mixed. One minute he's pissed and the next he's horny. Damn, he knows the buttons to push. I love this side.* "You're so right, baby. I'm not a man, and all I want is for you to fully protect me … inside and out. Now."

"Your want is shameless. I need to get to all of you to protect you." His voice husky with desire, he removed his hand from under her and reached around to find her bra clasp. "Where are the kids?"

"What kids?" she whimpered. *His moods are ferocious to understand, but his body language is clear right now. Stay present.*

"Ha ha. Activities. Got it. How long do we have?"

"Forty-five minutes 'til I leave."

Gabe already had Julie's shirt over her head and bra unhooked by the time she'd panted out her answer. Breasts freed, he laved her already-erect nipple with his experienced tongue. He knew her body so well. One hand returned between her legs. "I can feel you need my care, need me in you." He reached for the small packet in his pocket.

"So prepared."

"You need protection," he quipped.

She laughed at the absurd remark, even as she unzipped his jeans and sprung him free.

As fast as he'd hardened, Gabe opened the packet and rolled it down his full length. Their time was limited.

He lay Julie back on the couch and slid off her jeans and wet panties. He looked from them to her softened gaze and growled, "You're so beautiful, so ready, and you're all mine. I protect what's mine." He slid himself all the way in her. "Mine." His heart thudded. She felt it. An alarm rang out in Julie's brain, like an intruder alert. Gabe raised himself over his wife, pulled almost all the way out, and gently started back inside her. "You. Are. Mine." Then …

As she fought to ignore that panicky doubt to stay present, feel the ecstasy of their union, Julie's eyes flew open in a soundless scream as Gabe slammed into her. That alarm in her mind shrieked, *What? Fuck! Holy shit! What's—?* "Mine!" He growled louder, only this time into her ear and put his full weight on her. He used his dominant male presence to make his point. "If I can't protect what's mine, then I'm not a man, Julie, and I am a man." He pulled out and slammed into her again, spiraling out of control.

We've had hot, rough sex before, but there's no love in his body suddenly. Panic clawed through her. "Gabe! You're hurting me. *Please* be gentle." Julie tried to move out from under her formidable husband.

"How can I protect you if I'm not with you? You want

to travel and do research and get blown up and shot at? Do you? How about this? Is this what you want, too? Am I not rough enough for you? You need to go out and find it?" He pulled out of her, again sending mixed signals he'd fulfill her pleas, but slammed into her harder. He snapped.

Julie begged, frantic. "Please, Gabe. Stop! You're hurting me!" She tried to stay calm, but her heart pounded loudly in her ears.

"I'm not hurting you the way they tried to hurt you. Don't you get that?" His sanity flashed but failed to return. That snap of temper, coupled with her being physically under his control, turned him on. He slowed down but was harder than he'd ever been. *What the fuck am I doing? What point do I make by hurting her? What is the matter with me?*

Julie felt all the slight shifts in her partner's body. "Gabe?" Frightened and unaware of what was happening, she caressed and whispered his name as she spoke it, praying for his lucidity. "Come back to me. Please."

"Did you lie to me about that reunion? Did you get tangled up with crazy shit back there that led to the auto exposé?" He began to pull out of her again in slow motion as he spoke through clenched teeth. *Oh fuck, her body stiffened. I'm on it.* "Julie, talk to me. Now!" He roared back into her hard, then picked up his pace. "Now I'll take us both over the edge. You can deny how you feel, but you're fucking soaked. I'm harder than I've ever been and then— we—will—talk. Do you understand?" He eased the ferocity of his penetration so his wife would feel their connection and find elation.

She nodded her agreement. *Thank God he's eased up. Wait ... what ... no!* She swallowed a scream.

"But first," he said as he grabbed both of her hands pushed against his chest and pinned them above her head.

He threatened her, ruthless, unhinged. "Don't you understand? They want to hurt you? Is that what you want? You want me to hurt you to get your attention, too?"

"No, Gabe. Fuck. No, baby." *Oh shit, please.* "You don't really believe I *want* to be hurt, do you? Is that what this is about? You question your fucking manhood? Well? DON'T!" She shouted at him, determined to take back her power in the midst of her loss of control.

"See?"

"What?"

"Look how you respond? Your hips thrust up to meet mine. You've wanted it more—"

"You've misinterpreted my actions. I'm just trying to meet you to slow you down. I want you to make love to me, not fucking violate me!" She screamed, broke down in tears, and sobbed.

Shocked by her vehemence, shame washed over him. Gabe backed off enough to salvage their connection and satisfy each other, but not without tears and complete confusion by what had happened between them. Julie withdrew to the bathroom and simmered, furious and humiliated with both Gabe and herself. *Our conversations have been intense, heavy, negative. But this? Why? That wasn't about his concerns*, she spat soundlessly. Emotionally exposed, as if an interrogator's spotlight pinpointed her anguish, she stifled sobs in the strangled silence of the tiny space. *My ability to communicate my emotions has become contentious, almost suffocated. I feel manipulated—no, betrayed. By MY feelings? His? Was this about control? Or ego? It wasn't love, that's for damned sure.*

Julie wondered what Gabe thought now. *I need to draw my boundaries and then guard them, not allow them to be violated ever again. GUARD them.* She questioned the need to guard herself with a life partner. *Is he that to me ... or isn't he? Maybe what just happened is the obvious answer. And what about Dane?* She recognized, too, with him she had to put logic before her emotions. *I won't get to the bottom of any of these issues easily. If I could at least determine which sides these men sit on, friend or foe? Who can I confide in? Share and process information with? Or am I alone in this?*

Chapter 82

GLITCH

"HOW COULD THIS be?" she roared into the phone. "*I've* checked *every* single detail on this project. I've *personally* vetted *every* one of those employees—down to the cleaners. Are you certain Tate, I mean, Mr. Parker knows? *How* is it possible that even a *single* detail escaped?" She stared out the kitchen window, suspicious of the manager who'd texted her. "You call this a *glitch*? If you don't want to see what rhymes with glitch in person, I'd figure out how an unapproved car even found our gates—and I'd do it within the hour."

She glared at her dogs as she punched the end button on her cell and paced the kitchen floor, wondering if they'd share her secrets. "You two know you've got it good here, right? Mum's the word?" she asked them as she scratched behind their ears and under each collar.

She pressed Tate's number to dial it but got his voice message instead. "Tate, this is Houston. We have a problem. Call me immediately." She hung up.

"Our run's gotta wait. I've got to find Tate."

Chapter 83

BAT PHONE

JULIE'S CONVERSATION WITH Bob yielded little information. Bob cited "client privacy issues." *I know, however, if Bob's shrew wife wasn't so damned insistent about being present for nearly every conversation anyone had with her husband, Bob might share a little more to help keep this neighbor safe.* She recalled an old adage from her mom. "There's more than one way to skin a cat, honey."

There was also this gem from her grandmother. "Julie, dahling, ya gonna catch maw flies with honey than ya will with vinega'." Julie chuckled at the memory. She was seven when she realized there was an 'R' at the end of vinegar and that it was supposed to be pronounced.

Prior to her knowledge that she'd been shadowed and her every movement documented, prior to bomb detonations or close encounters of an ugly kind on airplanes and even her own home, Julie didn't think twice about leaving her house to *do* period. Now, as she prepared to leave, she was rattled. "Shit," she muttered to herself. "That means a 'W' for the bad guys—and that just won't do." She picked up her cell. *Think I'll check in with Aubrey again.*

"Hey, good morning, Aubrey. I didn't expect you to pick up, truth be told."

"Why? You have my 'Bat Phone' number. I answer

161

this one without fail. What's up, my friend? You okay?"

"Yes, I'm fine," she grumbled.

"You don't sound fine."

Julie wanted to confide in someone about Gabe's behavior and what happened between them but was uncertain who to trust ... especially her law enforcement friend. "So an item of concern we *must* cover, just so I have some peace of mind, is the fact that Gabe, the kids, and I are supposed to go to Maryland for a basketball tournament. This trip's been planned for months because of Katie's travel ball season. This was, of course, B.A.I.T."

"B.A.I.T.?"

"Before arousal ignited temptation, shall we call it? Before the 'excitement' began."

"Wow. Clever acronym. Dare I ask? What's the aroused issue? What's the ignited temptation?"

"The issue? I'm still under surveillance. You probably know this, though."

Aubrey said nothing.

"So I'm concerned about leaving Arizona. To be perfectly honest with you, I'm worried about my home. I'm worried about my dogs, my friend who takes care of them. I'm not comfortable."

Still no comment.

"Aubrey? Still there?"

"Yeah, sorry. Keep going. I was making a few notes."

"Okay. The flip side. I wonder if it wouldn't be a bad idea just to get out of Dodge? Perhaps it's a good time to not be here and just be somewhere else?"

More silence.

"Which will be most helpful? How will I not put others at risk? Should I just send Gabe and the kids? Would that leave an easy target and me alone? Or would it be better to give you and your people time and space to get ahold of whoever wants to play 'Follow Julie'? Unless it's you who's got an eye on me. That's weird. I'll take your silence as an answer, cuz shit, I just love to hear myself talk. Perhaps you've got someone in your office?"

Aubrey smiled, thankful. *Finally, she picks up the cues.* "Yes. You've clearly given this some thought. Let me talk to my direct superior and banter the options around, okay? You raise many good points. You haven't shared what you think is the temptation, though."

"I can't say for sure because I'm not clear on much myself yet. But here's what I am certain about—I somehow invite trouble right now. When I consider all the creepy and often scary shit that's happened since my high school reunion, my mouth dries, my gut flip-flops."

"Ah … the ole sixth sense kicked in, did it?"

"Aubrey, you're making fun of me. I recognize the art of distraction."

"You know me so well. You sure you don't want a job? You're solid with details."

"Very funny, my friend."

"I'm not being funny right now. I'm serious."

"You can't be serious." Julie laughed at the absurdity of her friend's statement.

"Why not? We have agents of all ages, you know. Though you're past the age range to start, you could be an independent contractor."

Julie hesitated. "You *are* serious."

"Since when have you known me to say 'I'm serious' and not mean it?"

"Well, I guess there's always a first. Writing about car restoration has certainly uncovered some weird-ass shit, hasn't it?"

"You haven't answered my question."

"Seriously?"

"Seriously."

"I'm a valuable ground person for now."

"You're more than just valuable for now. You think. You're clever. You ask tons of questions to yield crazy amounts of information from people and follow directions."

"Wow. Thank you. I needed the confidence boost." Both women laughed. "Coming from you? Not just because of your position, more because of our friendship and our awesome history together, it feels like we ... well ... don't take this the wrong way, like we're partners in crime again!" Julie giggled. A flash from their college nights reminded Julie of both naughty and nice experiences. They'd always been accountable to each other whether in trouble or whether they followed rules to the letter.

"I feel the same way! I know when we speak, we can trust each other. In this business, that's hard to come by. Maybe now you understand why I ask if you might want a job? We'd put you through a bit of coursework and have you do legwork. There's upward mobility, as slow as it may be. I'm serious."

"Well, you sound serious."

"One hundred percent."

"So do I gather you need more info on this car stuff?"

Aubrey ignored Julie's comment. "Think about it, if nothing else. Rare exceptions exist to rules. Besides, you already comprehend the world of acronyms." Aubrey chuckled and again hoped her friend understood others were still present during the call. "What did you mean by 'arouse or ignite temptation'? Lure trouble?" Aubrey needed more information.

"As I'd mentioned, from the first time I ran into Dane here at the airport before the high school reunion"—Julie waited for Aubrey's acknowledgement—"he's been aroused, you could say, and we've stirred up unresolved issues I didn't even realize we still had." She hesitated. "Um ..."

"Julie?"

"Issues with Gabe, too."

"What does that mean?"

She hesitated, sighed as she felt her cheeks blush. "Apparently, Gabe's ego has been ignited by fear, I think."

"Are you okay?"

"Sure ... no ... I don't know," she conceded.

"Julie, did Gabe hurt you?"

"Please, Aubrey."

"Son of a—"

"I have to process—"

"You mean make more excuses."

"No. I'm finished with excuse bullshit. I've managed and contained our state of affairs, let's call it."

"What does that mean?"

"I'd rather not discuss this further. Back to your question. I've aroused strong, fearful sentiments and ignited enough temptations to have me followed—again, as well as tempt unsafe actions from others. Does any of this make sense to you? I'm an emotional, freakin' cluster. Ergo my loads of questions."

"Give me till the end of the day. Is that a possibility?"

"Yes, that will work. That'll be all the time I've got, though. If I have to make any changes to our reservation, they'll need to be made today."

"Very well. And we're not finished with the other

topic, missy. Talk to you soon and stay safe." The quiet disconnect static hung on Aubrey's last two words like a storm cloud's approach when she heard bags rustle and felt her home's energy shift.

Chapter 84

DISCONNECT

WHAT HAD STARTED as conciliatory lovemaking, tender and hot, after an impassioned apology one afternoon, turned painful, harrowing, and dangerous. Gabe and Julie's emotional states never caught up with their sexual ones. Gabe's brash threats hurled a volatile mix of despotism, affection, and fear. Julie felt battered and exhausted by his impetuous switches. Defiant, she insisted Gabe move out immediately. He didn't argue. He just packed a bag, tormented by guilt, wordless and dismayed.

"I need to ask you one question, and then I'll leave."

Julie leaned against the doorjamb and hugged herself tight, braced for another of his impulsive tirades. Jaw clenched, upset and confused, she raised her chin with familiar courage and dragged her eyes up to meet his. She opted for bold instead of compassionate.

His tone laid bare his bewilderment. "We ended on a total high. We both climaxed, we cried, we conquered what happened ... together. Why do you want me to go then?"

His smooth, savvy, adaptable side's resurfaced. Julie shook. "The words you snarled at me as you rammed me so hard, I cried out in pain for you to stop? They were ominous, enraged words. You hadn't been drinking. You hadn't just come home from a long day at work, exhausted and short-tempered, not that any of that would excuse what you did. Your spontaneous, vicious mental state forewarned us both. You're not even aware of the mixed message you send now, are you? A real-life Dr. Jekyll/Mr. Hyde." Though the quiet hum of the air circulation fan kicked on, Gabe's face dampened, childlike in his anxiety. Julie barely contained her own screams of fear as her fisted hand crushed against her lips and dropped her voice to a fervent whisper. "Gentle, almost nervous? The fact that you've got to ask me why—wow. Right now, you're not the powerful man I married. The Gabe Archer I married liked his way, but he never needed to threaten me in his attainment of it. My Gabe can command, dominate, be aggressive and hot in passion, not brutally intimidate and savagely hurt me." Julie turned away to breathe and clear the tears that welled up in her eyes. "Something's toxically wrong, and you need fucking help before forgiveness is a reality." Her bravura gained traction, her frame commanded respect.

Gabe bowed his head, looked at the floor, and whispered, "I'm sorry. I've got some thinking to do." The door closed with a low click.

HOUSTON

"GOT YOUR MESSAGE and put a priority on this 'glitch.' I await the report about what's been tampered with. There's zero doubt there. Two concerns. The fact that such a system was guaranteed to be tamper-proof, especially given the extreme temperatures, and has failed is unacceptable."

"And the second?"

"It was a human. A highly skilled human."

Chapter 85

MALL MISSION

JULIE DIDN'T HAVE to wait until the end of the day to hear back from Aubrey. Hours later, after she'd dropped off her kids at school and run a few errands, her cell phone rang. Julie knew instinctively to be alarmed. Speed and The Bureau were usually mutually exclusive concepts.

"Hey, I need you to call me from a landline." Aubrey was abruptly silent for a moment and hoped Julie understood.

"Okay." The silence was an unspoken message. "Give me a few minutes, since I'm in the car. Which number did you want me to reach you on?" Julie asked.

"Same number." The line went dead.

Julie shook. *What's happened? I know that tone. It means there's a problem, and we needed to deal with it differently than the usual straight-up way.*

Julie pulled into the closest strip center parking lot. A local Target store had pay phones that she could use to contact Aubrey. "Reliable Target." After two rings, Aubrey picked up.

"Julie, listen carefully. I've less than fifty seconds. I want you to drive to Desert Ridge Mall now. You know where that is, right?"

"Of course," Julie confirmed.

"Good. Sam, one of my agents, will bump into you in

the Marshall's store in the home goods section. You'll say, 'oh, excuse me,' and he'll say, 'no problem' and wander away without another glance at you. Pay him no further attention. He'll have put a cell phone into your open purse. Head to the handbag section via children's sleepwear. Touch some fuzzy pj's or whatever. Spend two minutes looking at a purse, and pull out your list of chores. You understand so far?"

"Yes."

"I want you to study your chore list for just a few seconds, then roll your eyes and throw back your head. Look completely fed up with yourself for having forgotten items to do on that list. Go back to the bathrooms and go into a stall. Flush, wash your hands, and quickly move to your car. Leave the Marshall's lot and go park in front of California Pizza Kitchen to the north. I still have you?"

"I'm with you."

"Get out of your car there, lock the doors, and walk to where the fireplace is. The cell phone will ring. Answer my call." Aubrey was gone again.

Julie wasn't sure whether to laugh, think she was in some sort of crazy TV show, or shake in her boots with anxiety. She knew Aubrey meant business, though, and followed her instructions precisely.

Once at the fireplace, Julie took a breath and attempted to steady her nerves. She knew she couldn't look around, other than when she approached the table of the designated area. *A couple of older guys and coffee,* she observed. Otherwise, fairly quiet. Of course, a cell phone rang. It took Julie a moment to realize the sound came from her handbag, Aubrey's agent's "drop."

"Hello?"

"Okay, we're good to chat for a moment. You okay?"

"I am now. How'd I do? Did I ace the exam?" Julie wondered if she'd followed the directions as well as she'd hoped, or at least as well as Aubrey had needed her to.

"Great! Ever think about getting into this line of work?" She teased her friend again.

"I'm relieved to hear I passed so far. I knew from your tone you didn't want me followed or traced."

"I figured you remembered how we operated in college. Awesome. Now let me get you up to speed. I'll need you to keep this cell phone only for as long as I direct you to. Once again, it might be a strange or cryptic directive, so don't ask me in the moment. Just have peace, know I'll share the information with you at another point. Okay?"

"Okay. How long do we have, and what's going on?"

"We've less than ten minutes left right now. Don't panic, and please don't look around. Your sixth sense has kicked in for good reason. Continue to stare straight at the fireplace as I speak. Understand?"

"Gotcha."

"For your own safety. This is highly irregular, as it is, for me to ask you to do this sort of … well … work."

"Understood."

"Good girl. Also, good job responding as if you're talking to an old friend, too. This is just in case your tracker figures out what's what and traces this call sooner. You are, in fact, under surveillance, though we're not clear who follows whom and why. Moreover, your shadow has a shadow as well. You've got your own little private paparazzi-like parade, Julie. What have you been up to, young lady?"

"If I'd known, Aubrey, believe me, I would've already shared it with you and probably ceased whatever IT is. I do have some new thoughts, though—ones I know now I need to share with you. Tell me what you're looking for specifically, or even a few things going on, and I'll fill in as many blanks as I can. Remember, we're here to help each other."

"One thing is certain, you're quite popular. You've both domestic and foreign followers." Aubrey chuckled at her own humor, while Julie stared at the fireplace in horror. "Though there are multiple options, from what you've told me thus far, our best guess is your domestic shadow works for a foreign entity and your foreign shadow works for a domestic entity. Does any of this make sense?"

"Not yet. Can you be more specific? Some company name or some sort of connection to perhaps what I've told you or my writings? The explosion, Gabe's ex-girlfriend, the auto industry, whatever?"

"Thus far, all research with reference to Gabe's ex-girlfriend points to her money need for the alimony she was expected to pay to her cop ex-husband, as well as for her drug habit. We knew she'd tried to stay domestic in her attempts at financial gains, but at some point, she turned to international sources for assistance. We believe she was connected to your international shadow.

"Also, she'd been in touch with Gabe a couple of times, according to phone records. We believe they spoke twice. However, she needed money because of her drug habit, as I'd mentioned before, as well as her new gambling debt. Her divorce left her little child support and even less money for her 'medicinal' habits, shall we call them. Those bad habits caused her to be fired a few months ago. Her mom's been with her kids, while she's scrambled for a way to make ends meet.

"Her ex-husband's connections for her drug use would no longer supply her. Thus, he inadvertently redirected her needs elsewhere. We've watched him for years. That's a different story. We knew she had a problem, but we didn't know the extent of it. Getting blown up in Scottsdale underscored her desperation but did *not* help us grasp it. I don't mean to sound trite, Julie, but her next step was to turn her female charms on Gabe to use his good-guy mentality in the poor-single-mother-with-fatherless-children routine one more time. It didn't work at your high school reunion years ago, but Gabe's in a vulnerable place right now."

"What do you mean?" Julie was concerned her friend knew about Gabe's attack.

"Just as you said yourself, it's a complicated time." *What* has *Gabe done to my friend? DO I tell her I know he's moved out?* "Business comes from multiple directions simultaneously. First, world problems! *But* he's stressed and exhausted. Marital challenges exponentially complicate the big picture. He normally has no interest or eyes for any woman but you.

"You've got problems, however. He does have a huge heart and is often moved to the point of faulty decisions. I'm glad you sat down because you won't like what I have to say. I want you to lean over as you listen and put your hand over your eyes. Okay?"

Julie did as she was told. She didn't have to be told to clench her core, too.

"Julie, Gabe met with her three times. The first time was accidental. You knew that. Our sources tell us that, without his knowledge, she was going to be there. They ran into each other at a gas station where he and many of his company vehicles fill up. Somebody had given her the information as to where his office was and what some of his usual habits were. As per the gas station owner, the couple spoke politely for several minutes as the cars finished refueling. Not unusual. Done it myself. What they spoke about, of course, we're not clear on—yet. According to phone records, the next time they spoke, just two days later, they also apparently met for coffee. Gabe must've been a little uncomfortable about where they might be seen, so they met at a Dunkin' Donuts off of 19th Avenue. You okay still?"

"Sure," Julie barely croaked.

"Now don't worry. Zilch came of it. Intel we gathered shows the conversation lasted approximately half an hour. She was looking for a job, and he wouldn't provide one. He did hand her a twenty, told her to take a cab to where she was staying, and go back to New Jersey to her kids. Clearly, she didn't listen. She called him one more time and stayed on a hold for approximately two minutes. Gabe never picked up. Her final call the next morning was again never answered by Gabe."

Julie took in a lungful and sighed it out. "I can feel, Aubrey, that you've left some ugly details out. What are you sparing me?"

Aubrey paused, then continued as if Julie hadn't asked the question. She knew Julie would understand the non-answer, just as she'd understood all those breezy, cryptic instructions to go to the outdoor mall. One day, perhaps, Aubrey would tell Julie what else had happened in that last meeting. Now wasn't the time.

"For the next several days, she followed you, had evidently planned to tell you things both true and untrue. Her goal, remember, was money. If she happened to snag Gabe in the process, this, too, would have been okay with her. According to our sources, however, since she wasn't exactly a brain trust, she hadn't yet figured out when or where to share with you, until that day you knew for certain you were being followed. Clearly, she approached your car in the police lot for a reason. She'd no idea her car had been rigged. The people who'd wired it, however, must have doubted her ability to handle pressure for long. The bomb was likely a backup in case she started to speak up. They'd kept an eye on her as well."

"Are they the international player who shadows my domestic one, who was Jennifer?"

"We believe so."

Julie groaned and moved her hand from her forehead to her gut. "Aubrey, for God's sake and mine, would you pull it all together for me please? Connect a few dots. Speed up the misery already."

"Furthermore, Julie, it appears that Jennifer's ex's drug connection is based out of Europe." Aubrey paused with her message-rich silence. Julie could barely breathe. "Seefeld is a small city near Zurich in—"

"Switzerland," Julie interrupted.

"You're familiar with Seefeld?" Aubrey questioned.

"No. I'm familiar with where Zurich is, though."

"Ha-ha, okay. You had me worried there for a moment."

"Why? Because of Seefeld? What's the big deal about that city?"

"Julie, it's where Dane lives."

At that, Julie felt the ground fall away from under her. She stood up and ran for the closest garbage can. Aubrey could hear strange noises on the phone. "Julie, are you okay?"

A bit indisposed, Julie couldn't answer. Aubrey gave the instructions to her man to move in close enough to see what was happening with Julie. Relief washed over

Aubrey as she waited patiently for Julie to come back on the line. Time was almost up.

Julie had startled the old men's coffee club—enough for one of them to ask her if she was okay.

Weak but always polite, Julie responded. "Yes. Thank you. Would you happen to have a Kleenex or paper towel handy, though?" The older gentleman turned to his friend and grabbed the napkin from the table. "Here you go, miss." He waited for some sort of answer.

"I think it was the chicken omelet I made earlier ... must've been bad chicken. I knew it tasted funny, but I thought it was my hormones." With a feeble smile, she thanked him again and remembered Aubrey may still be on the phone.

"Aubrey?"

"Nice cover. Are you okay?" Aubrey was compassionate but very professional. Clearly, she was good at what she did.

"Mmmmhmmm."

"I'm sorry to share such intelligence with you. Do you have any reason to believe Dane had anything to do with any of this?"

"In hurting me? Absolutely not. In being involved with drugs? I have no idea. Based on my former knowledge of him, positively not. Based on what he does for a living now? I don't believe this is what motivates him. Corporations as well as individuals retain him for lots of money. I don't believe he has anything to do with drugs. Perhaps, however, one of his clients is involved?" The New York detective flashed in her mind. *Why?*

"I agree with you on all of it. So far, that seems to be the case. Have to consider it, all the same. I believe it's possible that's why Dane's driver in New York was gunned down."

That night's carnage darted between Aubrey's words. "Whoa, Aubrey. Mind reading now? That would make a lot of sense. It didn't seem random to me."

"Why not?"

"Dane definitely appeared troubled about Paul's death, distracted by it, yet he didn't seem overwhelmed with shock or surprised by the incident."

"Observation nailed, Julie. Nice. That's all information you wouldn't normally think to share with any detective or investigator. That's exactly the kind of intel I *am* looking for, however."

"Then again, you're not just any detective."

Aubrey smiled. *That's what I've explained to my boss about your help.* "Thanks. Now put personal aside. Dane was clearly not surprised because he knows some of these guys cross lines to make ends meet or just because narcotics are big business. By the way, he paid Paul very well."

"What was Paul's background? Perhaps Paul had been involved in other shit prior to Dane hiring him."

"We haven't found that connection yet, but with what you just shared with me, we will. We're only aware of his military experience."

They took a breath for a moment.

"Julie, seriously, are you okay? I kind of threw a lot at you all at once."

"You did leave out the Gabe details."

Aubrey smiled, remembering how Julie always had an excellent memory. "He didn't do anything ultimately so bad. We'll cover him again another day."

"Why don't you just give them to me now? I don't think there's much left in my system to come up."

"Because we're out of time. Don't turn around. Shadows are back. Stand over the top of the garbage can again. Turn nice and slow, wave back at the older gentlemen, and give them thumbs up. Head back to your car. I'll stay on the line with you. Take the phone and put it in your purse, face up, so nothing disconnects us if possible."

"Okay. Good talking with you. Sorry for the upheaval."

Aubrey smiled. "Witty. Do you think they're within ear range?"

"Yes. No worries. I'll feel better soon. I'm sure it's just a case of self-inflicted food poisoning." Julie outdid herself as apprehension washed over each step behind her.

"You're doing great, Julie. I want you to find another garbage can on the way and hasten your pace to get to that garbage can. Sense them, but don't look. My men are close behind them."

Julie put the phone speaker-side up in her open purse. She again followed Aubrey's directions precisely. She clutched her torso, hastened her pace, used her hand to cover her mouth, and clearly looked for a garbage can. She heard the hastened movement behind her but dug for her college acting skills. *I must be getting closer to the answers I so desperately seek.*

She didn't have to throw up for real but decided to fake dry heaves with the hope they didn't legitimately produce anything from her nerves. As she once again stood around a garbage can, a look of desperation on her face was perfectly clear. *Who wouldn't feel nauseous from bad chicken, not to mention strangers who follow you?* She felt their presence beside her, and her gut clenched for real this time. The one spoke softly.

"Miss, are you okay?"

"Yes. I … think … I had … bad chicken in my omelet. I didn't know I could feel food poisoning so fast."

Aubrey heard every word and instructed her men to pretend they knew Julie.

"Julie? Is that you? Hey, Danny, that's my sister's girlfriend."

Julie just stopped, turned for a moment, and looked over her right shoulder slightly to see two more strangers speak with her. The two tails were not sure what to do. Julie nodded her head numbly and smiled weakly as the one continued. "It's Mikey, Aubrey's brother? She *said* I'd made a good impression on you in college, but I guess it's been a while." Julie's eyes lit up. *Aubrey sent in the cavalry.*

"I'm so sorry. I'm so embarrassed. Forgive me, but I don't ... um ... er ... want to remember anybody right now, Mikey. Especially not you." She groaned. "A girl's got her head in the trash can with a handsome man next to her? Really? Where've you been all my life?" She tried a sickly chuckle to sell the whole act.

Mikey continued. "Are these guys with you, too?"

Julie shook her head no. "No, just kind bystanders who took pity on a distressed woman." She turned to the strangers and said, "Thank you, gentlemen. It's so nice to know chivalry's not dead. My husband will be relieved to hear strangers helped me. You guys have definitely done your 'kind deed for the day.' But seriously, everybody, I'm okay. I just need a minute. I'll go home to rest and wash this out of my system."

The two foreign tails said their "no problems" and left. Mikey and "Danny" stayed by Julie's side. Aubrey knew those "kind bystanders" waited and watched from another vantage point.

"Julie, it sucks to see you look like this. Aubrey wants us to get you to the ER or your doctor's office right away.

179

Danny will drive your car. He'll follow us to wherever we go. You're bound to feel better after you've gotten some fluids, then we'll take you home, okay?"

"Okay," Julie conceded. *Gabe's gonna just love another call from a strange guy about his wife,* she realized. *Too bad, though. He deserves it after what Aubrey shared. Why didn't he tell me his ex had contacted him multiple times? Seen him multiple times? Not his fault!*

After Mikey helped her climb in his car, Danny immediately started through Julie's purse. He knew the shadows had somehow either dropped a "bug" in her purse or attached it to her. After all, that's what they'd do. He looked at Julie with his index finger perpendicular across both of his lips to keep her quiet. This way, she wouldn't question what he did or why. She knew, then, to make it sound as if it was her.

"I know I put those keys in here somewhere," she groaned.

Mikey gave her the okay sign. That's exactly what he needed her to do to allow him a little more search time. "Here they are," she exclaimed, as Danny held up the planted device from the strange pair. "Need a breath mint. I'm so mortified." Her eyes opened wide in amazement. In his next move, he winked at her as he held up a box of mints and handed them over to Julie. She took one, he dropped the device in the mint's place, and she snapped the tin lid shut. The little device slammed against the tiny, hard breath mints wrapped in crisp parchment paper. *Go figure. Tin mints and paper can deafen.*

Mikey used the brief travel time to communicate with Aubrey that Julie was okay. The tails were still intact, however. She advised Mikey to take Julie to the local ER, since she'd already called and advised the hospital staff of what they needed to do to help out this investigation. Aubrey reminded Mikey to explain to Julie what to say and not to say to hospital staff.

"Mikey, you know what to do with the extra ears. Have Danny take her car home. Another squad car will pick him up. Return to the office for a debriefing. I'll talk with Julie from there."

Chapter 86

AWAKE

DANE SAT UP in a panic. *Whoa. What just happened?* He looked around his intimate bedroom and confirmed he was alone. He gasped for air, trying to calm his pounding heart and soothe his rattled nerves. *That was how I went to sleep—alone. So how? Who? No ... couldn't have been, could it?* "It's *always* been her, but now she just won't stay out of my head. She was vividly ... I ... oh, shit." Just then, he was aware of how wet his thin, cotton pajama bottoms felt. "You've got to be fucking kidding me." He jumped out of his king-size bed and headed for the shower. He was covered in sweat from head to toe, as if he'd just made love to Julie.

The shower restored Dane's composure and reorganized his thoughts. *Time to focus on issues that need my ... um ... management. Tate's blackmailed me. Why? He's also not in this alone. How and why is Rachel involved? Who else is involved? And why?* He dressed as if he was headed to court in a charcoal, Hugo Boss suit, crisply laundered white shirt, and gray, silk tie. Dane knew he looked sharp. He also knew he needed to when he walked into the office today. "I better present a strong, unruffled image," he told his mirror.

He started his workday from home for a few hours. Leaving his suit jacket over the back of his chair, Dane sat at the desk that once had belonged to his grandfather and stared at a blank legal pad. He texted Isabella and hoped she had some answers to the questions they'd come up with together.

Talk?

Isabella took orders from her boss. Dane gave them. A collaborative effort was novel for them both. After the last accusatory phone call from Victor, they agreed trouble lurked. They needed each other to think, sort, and strategize—fast.

Isabella rarely took more than a few minutes to respond to her boss's texts, as she knew there was always a reason for them. She chose to call him back in response.

"Morning, Boss." She began carefully, like dipping a toe in a pool to test the water's temperature.

"Morning. Cryptic text. What have you found so far? I'm about to head into the office."

"Well, are you sitting down?"

"Do I need to be?" he challenged back.

"Probably. You see, my sources tell me you're definitely being set up from multiple angles. It appears as though you embezzle funds from the firm and funnel them into your exwife's account. The logic behind that is, since you're on friendlier terms now, she'll help you hide money. Her eagerness to hide money stems from the fact that you take care of her and the kids and, of course, compensate her for her silence. Assume this to be true."

Dane finished her thought. "Why would Rachel say anything, then, especially to Victor?"

"Exactly, unless Rachel was in on it as some sort of diversion. I just can't quite make out how or why."

"Come on, Isabella, the why is the easy part. She's still angry with me for never loving her. She's claimed she's called a truce between us—again—recently, to be accurate."

"What do you mean 'again'? How recently, if you don't mind that I ask?"

"At this point, I'd think you'd be a fool to not ask. Within the last few months ... about the time I returned from my high school reunion and was headed back to the States on more business. Oh, shit!"

"What?"

"Isabella, be very careful who you speak with about any of this."

"Boss, you've told me this before."

"I know, but there've always been those in the firm who'd seen me as a cad and even called me neglectful of both Rachel and my children."

"Dane, no one's ever thought you negligent where your children are concerned. Who told you that?"

"In the midst of the mediation process, Victor counseled me. ..." Dane's voice suddenly trailed off.

"Victor? *He* told you that you were negligent? When? Whenever he was in our outer office, I heard him commend you about how generous you were and how Rachel was just hurtful." Isabella sounded confused.

"Yes, that's what he said in our offices in front of whoever was in there. You all became his witnesses. You also, though, became mine, too. But in those few partner meetings he insisted I attend, don't you remember how I'd return to my office with my head down, depressed?"

"Yes, but you looked depressed more than you ever looked ... well ... happy—until you returned from your reunion trip."

"My reunion trip was years after the divorce, Isabella. What does this tell you?"

"It tells me, and probably everyone else, Rachel included, you were miserable with her. Of course, you know what I think of her, so that's no stretch for me."

"Isabella, let's talk through these facts again. A few have clicked together here. Fact. Victor clearly made sure I had the right reputation for the office staff because he knows how all of you talk. As long as I produced, his money flowed as the partner in charge of me."

"Okay, so that's a fact. Why would a partner say one thing about you in front of the staff, but speak less charitably with you on the side? That doesn't make sense to me."

"Yeah, me neither, unless *he* was coerced to pressure *me* for more information for Rachel."

"Okay, now I'm confused. I followed you for a while, but you've lost me. Do you suggest—"

"I'm not sure what to suggest. Whatever comes out of my mouth right now will sound critical or imbecilic, neither of which are acceptable. I can't emphasize enough caution while you covertly investigate. Do *not* go out of your way, other than for usual reasons or while on your breaks. Keep up with our cases, like normal. I'll head into the office after I make one phone call. I'm about to test a theory before we speak again."

Chapter 87

Q'S & A'S

A FEW BAGS of IV fluid, a good night's sleep, an early morning warm-up run followed by a yoga class and Julie knew she'd be as good as new. She wasn't worried about her safety on the run because she wasn't going to live her life in fear. *I know that if anybody had wanted to cause me harm, they would've done so already. I'll remind Gabe of this, so he backs off—at least enough so we can talk about the kids with calmness and logic. Whoever followed me clearly just wanted me to know they were there, as well as know what I was up to and with whom. But why?*

"Eventually, I'm going to figure it out," she avowed to her dogs. "I know you hang on my every word. This *is* what I want to do, right? Poke around, ask questions, dig deeper into something, and write about it? Well, we're just gonna have to get used to people following us and maybe not being so happy with us. Right, guys? Sheez, why does it feel so … so … come on, help me with putting this all in words so I can process it and move on." She waited for her dogs' expressions to change. "I can see you two will support me on anything—as long as I give you cookies."

At the mention of cookies, the complacent canines raised their heads awaiting further instructions. She fluffed their fuzzy ears. "Relax, relax. I'm just checking to see if you're still listening as I talk through my own roadblocks. *What* is bugging me about it all? So many facts are just not connecting. Maybe I need to write it all down. See what it looks like. Then play 'Connect the Dots.'"

Once home, she unclasped the dogs' leashes and hung them up. Arizona's "dry heat" wasn't expected for months. Still, Julie's dogs lapped up ice water from their bowl and collapsed in heaps on the cool, Mexican tile floor, as if they were in the midst of the monsoon season. She chuckled at them, then headed for a blank legal pad and pen.

Her first notes were a list of names. "Gabe, Dane, Jennifer, Tate, Bob. Hmm ... maybe I need to draw a Venn diagram, like my kids had to in middle school. Might make it easier to discover the common factors of these people. Nope. I know what I'll do!"

Julie headed to her kids' arts and crafts boxes, snagged a handful of colorful markers, and designated a different one per person. She wrote down as many unanswered questions as she could conjure—some highly absurd—and highlighted each incident in colors different from all names. *It's at an adult moment like this when I can deeply appreciate Crayola's cleverness.*

After almost an hour, Julie stopped. *Don't look. Don't look. Let's see what else I come up with after yoga and a shower,* she convinced herself. "'Sometimes a mental recess allows greater clarity,' to quote Bryant McGill," she shared with her dogs. "'Your calm mind is the ultimate weapon against your challenges. So relax.'"

Ready to walk away, Julie realized she'd left one important name off her list—her own. She cringed as she gathered her mat, water bottle, and towel.

PUZZLE

DANE AVOIDED CALLS from Victor, aware avoidance both bought him time and invited hostility. "Chance I have to take," he told Isabella.

"He's had me schedule several phone appointments with you and doesn't understand why you won't confirm them."

"You've followed through. He sees that on our shared calendars. What have you said when he asks?"

"I've told him I'm responsible to schedule for you and then reminded him I'm not in charge of you."

"I had another issue come to light, a small detail I've failed to mention because I hadn't processed it myself. I wasn't even certain it was them."

Isabella waited. She was fully aware that to push her boss mid-process was to kill his trains of thought.

"Recently, I went to the Widder to meet with a client, right?"

"Right."

"Tate Parker was there with a companion. We made eye contact."

"What?"

"He was with a woman."

"Why do I feel like what you're about to tell me is—"

"Because I am." Another pause. "He had his arm around the back of his table lunchmate's chair." Dane debated once more if he ought to share this revelation now and accepted the fact that he needed to trust his assistant.

"Boss?"

"Grabbed her to kiss her, quite passionately."

Isabella heard Dane mentally debate.

"He wanted to make sure I'd seen them, or he sought

to prevent me from identifying his companion, perhaps. In either case, I recognized my ex-wife."

"Well, isn't that rich?"

"Pardon?"

"Recent hushed voices I overheard tangled your ex with your boss." She knew to remain silent, motionless, especially after that bombshell.

More vanilla flavored than salty, Dane's mild tone didn't surprise her. "When did you hear that? We just spoke yesterday."

"In the last few weeks." She grabbed a breath. "Before you freak out on me, remember you've told me to exceed simple caution, right?" She heard Dane's silence and continued. "I wanted to verify what I'd heard before I shared it with you."

"Have you?"

"No."

"He's acknowledged cases are completed, etc., correct?"

"Correct."

"He's pissed in emails, threatened me, but I minimally answer as required. I'll deal with him soon."

"Shall I warn him?"

"Not yet."

PROCESSING

SHOWERED AND THIRSTY post-yoga, Julie scratched out more questions than she'd first considered. "Holy crap! There are *so* many unanswered questions, yet I feel like I'm only a hair's width away from all of the answers." *The list of questions and inconsistencies seems to just go on*—until she remembered another recent conversation with Aubrey.

Their call bared an unusual fact for Julie to know. Somehow, Aubrey had turned up Dane's client list. When Julie had asked her how, she simply said, "Now *that* I can't tell you." Part of the client list shared with Julie gave her background information from which she could ask Dane innocuous questions. She began to understand why he had his own shadows on her after their high school reunion. Naïvely, she thought it was just his interest in her. "Had he made it seem that way, or am I so emotionally lonely that I wanted his interest, perhaps assumed it?" She shook her head and rolled her eyes at her private admission.

Dane's connection to her neighbor Bob wasn't just from being a client of Bob's with his boss, Victor. Dane represented Bob, too. From the outside, this detail seemed innocent. However, one of their many common clients included Tate Parker. Dane needed to make sure Bob's closest neighbors weren't nosy ones.

Julie recalled Aubrey's explanation. "Tate Parker is less than on the up-and-up—always has been, as you may know. Parker likely wanted both Bob and Dane to protect his privacy. Also tenable, Parker would have wanted to know more about Bob's neighbors. Your identity became apparent as the closest neighbor geographically while Dane attended the reunion with you. Dane found out the same information after he returned to Zurich."

"So, to clarify for my own sanity, Dane attended our high school reunion before he'd found out I was his client's neighbor?" Julie pressed Aubrey.

"Yes," Aubrey confirmed. She heard Julie breathe a sigh of relief. "I'm glad I could at least offer you some peace. There's not a lot of peace to be had here."

"What d'ya mean?" Goose bumps came over Julie.

"Well, I mean, you've definitely stumbled onto something rather significant here and somehow become tangled up in it. I'm pretty certain after the reunion not only did Dane have you shadowed because of Tate for Tate, but he had you shadowed because of Tate for himself."

"Well, that makes everything as clear as mud," Julie teased.

"In other words, Dane had you shadowed to keep you safe. We're very certain Dane had been forced to take on Tate Parker as a client. Also apparent? Tate Parker hasn't changed much since high school, as I've already mentioned. He may have attended a fine college, but he uses his education, for this discussion's purposes, for evil not good."

"Okay, Aubrey, what *are* you and *aren't* you telling me?"

"I can't tell you much more. I can only answer questions—to an extent, shall we say." Aubrey hoped her old friend would read between the lines.

Wise to Aubrey's pregnant pauses, Julie deliberated and proceeded to think aloud.

"Hmm. If I understand correctly what you've been comfortable to share thus far, Tate Parker is involved in something 'evil,' to use your word. He's doing it through the cars he brings to Bob. He wanted to make sure neighbors weren't nosy and had all of us checked out. He was surprised—something he appears to dislike—when he found out the closest neighbor was me. He was further bewildered when Dane and I had reconnected … ah … hence his early appearance for a meeting with Dane when Dane and I were having coffee here in town a while back." Julie's mental light bulb was flickering on and off.

"You're doing great so far," Aubrey offered.

"Tate wanted to confirm my identity as well as figure

out why his legal counsel seemed upbeat, an unusual state for Dane for many years. Still good?"

"Spot-on so far."

"Tate wanted me to know Dane wasn't the goody two shoes he portrayed himself to be. Dane didn't want me to know Tate was a client. He also didn't want Tate to know we'd reconnected. I'd completely forgotten about Tate until he surfaced. To be further straight up, Dane was forced to reintroduce us. Even then, I hadn't made the connection. Tate had been jealous of Dane in high school, as I recall. Our association at this point in time could make him a more challenging client, possibly even a dangerous one."

"Sounds like lots of history there. Very helpful. Keep going."

"Meanwhile, Bob may or may not know what Tate is all about. He just knows to keep Tate's name off of any referral lists, shall we call them. Consequently, Bob is secretive about *any* questions I ask about *any* cars, and most especially about Tate's. My recent chat with Bob yielded perhaps a small pearl—Bob regrets taking on Tate as a client."

"How do you know?"

"Well, he didn't mention Tate by name, but it's the way Bob described his most recent client. I've seen Tate around without him seeing me, and Bob's description of his newest client fits Tate. I'm guessing you could confirm this information. Perhaps Bob is watching his own back as well as mine. Am I missing anything?"

Aubrey smiled. *Phew, her deductive skills are still intact.* "Up 'til now? No. But yes, and I'm surprised you missed it."

"You're not gonna have to kill me and eat me after

you tell me, are you?" The old friends laughed easily after all the tense talk.

"No, thankfully. This is above board." Aubrey debated if she ought to open up this other subject, full of potential conflict, since Julie seemed to have enough on her plate.

"Aubrey? Ya still there?" Julie prodded.

"Yeah, I'm still here."

"What's the matter? You leaving me hanging now though you've started?"

"Julie, Dane had you followed to keep you safe."

"Okay, already got that. What am I missing?"

Silence.

"Christ, Aubrey, what the hell are you talking about?"

"Julie, Dane's still in love with you. You *must* get that, right?"

Nothing.

"Julie? Now it's my turn. Ya still there?"

"I ... I ... don't know what to say, Aubrey."

"I figured. A married woman with kids, separated from her husband of twenty plus years, bombs, dead limo drivers, druggy ex-girlfriends and, of course, an old flame resurfaces. What more could this story have? Oh, and, yeah, a bad guy!! I know. Kind of cliché, but kinda cool, if you ask me."

"Wow."

Aubrey chuckled. "Wish it was me—just the old flame resurfacing part, not the rest of it."

"How can you be so corny? I mean, I'm married." Julie was puzzled.

"Well, Captain Obvious," Aubrey reasoned, "for one, he's hot—"

"Aubrey!"

"What? It's true! You're separated and about to be divorced in no time. How lucky are you the man you should've married is available now, too?"

"Holy shit, Aubrey, I'm *not* having this conversation with you."

"Suit yourself, girlfriend. Have I ever lied to you?"

"I don't think so. I'm just not ready to hear all this."

"Divorce sucks. I know. I also know being alone 'ain't no picnic eithu.'" Aubrey poked fun at her heritage.

"I need time to think. There's just been so much coming at me all at once. Truth? I'm just trying to process all of it with some level of intelligence and logic."

"Well, since you brought up the processing topic, let me throw a few other things at you to chew on together. Besides, it'll help your investigative writing style."

"Oh crap, there's more?"

"Um … 'fraid so, sister. Guess I better throw it at you fast. I've a call waiting I *also* need to take. Not only is Dane still in love with you, his ex-wife has resurfaced on the scene as a formidable character, Dane's boss has been breathing down his neck about some inconsistencies in Tate's account's billing and receivables, and some people aren't who they seem to be."

"Aubrey, are you kidding me? What kind of information was that last one?"

"Julie, I can't explain right now. Must take another call, so we'll talk later. Sorry. Bye, honey." The line went dead.

"Aubrey, you can't leave me hanging … here just like … I can't believe she left me hanging. What did she mean? What a cryptic and creepy thing to say. No wonder she does what she does for a living."

Julie walked around her kitchen muttering for a minute. She headed for her lists and added Rachel's name. She shook her head and again turned to her faithful, fuzzy companions to assist her in sorting out new information.

"What the hell did she mean when she said 'some people aren't who they seem to be'? Come on, you two. Any input would be welcome." She looked at the two mutts. "That's it? Nothin'? Thanks a lot. Who isn't who they seem to be? Dane? Gabe? Bob? Tate? Aubrey? Rachel? What did she mean by the ex is a 'formidable character'? Grrr." Her dogs' ears perked up.

Some of Dane's clients—who they are and what they allegedly do for a living—have tainted the lens through which I'm now regarding Dane. Is that right? Fair? Perhaps, if nothing else, I'll be able to maintain more emotional distance from him. She feared their attraction. It couldn't be denied when near each other. *Good thing he lives a world away from here.* Since still technically married to Gabe, Julie could and would use her separation from him to safeguard her emotional space from Dane.

Still, she felt drawn to him. *He's probably a criminal! His clients are mostly criminals. Get a grip!* Finally, she did and picked up the phone.

Chapter 88

TAKE NOTICE

JULIE UNDERSTOOD THAT the moment she and Tate made unanticipated eye contact, they'd definitely speak soon. When he decided to fold his tall frame into his small, rental sports car then drive away slowly, she half expected him to turn around. *Though Bob said he wouldn't divulge private information about his clients, what's to stop me from asking those clients directly? I'm certainly not going to stalk Bob's property. If, however, the door of opportunity opened,* she reasoned, *I won't just knock on it. I'll take full advantage and run through it.*

She recognized her brand of directness could disarm anyone. *Tate Parker won't be any different. Let him speak for himself. I'm quite certain when asked to brag, he'll be like most humans—so proud of his newest deal, he'll answer just about any question asked … unless he has something to hide. I know my way of questioning almost always yields honest responses. Have no clue why. Doesn't matter at this point, though.* She weighed, "My husband seems amongst the few virtually immune to those particular charms of mine."

She dismissed her distracted thought and forced her attention back to Tate Parker. *He knows we'll most likely speak at the next auction.* Julie knew Tate held the answers to many, if not most, of her riddles. *All auction participants eventually speak with me in person or via phone. They're too damned nosy, proud, and competitive not to. Something is holding Tate Parker back.*

Julie was well aware she'd made a solid name for herself in the car auction industry. She humbled herself as a mere reporter of the varied auctions' results. The reality, nonetheless, was the opposite. She served as a liaison for the auction organizers, who had zero time to answer questions about car owners to one another. *My summary's well read. Tate knows this.*

She also wondered who was playing whom here? *Why am I starting to get the feeling I'm being used, but I don't know by whom or why—yet.*

SEEN

SHE LOOKS GOOD … even after all these years, four kids later. Tate knew, without a doubt, he shouldn't have racy thoughts about Julie Archer. *Boss lady would tear me to pieces for having them for several reasons.*

His draw toward Julie, though, was basic, primitive. Zero rationalizations made any sense to follow his gaze further. *I'm stunned that I, Tate Parker, multimillionaire, international gold mine owner, feel paralyzed in my perfect, polished, black Magnanni loafers in Bob's driveway. Walk away, Parker. Get in the damn car, Parker. Do NOT go over there and talk with her. What the f—?* He hesitated but finally got in his rental car and slowly pulled away, shaking. *HOW can this still be possible? I'd spoken with her in that Starbuck's, shook her hand even, but didn't shake—probably because Michaels was there, and I didn't want to look weak. Yeah, that's great. I better get a* complete *grip on myself before I call in. She's so sharp, she'll know the minute I say hello that something's happened. We can*not *have that. Okay, breathe.* Tate talked himself into a calmer state.

This was definitely not something he'd expected to feel

or think. *Focus on the mission. That's all I have to do. After this car auction, maybe a chat with Mrs. Archer, if necessary. First, deposit checks, confirm monies have been cleared, and get back to Canada. Focus.* Tate knew he'd dodged the proverbial bullet this time. *What will happen when I am required to speak with her? I don't know, but I've got to do my best to avoid her.* He brooded.

Chapter 89

CLUE

HE WASN'T A big man at a mere five feet eleven inches, but his physical strengths were evident in more than a strong, solid physique. Large, broad shoulders, a trim waist, and unyielding legs clearly indicated a man who took regular care of his anatomy. *No doubt a diet well tended to also*, Julie considered. Conscious of his presence and in obvious command of his body, his full head of salt-and-pepper hair kept neatly tied, almost slicked back, in a short ponytail added to this man's look as a whole. He didn't walk with any kind of pseudo-swagger. His stride was confident and commanding.

"I know you're not from around here."

After he crossed the parking lot in front of her, he turned and looked deliberately back at her, as if he'd heard her through the closed car windows. He caught Julie staring at him with a puzzled look and guessed she'd not identified him—yet. *She's a smart one. Won't be long.*

"I've seen you before. But where?" she asked her empty car.

A slow smile spread across his face but twisted unseen into a sneer as he stepped into his small pickup. He knew why she'd been looking at him. He was aware all women looked at him, and he no longer felt any guilt about using his God-given gift to get what he wanted.

"I know it'll come to me."

And it did. Her awareness was sudden and shocking.

Chapter 90

CALL

AFTER A DELICIOUSLY productive and sated afternoon with Tate, Rachel arrived home. Calmer than she'd been in months, she relieved her nanny, who doubled as her assistant. Unfortunately, the older woman had to leave early for a doctor's appointment, which left Rachel to assist her children with activity forms and dinner preparation, a task her efficient P.A. typically dominated. *Going with takeout tonight, then my being on the phone won't be so odd for a school night,* she decided as she searched through her purse for her cell phone.

"Good evening, Elena. Is Victor home?" Victor's sporting wife never gave anything away with her voice. Rachel revered her even temper as well as her sophisticated looks. "He's just arrived home and will need to return your call, dear."

"Thank you." The line went dead.

Right after placing the dinner order, Rachel's cell rang back with Victor's home number. *Odd,* she considered. *They're both home.* So was the brusque greeting she received. Her tone betrayed her usual velvety, though affected, demeanor.

"To be clear, there won't be even the slightest trace back to either of us. I've been assured," Rachel confirmed. "Just make sure the amounts deposited and withdrawn are different, so totals won't be related easily, if at all. Oh … I need to run. Dinner's arrived for my girls. I'll be at the bank tomorrow confirming all transactions, so I won't need a different computer. You'll hear from me afterward."

Chapter 91

BREAK

NOT LONG AFTER Gabe moved out, marriage and business collided. While thrilled and flattered for Gabe's company to be highly requested, its event reservation book was oftentimes overfilled. Gabe's customary excellence in handling crazy amounts of business missed his normal standards, as he worked himself to near exhaustion. Dumbfounded and preoccupied by his wife's apparent lack of concern for her own safety, guilt tormented the executive more so than normal. While he generally accepted this to be true, he was stymied as to how to address his extreme swings. His work, and even his kids, failed to serve as the usual diversions. When he arrived at the house to pick up their kids, he snapped at them and then lost his cool, even more with Julie.

At first, Julie stood up for herself, which always led to arguments and upset everyone. After but a few ugly interactions, though, her anger subsided. She walked a few emotional miles in Gabe's shoes, aware of his need to safely vent frustrations. However, Julie recognized she wasn't a healthy outlet for him. She was, after all, his principal cause for concern. She also recognized that to sidestep his behavior wasn't healthy for her. She couldn't fix how he handled what upset him.

He wasn't just vocal about his fear, which overtook his

instinct to protect. He showed her when physically close. His muscles tensed, dark and ominous like a thunderstorm cloud. The smallest bait of instability, like his wife's instant, frightened, cool distance, triggered its explosive release. "Regardless of what you may think, a man doesn't feel like a man when he can't provide for and protect his family. Call me old-fashioned. Call me a control freak. This is pretty primal stuff, Julie. Men and women are physiologically made different. I could be like some men who don't care." Just as tornadoes extend down in seconds to cause a huge swath of destruction, Gabe veered wild and cruel.

"I've never disputed that you care. I've also never disputed that men and women are made different. But"— she took a deep, calm breath—"physiologically different, or any other way different, does not give you the right to bully, intimidate, or assault me. Since when would it? *You've* always called those kinds of men cowards. And since when does violence show care or protection?"

Nevertheless, Gabe's tirades multiplied and escalated each time they saw one another. Julie stayed in the house several times to steer away from his verbal storms in a show of goodwill and suggested the kids run out to their dad's car. She hoped he appreciated the space and took the time to connect with them. When the children flew back into the house out of breath, hysterical, it was clear the respectful approach backfired, too. A few times, Gabe charged in, slammed doors, and demanded to know how they were to heal together if she avoided him.

One late afternoon, she stood at the kitchen counter. Alone. And waited. He gusted in, out of breath, and skidded to a stop. "Where are the kids?"

"Hello to you, too."

"You don't want to talk to me, so why bother? Where are the kids?" Darkness swirled.

"Basic civility. Good manners. Kids aren't here." Julie worked to keep the interaction light but confusion snaked through her.

"What do you mean they aren't here?"

"We spoke about their activities, schedules, hours, two days ago."

"We did not."

"Gabe"—her tone calm and level—"the kids chirped their excitement in front of you and reminded you just this morning on the phone."

"Bullshit!" he spat.

"I heard them, honey."

"Don't fucking 'honey' me when you don't mean it."

She bowed her head, opted once again for a calm approach, and raised her eyes to meet his. "I do mean it because I love you. I called you back to confirm that you understood what their schedule change was. Remember?" Gabe just stared at his estranged wife. "Do you need to sit down a minute?" He shook her off, squeezed his eyes shut, eyebrows knitted. "What does your business partner or our counselor say about all of your ... um ... challenges?"

His eyes flew open. "What do they have to do with your invitation of danger into our lives?"

Subject change, Julie's brain warned. "Everyone needs time, exercise. I'm hardly the only problem you face."

"Your constant criticism is debilitating," he said, accusing Julie.

"Earlier, when I called you regarding our kids, I asked you if you needed anything on the grocery list, since the girls planned to shop for us later, and you said—"

"I know what I said. My stomach's had some challenges. So what?"

"So you do remember that conversation?"

"Don't fuck with me, Julie." His tone grayed.

"Gabe, you don't recall the schedule part, but you do recall the stomach meds? I just want to be clear. Maybe we need to make sure there isn't a more serious issue to—"

"Yeah, I have a wife who's seriously unconcerned about who she's pissed off enough to want to hurt her. That same critical wife threw me out of my home. So, yeah, I have problems!"

"Since when is, 'Honey, I'm concerned about how many boxes of Alka-Seltzer you consume in a week' criticism?"

He refused to hear her concern for his health and blew out through the garage. *That's what I'm supposed to do, isn't it? Damn.* She questioned herself as a wife and mother. She reevaluated every word she spoke and every action she took. *This is bullshit. I walk on eggshells while he fucking blanks out! Reality check time. He's not normal.*

DOWN

THEIR CONVERSATION RESTARTED a few days later with calmness and Julie's genuine concern. Gabe shifted into a feverish, almost rabid, gear.

"Gabe, I know you work hard, been understaffed, dealt with pushy clients, and neglected yourself. You've shown extreme signs of fatigue, more than even usual."

"Tired? You're damn fucking *straight* I'm tired!"

"Listen to yourself. You're over-the-top belligerent. Why are you yelling at me? Why are you doing this to yourself, your employees, managers, and, most important-ly, to our kids and us?"

"Do what? Provide? Us? What us? You threw me out, remember?"

"Gabe, I didn't throw you out, I—"

"You threw me out, Julie! What else do you want to call it?" he roared.

"You assaulted me. What do *you* want to call it?" She gritted her teeth in an attempt to stay calm. "I don't consider a need to protect myself while you get your shit together away from here throwing you out. I call that a time-out to regroup."

"Oh, I know you don't. You're the only one who doesn't. I was a little too passionate and—"

"Too passionate? Call it whatever you *want*. It wasn't okay. I call your not living here 'time-out,' a breather. It's giving us a chance to retreat to different places, catch our breath, space to think. Find help. Do you think it was okay, now?"

The next words out of Gabe's mouth were damning. "Retreat? Ha! That's what you call it now? Interesting choice of words." Then his tone darkened. "I'm tired, all right, but I'm also pissed. I've been thrown out of my own home. A home I work so hard for. A family I work so hard for. I've grown our company to be worth millions so we could sell it at some point and live more comfortably in our retirement. I don't think I can take much more of this."

"Me neither! Our kids can't, either. They're scared. I'm scared and relieved! At last you're aware of how unhealthy this is! What exactly do you mean by 'can't take much more of this'? What help do you have in mind?" Julie heard this before, but somehow, she knew this time was different, more like a punch to her gut. She watched his body slump into a chair and stifled a gasp when her hand flew over her mouth. *Holy shit ... something is truly wrong with him.* She was barely able to breathe, and core fear twisted her gut. Even though she tried to stay calm and composed externally, she found her hysteria levels rising inside. Her mouth dried. *All I can do is be patient and wait for his reply.*

"Us."

Julie shrieked with a strained silence, tears brimming, when Gabe's head snapped up. He finally lifted his eyes to hers and rained on her what he felt he'd gotten. "You constantly criticize me. You won't listen to my concerns and me about your new projects. You just always seem to want to fight with me."

Julie blinked a few times and swallowed hard. "I think I'm hearing things."

"You're not hearing things. I said 'us.' I can't take more fighting, criticizing, feeling unappreciated by you, and now you're telling me our kids are scared of me. I work my brains out for us and. ..." He shook his head and just looked down pitifully.

"Don't you understand I'm not critical of you when I talk about how hard you work and how exhausted you've become and ... I'm worried about you?"

Gabe said nothing, oblivious to her presence. Julie's panic level rose. *Fight or flight? I don't know where this is going.* She studied him. Soft, calm but urgent, she attempted another appeal. "Please, Gabe, please come with me to see Doc. I think you've hit a very, very ... um ... unhealthy point."

Gabe just stared down in his lap. Julie was hit by a sudden wave of nausea. *Is he about to spring or pass out?* Sweat dripped one drop at a time down her spine. *Deep breaths. Regain calm.* She spoke with metered control. "Honey, I don't want to argue with you. I think you need some downtime. I know I do, too. Maybe a nice hot bath? A cool glass of water? A little quiet will help us both." Gabe didn't move. He didn't blink. He sat emotionless. *Is he breathing?*

Julie scrambled to the medicine cabinet and grabbed two ibuprofen. A sprint to the kitchen for a short glass, she filled it halfway with cool water and swiftly skittered back to Gabe. *Holy shit! He's frozen, motionless, immobile.* He barely even picked up his head enough to see Julie put the two small tablets in his right hand and the glass of water in his left. When he nearly missed his mouth, Julie held back a small gasp. *What the fuck's happened? Some sort of breakdown. Need to stay calm.*

"Just stay right here while I run your bath, honey. You'll feel a lot better after a nice Epsom salts soak. Remember how you did after that last huge function a few months ago? Just stay right here. I'll be right back," she said soothingly. "I need to go and get the towels out of the dryer. They'll be nice and warm and fluffy for you. Stay right here, and I'll help you." She bolted for the kitchen, snatched up Gabe's cell phone, and as fast as her fingers could find the number dialed his longtime business partner, Ben Quattrone. It rang and rang, but he finally picked it up.

"Hey man, glad you called."

"Ben, I'm panicked. It's Julie."

"Oh. Hey, Julie. I guess I can't sound happy to hear from you then. What's the matter, sugar? Where's Gabe?"

"I think Gabe's had some sort of breakdown. I thought he was just overworked, stressed, depressed even. I'm not sure whether I should check him into the hospital, or if I can care for him by myself, or, my God, Ben, I'm completely panicked."

"Well hang on there, sugar, you know you got to take it one step at a time. What exactly do you mean he's had some sort of breakdown? Where are you? I know he moved out—I mean, what's going on? Are you both safe? Does he know you're on the phone?"

"No, he doesn't know I'm on the phone. He came by to pick up a few things for himself and the kids when we started ... um ... to talk about ... well ... things. I left him sitting in our bedroom on the chair, and I'm running a bath for him. I gave him a couple of ibuprofen with water. Within minutes after he stopped by, he's been completely—I don't even know what the right word is—he's been weird and now motionless. He started to tell me that we're over because he feels criticized. I've not criticized him, Ben. I've been *worried* about him! I've expressed to him I'm very concerned about his overworking, overbooking, over-stressing."

"Sugar, you're right. I've told him the same thing. I've warned him to take time for himself and his family, or he'll end up divorced, kids hating him, and never make it the whole distance we have still to go in this business."

"Oh shit, I'm so thankful to hear you say all that." Julie let out the breath she held. "You have to know I've not been some nagging bitch. I know he works his ass off. Drives back and forth. With the amount of business that's been booked, and not just the shortage of staff but the shortage of *trained* staff and the shortage of managers, he can't do all this and neither can you." Julie neared hysteria after she'd stayed so calm with Gabe. "I know this isn't the time for drama, Ben. I'm sorry. Since his tirade, he's been immobile, frozen." She took a few deep breaths.

Julie slowed herself down and breathed in and out

deliberately while Ben waited patiently.

"You okay?" Ben masked his own dread.

"No, I'm petrified. Ben, I need your help. Would you please call your brother and ask him what I should do? Tell him I'm desperately worried and—need you to call right away. I know we can't share this with *any* other people. He's sitting ... well ... like in a catatonic state they talk about? Holy crap! I just heard a fall! Yes, Ben, I think that's exactly what's happening. I think Gabe's having a nervous breakdown!"

"Julie, go see how he's doing, and I'll call Sandy. Keep *your* phone near you, okay? Bye."

As she'd suspected, Gabe had fallen out of the chair and onto the floor. The glass of water had spilled near him but luckily hadn't broken or cut him. She ran into the bathroom and turned off the tub. *He won't make it in there. Even if he did, he might drown.* She scrambled to her office to grab her cell phone and awaited Ben's return call. *Thank God the kids are all out. I've no idea what to say to them when they come home later.*

Though it had seemed like an eternity until Ben called Julie back, he'd actually done so within fifteen minutes and spelled out very precise instructions from his physician brother she was to follow.

Chapter 92

STUNNED

GABE HAD MOVED out months ago, but Julie hadn't told Dane. In fact, she'd barely spoken with anyone about the breakdown, either. Outside of the help they sought, even her closest circle of immediate family and friends was in the dark, except for one person. Julie was ashamed and saddened, since the couple was at a standstill in sorting out their inherent problems. Her sense of failure acute, acidic, she avoided people at every turn. Her patent answer when asked how everything was—"great"—made her physically nauseous each time.

Though Gabe's physical state improved daily, he wasn't in any significantly better mental or emotional space. Neither understood the other's frame of mind. Counseling hadn't triggered vital growth or honed crucial skills, so an extended separation remained their only option. "Perhaps you'll learn to appreciate and miss each other," was the dispensed advice and hopeful outcome from a mutual colleague frustrated by the couple's unabashed stubbornness. Gabe kept to himself as well. Only a couple of his buddies sensed he and Julie even struggled, let alone were separated.

Stunned, Dane stumbled onto the information when Tate taunted him while on a recent business trip in Arizona. They'd finished with a transaction for a renovated sports car on which Bob neared completion. "So, Michaels, that will satisfy my current concerns regarding Bob's latest beauty. Speaking of Bob, I wonder what you make of his most recent neighborly insight?"

Though Dane was clueless, he knew enough to stay on alert with his former classmate. "Hmm ... which one?" *Play it cool.*

"Fascinating you're even aware of one, let alone more." He paused for effect but knew Dane wouldn't give even the slightest hint of what he did, or more likely didn't, know, so Tate continued. "She spends more time than usual quite alone—with her dogs and children to be specific, but all in all, alone." *Still nothing.* "You're shockingly impassive. What do you make of it?"

If Dane hadn't been vigilant whenever around the malicious Tate Parker, he'd swear he'd just been gut punched. Instead, he took his typical slow and deliberate breath. "What Mrs. Archer does when your people aren't following her is none of my concern, nor should it be any of yours."

"I thought your job was to keep an eye on all neighbors, especially those closest to this venture of ours. Closest would include *your Mrs.* Archer." *I'm such an asshole, but he's had this coming for a long time. Maybe I'll share my locked eyes story with him.*

"Has Mrs. Archer asked questions of Bob or peered into his windows surreptitiously? Bob's not mentioned any concerns such as these to me."

"Well, not that I'm aware of, but now that you mention it, maybe I need to ask him."

"Clearly, I already have, so leave Bob alone. You know he's not thrilled with you as an aggressive client as it is. He's quiet, private in his business, and doesn't allow any of his clients to press him, which includes you. If Bob needs to share, he's always been rather forthcoming with you, has he not? Take my professional advice, or leave it."

"Michaels, you're a fucking smug bastard, but you're right. Have to give you that, though I'd prefer to give you nothing. *Shit. Thought I had something on him. Never mind poking him with the other story after all.*

After Tate's abrupt departure and multiple deep calming breaths, a brutal mental debate ensued. *Go next door to Julie's or back to Bob's? Fuck! I'm glad no one can hear my insanity right now.* Dane's business brain won—sort of. Dane bribed his attention away from where it wanted to go and headed to Bob's renovation garage for clarification. "Thank you for the extra details on this job. I'm sorry our client is such … high maintenance, shall we say," Dane humbly offered.

"Listen, Mr. Michaels, I've handled tougher guys than Tate Parker. Something very off with him and his cars, but can't put my thumb on it. I scour his auto bodies for clues as they come in, and, just between us, there are marks in places considered highly unusual in this business. I share this with you—and only you—not even Victor. You're the attorney for this client now, and what I used to share strictly with Victor, I'm sharing strictly with you now."

"Is Victor aware of his non-inclusion at this point?"

"Not exactly, though he's asked more about my neighbor lately. Mentioned some detail about your knowing her a long time ago and to keep an eye on her. I asked him why, and he shocked *me* with *his* elusiveness. It was at that point I decided my longtime friend didn't need to know any more of my business here with his former client. Client-attorney privilege and all that," Bob said with a gleam only an old fox could make.

"I sincerely appreciate your discretion. And in the spirit of full disclosure with you, again, please keep this between just us—for now." Dane paused as he confirmed Bob's agreement.

"Mr. Michaels, plainly, you know how I feel about discretion as well as being straightforward."

"Of course. I just want you to be aware of clarifications I, too, seek. I must be not only discreet but also leery. Mr. Parker's 'boys' are likely watching us. Technically, they tail Julie Archer. However, I'm certain they keep an eye on you, too, and I've complete faith my presence here has given their day a small thrill."

"Well"—the craggily senior droned but winked—"we ole farts are hardly a thrilling lot. We stumble between the house and the garage and back, though I did have a brief but nice visit with my lovely neighbor." Bob placed his pen down on the clipboard with determined precision, looked up at Dane, and awaited the rest of his disclosure.

Dane took the hint. "Julie Archer and I did attend high school together." Dane watched Bob's reactions in an attempt to discern how much information would satisfy the elder statesman. "We dated, went to our senior prom together."

"Is that all, Mr. Michaels?"

"What do you mean, sir?"

"I may be a few years older than you, but I'm not dead." A twinkle in Bob's eye gave him away.

Dane looked toward Julie's house, then back at Bob. "I'm divorced, have two children with my contentious ex, live on another continent, and—"

"And you still care for her. Rather obvious. She's a looker ... smart, too. I'm not sure if she's still married or what, though."

Finally, what I've wanted to know. Dane barely composed himself. "Why would you say that?"

"Mr. Michaels, I'm married four times. My current wife and I have been together many years. In fact, she and I are married the longest of them all. I know trouble absence versus travel absence. Her husband leaves when most husbands are home for the night. He doesn't take the kids to the bus stop anymore. He's not even in charge of trash duty."

"You're, without exception, quite observant, and I appreciate you sharing this information with me."

"I'm not sharing it with you for your sake. I share it with you for her sake. I'm concerned about her safety. Parker's a bit of a loose cannon. She still has fairly young children at home, or with her, constantly. She's begun this new writing career"—Bob shook his head in dismay— "some of which has drawn unintentional heat with new car owners who feel left out of her summaries ... and then there's Parker." The eccentric older man's keen eyes bore into Dane's.

"As your lawyer, I have to advise you to keep me abreast of any further developments with her, since your privacy is imperative to me as well as to the firm, of course."

"Of course."

"As her former prom date, I don't want to see her harmed, either."

"How about as a man still in love with her?"

"That obvious, huh?" Dane's gaze fell to the ground. He tracked a bug big enough to saddle up and ride as it passed in front of him, before he looked up and met Bob's humored eyes. "Planned to leave that minor detail out, did you?"

Wily bastard. "To be quite honest, I was, but I can see it wouldn't have mattered to you if I had." Dane had to smile and shake his head as the senior raised his eyebrows.

"Haven't I already mentioned I've been around the block a few times? Appreciate your honesty, Counselor."

"Yes, Bob, you've mentioned this. Victor's never let on about how wise you are beyond cars."

"Victor doesn't need to know at this point, and I highly advise *you* to keep quiet about it, too. Hmm ... I need you to keep quiet about one more topic." Bob pretended to have a coughing fit and lowered his voice. "I'm sharing this with you to keep us both safe, plus I can't tell my wife. She's apt to make me give up this business, and I refuse to be bullied. I play nice-nice with Mr. Parker, and even sass him back, to have him think I'm not intimidated. Main point? I shared before, these cars are off when I get them. Their weights are far beyond what bodies in these conditions ought to weigh. I'll be damned if I can spot where the extra weight is hidden, though. However it's done, it's by professionals, ones with whom I'm unfamiliar."

"Bob, be very careful. If you find any clues, please call me. If, for whatever reason, you can't reach me, because I'm on a plane or with a client, share this information *only* with my assistant, Isabella Breslaux. Ask with whom you're speaking, in case a sub is there. It happens when I send her out on varied assignments. If she says her name is Isabella, ask her any random question. If she answers the random question, you know it's not Isabella. If her response, regardless of your question, is 'absolutely environmentally humorous,' you know it's Isabella."

"You don't mess around, I gather."

Dane smiled at the older man. "Bob, you know me better than that. And if you didn't before this, you do now. You can be certain I don't mess around—period. Not when it comes to the law. Not when it comes to our lives."

Chapter 93

NOW YOU SEE IT ...

BESOTTED, BUT AN ugly duckling early on, Elena had always wanted to impress Victor and his family. Although generations of her family were longtime landowners, the Boskos' oldmoney world snubbed hers. A family of hard working, self-employed miners, who for decades worked with their hands, clearly signaled a bourgeois lifestyle, especially to aristocrats.

The young law clerk had shocked his family when they began dating, after reconnecting through friends and coworkers in a small-world scenario. Thought to be lovely enough for marriage, bright enough for breeding, and a solid partner-to-be in a wife who lent stability and freedom from drama, no one ever believed Elena would be much more. The common consensus within Victor's life's circle was typical of the very well-to-do. He'd surely need a girlfriend on the side to keep him engaged enough to stay married to the quite plain, but "sturdy" and "secure," young, working artist. Meanwhile, he'd impressed her parents not by merely appreciating their only child for her brightness, but by seeing past her downplayed beauty.

The handsome barrister disregarded naysayers as shortsighted and shallow and enjoyed lively conversations with the understated young woman about the law. Besides her education and brilliance, he was also drawn to her creativity, so antipodal to his legal pursuits, and cherished her tolerance of his extensive work hours as he aimed for a partnership.

On their wedding day, his stubborn determination to marry her was more than rewarded. When the music began and signaled the escorted bride's entrance, Victor beamed. Elena stunned all who were in attendance. She'd waited until this perfect moment to reveal the creature hidden beneath the plain façade. He knew just from her gown he'd hit the lottery. In fact, he couldn't take his eyes off of her.

The church energy shifted, too, from a formal-looking, floral-stuffed, obligatory function to a breathless, captivating one. Attendees stood up straighter, voices hushed, and jaws dropped in the pews as the procession began. The musicians took notice, too, and adjusted not only their attire but their attitudes. Some said the music brightened.

The bride's father in a handsome, black tux, cummerbund, and matching bow tie, patent leather wingtips, and a crisply pressed, white dress shirt, escorted his statuesque and beautiful offspring down the aisle. His eyes outshone his perfectly polished cufflinks.

Her mother, in pearl-pink, silk shantung, mother-of-the-bride dress, had been the last one seated in the front pew. She remained expressionless, justifiably smug from the hurtful rumors she'd endured during her daughter's courtship. She'd already decided to dismiss all the naysayers at the reception, regardless of their apologies. She knew they'd come.

As the father of the bride proudly ushered his only daughter into the adorned church, her candlelight, satin-and-lace gown appeared demure, until she passed the onlookers. The details were anything but. A form-fitted bodice revealed a slim, toned body, nude tulle exposed creamy, cared-for skin. Sheer, long sleeves were accentuated with hand-sewn lace and tiny pearls, and a low-cut back divulged a risk taker. A whisper of Chanel perfume trailed close behind her.

No one but the groom had seen the transformation approach. Few missed it now.

Just a few weeks after their honeymoon, the new husband reveled in his bride's shameless strength, the opposite of demure or plain. Her high energy, unique creativity, and ambitious sex drive, which exceeded his own, exhausted the elated young lawyer for a while. He expected to get used to their breathtaking passion— eventually. His friends at work winked at him, as he'd explain his groggy mornings due to late nights. Still incredulous, they wondered how soon he'd introduce them to his "concubine." He laughed at their disbelief, and then marveled at his good fortune.

Chapter 94

DREAMING?

LOCKED EYES PENETRATED. The connection was fleeting but intense, real.

What the hell was that all about? Not normal for our interaction to be so … intrusive, palpable, or am I deluding myself? I'm dreaming, right? I need to wake up.

Julie tossed and turned.

His look was undeniable. What happened? What shifted? He didn't look into my soul. His eyes barged in and begged my inner being to remember that we've met before. Well, of course we have! We went to school together, right? Not that kind of "before?" Is this possible? It was mere eye contact. Wasn't it? No. It's also not just a dream.

Why does he assume I want to know him now? Does he know something I don't?

Yet not a word beyond our normal banter is spoken, and I can't seem to awaken.

I smell something.

I know now something's changed somewhere in his life. My knee-jerk reaction is to tell him to go home, call his ex-wife, fix things, figure it out. I want to emphasize to him I'd never hurt my estranged husband or our children. My children! Late for school. I can't wake up, but what is that smell?

All of that was left unsaid, yet every letter a truth emblazoned like a neon billboard flashing in the middle of the night. Yes, it's the middle of the night. That's why I can't wake up.

What's happening? What's ignited? What vibe have I given off? Had what I thought to be resolved between us now been misconstrued? Perhaps what I thought were simply innocent, flirty exchanges have gone too far?

I know I'm dreaming, but I still test my theory during an imaginary meeting. I commit myself to being ultra professional, curt even, as it is necessary. He feels a need to confess feelings, needs, wants to me, despite my not asking. He does so without voice, without words. This is bizarre!

There it is. Again. I sniff the air. It's not offensive.

He confides how long it's been since he's left his wife. He shares that he's dated various women. His ex knows, he stated again. Has he mentioned this already? I've not asked for any of these outlandish admissions. He reports these insights as assurances, wordless, imploring with his eyes.

It's ignited but not burning. I just want to know what it is.

But I speculate aloud with him. Those dates likely had not been with any of our common friends. That's the real difference. A stranger was barely tolerated. A friend would signify betrayal by all parties.

Enough time has passed, he argues.

Define enough, I challenge.

Enough that she's remarried, so why can't he also do as he pleases, he surmises. He doesn't parade women around or shove them under his ex's nose.

Ask her permission, I counter. At least it'll have been above board, open.

She'd rather die than see us together, he acknowledges. Seeing us together would validate what she'd suspected all the years of our marriage—there'd been another woman all along. She'd probably get a P.I. again to find out if I'd been lying.

Still, he sees my point.

We can't hide. That's not living. We also aren't one hundred percent certain this (I encircle the energy between us) is it for us, are we? How do we know that this isn't basic animal attraction? Old business unfinished from when we once knew each other? Make anything about us public, and we invite unwanted and unnecessary drama, chaos, into our already complex lives ... unless we're ready.

So you're going to try to deny every word?

What word? We've not spoken anything. I know this is a dream. This conversation isn't real.

Bullshit. You know that's bullshit. When we lock eyes, we both nearly panic because there's so much there.

He closes the door with a quiet click to the window-shaded room and moves with stealth speed to me, taking me in his arms. I'm breathless when he kisses me, deep and passionate, my every sense overpowered. His scent ...

What are you doing? I gasp for air, not wanting him to stop but scream in my mind this is wrong. Shit! There it is again. Wait. Is that—temptation?

He kisses me again, hungrier than before. When are you going to get me? Us? I know I can convince you this way. I just need to turn off your brain. He begs with his kiss. He knows if he can somehow make his case clear and absolute, neither of us will ever walk away again.

Your sense of loyalty is admirable, enviable even. It's misplaced, however. Your husband doesn't appreciate your sensuous, carnal appeal. You radiate it. He asks me if he imagines our attraction? Is he presumptuous? He knows a few other ways to make a strong impact with me. He rationalizes, dips his strong chin. Either I'm oblivious, disinterested, or he's not communicating his thoughts or emotions well. Perhaps I need to be obvious, he taunts. Showing is better than talking. His hand moves from my shoulders to my lower back. Oh, the power his pinky possesses over my tailbone!

I come up for air, attempt to reason with him. He shuts me down again, first with his fiery eyes as he bores into mine, like the rake who lures a woman from across the room to look at him. A caress of his lips on mine, slow, deliberate, he tastes me with his tongue as he whispers unrecognizable words. It's hot, devastating. How's this possible? He's fixated by a need to make crystal clear with his lips all the words he can't seem to speak.

In turn, I render him mute, confused with cool, aquamarine eyes and wanton body warmth. He accuses me of haunting him at the most primal level. That's what I smell. Arousal. A memory. We've been here. Before arousal ignited temptation, together, in each other's arms, terrified to let go. I more than feel it. I inhale it. I taste it.

He further accuses me of imprisonment. How, I challenge. You hold me.

We hold each other captive, helpless when the other is near. Like bees drawn to flower nectar, we're defenseless against the pull of an evocative, unearthly scent only we detect. At least I'm aware of this, though I don't yet understand why. Does it matter? An unidentifiable scent, let alone what we do to each other when we breathe the same air.

Reluctant, he withdraws his full mouth from mine. I know to be quiet and wait for him to speak first. He feels me relax, just a little, in his arms. I watch his eyes, await his command, search each fraction of movement as he drags his appreciative gaze from my lips to my eyes. Who are you? He's amused.

Shakespeare said it first, or perhaps it was in the Bible, and I happen to agree. Your eyes are doubtless windows into your deep and fiery soul, like a magical key. I've seen this soul before. He gasps as he stares into them, like an ocean, vast and seemingly infinite. How had I seen you like this in high school and let you go? He grieves, tortured by memories.

Unbeknownst to the other, Julie and Dane awoke in two different parts of the same city having had the same dream. Each knew they needed to figure out what happened between them. It didn't have a name yet, but it was powerful.

Chapter 95

DINOSAUR

BEN'S INSTRUCTIONS TO Julie had been clear. Gabe's collapse required professional help. Also clear was Julie's inability to be her estranged husband's professional caregiver, never mind unaided. She still had to take care of their children as well as tend to her new business.

After Gabe was allowed to leave the care facility, he gave Julie an unexpected gift.

"Wow. It feels amazing to be home." He took a slow, deep breath in and out, then continued. "I want to thank you."

Julie's small smile signaled she barely listened, so preoccupied by her natural caregiver instincts. She made sure Gabe was comfortable for the few days he transitioned at home before he moved back out and returned to work part-time. "For what?"

"For your advocacy, showing up for me just about every day at the Center, for standing by my side throughout this whole ordeal."

"Of course. I mean, you're welcome. In sickness and in health, right?" She realized they headed in the exact direction Gabe's doctors warned her against—tough topics, which included their marriage—until after his next doctor's appointment.

Gabe sighed as Julie suddenly looked up. "You

could've done what several of our friends' spouses have done ... dump them while they were in treatment or right after their release. Sounds like prison, but you know what I mean. I know we've filed and that I move back out in a few days. Don't worry."

Julie's blush went unnoticed by Gabe. After his shocking collapse, sometimes at night when Julie laid in bed alone, she wondered. *When will the right time be to bring up the "purple dinosaur" from our greatest confrontation? Do I need to just hope Gabe completed enough therapy to broach the hard subject on his own, or, better yet, that the attack had been covered already?* Like a young child playing hide-and-seek with an adult who chose to "hide" behind the broomstick, there was no place for the troubled couple to hide.

"Gabe—"

"Listen, I'm gonna be fine. The bad news? It's gonna take me a few weeks to get back up and running one hundred percent. The good news? I will. When I do, you won't have to worry about me."

"Gabe—"

"I don't need you to feel sorry for me or to make excuses. You've asked me for years to take care of myself, right? To go to the doctor when I needed to, whatever. I didn't listen. Pretty obvious, huh? I ignored all symptoms, and then physically, emotionally hurt you. You don't get as fucking low as I was unless you're just a hardheaded asshole. I've got a lot of work ahead of me," Gabe owned. "I can at least be thankful for your help, and I promise to figure out my shit for myself and our kids, even if it's too late for us."

Julie didn't look at Gabe. Perhaps if she didn't stare at him in this state, he was left some space, some sense of privacy to restore his pride. Not for her sake, but for his.

She blinked back unshed tears.

Now for reality check. "How many people know what's gone on?"

"At work, just your partner."

"It's been almost a month, Julie. Do you really think my employees haven't noticed I'm not there?"

Concerned about his stress, she offered, "Gabe, Ben is the only one who knows the facts of what's gone on. Your staff was told a ... broader version of a truth."

"Care to explain what that bullshit means?"

"It means we told them you had a severe asthmatic attack."

"You told them I had a severe attack, and *that's* why I'd miss almost a *month* of work?" Gabe's body language signaled disbelief and relief together.

"You're not the only one who found that a stretch. So in order to dispel any concerns about the company folding, or address whatever people wondered about, and to proceed with business as usual, I had our primary doc come in and talk to our employees, answer their questions. He shared how to avoid any kind of similar illness, as well as to reassure everyone you weren't contagious and would make a total recovery. You had undiagnosed asthma, which you thought was a cold and foolishly worked through. Never saw a doc, ignored your wife's and your partner's urgings—hardly a stretch—caught a horrible flu virus, couldn't breathe, and had to be hospitalized. When you think about it, that's essentially what happened."

"No one but Ben knows about the ... um ... state I was in, then?"

"Nope. None of their damn business."

"Wow. Impressive."

"Thank you. I've always been on your side." Julie

looked at Gabe impassively, checked her watch, and exhaled. "I've gotta pick up the kids. You'll be okay for thirty minutes?" She was genuinely concerned to leave him for even five, though his temperament remained calm.

"Yes, I'll be fine."

"The kids will be so happy to know Dad feels better. I'll warn them to take it easy on you, though. Okay?"

"Whatever you think is best."

"I'll be quick." As she fished car keys from her purse, Julie gave her estranged husband a small nod and left without another word.

Chapter 96

TRACE

NAUSEATED, JULIE TRIED to stay calm as she drove to pick up her kids. She felt for her cell phone in its usual spot in her purse, touched a number to autodial Waffles, and urged, "Please pick up. Please pick—"

"You okay?"

"Kind of." *No.*

"Great answer. What does that mean?"

"Short version?"

"Please."

"I just brought Gabe home from the hospital. He'll be with us for a few days before he moves back out."

"I'm sorry."

"There's more." She took a deep breath, her intent to calm the quiver in her voice. "I have multiple parties following me. Any chance you know this?"

"I know of one. Are both following you, or is one following the one following you?"

"Sounds more like a riddle than real life. I don't know for certain, but I believe, well, both."

"How've you come to that conclusion?"

"How am I supposed to know who's following whom?"

"Give me your best guess."

"Supposedly, one set was called off—by someone I

know—and then a different set surfaced. Then Gabe's ex's car exploded, and she was definitely following me, as you already know. The same guys who followed Gabe's ex just before the car blew up appeared at the mall. Thankfully, a Fed friend had my back that day and had her people intervene before the bad guys activated their own plan, whatever that might have been." *Please no more questions.*

"Okay, hold up, a Fed friend? You recognized *and* made contact with your shadows at the mall? You're in over your head, my dear. It's time to call this in to a higher authority."

"Hear me out first. Besides, a 'higher authority' already knows, obviously. I just wanted to make sure someone local knew. Maybe in your line of work you hear things? I know guys talk and all. Wait, how do you know I'm in over my head? What do you know?"

"What did these guys look like? Any particular physical features? Accents when they spoke? Weird eyes or jewelry?"

"You know something."

"I've done some checking around. That car bomb is in my jurisdiction."

"Okay, and?"

"And it led me to question varied people."

"Does the car renovating industry have anything to do with these people? You know I'm writing basically a 'Who's Done What' for local car shows, right?"

"You're not writing anything controversial, correct?" Julie's insider confirmed.

"What's with the 'Twenty Questions' game? Not that I'm aware of." Her tone turned testy.

"Are you sure?"

"What do you mean, 'am I sure'? Haven't you read

any of my pieces? As far as I—"

"What's the matter?"

She'd felt his stare before she'd seen it. It was the kind that locked on to the skin, willing the eyes of the observed to seek those of the observer, pain inflicted if the gaze went unmet. "Um … I stopped to get gas while speaking with you and … and. …"

"Are you safe? What are you seeing, Julie?"

From her peripheral, she'd spotted the old Ford pickup waiting across the parking lot from her small gas station. "Since when is some mom pumping gas worth watching? I'm being so paranoid." She thought she'd whispered to herself.

Waffles' volume dropped almost to meet Julie's. "Talk to me."

With his feet up on the dash straddling the steering column, his slicked-back, salt-andpepper ponytail and beat-up T-shirt blended in with the look of many day laborers in the area, except he seemed fairer skinned. He more than observed her, however. His scrutiny was the kind that made her skin crawl, the kind that dared to be resisted. When she succumbed to the pull, she glared back in defiance. His poker face chilled her in spite of the day's warmer temperatures.

"I've seen this guy before," she confirmed more to herself.

"Where? What does he look like? I can't help you if you don't talk to me."

Julie's description matched the account given by the artist with whom Waffles had spoken. He was the same man the artist had allegedly thrown out of her apartment.

"I saw this guy in a grocery store parking lot a few days ago."

"Julie, are you done filling up your car?"

"Just now. Yes. I'd seen him before that, too."

His tone level and voice calm, Waffles directed, "Where are you headed?"

"To pick up two of my kids from after-school activities. Gabe's home alone, and … oh, shit, I'll lead this guy right to—"

"Julie, I need you to stay calm and focus with me. Okay?"

She nodded her reply as she recapped her gas tank and straightened her spine.

"Julie?"

"Yes, I'm here. Hang on, I'm walking toward him."

"You're doing what? Julie, stop! Listen to me, and go back to your car." *Shit.*

"You know, I'm so fed up with all the frickin' male egos. I deal with them at the auto shows when I ask questions to get details correct and learn, and even at home, at least until he's moved out again. I want to know who the hell this ponytailed asshole thinks he is trying to intimidate me at my own gas station in my own town," she growled.

Waffles implored Julie's shoulder, where her cell had been relocated, to return to her car. "Oh fuck," he muttered, frustrated and alarmed as he paced in his office. He strained to listen to her muffled conversation and was surprised to hear a string of obscenities from her instead. Relieved, he suppressed a smile and waited for her to share what he guessed had happened.

"Cowardly bastard. He drove off, smirking no less, when I crossed the parking lot to where he hung out, leering at me. What—"

"Julie," Waffles interrupted firmly.

"Yes?" She snapped back.

"What the *fuck* were you thinking?"

"When?"

"Just now? When you decided to cross the parking lot? You're aware that maybe these people aren't all nice, family-oriented folks, right?"

"What was he gonna do, shoot me in broad daylight? I mean, seriously." She didn't get a response. "Right?"

"Julie, I hate to be the one to do this." *Love her spirit, but it's recklessly directed.*

"What?"

"Be honest and scare the living, hot shit out of you, but yes, he could've shot you right there, with or without a silencer, driven off, and disappeared. Even if you *were* lucky enough to have been watched by *someone*, and assuming that someone got the truck's license plate number, I guarantee you, Mr. Ponytail drove a stolen vehicle and will easily disappear. These are some rough people, Julie."

She shivered at the reality check as she slid behind her steering wheel and started her car.

"I don't know exactly who they are yet, but I *do* know that car bombs and multiple vehicle tagalongs are not to be ignored ... not by the professionals or by pissy moms who get a hair across their asses. Ya feelin' me here? You have children to think about."

"I'm feelin' you," she conceded with a pout. "But I also don't want anyone to assume I'll be easily intimidated, even if I am," she whispered in her car alone. "I despise bullies ... anywhere."

"I don't blame you. Nobody likes 'em." He paused, allowed his warning to sink in a moment, and then continued more gently. "You okay?"

Julie drew in a slow, deep breath through her nose and let it out, slower, to steady herself. "Sure."

"Well, that was completely unconvincing, but it'll have to do for now. Listen, pick up your children, be mindful of who's around but not obvious, and get back to Gabe. You have enough on your plate without Mr. Ponytail and his intimidation tactics. We'll figure out who he is. Continue to write your stories, do your research, attend to your kids, and quit looking for trouble. Stay in touch, okay? Oh, and if this helps at all, you were pretty convincing with your rogue move." He chuckled.

"Yeah, thanks. That would be one of us."

"Certainly, you surprised him this time, or he wouldn't have sped off. He'll expect you to approach next time, though. Watch yourself."

Chapter 97

... NOW YOU DON'T

VICTOR RECALLED A question his wife had asked him recently. Just before he picked her up for their first lunch date in years, he'd shared his concern for Dane with her. "Whose side are you on and why?" she'd asked. Victor had considered his answer carefully, since he recognized his inability to do so at the time asked. Finally ready to decide, the seasoned legal partner prayed he wasn't too late, as his choice would bear severe impacts on the unchosen.

His dalliance with Rachel a few years ago had been pathetic enough, though Dane hadn't ever discovered it. Victor hadn't meant to get involved with her. He'd initially just felt sorry for the young wife and mother. Dane Michaels' ambition was admirable, but his inability to recognize Rachel's desperate attempts to capture his attention frustrated Victor. His own wife had gone to similar lengths early on in their marriage, and Victor had done his best to keep up with her voracious sexual appetite. *We all have our languages of love, don't we?* He mused.

Dane's inattentiveness, however, made it clear he wasn't looking to hurt Rachel. It was more like the movie title, "He's Just Not That into You." Sad, yet stark and obvious, Victor believed Rachel had misread Dane's cues, but somehow they'd ended up married. Very few personal conversations had happened between the two men, but Victor soon grasped his pupil's perspective—especially after several of Rachel's hot seductions. He reflected Dane's same disinterested behavior. By the time he'd awakened to the shrewd young woman's intentions, his wife had caught them leaving their "lunch."

Elena's frustrations by her husband's thwarted affections prompted her to hire a private investigator. He followed the unwitting couple to Zurich's largest casino as they attempted to disappear among the tourist crowds to their prearranged room. To the P.I., it was evident they'd done this before—regularly—which, of course, made it easy for his client to catch her husband.

They'd left Rachel's car parked on the street several blocks from Victor's office, and Victor parked in the City Parking garage next door. They raced hand in hand up the escalator, through the prepaid turnstile to the elevator, breathlessly unaware of their "company."

Typically, a well-dressed clientele frequented this establishment. Exceptions happened. Any time alcohol shaded a scene, casino management knew their security panorama was painted the color strange.

Passed out drunk in a wheelchair and held up by its arms, an unconscious young woman was nearly dumped face first by her giggling, skanky companion who couldn't see more than inches over the front of the chair. Their acquaintances weren't in much better condition. In the elevator, a kelly green-haired girl tatted from head to toe, twig skinny and tweaked on something more than vodka, blanched and slid down the moving box's back wall. Her desperate girlfriend looked for help just as the doors opened to the lobby. Thankfully just entering, management assisted before Victor and Rachel were forced to choose between their tryst and their day's good deed.

The private eye followed them all the way past their door to another room, grumbled something about a key, and returned to the elevator. Once back in his car, he turned on the radio to catch the last of an exhibition American baseball game. "Bounces that one and the count is full," the announcer's play-by-play described. He knew the couple would be at least an hour (their rendezvous never went less than that). He called his client and awaited the doomed forthcoming scene.

It wasn't until he'd been caught leaving that day when the very real possibility had occurred to him—Rachel had set up Victor. He didn't know why. He couldn't see it. He just knew he had been.

Chapter 98

INTERNAL ALARMS

DANE'S CAUTIOUSNESS APPEARED to soothe his client, but it triggered a deep-core alarm, one with which Dane was unfamiliar. *The law spells out how to handle a variety of facts, circumstances, and incidents. It doesn't spell out how to handle humans and their opposing choices, be they good or bad.* He sat in his parked rental car around the corner from Bob Couvey's house, gathered his uncharacteristic mess of papers to organize, and realized his thoughts were even more scattered. *What the hell is going on?*

During all his years in college and throughout law school, Dane Michaels had never felt such mental strife about his profession. He'd been part of straightforward as well as cagey businesses. However, when his driver, Paul, had been killed not long ago, he'd felt a shift. Normally unruffled and determined to remain focused and collected, he fought disengagement. Though he'd spoken to Bob with a calm tone, the current dialogue in his head was anything but as it unraveled and pounded to be released. *What the hell is happening with me?*

Startled by a single-minded vulture hawk as it snatched a young rabbit in the desert neighborhood, Dane's primitive, protective instincts wondered where Julie was. "Something's wrong." He picked up his cell and punched in Isabella's programmed number.

"Hey, Boss. Are you okay?"

"I'm not sure. Sorry to call so late."

"What does 'I'm not sure' mean?" She hesitated as she asked.

"It means I'm physically safe for now, but I'm certain Tate Parker's up to something, especially regarding Julie Archer. I just left Bob Couvey's house after meeting with both men at first and then just Bob alone. Bob and Julie are neighbors, and—"

"Boss, I know where Mrs. Archer lives." Dane wasn't sure if he'd heard a slight emphasis on the missus by his assistant, or if it was his newly acquired paranoia. He chose to let it pass for now, determined to trust Isabella.

"Right, sorry. Just trying to be thorough. Anyway, Parker thought he was taunting me with information, but instead, I picked up on his searching for my Achilles regarding her. He's doing something with those cars, and he doesn't want anyone to find out."

"Doesn't Bob know? I mean, he works on those car bodies."

"Bob actually shared he's been searching for clues as those frames have come in. He's got reason to believe something's wrong, too, like marks in highly unusual places and Victor suddenly being evasive about details. This means Victor clearly knows something we don't yet. We need to keep all of this information just between us. Bob's no longer sharing anything with Victor."

"Really? He and Victor have been friends for years. Did he tell you that? Are you sure you heard correctly? I don't mean to question you. It's just this file is getting more and more bizarre."

"Bob was quite adamant. He cited client-attorney privilege, reminded me Victor was no longer his attorney, and felt the need to remind me I *am*. So, yes, this file *is* getting more bizarre." Dane paused. "Tate Parker needs to settle some score with me, but for what? I wish I knew. Today, just now, I got a sinking feeling Julie Archer has somehow gotten mixed up in it. Any updates through the office gossip?"

"First of all, I agree with you. He wants to exact some sort of revenge on you. And yes, the coffeepot gossip has been percolating." Isabella snickered at her wit. "There's been reference to Mrs. Archer as an 'unwitting,' even 'coincidental' freelance writer, and to our illustrious Mr. Bosko for his fabulous timing to turn over such long-held accounts. When your name came up, most agreed you were the oddest yet clearest choice to take over such a long-considered 'dirty account.' Fascinating dialogues, in fact."

"That relieves and disturbs me. Why was I the 'oddest yet clearest choice'?" *But there's no such thing as a coincidence. Does Julie know something I need to know?*

"Yes." Isabella responded so fast to Dane's thought, as if she'd heard him. "Both. And more to disturb us is the whisper of gold smuggling with Parker's other account."

"What are you talking about?" Dane scowled at his cell phone.

"Boss, when are you coming home?"

"Excellent question. Isabella, what do you mean gold smuggling? Explain."

"There's been an increased number of shipping trans-actions with Mr. Parker's mining company, but the shipments once cleared through customs ... um ... well ..."

"Spit it out, for God's sake."

"Disappear."

"Disappear?"

"Yes. Disappear."

"And where does the coffee-klatch chatter believe it's going?"

Just as Dane finished his question, he noticed the increased action around him. The neighborhood began its late afternoon hum. Parents drove minivans and SUVs as they returned from after-school activities with their children, contractors headed out in pickups from varied home improvement projects, and an old Ford Bronco ... "Hold on, Isabella, I know that driver." The ponytailed driver was pulled off to the side of the neighborhood road. He didn't fit in as resident or contractor.

"What driver?"

"A guy parked facing me on this residential street. He's out of place."

"How do you know?"

"Because he's staring at me."

PAY ATTENTION

"MAYBE *YOU'RE* THE odd man out of place."

"Why would you say that?"

"Why did you say you know that driver?"

"Because ... fuck it. Let's find out."

Dane put the car in drive and eased from his side of the road toward the old pickup. Without a break in their eye contact, the ponytailed driver moved backward.

"Holy shit. He's not even looking at where he's driving."

"Boss, be careful."

"I'll call you back." Dane hung up with his assistant and dialed 9-1-1.

"Nine-one-one. State your emergency."

"There's an out-of-place truck in my senior dad's neighborhood driving in reverse without looking where he's going, and I'm worried he'll hit someone. Can you send help? Please? Uh … ASAP!"

"What is your name, sir, and where do you live?"

"My name? Michael. My dad lives around the corner at … oh, shit … oh … sorry. He just missed hitting that boy on a bike! How far is help?"

"One minute, Michael. Stay on the line with me, please, until police arrive. Do you still see this truck?"

"I do."

"What kind of truck is it?"

"An old, Ford Bronco pickup."

"What color?"

"Cruiser is following him, so I'm outta here. Thank you, ma'am." Dane knew when he hung up he'd frustrated the emergency worker. His cell phone number was permanently blocked through the carrier. "Who was that?" he questioned aloud then called Isabella back. "Hey, about the missing gold—"

"Are you okay?"

"No. My client hasn't mentioned anything about missing gold, and you say my name has been brought up in the same breath?"

"Only because he's your client. Your name hasn't been specifically linked to the theft—yet—but your signatures are on all the paperwork."

The lawyer rolled his eyes. "Terrific. Sounds like it won't be long before it is." Through his nose, Dane pulled in a long breath to fill his lungs to capacity. He rested the back of his head against the car's headrest as he moved with traffic on the busy side streets of Scottsdale. To any onlookers, he was a businessman en route home from a harried day, his tie askew, sunglasses positioned on the end of his nose, and visor pushed forward on the windshield to block a low-horizon sunset.

Chapter 99

WAIT, WHAT?

JULIE COLLAPSED INTO a hard, unbroken sleep. After she picked up their younger ones, fed the whole family, and situated Gabe in their guest room, she started a bath for herself, lit a few candles, and searched online for an extended music playlist of soothing sounds.

"Soft candlelight? Check. Epsom salts. Check. Essential oils for relaxation ... perfect." She reached for her little bottles of lavender, bergamot, and clary sage. "One, two, three." She counted out nine drops from each. "Three of this." She uncapped the precious vial of rose oil. "Three of you," she whispered to the tiny containers of jasmine, sandalwood, and patchouli.

After dropping her clothes into a pile at her feet, the exhausted mom stepped toward her tub. She gathered her hair above the nape of her neck in a soft elastic, then sunk into the healing waters. Several slow, deep breaths in through her nose followed gentle exhales through her mouth. Peaceful music filled both her physical and mental space. Her weary eyes closed, intent on dismissing the day's formidable events. Julie felt the clenched traps in her neck and shoulders begin their welcome release and drifted into the music.

Rather than process the day, though, flashes of naked legs entangled in rumpled, white sheets appeared. Anxious about who they belonged to, Julie's eyes popped open. She searched her memory for something she'd just read or watched. *Must have been carpool line babble.* She dismissed that thought, and once again sought to shut down her brain, to just be quiet—even briefly.

Her brows were sweaty, her forehead damp. "Okay, a little better, even if that's all I get tonight," Julie noted wryly. "I'm lucky I've had this thirty minutes to myself. So grateful." She toweled off, ready for sleep. "Finished tucking everyone in?" she asked her loyal, four-legged friends, then patted her mattress, the signal for them to join her. "My turn." A sigh, and she was out before they'd even finished circling for the perfect position snuggled next to her for the night.

Passion came tenderly, gropingly, and transformed into wanton, steamy, needy grasps. The phone rang unanswered, but the interruption allowed them to catch their breath.

He left her side for the bathroom. "What's happening between us?" he pondered aloud. "What am I doing?" Without thought, he undressed before he could stop himself.

She followed him in reply. Wordless. Captivated by his naked skin, she watched him from the doorway as he turned on the shower. He lured her with promises of a relaxing neck massage, though she knew where such promises led. She remained silent, slipped off her clothes into a pool on the floor, and walked through the open shower door.

As his one hand closed it, he reached with the other for the musky-scented shower gel. "Massage always feels better when the masseuse's hands move smooth and easy over the skin." He stared into her eyes, mesmerized, leaned in as if under a spell, and grazed her ear with his lips. "You are stunning." His husky voice made her quiver. He smiled at her responsiveness and struggled to remain a gentleman. Still, he pirouetted her away from him. His hands moved with fluid strokes along her graceful neck, hoping to release any tensions or doubts. Her shoulder blades relaxed as he kneaded and caressed her flushed skin. He wanted to touch her everywhere all at once but knew his advances would overwhelm her. He took an unhurried breath as he willed himself to slow down. Enjoy her skin, he told himself, and take in all that she's become.

Basking in the warmth of their closeness, she turned herself to face him once again. This time, he couldn't stop himself from massaging the fragrant liquid into the front of her shoulders, down her chest to her glistening breasts. He groaned as he touched them, and she pushed him farther when she felt how aroused he'd become.

She, too, wanted all of him at once, yet glided, unhurried, up and down his torso on her tiptoes to communicate her desires. She positioned him at her slick entrance and teased him to near connection. His focus intensified. His breath unsteadied. When her naked, erect nipples touched his, she shifted his hands to reach behind her. Their hands found more places to spread the woodsy-scented gel. She continued her sensuous slide up and down him, hooking her ankle behind his calf, when he surrendered to their mutual hunger. Their bodies moved rhythmically as the shower's steam enveloped and camouflaged them.

Afraid of it all ending too soon, he moaned as he grasped her shoulders and moved back from her. He rinsed off and left the shower with an enticing grin. With a lick of her lips to calm her near breathlessness, she followed his lead.

No longer twilight, the full moon's impact was breathtaking on the backyard landscape. Like a noiseless spy on a mission, he moved to a chaise lounge and waited for her to catch up to his thoughts. She didn't miss a beat and had already guessed his next move. As stealthy as he'd been, she positioned herself astride him, then lowered herself to accept all of him.

"You're dizzyingly beautiful in this light," he whispered. "I'm so close. Go slow."

She saw it in his fiery eyes and stopped riding him so fast. He *clutched her hips to him hard.*

"What's wrong?" he asked, worried.

"Wrong?" She chuckled. "What would be wrong at this perfect moment?"

"You stopped so suddenly, I got a little nervous, that's all," he murmured. He pulled her down to kiss him, her hair shrouding them in a curtain of privacy.

"I had to. I'm not ready for this incredible feeling to be over. It's got to be a sin or a crime to feel this connected, this ... I don't know ... spiritual, seriously," she whispered.

He smiled and all but begged. "Please keep going." Perversely, she eased off of him, left his slicked hardness directed at the stars, and strolled a lap all the way around the pool to the chaise positioned near him where she lie naked. "Don't move," she tempted with a siren's call. She knows exactly what she's doing to me. I accept I'll lose my mind. "Why am I listening to her," he begged the stars, "instead of jumping up, pinning her to that lounge chair—and I mean pinning her—and finishing what we've started?" he puzzled aloud, shaking his head. "I understand she's just taking another breath, but does she know it's my breath she's taking?"

She squirmed as she touched herself in the moonlight. "You're delicious. Let me imbed this visual of you in my dreams." Taunted, he started from the chaise. Again, she cautioned him with a whisper. "Stay where you are." She stretched her legs in a slow tease and bent her body in ways that nearly drove him out of his mind. She paused, looked over her shoulder, and watched him watch her. Amused by her effect on him, she was completely at ease modeling for him in the moonlight. He held his breath, watched her strut away again, like on a runway, and then she turned back toward him at the painstaking saunter of a huntress stalking her mesmerized prey. Though temperatures outside remained a remarkable ninety-five degrees, he shuddered.

Instead of slipping him back into her, she kissed and nibbled him from his toes to his head and back halfway. He honored her demand and lie motionless with extraordinary selfcontrol. Desiring her more than he'd ever desired anyone in his existence, he was indeed mesmerized by her scent, her movement, her touch, paralyzed by her lips and tongue, her hands and skin.

"This must be what heaven feels like," he groaned. "I. Have. Never. Felt like this before. You can't imagine what you're doing to me ... how you're making me feel." She replied with a small, pleased smile and a lick of her lips.

As she descended halfway down his body, she lingered, pausing in appreciation and wonder at how his entire body responded to her every touch. The sensation of his skin against hers warmed her from the inside out—right from her very core. A warm sheen of sweat deepened into a hot, instinctive desire to have him at that moment. Passion was no longer a yearning. It was a staggering, urgent need, an ache at a primal level. He sank farther into the lounge chair, not realizing that he'd been anxious for more than her skin against his. "Slowly," he panted. "Need you ... now ... slowly ... please."

When she effortlessly realigned their bodies, they disappeared from the physical earth, as they knew it. Beneath the stars, the full moon, and the cloudless night sky, they made love, slow and tender, holding, touching, kissing, looking into each other's eyes to cement these sensations into the very essence of their beings. Intense, glorious climaxes seized then calmed their near hysteria, their physical edginess, but presented soul challenges, an almost unbearable effort to postpone reality's imminent and eventual return.

Julie rolled over, awakened by her alarm to an empty bed. "Oh my God." She panted. "Whoa ... what the ... who's eyes ... who was that? *What* is going on?"

Chapter 100

SPELLBOUND

SOON AFTER GABE'S return from his "treatment," as they referred to it, he moved back out. Julie's writing world began to spin faster. An editing opportunity, magazine stories, and the continued auto auction series needed her attention. *Of course*, she reflected, *they'd all surface concurrently as I speed up the book's completion and juggle kids' schedules.*

Upon Julie's return from New York, having completed more research for her book, she felt another pull, different from the ambition to finish her current manuscript or pay attention to family schedules. It was undeniable. *Damn. That's all I should've needed, right? A few weeks? Certainly, a spell could be broken in that time period. Isn't that what it was? A spell? Sure as hell feels like one. Is he aware he cast it?*

Once past much of the family turmoil, Julie announced her availability, via group email as usual, to assist the auto show's marketing team. She received a colleague's request to fill in at a meeting in downtown Phoenix.

"We've already paid for a hotel room for your out-of-town counterpart, so you might as well use it," she'd been instructed by her team's lead.

"You know what? I will. Thank you. It'll cut down on any chances of being late and increase the amount of sleep I get." She inhaled the promises of a little more space from her daily parental responsibilities, like making lunches for her brood, helping with homework, and driving carpools. *Coverage. Need to call ...*

"Something that's likely at a premium for you anyway. With all of your kids, your ... um ... well ... personal challenges and. ..."

Dismayed by her distracted thoughts as well as her boss's attempt at sensitivity, Julie skipped to read another email when a new message alert popped onto the computer screen. Dane's seemingly innocent note to the untrained eye was the hook she couldn't have anticipated.

"You doing okay? I'm presuming your phone works now."

And there it was ... that pull, like a spell. When she awoke, she thought about him. She resisted sending an early text to ask if he'd had the same dream, as she tried to keep her distance. A song on the radio, however, triggered another thought of him.

Damn, a lascivious thought, of course. Why deny it ... like denying the guilty pleasure of ice cream on a hot day. She pictured his insightful look. Certain it wasn't innocent, it would indeed entice, even bait, her.

"We aren't even in the same country, yet I feel his presence, as if he stood right here next to me. If we were in the same room, we'd be drawn side by side. Another human would need to physically stand between us for us to keep our hands off of one another. To shake hands would be an insufferable form of contact. Even such minimal touch would cause pain, like an electric current jolting through us. The energy that remained would sizzle between us." *Sizzle leaves unmistakable clues for a nose to follow. Hypnotic and powerful like pheromone-riddled perfume, those who witness us will teeter between delicious burn and cheap greed.*

She closed the message, unanswered.

Chapter 101

DELUSIONAL

ELENA COULDN'T DECIDE if her heart was broken or simply numb. She'd tried to steel herself for the possibility of Victor leaving in the past. He'd threatened to go, stormed out several times, as he made sweeping relation-ship-ending statements. She'd felt his abandonment deeply, like all the air had been knocked out of her, each time he'd moved for the door. Considered a surprise choice in a wife for Victor, the young beauty understood from friends there was no right way to prepare for his potential loss, just as there'd been no right way to prepare to marry him. Loss through death or loss through divorce, loss through growth or loss through transitions are all still losses. Good or bad. Happy or sad. She never imagined they'd have so many disagreeable, boxed-in moments.

Victor left Elena for a time after she'd exposed his torrid affair with Rachel. At first, the feeling had been unidentifiable. Elena vacillated between relief and fury, between long, hot showers and throwing framed photos against his office wall. Then terror took over her gut. It shifted, ebbed and flowed, morphed, and then it stopped.

Elena's parents explained. "When overwhelm of any kind subsides, be it temporary or permanent, there's a peace and stillness. Like an ocean calmed after a storm, the waters are still murky and harder to navigate, but they're calm."

There were moments back then when she'd just need-ed to get out of her own mind. *Looking back, I remember seeing this with our kids,* she considered now, *as they grew more competitive in their sports, victories, and defeats. I, too, recall facing mental anxiety as an ambitious, young artist in both high school and college, but no one spoke of those feelings then ... ambitious, tough feelings as if too many voices had a right to an opinion in my head. A stigma was attached to aggressive, competitive feelings in those times. The stigma meant you might be unstable or imbalanced—a "crazy" person, instead of an unfocused or distracted one, one that merely needed guidance. Thank God for my parents!*

After each threat and incident passed, though her insides went from calm to clenched, then to sick and starved, she knew. Victor's wife knew it was vital to take care of herself on all planes of life—physically, spiritually, psychologically. *So,* she reminisced, *I prayed during this challenging time for sleep.*

Common wisdom shared that the morning after any trauma always brought a new peace and perspective. The mind had all night to process. Sleep was always the best medicine to aid coping. *I'll never forget the day I received the P.I.'s call and confronted Victor with that desperate little bitch. What an upsetting and bewildering night!*

"It's as if we've traded places." Victor sought to stay up, talk, and process.

"Get out! I ... I ... can't do this right now." Elena simply needed to shut down and go to sleep.

The following morning, she knew exercise would help give her perspective. *Shit, now, as well as during that time, I'd have given anything to have a nightcap to facilitate "processing" if it wouldn't label me a drinker.*

So many years later, this morning was no different for

her as she took her dogs out for a fast lap around the neighborhood. Gray clouds spotted the skies, remnant, patchy edges from a rare hurricane off the West Coast. As the sun began its early ascent, wispy, pink, cirrus skies took charge, and so also did Victor's wife.

After too many threats, Elena had just about run out of patience. Still, she explained the next time he threatened their marriage would be the last time. "You see, my dear Victor, over the years, the impact of your threats hasn't been a one-off occurrence to be forgiven and forgotten, moved past. Rather, they've been exponentially negative."

"I don't understand what you're talking about." She recalled his reply.

"Threatening to end our marriage has come in varied styles over our years together. There's the often used 'we're through' with a flourish followed with a dramatic exit from the room or even the house. There've been the harrowed words 'I'm over you' and 'we're done with this' thrown around. Perhaps it's all been part of an adult temper tantrum you throw when you don't get your way. While it's never been an acceptable means through which you communicate your frustrations with our discussions, I've tolerated it. I've allowed you to control me through them. You want control? Stick to our debauched bedroom communications ... if I ever allow those again." She smirked. "In other words, if you threaten me or our marriage again, we'll be done. No threat. You know me. I'm one for follow-through."

And now the shoe sat on her foot instead of his.

A high-flying airplane broke the morning's quiet as a student pilot earned more airtime. Victor had chosen then to walk out, call it quits, and not seek other answers or remedies. She'd always appeared to be in charge of all things home related, which included their relationship. Because she wanted peace and didn't recognize that she'd taken on management of all aspects of their marriage, she used to figure out how to patch up fallouts just enough, then accept paltry concessions thrown to her, as if to say "nice job" or "all better." She realized later how much she, too, had contributed to their problems.

"See, dogs? Because I believed I was much to blame for our problems, I believed I was able to fix them, right?" The deep-seated pit in her core had been fear—fear she hadn't given their marriage her all. "How many times," she wistfully asked her faithful running companions, "I'd resolve to move forward differently than I had in the past than be seized by a fear I'd failed to expose. How many times did I take responsibility for issues that weren't mine? How many times did I go through such an emotional roller coaster only to be left more bereft after each? The only one who abused me was me."

On a flight home after an art show, she sat next to an elderly couple. They'd been married for over forty years, their children long since graduated from college. Now they watched as their grandchildren managed contemporary schooling, thankful to have passed on the "baton of raising children." As they marveled at how they'd survived marriage and child rearing, inevitably the conversation drifted toward how their marriage endures. "Do you always resolve things?"

"We don't!" They laughed.

"Seriously?"

Taking a thoughtful breath, the older man clarified. "We don't always resolve things on the spot. We just don't go to bed mad."

"How?" she asked. "How is that possible when you're not agreeing or in the heat of debate and discussion?"

"At one point in our marriage, Henry travelled so much, he even lived across the globe while I was home raising our three children. It was brutal, to be perfectly honest ... wouldn't ever recommend this, especially at such an important stage of our lives—raising younger, very impressionable children."

"How did you typically work things out?"

The kind, bright-eyed grandmother of nine shared. "We both agreed nothing good could come of anguished discussions late at night. We admitted we were too tired to generously process our disagreements, but we loved each other and had faith we'd figure it all out after a night's sleep." She quieted her thoughts, reached for her husband's hand, and smiled at their connection. "We'd always resume our discussions the next day. We were determined to figure them out. Either of us being angry when going to bed would never have allowed our souls to solve our problems."

"Wow. That's so practical. You make it sound simple, easy even."

Both women grinned. "Oh, I assure you, it wasn't easy in the heat of the moment, as you mentioned, especially since we considered ourselves sophisticated communicators. But our great respect and extraordinary love, coupled with knowing the saneness from a night's sleep, always rewarded us with solutions. Leonardo da Vinci said it best—'Simplicity is the ultimate sophistication.' We opted to exemplify sophistication and be simple! Sleep on it, and the answers to the problems would come. They always did." Her eyes reflected a patient intelligence as she glanced back at her weathered and wise husband, who dozed in his window seat.

Victor's wife accepted these sage words. After all, she'd heard them even in art school. "Keep up with homework a little each day, and college isn't hard. Same applies to relationships. It's rather simple." Her business mentors advised, "What is easy to do is also easy not to do. Just because it's simple, however, doesn't always make it easy." For all of Victor and Elena's sophistication, somehow one piece still eluded them—mutual love and respect.

Chapter 102

QUESTIONS

HE KNEW SHE couldn't have known of his attendance at this meeting. Dane subbed for the usual attorney on this case, since she went into premature labor the night before. He'd already been in the U.S. when his firm asked him to cover this conference. To fill in was a no-brainer. After he'd received the agenda with an attendees' list, Julie's name caught his attention under the support and media staff. Shocked to see her name in ink, he'd the luxury of time to process his approach when she arrived—time Julie wouldn't get.

He stepped back from the rail on the mezzanine level as she entered the lobby as scheduled. He watched Julie take a cursory glance of her environment. *Thank God she didn't look up.* Dane breathed. *I'd prefer our first encounter to be within arm's length distance and not as if I'm some stalker tracking her, which is, of course, what I feel like right now from up here.*

The line at the reception desk gave Julie enough time to look for her reservation forwarded by her manager. It was also long enough for Dane to take a few deep breaths and head downstairs.

JULIE QUESTIONS

AS JULIE FINISHED getting her room key and the

directions to the elevators from the front desk clerk, she turned and almost ran into Dane.

"Oh! I'm so sor ... what are you doing here?" There was none of the usual preamble of strangers' hellos exchanged, no handshakes or hugged, familiar greetings. Julie shuffled out of the way of the next guest checking in and toward the nearby couches in the lobby.

"Is that a 'what are you doing here' good, or a 'what are you doing here' bad?"

"That depends." She regrouped, clearly thrown off her check-in game plan.

"On what?"

"On why you're here."

They exchanged shocked expressions for guarded ones, as they half-eyed the other and still checked out who may be in the lobby. Careful at first to avoid long, direct eye contact, they settled on an initial, almost provocative, stare down. Fixated silence ensued and allowed for them to catch their breath. The energy around them shifted as their harsh façades liquefied. Unbroken glares softened and became gazes. Neither had expected to lose their ability to exhale. Overwhelmed by her emotions and the rising heat of the moment, Julie's knees weakened. She nearly missed a lobby couch. Dane reached out in time to grab her arm as she righted herself in the available seat. *At least I'm touching her.* His tenuous delight starkly contrasted her selfconsciousness.

"Thank you," Julie whispered, embarrassed. "I'd wondered what it would be like the next time I saw you, because well ... um ... I've been certain ... uh ... I knew it would happen at some point." Dane's puzzled look prompted Julie to continue. "I know why you're here."

"There's a client meeting." *So much for sounding casual.*

Dane continued to look directly into Julie's eyes, his soft focus now camouflaged by the business rhetoric he'd rehearsed.

"Funny if we were attending the same meeting."

"And why might that be?"

"Why don't you tell me?"

She noted the change in his expression, checked her own, and relaxed the butterflies of which she'd suddenly become aware. Without thinking or hesitation, he tucked loose strands of hair behind her ear, skimmed her face, and felt another shift in their connection. As their eyes catalogued every detail between them, their restless energy increased and caused Dane to adjust in his seat just inches from Julie's side.

Her eyes softened. "I'm fine. I promise. Thank you." Her small, smiled reassurances cast him off balance. Reluctant, he released her arm, a subtle change but enough to cause a brief pause in their eye contact, allow each an attempt to regroup.

"I've heard." He waited for her to be tempted. *She's not. She's strong.* He thought to himself but decided to wait another moment anyway. *The quiet gives me a chance to just look into her eyes. I can see her mind racing through an index of response options. Fascinating.* He smiled inwardly.

Surprising Dane, she asked, "How?" Julie noted his pupils dilate. *Surprised him?*

Holy shit! That wasn't the response I'd anticipated AT ALL! He swallowed and decided to show a few of his personal cards. "Does the circuitous route truthfully matter? I don't understand why *you* didn't tell me."

"How was I going to tell you? Seriously. I'm still in a state of confusion and embarrassment myself." Julie looked down at her hands, a white-knuckled grip on the side of the small, lobby love seat.

"Why are you embarrassed?"

"Dane, I'm separated because I've failed. Failure is a part of life, but it's still, well, at least until sorted out, embarrassing."

"So are you telling me I ought to be embarrassed *still* because of my failed marriage?"

"What does this have to do with you?"

"If you're embarrassed, does this mean all who've divorced ought to be, too?"

"No, it's just—"

"If so, how and when does one move forward in life?"

"Damn. Um ... well—" She hesitated.

His complicated lawyer side pressed her further. "Regardless of success or failure, the real question is have you learned from what's happened? Do you have a clue as to what to change within yourself and why, so you're able to move forward?"

"The shoe's on the other foot now." She chuckled, shaking her head.

"Sorry?"

"I once dispensed sage thoughts regarding marriage and child-rearing to you. Now *you're* sharing them with *me.*"

"I'm honored you even consider me *part* of the same set of feet." Humored, Dane's eyes dropped the subtle coolness of just moments ago. He reached out to put those same errant strands of hair back behind her ear, lingering a moment longer than he knew he should have. *Fuck. That was bad. Keep your hands to yourself until you're given any other indication.* Julie closed her eyes as Dane withdrew his hand.

Soft as a whisper but solid in intent, she adjusted her hands' grips on her belongings and looked him in the eyes.

"I need to go and settle into my room. I'll see you at registration."

Dane responded with a faint nod.

Chapter 103

MAGNETIC

THE AFTERNOON REGISTRATION process for the meetings was efficient. The young administrators had clearly done this before, so tables and staff flowed logically. A three-minute procedure with few in line, attendees were given their nametags, a bottle of water, and the most current agenda. A painless process in a standard hotel meeting space.

She felt him enter the room. He'd checked in with coordinators earlier but stood in line behind her.

Quietly, his lips barely moved. "How are you doing?"

"How do you think I am?" came the frustration-laced reply.

He smiled sardonically. "I know exactly how you are."

"Do you?"

"I feel the same way."

"Can you feel it?"

"Who in this room doesn't?" He teased gently.

"I don't care about anybody else in the room." The edge was so clear in her voice, it raised a few eyebrows at the desk. She collected her thoughts and stated simply, "So you think it's that obvious?"

"Only to me, baby."

She glimpsed at his small smile when she glanced over her shoulder and closed her eyes in a deliberate, brief blink. Julie steadied her breath and relished the endearing term Dane used for her. It had been so long since she'd been called by anything but her own name. Gabe just had never called her anything but "Julie."

"Our pull is undeniable," he murmured. "I felt magnetized from states away, hell, from across the ocean from you. It's the most insane feeling."

She glanced at him, letting him know of her concern.

"I'm powerless to resist being at least near you, if not with you. Period." He watched her body language. "I can't believe I'm telling you this."

Holding her breath, Julie murmured, "Me neither."

"I'm sorry. I'll shut up."

"Shut up only because it's my turn." She turned back and winked at him.

As soon as she had her attendance packet, she stepped aside to allow the next participant to speak up. Dane had moved away from the line and waited for her. When she joined him, he politely put his hand on her lower back to guide her to a table, a small but powerful intimate gesture. A gentleman's gesture, he pulled out a chair for her.

"Right now, just standing near you is painful, but better than not standing near you. It physically hurts to not hold you, touch you, to try *not* to react to you publicly when I lean over and brush against you—in even this small public gesture. Those around could easily misinterpret us, not see us as professional." He leaned in as if they conspired on a case.

He bowed his head to acknowledge her trepidation. He needed this connection with her, though. *I have to feel her, touch her, like a junkie needing a fucking fix. This is insane, selfish.*

"What?" She questioned the look on his face, fear and

anticipation blatant in her eyes. "You're being really forward. Rather unusual for you."

He glimpsed at her with a small, puzzled smile on his face and looked away. His head shook, an attempt to deny her ability to read him so easily. "I laugh at myself because I don't know another way to explain my longing to touch you—even to myself. I *need* to touch you. Such a magnetic desire is inappropriate and by all rights selfish." He stopped speaking, abrupt, looked at her profile, and willed her to look at him.

"I know." She swiveled only her eyes to peek at him. What was meant to be a brief glance grabbed them, like an optical ambush, and hypnotized them, trance-like. Like the awe of being caught off guard by an early morning rainbow, the warmth and promise in his eyes held hers captive. "What do you see?"

"That I'm going to need the next fifty years to understand you," he whispered.

"Oh, excuse me. Sorry to interrupt. Aren't you Mr. Michaels?" the eager young attorney asked.

"Guilty." Dane struggled to drag his eyes to the speaker.

"I've read your summary about …"

Julie smiled, always polite, and excused herself from the conversation, amused by Dane's complete calm but pained facial expression. She wanted to throw herself at him, even in a broom closet, but recognized how wrong such a desire was for so many reasons. Professional courtesies aside, Julie was here on multiple missions.

Exhausted by the familial logistics all moms deal with prior to their unavailability, she was more drained and frightened by her emotions and the temptations of being alone with Dane. Julie slipped out of the meeting area, asked for directions to the ladies' room, and stole away to her hotel room.

The young lawyer engaged Dane in a conversation, but Dane still noted when Julie left the conference room. He'd kept track of her every movement and interaction, which also meant he'd noticed she hadn't returned to the meet-and-greet. "Excuse me. I need to follow up on a … time-sensitive issue. I apologize. Let's finish this tomorrow right before the first session."

Julie paced in her room and debated her retreat or surrender choices, since she knew the "fight" option didn't exist for her. "Those are what my only options are, aren't they? How am I to stiff-arm a situation, some*one*, I want, I'm drawn to? I can feel now … inside me … that won't happen. My resolve to steer clear of Dane Michaels is melting. If it wasn't for my children still at home, there is *no* doubt in my mind I'd run away with him. How evident is it that I struggle to think clearly when he's around? As a professional, this could have repercussions. I wonder if such sensory overwhelm could ever change if we're around each other every day? Oh, shit. Who am I kidding? WHAT am I thinking? Shit! He's not even in the same room, and my brain's scrambled like an egg. I've got issues." She chided herself.

She grabbed her running shoes.

SALVAGE

DETERMINED TO SALVAGE control of her emotions, Julie chose to forego the optional networking cocktail hour for another visit to the hotel's workout room. She hurried through a shower and protein shake. Aware of the importance to make a positive impression with new clients, she returned to the conference room calm, focused, and all business. Now privy to the agenda and updated attendee list, it was time to use it to her benefit.

At first, she'd been shocked to see him at check-in and now again to see his name in print. Little time remained before he returned to the meeting and even less to figure out whether he was on the right side. *There'd been a time*, she felt, *we'd have been an invincible and powerful team. Now he just overwhelms me. I wondered yesterday if, like a new habit practiced, consistently, I'd gain more focus the more I'm around him, get used to him.* Innately, Julie knew the answer. "Right now, I need to be steadfast in search of allies. Instead, just like that, it's like I'm drunk." *Dane also somehow levels and focuses me. I'm not sure if it's his lawyer aloofness or ruthless pursuit of facts.*

"Why am I spending more time analyzing the man?" She shook her head, dismayed. *I can't believe I'm even thinking about him this way. Ridiculous. We aren't a team.* "Get a grip, girl." An admitted attraction expressed practically between them seemed more challenged each time they breathed in the same air.

She accepted the need to put reason and logic before emotions. *I likely won't get to the center of this issue just yet, but if I could at least ascertain on which side he sits … sure would help. Friend or foe? Partner/thief or upright lawyer? Can I confide in him and share information, or am I alone in this?*

Chapter 104

BREACH

"Sir, the 'glitch' was more than an 'unapproved' car," the efficient facility manager briefed Tate.

"I assumed as much. Go on."

"It was a delivery van."

Tate stared at his computer screen and waited for the video call to resume. *Technology can be such a pain in the ass.* "And?"

"And the driver claimed he was delivering parts for our current project. Unaware of any schedule changes to anticipated shipments, I checked with all departments from where this change may have occurred and found nothing. I advised the driver of this, he cursed in another language, apologized, turned around, and left."

"Which language?"

"West Slavic, I believe. We're confirming Czech versus Slovak, as we speak, sir."

"Fine. Let me know when you do find out. Did he share who'd sent him? The company? What did he look like? I need details."

"Here's his picture from the gate's cameras. Ponytail, slicked-back hair, so it's hard to know the actual color, angular face with strong jawline. He drove your standard European Mercedes delivery truck—"

"Standard *European* Mercedes delivery truck, did you

just say?"

"Yes, sir, I did. Clearly unusual for around here, so we're running a plate search, as well as his photos through biometrics to ID him. Just don't like the feel of this situation. Obviously, there's been a breach somewhere, sir. We're too far away from civilization for some 'random' delivery driver in his 'standard Euro' truck to have happened upon us."

"Obviously." Tate dripped with emphatic sarcasm. The manager's flinch, as imperceptible as it may have been, didn't escape Tate's shrewd eyes. "Did you send guards out to search his truck?"

"Our protocol requires a search prior to entering this compound. Since entry to the compound was refused, and the driver didn't argue his case, it initially appeared to be a mix-up in delivery dates. We did escort him several miles down the road, however."

"Have delivery dates ever been mixed up before?"

"No, Mr. Parker."

"I want all details, regardless of how minuscule you believe they are, within the next twelve hours—and I mean all details. Hair color, names, aliases, truck make, model, where it's driven, who owns it, for how long, etcetera. Do you understand?"

"Yes, sir."

"We need to figure out where our system's not working as fast as possible, or we won't just be out of jobs, my friend ... we'll be dead."

UNDETERRED

ONCE HE SATISFIED his well-armed escorts that he was no longer an immediate threat, he continued far enough down the road so they'd turn around. A brief glance through his highpower, compact, Fujinon binoculars confirmed time to disappear. He pulled off-road, took off deep into the trees, and cursed. He knew what he had to do and wasn't happy about it. Doubling back wasn't strenuous. It was just time-consuming, at this point, and cold.

He grabbed his gear from the back of the truck and locked the doors with a smirk. *Why bother?* The second push of the key fob set the timer in motion. He knew he'd double back about half a mile before he heard and felt the muffled impact of the charge. Someone always set off explosives in this area, so it would go unnoticed. He headed back to the factory.

He had a mission to complete.

Chapter 105

WARY

DANE OPTED TO give Julie her space on the first meeting night, though it wasn't his preferred choice. *Besides*, he reasoned, *that text from Isabella concerns me and warrants my immediate attention.*

"Klatch chatter yielded unexpected windfall today."

He checked his watch and knew it was late in Zurich, but Dane also knew Isabella would wait for his call. She understood his modus operandi and would assume he was in meetings. As a habit, he replied to her as soon as he was available.

"Good evening. Sorry so late. Windfall?"

"Hey, Boss. I'd hoped you'd call sooner. Olivia just got home, so we've rather limited time."

"So you're not totally free to talk. Throw me some keywords, and I'll ask the detail questions."

"Brag about horrendous hangovers?"

"That's my first hint?"

"Indeed, Boss." Isabella took on a suitable scolding attitude for this "game."

"Who?"

"Guess assist here, please."

"This isn't an easy game. An assistant to one of the other attorneys?"

"Yes." She sounded relieved. "Your boss, too? Really?"

"Victor's assistant?"

"Ah ... the same one."

"So, to confirm, Victor's assistant tied one on last night, and you overheard her brag in the coffee area."

Isabella held her hand half over the receiver and loudly whispered to Olivia, "Turn down the heat when the timer goes off. Got it. How long will you be?" She paused. "Okay. Boss, Olivia's just decided on a shower, so let me share fast. Victor's assistant danced and drank her way around Barrio5 and finished at the Widder's makeshift jazz club, Aries Garage, with her girlfriends. She said for an old carriage house it was pretty cool, except for this ponytailed guy who just seemed to take up space, kind of propped up in a corner on one of the leather chairs, and leered at them all night."

Dane's ears perked up. "And?"

"One of her friends showed off how impervious she was to him by sitting with him, when he asked her if she'd ever been to Alaska. The girlfriend giggled that she'd barely heard of Alaska, let alone been there. He boasted he'd been there on a special mission to find some secret place that makes golden cars and buries big-mouth employees who speak of it. She snickered and challenged him about such a ridiculous story. He bolted upright in his chair, grabbed her jaw with one hand, and, red-eyed, spat bourbon droplets as he enunciated drunken words. Said he could be killed for sharing this information unless he killed her to prevent her from talking. The girl only stared at him at first, then burst into hysterical laughter, broke from his grasp, and kissed him before she stumbled back to her group."

"Is she okay?"

"As far as I know."

"Did your coffee mate spill anything else?" *I can be witty, too*, he thought smugly.

Isabella rolled her bemused eyes. "Just that she desperately needed strong coffee and could anyone believe such a crazy story."

"Your thoughts?"

"Those pieces belong to our puzzle. Okay, she's out of the shower. Have to disconnect but reach me tomorrow."

"Nice work. Stay safe, Isabella."

Chapter 106

FLAWED

YEARS AGO, VICTOR assigned his ambitious, new associate to represent a newly successful but emotionally immature model. Her ruthless, social-climbing pursuits hooked her new lawyer into marriage and grown-up wealth. Still, Rachel failed to understand she'd never had her new husband's attention from the start. Victor felt sorry for the young beauty—too sorry—and "helped" her cope with her hard-working husband's dreadful hours. Like a kindly uncle, he slipped money to her to spend on lingerie and clothes to catch young Dane's attention.

Instead, it caught his own.

Rachel didn't need the money to purchase anything, let alone lingerie she modeled. As she'd share her purchases with Victor, however, it was clear how she preoccupied the elder counselor.

When Victor's wife, Elena, figured this out, she was stunned, hurt, and embarrassed. There'd been zero signs or apparent reasons for his wandering. She served Victor three ultimatums—choose a new hobby or activity they'd do together and drop his affair, keep the "poor" girl, *and*, in typical European fashion, allow Elena to share her affections elsewhere, too, or be dragged through a costly public divorce.

Opting for the least embarrassing and most dignified

of the alternatives, the easy choice for Victor, since he still loved Elena and valued Dane, was to end his relationship with Rachel. He couldn't bear to share Elena with anyone. She was everything he'd desired in a lifetime partner. *Why did I do it then?* he questioned himself. Rachel, however, played Victor's heartstrings like a professional harpist. He continued to fall for her tormented pleas and secretively funded her, even after "cutting off" their relationship.

Since Victor liked to tinker with mechanics, he and Elena became involved in a local car club. Over hundreds of miles testing newer cars, as well as renovated ones, the couple healed their wounded relationship. Soon Victor forgot about the automated payments sent to his young associate's wife, even after their divorce. He focused on an expanded roadster activity calendar with Elena. The couple attended car shows of assorted sizes all over Europe. Friends met along the way encouraged them to attend the Barrett-Jackson in Arizona and bragged about the weather, fabulous array of cars, and global audience. It was there they'd met Bob Couvey. Because of his specific renovation skill set, Victor and Elena felt confident as they searched for a classic auto frame needing only mild work.

On one trip to Arizona to which Elena had travelled with Victor, they were excited to make friends with the brash Americans. Elena and Carol, Bob's current and second wife, managed to get along on the surface. Elena's superficial tolerance soon converted to open loathing when the gaudy, drunk American tried to seduce Victor one night during a car club event.

Too much alcohol flowed, and Carol fawned all over Victor. Bob hadn't seen his wife's antics, since he'd been preoccupied wooing business with another member during a networking period. Elena wandered to an upstairs bathroom and sat in one of the elegant powder room chairs to take a break. Hushed voices always trigger the human instinct to listen more carefully, a typical fear of missing out. While she listened, her jaw set as she figured out to whom the female voice belonged. It was the male one she hadn't yet determined in spite of the goose bumps on her arms.

Like a spy out of a movie, she inched open the door to the washroom area. Thankful for the noisy ventilation fan, she squatted down at the base of several stalls to determine the shushing's location.

What she'd not anticipated was who'd been silenced. She knew the scent of his aftershave.

Elena crept on top of the neighboring stall for a look down into the incriminating one and saw Carol's left hand covering Victor's mouth, and her right one with his flaccid cock outside of his unzipped pants. Victor looked up with culpable eyes. He sensed Elena's presence. Wideeyed, he shoved Carol off of him.

"At least she undoubtedly isn't doing anything for you," was all Elena could manage to say.

She hustled down to lock the stall door, contemplating her next move to leave not only the bathroom, but also the event without her husband.

"Elena."

"I'd understand if I didn't like sex, Victor, oral, anal, or vaginal, with you."

"No need to be so explicit."

Carol's eyes widened with disbelief! She yanked open the stall door, moved without any delay to the sink, and lathered her hands with enough soap for three.

Elena smirked at the nasty woman's obvious attempt to escape the scene to which she'd contributed and continued. "I'd understand if I was a fucking puritanical, goody-two-shoes prude."

"Elena."

"What's the matter, Carol? Didn't know Victor might bend you over and ram you in your ass after being in mine this morning?"

"That's enough, Elena," Victor warned.

"In fact, it was so fucking hot, you know now why he's not responding so well to you."

"Elena!"

"What? Didn't get enough this morning? Wow! That'd be a first in quite a while. Why not share it with the one you claim to love? I would've been more than happy and willing *and* extremely capable of giving you whatever you wanted—and then some—as you know." Her tone shifted from naughty to haughty. *Might as well drive my point as deep as he was in me this morning.*

Carol ran from the restroom while Victor fumbled and cursed with his zipper, nearly catching foreskin. Elena crawled under several stalls in the commotion and slipped out of the ladies' room. Victor pounded open the stall from which his wife had made her discovery.

Ever since the bathroom scene when Elena drove home several vulgar truths, Carol refused any physical contact with the couple. She did keep up her phony front, however.

Elena "slipped" about the incident later in the evening to Bob. Victor at least had the grace to appear genuinely sorry and disinterested in the tacky female. Bob wasn't upset with Victor, though. His ire was directed at his wife. "Why the sudden interest in oral sex with someone else, when I've begged for years?" Elena's fury superficially faded but took a darker turn against the only man she'd ever loved.

HARDENED

FROM THEN ON, as a rule, the two hardened wives avoided each other and each other's husbands. Appearances the two couples made together at club events suggested bygones were bygones—minus the friendship—especially with each year passing.

However, Elena's upbringing didn't allow her to tolerate such pretentiousness without repercussion. She'd listened to her parents fight over just one topic throughout her entire childhood. Her father was often disrespected for his tolerant heart and forgiving nature when people's humanity struck. He appreciated their imperfections, understood their shortcomings, and bore no malice toward their mistakes.

His wife, however, hated when she'd go into town and hear people making fun of him for his goodness. She argued with her husband to stand up for himself. He'd do so with his daughter, their only child, however, as if practicing on her would empower the whole family. Despite tolerance with others' flaws, he expected perfection from her.

She worked hard to attain such approval from him. Elena knew to be above reproach in her art and well-read in life's events, to use impeccable manners and have exquisite taste without arrogance, and to embrace her business education, as Albert Einstein once cautioned, to "be not a success but of value" to bolster the family's good name.

Her mother warned her as a plain teenager, though. "You must possess an unflinching reserve." The quality served her well in the wretched, formative years. Sadly, her mother failed to revise the warning after she'd come into her own exquisite beauty and graduated from business school.

Potential embarrassments triggered her innate childhood story of not being enough. Despite their marrying, Victor and Elena never validated their love for one another. Instead, they stirred the drama pot of family disapproval and compounded an inability to forgive in their marriage. Elena grew more determined to not just get Victor's attention but to secure his respect.

Chapter 107

HUNTED

A RARE MOMENT. No meetings. No one around. Julie recognized and treasured the quiet. She experienced it in her heart, body, mind, and soul. Not a scary quiet, but one focused on contemplation, one that allowed her to think, process, and wait. She listened for guidance. She needed some, and not from an inexperienced girlfriend or cynical cohort. At first, she hadn't a clue if she'd even recognize any response. So when an answer came with such clarity, her eyes flew open and her quiet was shattered. *Need him, talk with him … now.*

"What?" Julie questioned herself aloud. "I'm desperate to understand my remarkable need for this man. I've not heard from, let alone seen, him in decades. Now he's resurfaced several times." She stood and paced. "I can feel him thinking about me, and yet, nothing's happening—even right now. Not a phone call … which is okay, I think … but why? What's he involved with? Why do I need to talk with him? And now? Will we go dark again for another decade? Assumptions made, questions unasked, let alone unanswered. I. Am. So. Confused. Is he?" Heavy in frustration, she plopped down onto the small sofa in her hotel room.

Surprising coziness emanated from the upscale surroundings of new finishes and fresh décor. The recently renovated property reflected a contemporary touch with clean, light bamboo wall coverings, sleek, matte finishes, crisp, white sheets, and fluffy, new towels. The neutral physical space allowed Julie's mental needs to reorganize instinctively. Deep in her mind, an entangled forest of distant memories, mixed-up feelings, and merciless desires fought each other to emerge. Just as fast as she'd process any of them, she felt Dane's presence. It wasn't his knock. There hadn't been one. She hadn't looked at the door, yet Julie sensed him and clasped her hands over her mouth. She swallowed hard, wondered how much he'd heard, and took a deep breath.

As she rose, she let it out and her hands fluttered to straighten her clothes. She walked to the door and unbolted it without even a glance through the peephole. She knew he stood outside of it. She pushed the handle down, cracked open the room's door, turned, and walked back toward the window.

Dane guided the door open enough to enter but didn't close it. His eyes bore into her, willing her to turn around. She did as he wordlessly commanded, then froze, as if he'd yelled. He moved, swift and decisive, to guide her by her elbow.

"Where are we going?" She searched his face, anxious, his expression so deep and intense.

"To my empty suite," he coolly revealed but concealed further intentions.

"Of course it's empty." She giggled in an attempt to lighten the nervousness that grabbed her gut. "You're here." Julie saw him register her comment but not even smile back. "Why *wouldn't* it be empty?" His grip tightened just so as she sought more answers.

Bewildered and even a little frightened when they

bypassed the elevator, she tried, "The stairs?" Half a step ahead of her, he opened the stairwell door and stopped a few treads down, where he pinned her against a wall. One hand was still on her elbow, but the other secured her in place at her waist. Trapped between his arms and the wall, his ruthless focus was zeroed in on her, just like when they were teenagers. This energy she understood and was no longer alarmed. Yet, when he touched their foreheads together, she leaned into his and closed her eyes. *Savor his warmth. Feel our connection again.* She breathed.

He closed his eyes, too, intoxicated by her faint perfume infused with anticipation. As they peeked up from downcast eyes, his shoulders let go an inch. Again, so much was said without even a word. All the years between them fell away. All the shrouded feelings rushed to be unveiled in the silence. Their foreheads shifted and cheeks grazed. Their bodies awakened, tender nerve endings, thought forever dormant, and rediscovered sensations, thought never recoverable. Aware of the bittersweet inevitable, the couple savored every scent, every touch between them.

Gazes locked, souls connected. Dane's hand, determined but gentle, moved behind Julie's neck under her hair and pulled her hesitant lips to his. At first, their kiss was tentative, sought permission. They bore into each other's eyes, reverent. The initial consensual gentleness snapped, and their next kiss deepened. Dane's left hand found the curve in her lower back and drew Julie flush to his body. She gasped mid-kiss, and he smiled at her sensitivity to the scintillating current between them.

"Feel it?" he asked her without taking his lips from hers.

"It's undeniable," she whispered.

His right hand slid down from her neck across her shoulders. His left lingered on her lower back but made its way across, locking her into his arms. Their kiss exposed years of pent-up passion. Tongues explored, tasted, delighted.

"This is insanity." Julie attempted to catch her breath without losing their physical connection. "It's as if we're trying to make up for all the time we've lost."

Hesitant to pull away from her, he dragged his mouth from hers along her cheek and whispered in her ear. "We know that's not possible. Let's try anyway." His kisses headed south along her jawline and left a sensual trail. "Your scent is mind-altering."

"Holy shit!" She panted, barely breathing.

They jumped, startled, when a stairwell door slammed uncontrolled on some floor not far below them. Hands flew to adjust clothes as they caught their breath and attempted to locate the direction of the footsteps. When another door banged shut, the couple assumed they were again alone. Dane reached up to caress Julie's face, then allowed his hand to slide down her neck and across her collarbone at the shirt's opening. Her face blushed. He smiled at the glow he'd caused, then slipped his hand between her shirt and shoulder to stay connected to her skin. Once again, he brought her flush to him.

Another door slammed somewhere above them. Immobilized, their breath stilled. The conversation they overheard overtook their attention.

"They're not in her room, either."

"You checked his," confirmed a different voice.

The breathless couple knew those voices looked for them but hadn't a clue who or why. Dane put one finger between their lips to signal to remain silent, then jerked his head in the direction they'd tiptoe. Julie's fixated look said all he needed from her. She'd question him later. He'd have to have answers, too.

"Right after he shoulda gotten off the elevator at his floor."

"Check this flight. I'll take the elevator down to his floor again and meet you at the stairwell door. We won't miss them then."

"Copy."

Stealthy footsteps moved to each landing, but Dane and Julie had already snuck out of reach onto the mezzanine level. He guided her into an intimate, empty meeting space near where he'd spied on her the previous day. The meeting room's cool, black, granite countertops and sleek, matching conference table were buffed to a shine free of fingerprints and streaks. The glimmering, chrome trim and knobs mirrored different parts of their bodies as they searched for places to hide.

"You okay?" He considered her body language as she surveyed the table's perimeter, her middle finger skimming the cool granite. *Hmm … calm again. Interesting. Is this shock, fear, or her m.o.?*

Her voice was soft, airless even, as she scanned the space. "I'm guessing we're both a bit shaken by the depth of our desires as well as. …"

Almost like in a dream state, Dane stood in her path and gripped both of her arms, confining her for the second time that day. This time against the table, he straddled her with his powerful legs and hoped to regain composure. "You're shaking," he confirmed, familiar with her response to fear. "Me, too. It'll be okay, and yes, I *will* answer all of your questions."

She licked her brooding lips with complex feelings of

anticipation and angst. "Dane—"

He silenced her concerns, and most of his own, with a breathtaking kiss. Unexpected but welcomed, she leaned in to kiss him harder when she heard his moan. He placed her arms around his neck and pulled her tight against him. One of his hands followed hers and grasped both. The other spun her away from the table, her back to the door. He walked them behind the service bar on the other side of the countertop and pressed her once more against a wall in the corner. "I seem to have a need to contain you."

He shifted her weight more to one leg. Julie curved an ankle behind one of Dane's legs. He exploited her enticing cue, tugged gently to unhook her ankle, and hitched her long leg up over his thigh. Her raspy breath and darkened look were all the approval he needed. He released her arms and placed his hands astride her head, since she was pinned by his body. He tilted his hips into hers and allowed their bodies to recognize each other. He slid his legs apart just enough for her raised knee to slide up his thigh and greet his hip. Her hips responded in kind, forgetting she wore a slim, tailored skirt from their earlier meetings. Several stitches ripped a little before she hiked it higher.

All of a sudden, her eyes widened.

Dane felt it, too … a peculiar breeze. He stifled her strained intake with his decadent mouth and curious tongue and reassured and shushed her gently. "Just focus on me. *Really* focus on *me*." He raised her up, swept her off her feet, and right to the floor under him, as he intention- ally ripped her blouse just loud enough for the intruder to hear and head their way. He unzipped his pants and shoved them halfway to his knees. As he secured her knee under his elbow high up around his hip, his hand on her seemingly naked ass, his briefs twisted as if he'd penetrated her. Then he didn't just kiss her—he ravished her mouth as he heard boots creep toward them.

And just as fast as the draft occurred, the door clicked shut and the air stilled.

For several extra moments, Dane's gentle hip thrusts continued, grinding into Julie's. They trembled, wanton, adrenaline coursing through their bodies. Conscious of the emotional chaos between them, and their ache and need for each other, Dane slowed and backed off their staged intimacy enough only to evaluate their safety. Satisfied they were indeed alone, Dane's panic took on a vulnerable quality. He was terrified Julie would run from him, only she looked as dazed and tormented as he did.

"Well," she stated through amazed inhales. Dane noticed she hadn't pushed him away. "If this was your idea of 'sweeping a girl off her feet' then 'hiding in plain sight' and 'pretending,' it was, well, masterful. There're just a couple of problems, as I see this ... this ... whole picture."

Not moving any farther from Julie, Dane wasn't sure if he should exhale what little air filled his lungs. "Dare I ask?"

"Okay, there's no tactful way to put any of this, so— I'm—just—gonna blurt it all out and hope you don't think less of me."

"Hmm. Let's have it."

"Awesome 'cover,' except ..."

Oh shit.

Julie's summoned courage bore a defiant edge. Her breathing appeared to resume some level of normalcy, yet she pushed her hips up into Dane's thinly cloaked hardness. "... Except I'm not buying the whole pretend part—from either of us—to be quite blunt. Just calling it like I see it, Counselor. We couldn't keep our hands to ourselves before the intrusion, and now—"

"And now, if you'll allow me to finish your statement," Dane interrupted.

"Please and thank you." She agreed. *Can't wait to hear this.*

"We're not just aroused, we're out-of-our-fucking-minds horny, and—"

"And I'm still married," she blurted.

"And we're ... Julie, you're separated ... for a long time and about to be divorced." Dane justified. "How long has it been?"

"Separated, true. It's been only a little more than a month. We've started the divorce process, but I'm still technically married."

"So that's why you haven't called me."

"Have I been wrong?"

"Yes ... and no."

"Not helpful."

"But accurate."

"Explain, please, fast, before I can't hear you. I almost can't control what my body dangerously wants to do." She squirmed against Dane, ablaze with desire.

"I'm not sure either of us could let go right now, unless we had to, which we don't. Do we?" Dane raised his chest off of Julie enough to look into her eyes, while mirth and confidence filled his own. "I can see you want me as much as I want you. We can't say we've been impatient, not waited. Decades." He awaited her confirmation, an expression, something to sanction his brazen statement.

She didn't flinch. Uncertain of how obvious her needs may have appeared, she opted not to make them any clearer.

He licked his bottom lip. "If you want me to stop, I will immediately. I don't want to. I've never wanted another woman as insanely as I want you—ever—not just now." He scrutinized her entire being for any sign of fear or doubt, like a body language expert assessing potential jurors. He waited. Still, she didn't move. "Just say, 'No, I don't want you.'"

Julie's eyes softened.

"I'll answer any questions, just as I promised before our visitor's entrance, okay?"

She nodded once.

"After our Q and A, I'm making love to you, Julie. Are you okay with that?" His sensual tone made it clear there was no room for debate. He spoke with shameless determination, zero tolerance for the usual questions and debate he faced in the legal world.

Julie's chin dipped a little lower, her eyes flickering as they looked up and nodded in agreement, tantalized. As Dane started to put a little space between them, Julie's lusty reaction confirmed all Dane hoped. "Talk here?"

With a small, devilish grin, he lowered himself against her again, leaned in for a chaste kiss, and whispered, "Fire away."

Julie shivered with goose bumps and took a deep breath. "I … um … shit … can hardly think when you're close to me, let alone like this. Maybe we need—"

"Julie." Dane reclaimed her mouth again, hard and hungry. Before she could say a word to protest, in what seemed to be one move, Dane stood up, grabbed her hand, and pulled her against his powerful muscular frame. "Let's get out of here and talk."

Dizzy with carnal anticipation and emotional confusion, Julie straightened her hair, smoothed her skirt, and led the couple to the door. She stopped abruptly when she reached it, though, and looked down at the handle.

Dane leaned into her, put his hands on her waist, and murmured, "You okay?"

The sensuousness of their earlier "cover" emboldened Julie. She felt his hands on her, traced them with her own, then turned and grasped his shirt collar. She delivered a provocative invitation and then left the meeting room. Dane stood there for a moment, dumbfounded and enticed, then followed her to the elevators.

Chapter 108

UGLY DETAILS

AT RACHEL'S PECULIAR prompting, Victor decided to take Elena on his next business trip to the U.S. He needed to meet with Bob on both business and personal issues, ample excuses to head overseas. Due to apparent account irregularities, Victor felt an in-person checkup was warranted. "Perhaps," he considered with his wife, "Bob's crustier-than-usual tone begs a visit anyway. Perfect time to check in regarding Dane Michaels' client service follow-through." *Perhaps THAT'S hypocritical. Still ...*

"Yours was just the first of several odd transactions discovered, highly abnormal for a legal professional of his stature. Still, he's human," he'd concluded with Rachel.

"Since you'll already be with Bob, you might as well test your most current renovation project—two birds, one stone idea." Rachel knew of Victor and Elena's luxurious hobby.

Recent marital challenges were the perfect additional justification to take a few extra days off while there. *A long drive to talk things through, followed by a ski vacation in posh Park City, Utah, ought to help our cause.* Victor patted himself on the back mentally. *Besides,* he further rationalized, *the drive to Park City would encourage any kinks in the refurbished car to either work themselves out or be listed for Bob to tend to when the car was shipped back to Arizona.*

What he hadn't reconciled mentally was why Rachel pushed him to go. Her excuse was that she was concerned her ex-husband had gotten into something "ugly with this Tate character" and that Victor "must check it out from all angles." Victor was wise enough to know Rachel tried to make him feel jealous. Translated simply, however, he knew the former model was concerned about one thing— money—though no one would contest she was a good mother. Cloaked as strict concern for her children's well being, she'd questioned Dane's apparent unwise choices. "What if whatever is going on affects his ability to cover his responsibilities of alimony and childcare?"

"You have plenty of money, my dear. Your children's welfare isn't an issue regarding your ex, either."

Lower lip aquiver, eyes misty. She's good. After she left his office, Victor struggled. *What the hell is she up to? Hate that I'm still ignorant about some detail.*

Chapter 109

DISTRACTION

VALET CAR PARKERS keep the "fun" cars close to the front. They'll use any excuse to drive them, regardless of proximity. Big tippers also make it worth any potential inconvenience. Dane's car was always next to the valet stand.

Silent and breathless as they regrouped, neither spoke a word during the long drive out toward Gold Canyon. Once convinced they hadn't been followed, Julie opened her window for some fresh air. Only then did she realize she'd held her breath since Dane assured her his rental would be waiting. Nevertheless, he didn't let up on the gas. He wanted as much distance between them and the interested party.

Remarkably, for the first time in months, Julie finally relaxed. The cool, dry desert air and the warm car compounded like a powerful narcotic and knocked her out. Emotional overwhelm had caught up with her. Not until Dane pulled into a parking space and turned off the car had Julie realized she'd fallen asleep.

"Oh, wow ... um ... I guess I was a little tired. Sorry. Great lookout I was," she mumbled as she pushed herself up in her seat, stretched, and yawned. Confused for a moment as to her whereabouts, Julie blinked and took a brief look around. "Where are we?" The breathtaking surroundings lent her a little time to shake the fog from her relaxed brain.

Dane catalogued the sequence of her movements and appreciated the complexity of such a small moment. He'd studied her as often as was safe during the drive. "The Superstition Mountains. Home to scenes in several westerns and lots of desert critters." As if cued, a family of quail fluttered past, the male, with his cluster of feathers atop his head, bobbed in procession. "Thank you."

"For what?"

"For having the confidence while with me to know you were safe enough to sleep."

"Truth?"

"Always."

"I haven't been able to let go like that in so long, I. ..." She turned in her seat to look at him and swallowed hard, a little dry-mouthed.

"I what?"

"I need to thank *you*."

Dane didn't just make eye contact, he delved into her soul—again. The back of his hand caressed her cheek tenderly. She closed her eyes, tipping her head just so into the small but intimate gesture. He, too, closed his eyes at that moment, savored her scent, as if it was his last time. A permanent groove in his memory formed. Unhurried, he opened his eyes to see her now observe him.

"We came here to talk."

"I know," he said, matter-of-fact. "I owe you a few explanations." He nodded in agreement. He got out of the car and rounded the front end intently. As he opened Julie's door, she took his proffered hand and stepped out. He guided her in front of him as he backed against the car body, fully committed and engaged.

Each searched the other's expression for permission to start. Dane allowed his head to lean in to Julie's, shifting his gaze from her eyes to her lips. She backed off, just slightly, licked her lips reflexively, and weighed her options. His eyes returned to hers. He barely moved his hand off her face, noting the softness of her skin. As they continued to edge closer, like unwitting magnets, a small piece of her hair strayed across her cheek. Dane thumbed it away with a caress as tender as the afternoon breeze. Almost reverent, he kissed Julie once, twice. His other hand found its place on the back of her neck, drew her closer, and deepened their kiss. Like lost halves of a heart charm that have found each other, their fit was unmistakable and life-giving.

Dane's hand shifted from Julie's neck down to a commanding place in the low curve of her back and pulled her tight to him. Dressed and in public, still he left no space between them. She shuddered when she felt every inch of his muscular chest down to his lower abs and his clear interest in her. His strong legs rooted them where they embraced, desperate to regain their earlier connection. Julie pulled back enough to catch her breath and opened her mouth to speak. Dane silenced her words with another sultry kiss.

"Please," she whispered into his mouth. He responded by kissing her harder.

"We need to talk." She tried again, but he continued. "We'll be late to return to the meetings." Breathless, she teased him.

"What's your point?" Dane grinned, satisfied at his rare disregard for an appointment. He felt Julie stiffen, though, enough for him to know she'd taken the comment differently. He barely separated their lips, a smile planted on his face. "I was making fun of me," Dane clarified, proud of himself. "I can be a bit—"

"Anal?"

"I prefer structured."

She relaxed in his arms. "We need to talk."

Once again, he distracted her. "Agreed." His hand wandered from the back of her neck across her shoulder and cradled her in the crook of his elbow. He embraced her even firmer, felt her body yield to his touch through the skirt's flimsy material, and dipped her like in a slow dance. As he exposed her neck, his lips travelled down her throat, captivated low against him. He stopped when he'd kissed her partially exposed breast. Their unimpeded connection caught his breath. It was just enough skin to leave him enchanted, desirous, and heady.

He brought her upright and fell back, panting on the car. "Shit. Thank God the car's there."

"Damn, what a kiss. I ... we. ..." Breathless and weak-kneed, she smiled up at him from his chest where he held her to him. "This is quite the private ... um ... chat between meetings, and we do need to chat."

"Indeed."

"Why did you stop? I mean, why are you determined to distract me? We have to talk."

Dane stared at her but volleyed back. "Surprised? Disappointed?"

"Yes."

They laughed.

"Why surprised? Didn't think I'd still be a gentleman?"

"I've learned it's best not to assume."

"Why disappointed? Didn't think the chemistry was pretty clear between us?"

"Oh, I knew it was clear between us. I just didn't realize *how* clear, or maybe how intense, it still is."

"Sooo?"

"So I'm disappointed you stopped because …" Julie looked up at Dane and wondered how much she ought to say. "In all the years that have passed, haven't you ever wondered what we'd feel like? I mean, as adults? I mean, sure, we did kiss in high school, hold hands, hug."

"But somehow we were always interrupted, almost like we weren't supposed to know how incredible we'd be." Dane raised an eyebrow as the question's punctuation mark. "Sounds crazy, doesn't it?"

Julie stared at Dane and debated while her hands moved from his forearms to his biceps. "I need some answers." She grazed his shoulders, clasped her hands together behind his neck, and drew her slender frame tight to his thick body. "I expect you to be honest." *Two can play this game.* She decided. *I think.* Her body shook with what little self-control she had, fervent in its need to be as close to Dane as possible.

"Interesting examination technique."

"Took my cues from you. You're not resisting."

Neither appeared to notice an older pickup parked at the other end of the scenic lot. The driver and front seat passenger watched as Dane's leg separated Julie's enough for her to lean into him even more so.

"Apparently I don't sound crazy, nor do I resist you." He panted. "Get back in the car." She looked at him, puzzled. "Stay dialed in on me. With another car having pulled into this lot, we've lost some privacy, don't you think?"

Julie did as instructed, grateful for the chance to gather her thoughts, and straightened her dress. She threw a casual glance toward the intruders. As Dane closed the door and bent toward her, Julie's calm lean toward the window to kiss him camouflaged her evident panic. "I think we need to pretend we still haven't seen the people in that car, but get the hell out of here as fast as possible." She fake-smiled. "I recognize the driver."

"And I thought you hadn't noticed them. Huh. Assumed I was more distracting than that. Must be losing my touch." With a small shake of his head and an amused smile, Dane headed around to his side of the car.

"Assume … a dangerous word. How can you be so vain at a moment like this?"

He clicked his seat belt into place and put the sports car in reverse. "Did you think vanity was only a woman's right, madam?"

She unbuckled her seat belt and straddled Dane. "Besides, you *have* been insanely distracting."

"You can rest your case now, Mrs. Archer. I'm sure if they thought we were onto them, this move definitely sent them a mixed message. Very smooth, once again, I might add."

"Maybe now you'll play 'Q & A' with me."

"You're totally blocking my view."

"You noticed," she sassed.

"Because?"

"Because you've avoided explanations and opted for making out *and* making us both more hot and bothered."

"My goal has been to get to the other side of hot and bothered, but we keep getting interrupted." Dane moaned. His eyes scanned behind the car, but one hand adjusted his pants where he throbbed. "Some things never change."

Julie chuckled but couldn't resist her bold whisper.

"Need help?"

"Clearly," came his strained response, but he shifted her back to the passenger seat anyway. "Just for the record"—his chest heaved as he pulled the car out of the parking space—"it took a Herculean strength because the last thing I wanted was to shift you off of me."

Calm and smooth, Dane left the scenic lot and returned to U.S. 60 westbound. This part of the commuter freeway, bumper to bumper in the morning rush, was almost empty in the afternoons. The pickup followed a mere car length behind all the way until, at last, they reached the hotel's lot.

Dane glanced over at Julie, but she stared out the window at the other vehicle. "Probably not a good idea to look over at them."

"You know the phrase, 'A girl's gotta do what a girl's gotta do'?" She turned to him. Dane's confused look was all the confirmation Julie needed. *This worked once before, so what the hell.* "Shit. Stop the car. I dropped my diamond earring out the window."

"What? I'll get you another one," Dane shot out.

"So sweet, but that's a bad idea. Please?" His discreet exasperation gave Julie just enough time to unbuckle her seat belt, jump out of the car, and wildly flail her arms in apparent fury. "A girl can only handle so much!" As she did so, she left her door open and stomped in the direction of the pickup truck as it backed out of its space.

"What the ... she's fucking nuts," was all Dane could mutter.

The pickup driver gawked, wide-eyed, as Julie headed his way. "She's doing it again!"

"I've never seen anyone, let alone a woman, do this before. What's she doing?" The alarmed companion pulled his ball cap low over his eyes.

"I haven't a fucking clue, but I never guessed she'd do it again."

"She's done this to you before?"

"Yeah. The other day when I followed her to the gas station."

"What'd you do?"

"I drove away."

"So why aren't you now?"

"Because she'd expect me to. She's pulled the unexpected—again. Now it's my turn." With that, he lowered his window and drawled, "What's a matter, sugar? Lost something?"

"Yeah." Julie was shaking mad.

"Pity. Your boyfriend? Need help?"

"What a gentleman." She rolled her eyes and jabbed with her temper barely in check. "I lost my diamond, not that you've likely ever seen one."

"Oh, missy, it's not very nice to be unpleasant to someone just trying to help. I'm so very sorry for such a tough loss."

"Are you now? Then why aren't you out here helping me look? Or are you just gonna try to get in my pants like he was?" They all turned to look in Dane's direction where the small sports car was parked closer than they'd expected it to be. "Yuck. Men." Petulant, she shook her head and stormed off past the back end of their truck, taking their attention with her. *Take the bait, boys.*

Confused, they backed up a bit, putting a little more space between them and Dane. "Get out and help her look while I keep an eye on him."

"But—"

"I can see her. Go and find it fast, then we'll 'talk' with

her. Hurry up. I've got a plane to catch."

Dane guessed Julie had offered herself as a distraction while he got to the driver. He'd backed up close enough to the truck to park his car but left it running, so the unwelcome company would more likely assume he was still in it. As the truck companion opened the door, Dane shocked them both when he reached in, drove his palm, heel up, into the base of the surprised man's nose, and knocked him out cold. Everything happened so fast, the driver didn't notice Julie disappear. He threw the pickup in reverse and hoped to stun Dane. Instead, Dane jumped in. Tires screeched. Julie shrieked "FIRE!" and brought more attention to the scene than anyone had expected—or wanted.

"What do you want?" Dane growled at the man.

"To ask a few questions," came the cold reply.

"Why not call?"

"A personal visit is such a pleasant touch."

"So ask."

"Not you, asshole."

"Julie? Why?"

"It's not your concern, regardless of your 'relationship' with her." The man's sneer chilled even the composed Dane Michaels.

Surprising them both, Julie yanked open the driver's door with a couple of hotel security guards. "Well, isn't this cozy. Need a match, gentlemen?" She spoke directly with Dane, though, and gave away little.

The ponytailed driver looked down at Dane's hands on his shirt, then back up at the lawyer.

Dane opened all ten fingers, the universal sign of cease-fire. "We're not finished here."

"You're damned right," Julie interrupted. "Why are

you following me?"

"You're observant."

"Hard to miss. Flattery won't get you far. Besides, either you've been trying to scare me, or you suck at your job."

"I'm a fan." He lied. "Your pieces about the auto restoration world are fascinating."

"What's so fascinating? I just report what's happened at the auctions." *I knew I was onto something!*

Dane froze, however.

"I have another appointment to keep."

The man Dane had knocked out started to regain consciousness. "Your friend needs help."

"Be a good fellow and look after him for me, will you?" The driver pushed Dane out of the truck and sped off. Julie and the indifferent guards instinctively jumped away from the tires, then she stared at Dane.

"Julie." He scrambled to his feet.

"I'll get more help." Distracted, she turned toward the hotel.

Dane caught up with her, though. "What are you thinking?"

"I knew this had to do with cars and you. I just haven't put it all in order yet."

"What do you mean this has to do with me?"

"Every time we're near each other, something car-world related seems to happen. Have you noticed that? I know you're working with Tate Parker, too."

"Of course you know I work *for* him. I told you that. And what are you saying? Do you think I'm involved in something wrong? Illegal?"

"Don't legalese me. What an interesting question coming from you, Counselor." Julie walked faster, but

Dane grabbed her arm to stop her.

"Look at me." He couldn't miss the hurt and anger infused with confusion on her face. "I told you I had questions to answer, didn't I?"

"Then why not answer them instead of distracting me?"

He laughed. "Do you think I'm intentionally distracting you? To avoid answering your questions? You're the distracting one."

"Oh no you don't. Don't flip this and blame me."

"I promise I'm not avoiding your interrogations." He chuckled and pulled her in for a hug.

"This is how you avoid talking with me."

He feigned innocence. "What? By hugging you?"

"This is how it starts. Then there's ... energy ... between us." Julie pushed Dane away. "Stop it."

"What?"

"Come with me, and not like *that*." Dane raised his eyebrows but followed her.

"What about them?" He thumbed behind him.

"I'm sure they've already called for an ambulance, don't you think? Besides, I want answers before the police come and question you. And this time, we'll start on opposite sides of the room."

Chapter 110

DISCLOSURE

BOB'S WIFE SHOWED him the document. Victor had indeed signed it. "Fool," he said under his breath.

"Has he paid for it yet?"

"Always your concern, isn't it? The man may be driving to his death, and your only concern is whether he's paid his bill with us. Cold. That's quite cold."

"To use your word, if the 'fool' wants to kill himself, then that's his choice. He's a grown-ass adult, Bob. He's a likable fool who can't seem to keep his hands or eyes on his wife, but a fool nonetheless. As long as he's taken care of his responsibilities, then he can do as he pleases."

"You're still just mad he wasn't swayed by your inappropriate affections years ago. 'Bout right?"

"Bob, honey, an unfortunate bit of poor character a long time ago, and I've more than made up with you about it, haven't I?" Carol winked at him, anxious to change topics.

He chuckled. "Yes, my dear, you have. I'm just not one to sit back and easily watch a longtime client, friend, and ass-coverer potentially kill himself. I have a bad feeling about this."

"You haven't done anything wrong," his wife insisted. "I heard you warn him. I heard you state very clearly he'd have to sign a full disclosure statement before you allowed him to take it. That's a first for you both. Victor even pulled the lawyer shtick on you. Remember? What was it he'd said?"

"He'd take what I'd said under advisement."

"Ah ... right. Then he sent you this signed statement, which he'd written himself. So you didn't sit back and watch, and you certainly weren't easy about it."

"Perhaps you have a point, dear. Is his account current?"

"Yes."

"Then why don't I feel any better?"

Chapter 111

THIN ICE

VICTOR STILL STUNG from his last phone call with Bob. The idiosyncratic older man took every car body he worked on so to heart, they were akin to his children. Victor understood. "He knows how I drive, how I care for our cars, so I don't understand the excessive warning this time," Victor shared with Elena. "He's known us *and* driven with us for years. It doesn't make sense."

"I think it was Jon Bon Jovi, an American singer, I once heard sing or say, 'There's a vintage which comes with age and experience.'"

"What's that supposed to mean?"

"What I mean and how you take it may be two different things. Here's what I mean. Bob's still around. He's been doing this car stuff longer than we have been. Maybe we ought to take his advice and wait until he's completely finished with this car."

"True. It could also mean I need to trust myself, since I've been around for a while and lean on my many experiences, right?"

"Victor, darling, that's exactly what I meant." Elena winked at him and returned to her packing. "Packing for a ski trip is always brutal. Oh, poor us." She laughed. "First World problems."

"I don't know how Bob could be concerned about car

weight when he knows I'm traveling with you. God knows your suitcase adds enough weight for additional traction." He teased her. She mimicked her husband's laugh as she finished the task before her. "Besides, good tires with chains and functioning heat are all we need. We're only driving one way from Phoenix to Park City. I took your advice and booked our return flights home from Park City under separate cover, as usual." He convinced his wife.

Chapter 112

TAG

DETECTIVE LIGHTFIELD FINISHED a round of questions with Julie, thankful it was Dane's turn. "Pit stop needed, Detective." He sent an officer with her who waited in the hallway, thankfully. "Appreciate that. I get performance anxiety when I have to pee in front of someone." She quickly slid the stall-door bolt into place and took her phone from her purse.

You're right.

The reply to her text came fast.

About what?

Needing to be careful.

Are you ok?

Yes.

Where are you?

Downtown Phoenix attending conference.

"You okay in there, ma'am?"

"Yes, sir, thank you. Guess I needed to do more than just pee." Julie knew men hated those private details and thus guaranteed herself a few extra minutes of peace.

What happened?

It'll be easier to explain when we talk soon.

What's wrong with now?

Too many ears. Bad timing.

Give me something, please …

Mr. Ponytail returned with a friend. No harm done. He's definitely connected to car restoration and my articles.

Great. Dare I ask how you came to this conclusion?

You probably won't like the answer

You didn't—

Kinda but different. We need to talk. He's got an accent.

From where?

Sounds Slavic but not sure. Have to go.

Ok. Text later when ok to talk.

Yes sir.

Waffles put one and one together, but again it came up snake eyes. "Who the hell is the ponytailed guy?" he questioned.

Chapter 113

DOWNHILL

DESPITE BOB'S PROTESTS, Victor's 1960 Karmann Ghia had just been delivered to the prestigious Royal Palms Resort & Spa in Phoenix, Arizona. Victor had wanted an elegant retreat, one that appealed primarily to couples. Since he and his wife no longer had children around, a family-style resort wouldn't set the stage for the intimate boost they needed. Bob confirmed it would "keep the wife happy while we're doing business, especially if you get her one of those fancy massages with lots of candles."

But the cordial conversation turned stern, almost fatherly, when Victor thanked his longtime associate and friend for the personal delivery. "Don't thank me yet. You haven't driven her, and let me tell you, the ride is rough."

"Bob, you've warned me multiple times. What's up with all the warnings? She's a beauty."

"An unfinished beauty-to-be without my usual finishing touches," Bob growled. "You're going to bring her back, no doubt at the very least, ridden hard, corroded from all the salt on the roads up there. Even with the minimal oil solution undercoating I've got on there, you can't guarantee me an unscathed body when she comes back here."

"Are you worried about the cost increase if there's an issue? Come on, Bob, you know I've already signed the waiver and included a little extra to cover most potential issues in an *early* final project payment. A 'just in case' advance for your concerns."

"Of course I'm concerned about the costs, Victor, but I'm also concerned about her driving safely. She's a lightweight. In conditions you and I both know are ill-suited for her even when finished, her tractability is dicey at best. Lacking the last coats of paint and sealant is bad enough, but your safety and Elena's? I wouldn't forgive myself if I didn't try to warn you off."

Victor's inner little boy couldn't wait to drive it, how-ever. "You've warned me plenty. Trust me!" He laughed despite his clear agitation with the older man. "I appreci-ate your concern and promise to pull over if it's truly unwise to proceed, okay?"

"Whatever. You're an adult, though I'm certain it's not the adult who's on this mission."

"Hey, with any luck, maybe my wife will agree with you later." He winked.

"Speaking of your wife, does she know how I feel about this? Is she aware of my warning you? Being totally against this?"

"Yes, I've shared your concerns, and I've calmed any of hers."

"I can only imagine. Well, this is all on you now. When you leave, the concerns are yours. I'm too old to carry this shit around with me. Got it, my friend?"

"Got it."

"Any further business to cover? I've got to get going before *my* wife thinks I've run off with both of you."

Victor winced a little at the mention of Bob's wife. "Yes, of course. I wanted to check in with you about how Dane Michaels is handling your account."

"Dane? A fine lawyer. Why?"

"Good to hear."

"It's unusual for you to ask. You know if I have any questions at all, or if I'm not happy, I'll call you right away. What's going on?" Bob hoped for even a small crumb of an answer to his nagging concerns. He didn't mention the car's abnormal heaviness yet ... though, in the case of safety in this model, it meant nothing.

"Well, there appear to be a few discrepancies in some of his paperwork, but I'm assuming you check it all over before signing off."

"Discrepancies? Like what? He seems like a very thorough professional."

"It's probably some typos, but nothing jumps out at you?"

"Like what? Typos sound more likely than Mr. Michaels' billing. *You* trained him, didn't you? He's been quite methodical since you introduced us, but I can look." *Come on, Victor, what's going on?* Bob silently urged.

"I'll have my paralegal double-check before I misspeak. I can email you if it's anything to look at, okay?"

Bob scowled. He didn't care for whatever deception he knew he'd encountered just now with his longtime friend. Fertilization of a mistrustful seed was unhealthy. Straightforward was his preferred approach.

Victor continued. "Since we're on the topic of Michaels, how's his old flame next door?"

"Fine, why? You expect her to suddenly need something?"

"She *is* a writer, so I don't know. I know you guard your privacy."

"She's my neighbor, has been for years, and, quite frankly, has never been a problem. I can handle her. Why are you and that character Mr. Parker concerned with her?" Victor was caught off guard for a moment at the mention of Tate Parker's name, and Bob caught it. "Victor? Is there something you need to enlighten me about?"

"Parker asked about her as well. I suppose it makes sense, since he's privacy-sensitive, too. His legal paperwork hasn't been as orderly, either, since you brought him up."

"Well, let me know what you figure out. If there's nothing further ... oh, come to think of it, there is one more thing." He paused as the young valet attendant opened the driver's side door of his chase vehicle. "Did you ask for the Karmann Ghia's frame to be reinforced before it came to me?"

Victor's taciturn look was all Bob needed—for now. "Why?"

"You're probably safer in this car from a weight standpoint than I remember about this brand. Bon voyage, and say hello to Elena for me. You'll let me know when and where to send the car carrier." A satisfying click of his car door and he left.

The experienced lawyer stood there, puzzled for a moment, and wondered what Bob hadn't told him. He also wondered why Elena hadn't shared their return information and made a mental note to ask her.

Compartmentalized for now, Victor redirected his attention to the matte gray roadster in front of him. He didn't even understand his own need to put "his new baby" through certain paces before it was shipped home to Switzerland. He knew to drive in such harsh winter conditions was irrational and would likely damage the unprotected undercarriage, as Bob had implied. *After all, I highly doubt I'd drive it in such conditions at home*, he accepted.

Bob's adamancy pushed my stubborn button. He's probably right, quite childish, but I've already convinced Elena. Besides, a little ice on roads has rarely prevented us from driving at any point, let alone our latest finished project.

Or so Victor believed.

ARRIVED

THEY DIVIDED THE eleven-hour drive between two days, enjoyed a relaxed pace, and spoke more than they had in weeks. The trip was fairly uneventful until the couple needed to get the chains on the car tires, always a tricky operation. Nonetheless, Victor and Elena finally checked into their Park City ski-in/ski-out condo, a lovely mountainside getaway. They unpacked the "little car that could," as they'd nicknamed it, and reached out to friends expected to have already arrived.

Snow was in the crisp, mountain air. Cloud cover hinted at an approaching storm. Flat lighting always challenged activities both on and off the slopes.

Chapter 114

IN THE LOOP

THE BUSY SPECIAL agent spent little time in her office of late. So when she picked up her hotline phone, Aubrey startled Julie.

"Need I be worried or honored?" Julie questioned. *It's never a bad idea to test one's timing when dealing with the Feds, even when a particular Fed is your best friend from college.* Such thinking allowed Julie to know the limits of what to share when, a trick developed early in their relationship during their college days.

Aubrey let out a deep breath. "Well, to be fair—"

"Oh, that's not good," Julie interrupted.

"Both was going to be my reply. Thanks for not making me track you down."

"Track me down. Hmm ... I guess that's my cue to say you're welcome?"

"I understand. Let me get right to the point."

"'Preciate if you would."

Aubrey pressed the speakerphone button. "Yes, I just put you on speaker. No, I'm not alone in my office."

"I figured both. With whom do I have the pleasure of sharing this call today?" Julie spoke as if with her youngest child's classmates.

"I'll let them introduce themselves. They're working a particular angle of this case with me."

"Ugh. I'm a case angle now? I mean, I've always been a case, but *now* I'm an '*angle.*'" She moaned as the pair of agents snickered and stated their names.

"Julie, listen. You aren't in trouble, but you will be if you aren't one hundred percent honest when you answer a few questions."

This isn't a normal thing for my close friend to say. Something's not right in her office.

As Aubrey went through a couple of "housekeeping" items, she then ended with another odd statement. "I know you've always been straightforward with me, so let's just continue with our tradition, okay?"

"Of course," was all she could say while she tried to discern the "between the lines" stuff and grab a notepad and pen.

"Is there anything noteworthy you want to share with us before we start the Q and A?"

"In fact, I do. I've just been through several hours of interrogation with local law enforcement, so I won't be able to handle too much of the fun and games you perhaps have planned."

"Why have you been through an interrogation?"

Julie explained everything that had happened with Dane, leaving out the more intimate details. Once finished, she breathed, slow and deep, to regain her composure.

"Well, that's all quite … um … relevant. Okay, you two know what you need to follow up on."

Julie heard a door close as Aubrey picked up the handset. *Hmm. A dynamic shift.*

"Julie, what the hell is going on?"

"What do you mean? I just told you everything going on. So no Q and A?"

"I mean with you and Dane? Have you slept with him?"

"Jesus, Aubrey, *that* was your takeaway? How? I said nothing about sex! I sure as hell hope you're alone in there, and why would you ask such a question?"

"You know I wouldn't ask if I wasn't alone, and I ask *that* because you sound more involved than I need you to be—especially now."

"What does 'especially now' mean? What's going on, Aubrey?"

"Well, have you?"

"No! Now what the hell's going on?"

"We've been given several leads to follow. One lead includes Rachel, Dane's ex, coming to the U.S. Another includes Tate Parker and his privacy concerns, and yet another includes you knowing too much about car renovation."

"Okay, if I sound confused, it's only because I am. What does I 'know too much about car renovation' mean? I do research about unfamiliar topics. Car renovation is unfamiliar to me, hence the necessary research to write intelligent pieces. What do I have to do with the other things? Dane's ex? Don't know her, don't care where she is or why. Tate Parker is certainly a curious being for me as well. Am I being accused of something? Please tell me. I haven't a clue as to what you're saying." Julie's heart started to pound. Her fear level rose.

"Since you're the person of concern for all these parties, we have to look more closely at you as well."

"Seriously? Wait, am I hearing this right? I mean, are you allowed to tell me these things? Do I need a lawyer? Is this a time to panic *and* freak out?"

"No, I'm technically not allowed to tell you these

things, but you're my best friend. If you're doing something stupid, I want you to have a reasonable chance to come in on your own and—"

"Holy shit," she muttered. "Okay, what do you want? I've told you everything that just happened. Ask me anything. I'll share what I know. Have I sounded anything but candid? Something you need to ask me? Or is this seriously about sex? A few weeks ago, you were practically cheering me on. Now, you're concerned I've gotten 'involved' and maybe, what, become a part of something? What are you saying?"

"Of course that's completely possible—a la Bonnie and Clyde—but, no, not at all. In fact, everything you shared earlier sounded honest, factual, and incontestable."

"Glad I've got *something* going for me."

"Julie, now is not the time to get snippy with me."

"You're accusing me of something, but I don't know what, and I warned you I'd just been through an interrogation. So, of course—"

"Was Dane with you?"

"So I'm gonna get a bit snippy. Dane? With me during the interrogation?"

"Yes."

"Yes, he was. Then he was questioned."

"Were you with him when he was questioned?"

"Yes ... no ... well ... part of it. I desperately needed a bathroom. Peeing is allowed, right?"

Aubrey chuckled. "Of course. You didn't hear everything he shared with the police, though, right?" She heard Julie's sigh of concession. "Julie?"

"No."

"Honey, we're not accusing you of anything. We're concerned you're being framed, and we don't know the who or the why. I'm … hang on," Aubrey murmured. The muffled phone allowed Julie to hear someone walk in then out.

"*What* is going on?"

"Julie, listen. I'm trying to help us both here. We've been able to locate Mr. Ponytail. He's getting on a plane, but we haven't anything conclusive to prevent him from doing so. Stalking, talking, and leaving town aren't reasons, unfortunately. Why would Tate Parker be concerned about his privacy? Do you know anything about Rachel's trip here?"

"Damn, Aubrey. Fire away! I don't know anything about either of them. Clearly, I'm not the one they're interested in. For me, I'd speculate they're interested in Dane. Rachel is his ex. Tate is his client. Are those two involved in something together? What does Dane know about them or have to do with them? Do you have anything I need to know? Aubrey, please, pitch me a hint because I'm falling for him all over again, which, by the way, isn't a good idea when I'm not even officially divorced yet. I'll see him in mere minutes. He's on his way to my room."

"Tell him you're concerned because of today's events. You need some answers. Your life has become a series of strange, even frightening, events—weirdoes following you and now almost running you over, bombs, his driver being gunned down, etc. Ask him what's up with Tate Parker and his increasing trips to your neighbor? What's his relationship with his ex? This gives you angles to work with. You've every right to understand what's up with him, if he's at all involved, etc. Ask him those things. Your woman's intuition and investigative curiosity will kick in, and you'll know which avenues to further pursue."

"Okay. I can make it work, but why do I get the feeling this isn't my choice? It's kind of your nice way of telling me I need to do this or I'll be in serious trouble?"

"Because you're right."

The knock came almost on cue. "He's here."

"Good luck, honey."

Chapter 115

ASK TO RECEIVE

"ROOM SERVICE."

Julie put her cell phone down and went to the door. She looked through the peephole, though she didn't need to. "I didn't order anything, but thank you." *Maybe he'll be put off by such silliness.*

"That's not what I was told, madam."

Guess avoidance was wishful thinking. And so the seduction begins. Julie filled her lungs slowly. *I can do this. Ha. Like I have a choice.*

As she unbolted the door's lock, her "server" stood in the doorway waiting for the signal to come in. "Good evening, ma'am." Dane looked at ease and shamelessly handsome in simple stonewashed jeans and an untucked, turquoise, button-down rolled up twice to mid-forearm. His hair was still wet from his shower. His fresh scent bathed her senses. *Mmm ... all male.* He carried a bottle of pinot noir in his right hand and two wine glasses in his left.

"Perfect accessories for your attire," she teased. His eyes followed Julie's down to his hands.

He raised his head but skimmed her body with appreciative eyes and a smug grin on the way up to meet her gaze. *Easy, Pal. You can't push her against the wall again quite yet.*

She peeked up, took in the entire scene at her doorway, and caught his once-over. His intensity zeroed in on her face. Julie broke their eye contact and glanced down, wondering what he'd seen to cause such a confident stare. When she realized she could've easily won a wet or dry T-shirt contest in her pajama tee and shorts, instinctively her hands flew up to cover her breasts. *Traitor body giving away everything. At least he can't see between my legs.* She attempted to console herself. She blushed but couldn't meet his stare. As she turned on her heel, she threw over her shoulder, as low-key as possible, "Come in and grab the door, please, while I grab a robe."

"No need on my account."

"I'll opt not to reply to your comment, other than to say my letting you in can't be a good idea." *All bad things happen at night.* She smirked. *Well, not all.*

I'm not in yet, at least where I want to be, Dane restrained from saying aloud.

"Oh boy, I can only imagine what you were just thinking." *Cuz I know what I was thinking.*

"No need to imagine. I'm fine with sharing—"

"No need." She cut him off, lighthearted but firm, and let Dane just inside the doorway. She waited for him to push the door closed, then turned around when she hadn't heard the click. Again, he analyzed her movements. She shook her head and smirked at him. *I wonder what's attached to his bottle of wine. Whatever it is, I'm sure I'll want it, despite what I'm supposed to do for Aubrey.* Aubrey sobered her thoughts, forced her to refocus. *A late-night visit means one of two things—a fantasy seduction or a cruel reality. Either way, this visit is going to deeply affect us both.* Overwhelmed with desire to grab Dane and kiss him fiercely made her shudder with restlessness.

His keen study of her edgy movements aroused them both. Julie's core muscles clenched in anticipation of the questions she knew she had to ask, as well as the willpower she sensed she'd already lost. She shook not from any cold but from the intense ache inside her, an almost merciless struggle. "I need to address this … um … situation, right now, instead of just allowing our irrefutable attraction to sweep us beyond a point of no return, kind of like a powerful current dragging us out to sea."

"I'm pleased to hear you say 'irrefutable.' I concur, your honor." He chuckled and closed the door.

Julie's fiery expression fueled Dane's desire. It smoldered just below his calm exterior. "Point of no return. Yes. That's what we need to avoid." Julie pressed her legs together, then saw Dane catch her. "If we can avoid or even conquer this point of no return, or never reach it, better yet, I'll be sa—*we'll* be safe." Even as she spoke those words and drew her robe tight across her chest, she knew the possibility of being strong enough to resist their pull didn't exist. "Morning's a safer time for us to meet." Their chemistry, their attraction, was so powerful, it enchanted them. She knew not *if* but *when* their skin touched again, that electrical current they shared would spark a dangerous path of zero resistance.

Backing up just inches, she took a deep, steadying breath. "Dane, what are you doing here?" She spoke in such hushed tones, the intimacy in her voice startled even her. She stood, frozen. Again, his fresh shower scent of strong male mixed with complete dominance, splashed with musk and teakwood, seized control of her judgement. *He's a powerful aphrodisiac just standing there. Oh shit, did the room get stuffy, or is it the robe?*

His slight nod acknowledged her question. "Safe. Noteworthy word choice, but safe from what or whom? Each other? Hmm." Again, he nodded. "The answer to your other question is I couldn't sleep." He attempted to sound indifferent. Inside, however, he felt anything but. He raised his eyebrows and shrugged his shoulders, a silent request for entrance farther into the room. As Julie let him pass, Dane breezed by so close, the audible energy between them crackled and caused both to gasp at the shock. He shot her a surprised, wide-eyed glance and was met by hers. *Oh boy* was all he could think.

Almost consumed by his own lascivious thoughts like fire embers, he summoned the last crumbs of self-control he possessed. He placed the bottle and stemware on the tall dresser next to the flat-screen TV and tried to be casual. "Crazy day's events. Nervous about tomorrow's presentation? I am." *Feeble, transparent excuse. I know better with her.* He'd stood in his hotel room and groped for any excuse to be in the same space with her. *Why hasn't she answered me?* He turned. *She's checking me out! No shit.*

"What?" *Uh-oh.*

"Not very original. All you could come up with?" she questioned, indignant with her hands on her hips.

"What are you say—"

"I call bullshit. You know me better than that, and since when are you nervous about any presentation? Do you think I was born last night?"

His small smile and lowered eyes betrayed the truth. Dane stared at the corkscrew in his hands. Julie watched him play with it for a few seconds. *Wish that thing was me.* He turned, as if he'd heard her thoughts. With a decisive grip, he opened the bottle. "Total transparency?"

"Of course." She swallowed—twice. "Always." *Holy crap! Had I said my thoughts aloud?*

Take your time. Dane advised himself. *Breathe. In and out. Slow and deep.*

Julie let out a steady stream from her lungs, too. *Have I been holding my breath since you entered the room?*

"I simply wanted to be with you. If I can't have you right now, then I could at least be with you and talk business." *Business. Meant to calm. Is it working?* Their soft smiles fractured the tidal pull between them long enough for Dane to finish opening the bottle of wine and pour a little in each glass. "Plenty of deals and agreements have been accomplished during a game of golf or over dinner and wine, right?" He turned around to hand her one and realized she hadn't moved an inch, legs pressed together.

Her nod was just perceptible. *How much of this do I buy?* "We need to talk."

"We aren't going to play a round of eighteen right now. It's 9:30 at night. We've already had dinner. I figured a nightcap might calm ... well ... perhaps *my* nerves." Still rooted where she stood by the bathroom door, where he'd brushed past her, he admitted, "Who the hell am I kidding? From the look on your face, not you."

He took a small step toward her and stretched out his offering. "You shrewdly assess me, as I've been doing to you since you opened the door in your ... um—"

"P-pajamas," she offered. Self-conscious, she pulled her robe tighter. *There's that smug smile again. Damn it, and it's so utterly hot. He knows exactly what he's doing. How am I supposed to ask about today?*

"Okay." His pause and smile gave him away. "We both physically felt and heard a spark, a current snap between us. A toast, shall we?" His deep voice dropped any remnants of professionalism. The personal shift intoxicated her as he took over. "Take the glass." Julie did as instructed. Her gracious acceptance camouflaged her body's need to touch Dane. "To our successful interrogation today, our preparation tonight, and our teamwork tomorrow." Emboldened by the alcohol's dominant berry flavor in their mouths, Dane strategically sat in the desk chair.

Just two places for Julie to sit remained options—the reading chair between the bed and the window, but she'd have to brush past him to do so, or the bed.

"Please don't tell me you plan to stand the entire time I'm here. Would you prefer to sit here at the desk?" He stood, showing his good manners and upbringing.

She glanced at the window and noticed they'd become steamy around the edges. *How did we do that already?* Reticent and uncertain as to how either sitting option might be construed, Julie took several more steps into the room, sunk to the floor, and leaned her back up against the bed.

Dane laughed aloud. He couldn't help himself. "Honestly? Do you think I'm some savage? I'd just accost you here in your room? Okay. If I thought I could get away with it," he teased, "if you'd respond and love every second of it? Total transparency? Of course I would. Now how do you feel? Better that we got this out in the open?" Julie couldn't help but laugh, too, even as questions from the day burned on her tongue.

The music she'd put on earlier to relax shifted the room's already-charged energy. Dane didn't miss its cue, either.

"I'd say *nice* music, but some Buddha Bar mixes are anything but."

She swallowed and looked down at her hands in her lap. When she spoke, she didn't recognize the sultry voice as her own, as it further bared another hint of her surrender. "I don't know whether to laugh but be aghast at your incredible honesty, be offended that you haven't already accosted me, or just thankful that you're a gentleman and know not to screw things up for the morning. I'm completely horrified I just said all those things, but ... um ... yes, definitely better it's all out in the open."

Then he was on her, unable to deny any longer the ache in his lips. His needed to be on hers. Crouched with both hands holding her face to his, he explored her mouth, which she gave into. As abruptly as he'd kissed her, he let her go, then he returned to the chair. *She is so damn delicious, like an addiction. I need more.*

Breathless, she sipped her wine. *What the hell just happened? Did I imagine it? Fuck, that was hot.* "Before we talk business"—her chest heaved as she caught her breath—"which we truly need to do," *what is wrong with me,* "and about more than just necessary preparation, we first *need* to decide how to manage this ... this ... hypnotic chemistry between us. Holy shit! I can't believe I just said that, either." Julie chugged the wine to dull her fragmented nerves, like a calm wave before an anticipated storm.

Her head sank back against the mattress as she closed her eyes and succumbed to the wine's heady effect. She felt Dane's energy shift again and, through the languid opening of her eyes, confirmed he'd moved to squat in front of her with the open bottle of wine this time.

"Are you trying to get me drunk? Take advantage of me?" she whispered.

"Yes." He waited for a slap, but it never came. "If you aren't open to being stone-cold sober with me, which *was* the original idea, as if we both didn't know this, I'd take you slightly drunk and enchantingly disheveled."

Her humored, shocked expression tried on indignant.

"Ah … so you *were* playing me a fool, were you? Just wanted in my panties."

"Julie, you're nobody's fool, least of all mine." He refilled her glass. "Yes, I did, and still do, want in your appetizing panties, pajamas, whatever you have on."

"Assuming I'm wearing any panties at all," she taunted. *Oh God, did I just say that?* Her eyes glistened, provocative and restless.

Dane groaned, closed his eyes, secured the bottle on the floor next to the dresser, and didn't dare shift the insane tightness of his jeans zipper. "Touché, Mrs. Archer." *Even nervous, she's still got sass. Damn.* "God forgive me for all the lies I've told you about how I was going to take this slow with you, perhaps just talk business over a nightcap or two, or three, and. …" He cursed as he needed to relieve the throb between his legs. "Christ, Julie, clearly I'm aware of the energy that crackles between us. It's intoxicating. Can't you taste it? It's almost tangible! You think I'm not aware of this powerful, shit, I don't know what it is … force field or something? I've never felt this intense passion for anybody other than you. It's always only been you. God knows I've tried to deny it, and God also knows I can't now." He leaned in and kissed her again, tender but commanding.

"Dane—" Julie trembled and tried to catch her breath.

He cradled both sides of her head and smothered her words with another kiss, more intense, determined, intimate. Her soft moan of approval awakened any shred of dormant longings. Dane wanted this vulnerability between them to last, so he used one hand to reach for her glass. Instead, she pulled back from his lips and took another sip. Sheepishly, she smiled. "Try some more?"

He shook his head, took the raised glass, and placed it next to the wine bottle. "On second thought, we don't want to rush into anything. So let's talk business first and enjoy our nightcap after." He re-established himself on the floor to Julie's left and smiled, very proud of himself.

"Wait. What just happened?"

"You wanted to talk. I'm just trying to be a gentleman and not a total cad."

"So now I appear to be a Siren and have to *attempt* to act ladylike while sitting on the floor dazed and panting, as if I've just come … um … uh … *in*—shit—arrived from a workout? Oh, I've been worked out, all right. Is *that* being a gentleman? I think you're a complete scoundrel *and* a cad." She crawled to snatch back her wine glass and then inched away from Dane to be on the adjacent corner of the bed to pout, thankful, very confused by her own mixed emotions.

Dane chuckled and shifted on the floor to Julie's end of the bed, so their shoulders touched. "Aren't they the same thing?"

"Whatever."

"You're the writer," he teased. "Know what I think?"

"Do tell." She sulked.

"You're cute when you sulk."

"One minute, our tongues explore wine in the other's mouth, and the next minute? Eh, we're talking about whether you're a cad or a scoundrel."

Dane's genuine laugh egged on Julie's sullenness. Still he offered, "I think you're teased, relieved, totally turned on, and confused."

"What's your point?" She stared at the glass and appreciated the light tannins. *I hate how his power over me has me so fucking turned on.*

"No point. Just an observation. Here's another one." Dane turned to nuzzle Julie's neck. His breath caught. "I'm dizzy you're so fucking delicious."

"I ... I don't understand. Why did you just kiss me like you meant it, twice, then stop? And now tell me I make you dizzy but won't touch me? Is this a game to you? Testing for an effect? To see if I still move you? Matter to you? Or what? It sure as hell looked like you were." Her voice whined in despair.

Sounding harsher than intended, Dane turned his head toward her. "Is that what you think? No effect on me? Are you kidding me or testing *me?*"

Julie glanced at their shoulder connection and placed her hand on the floor between their hips. Her knees fell together on Dane's leg. The change in his tone felt like a punch to her gut. "I know why you stopped, but I don't want you to. It feels wrong but right. I want you to kiss me again." She placed her cheek against his shoulder, and Dane shifted just enough to kiss her forehead, then her nose.

"Julie, I won't stop there." He waited for her to lift her eyes to his.

As she did, she raised her lips, too. "Then don't."

He accepted them, brooding and hungry but gentle at first over his shoulder, just the way she offered them. Desperate to feel her against him, he reached his left arm across his chest, brushing past her breast as he secured the back of her neck. *Oh damn, I want more of her, any way possible.* He slipped his right arm behind her and pulled her gently into his lap in one smooth, powerful movement and cradled her. He drew in her perfume of fresh, soft flowers, the allure of springtime.

Julie's arm was tucked in with her palm against Dane's

muscular chest. *Holy shit. Is he real?* She felt his strength pulse through all of him, rock-hard through those jeans, his heartbeat so wild it felt ready to burst. He tensed when she looked up at him with searching eyes.

"I do have so many questions I need to ask you," she reminded him, mesmerized by his eyes. "Years of questions and unshared feelings. Instead, we act like sixteen-year-olds in heat."

The confident lawyer hadn't expected the vulnerability he felt. Watching her observe him grew fears he didn't recognize. "Are you positioned to push me away, because I won't let you." His heart braced for a reply it wouldn't accept.

Her gaze dropped to her hand and followed it up his chest, deliberate and slow, like it may never happen again and needed to be savored. When Julie cupped his broad, athletic shoulder, their dance at the reunion flashed in her memory. *I'd become weak-kneed with guiltriddled lust.* "Thank God I'm sitting down." She explored the skin on his neck under the collar and pulled herself to him as close as possible to erase his doubts as well as her own. *And now I just want him … no guilt.* She allowed herself to look up and stare into his warm eyes. Tears began.

Don't ask why. Dane guessed but just pulled up his knees to support her back as they kissed without hesitation, unhurried. It was thoughtful, yet almost primal, as their lips sought out undeclared truths. *I need to rip off her clothes.* Dane pulled back just enough to silently check in with her, no words, no business. Julie's tears had been exchanged for a smoldering gaze. *Need your skin.*

She lifted her chin just enough to consent to whatever he wanted. Dane grazed her lips with his and felt her body quiver. *Yes*, he hissed in his head. *Breathe.* His firm hand travelled down Julie's robed back to trace the tie around to the front and tug at it. She allowed the robe to fall open and stilled as his hot fingertips traced her thin shirt's strap. As he pushed the robe off one shoulder and exposed her neck, his lips left hers to kiss and nip a path down her graceful neck.

"What do you think?"

"I can barely breathe, let alone think, when you're this close. Do I have to?" she whimpered.

His impish smile and passionate kiss liquefied her insides. "Damn," he rasped. Another nip, a soft moan as he touched her skin, his hands sensitive to her body heat. As he slipped off the rest of her robe, Julie arched her sheer-covered breasts, nipples taut, into Dane's chest with an unfamiliar sensuality. His hands explored her back under the thin camisole and waistband of her bottoms. He cursed his amazement. "I had no fucking idea this feeling even existed. We've missed out on this—"

"Shhh … I need more of our skin to touch." She panted, now confident as her hands and knees straddled his thighs.

"You can't sit like that … impossibly provocative."

"Your point?" Julie gathered Dane's shirt by its hem, her fingers unhurried as she unfastened each button. He watched her hands, studied their sensual pace. She peeled the shirt off of his shoulders, then leaned in to feel his naked flesh on her lips as each inch of it was exposed to her. "Oh my God, you're not real … you're divine." Her tears free-flowed again, but Dane's head fell back on the mattress, entranced. She shimmied backward on his thighs and buried her nose in his skin on a path where his hip bones met his jeans and soaked in his heady, male scent. She retraced that path, fascinated by every kiss up his cut torso, and stopped only to lick and tease one nipple harder. She pushed his shirt over his shoulder tops but tangled his arms in it, delighted in her boldness. "Oh ... my ... look at this." *These pecs ... his heaven-scented neck.*

She tasted every inch of his neck at a mischievous, unconcerned pace and coaxed the other nipple with her fingers to insane sensitivity. When she reached his belt and began to unbuckle it, Dane grabbed her hands in one of his and flipped her onto her back on the floor before she'd even processed his possessiveness. Her hands above her head, his kiss scorched her senses while he rocked his hips into her thin bottoms, his belt and top button undone. *Oh shit.* "Don't stop. Please." She rose up to meet his incendiary rhythm.

He shifted his weight to hover above her again. *Whoa—* "My turn," he croaked. Almost unable to grasp their surreal scene, his warm lips left hers and swept across her soft cheek to caress below her ear. His slow release of her hands came with a quick but clear command to her with hypnotic eyes and a husky reminder. "My turn, baby. Be still." Her anxious gaze agreed.

His fingers spread wide to touch as much of her through her delicate camisole as possible down to its hem. Julie shuddered, her self-control teetered, but Dane was done playing the polished professional. He pushed up and over Julie in a plank and pulled his knees even with her hips. He looked straight into her eyes. All restraints in his brain snapped. Dane bent down and reclaimed her mouth while his hands reached under his chest, grasped the neckline of her thin top, and shamelessly ripped it apart, her bare, sensitive breasts now covered only by his warm, naked skin. She sucked in a startled breath from his mouth, wild and erratic. Her eyes flew open wide to meet his, her heart pounded. "Oops." His smirk was lascivious. "See what you do to me?"

Despite the erotic moment, she couldn't stop her flippant, insecure words. "Bet you say that to all the girls—"

"Julie." Dane's fierce interruption jarred her from a playful reverie. "I've never said or felt or thought anything like this before—to or with anyone—ever." She stared at Dane. Her mouth went dry, and she licked her lips. "Could you, right now, picture me doing this with another woman? I'm straddling your half-naked body, worshipping your soft breasts, and teasing you, making you squirm, wet, nearing *that* point of no return to which you so poetically referred when I first walked in." Julie opened her mouth to say something and thought better of it. "Could you? Answer me," he said, calm in his forceful-ness.

Hypnotized by his vehemence, she took an uneasy breath. Her eyes darted between him and anywhere else in the room.

"I'm waiting ... and I won't be *nice* about it in a minute."

"You've been with—"

"Look me in the eyes and just spit it out."

She raised her chin in defiance she didn't feel and did as he demanded, more aroused at his bare honesty and blatant control of her than she'd ever believed possible. "You've been with incredible women since we once knew each other, and. ..." *Okay, just brace yourself. He's going to leave, but you can deal with it. No matter what happens.* She checked her thoughts before speaking.

"And?" Dane snapped. *"Julie."*

Her worries tumbled out of her mouth. "And I'm

worried I don't stack up! There. Are you happy now?" She glared at him. "I mean, I know I'm pretty amazing, blah, blah, blah, but your dating résumé is a veritable list of 'Who's Who in the World of European Models,' if there is such a thing. Granted, some may be pretty smart, but I'm no damn model, that's for sure, and this is such an awkward conversation with me lying here like this and. ..." Her hands gestured frantically when Dane cut her off with a burst of laughter. She glared at him and tried to push him off of her.

"Not a chance! I told you it was my turn." He shook his head enough for her to see his amused scowl. As she began her protest in earnest, Dane clasped her hands and pushed them above her head again. "Irrational, stubborn, some things don't change." He laid on top of her, his bare chest on hers, and kissed her breathlessly. *Finally.*

She froze just long enough to catch on, felt the realization. *Oh. My. God.*

He kissed her again. "We'll simply restart my turn until you get it, until you come back to me, us, here, now."

"O—"

At last silenced by another lusty kiss, Dane smiled into it when he finally felt her body's acceptance. Julie looked drunk when he pulled back, grazing her cheek with his. His free hand roamed her naked side. "Thank you," he said softly.

"For what?"

"For not overthinking this anymore, for being present with me."

"Your bare chest is on mine."

"You figured it out." He lightly rubbed his body against hers to heighten the awareness.

With a sublime smile, her lips reached up to kiss him.

"Mm-hmm." Lips still connected, "Mind-blowing."

"We've waited so long to know what we feel like to-gether. I want to feel the rest of us the same way." He pressed his hips into her and felt her rock into him in response. Dane slid his hand off of Julie's and down her arm. "Your skin ... I want to touch all of you, cherish every bewitched inch of you." Dazed, he asked Julie, "Is this what you want? I have to stop now if it's not. I can't be like this with you much longer and stay in control of myself. I need to know, Julie." Like an imprisoned man starved from all human affection, Dane just stared into her limitless, teal eyes, mesmerized.

She shuddered. "Isn't it obvious? We passed that point of no return when you pressed your bare chest against me."

"That's not what I asked." He growled his demand and retracted his lips.

Without hesitation, breathless, Julie rose up to recon-nect their lips. "I want this, too, Dane. Please don't make me beg."

Chapter 116

LUNCH ERR-AND

WHILE VICTOR AND Elena enjoyed lunch with another couple at Legends Bar and Grill in Park City, Victor realized he'd left their new auto project plans at the rental house. Open to new investors to share expenses on this endeavor, Elena suggested, "Darling, why not run back and grab them?"

"Great idea, my love. Why not? It's not far from here."

"Be careful, though. The forecast has called for several inches this evening, but the skies look ominous now. Do you want me to go with you?" She shuddered, though they were settled in front of an outdoor fire pit, and pulled her ski jacket from the back of the chair to drape over her shoulders again.

Victor smiled at her as he shrugged on his parka and pulled up the zipper. "No, honey. I'll be fine. I won't be too long. I know right where I left them. Finish your coffee. Be right back, folks." He gave her a peck good-bye and turned for the door.

Chapter 117

OFF-ROAD

MOST TIMES OF the year, delivery truck drivers found the resort neighborhood reasonable to navigate. As spacious as roads were in the summer months, however, they turned perilous, slick, and clogged with stranded vehicles imbedded in snowbanks throughout the winter. The furniture delivery driver experienced nothing different that midafternoon. Angry, darkened skies promised several inches of snow and camouflaged small pools of black ice on poorly drained roads just to complicate matters.

"Hey, ya gotta pump the brakes, Pal," the shift supervisor offered his new driver. "Have ya ever driven in these conditions before?" Silence. "Concentrating. I see. Oh SHIT! Watch OUT!" Neither had seen Victor's small sports car skate across the road until it had bounced off of a snow-entrenched vehicle. They'd bisected it, much like a hammer through a slim tree branch.

The delivery truck slipped and skidded down the small hill, then crashed through a home's glass front door. Shattered pieces gave entry to the heavy truck, which hadn't met anything to stop its cruise through the house over the backyard deck. Like a seesaw at the park, the front end teetered at the swollen creek's edge. Each exhalation moved the cab and creek to their inevitable kiss.

The older man's head had smashed against the cab door's window. At first subdued, his survival instinct and the near-freezing mountain temperatures awakened him just enough to struggle with his underling for control of the steering wheel. "Shit … my head. What the hell happe—"

In mere seconds, the stronger man, however, scrambled to unbuckle his own seat belt, open the door to jump out, and pushed away his injured boss. "What are you doing? Hey! Where are you going? Help me!"

The truck lost its fragile balance during the struggle and lurched into the numbing waters. Jostled by the new danger of drowning, but woefully bewildered from his head injury, the old man grabbed at anything for help and landed on the new hire's long hair just as he was about to jump to safety. The driver's cursory moment of compassion compelled him to unbuckle his boss, free his ponytail, and jump into the racing waters to escape.

Left to save himself, the older man hyperventilated as he fell out of the submerged truck into the swollen, frigid flow and tried to gain some sort of bearings in the rising icy river conditions. "H-H-He-Help." He panted, short of breath, and clutched his aching chest. His legs sought something to stand on while he twisted back to the unstable truck. He couldn't catch himself as he again slammed his head on its hood and fell, unconscious, into the freezing waters. He slipped, wordless, below the surface.

The ponytailed driver watched from the bank, shivering, patient. "Thank you for sparing me from shooting you. The rule is no witnesses."

Chapter 118

HELPLESS

THE SLICK ROADS caught Victor a bit unaware. "Damn. Even just since lunch, they've become rather treacherous. Better grab those sandbags from the garage to bulk up this little girl while home." But as he rounded the turn, made blind by a snowplow's handiwork, Victor's small sports car lost what little grip it had on the road and skated diagonally across until it bounced off of a snow-entrenched vehicle. "Oh shit!" was all he could yell as the delivery truck carved his engine from the rest of the vehicle.

He swerved into a front yard and finally stopped when he hit a tree head-on. The lightweight roadster's crumpled front end hadn't done anything to protect Victor, either. Just a few lots from the same icy plunge the delivery truck had just made, Victor shivered from shock as he took inventory of his physical body. *I need help ... likely lucky in comparison to the truck's passengers. Still ...* "Where's ... phone? Need help ... now." *Painful breathing ... pooling blood ... not good.*

Victor had no idea exactly where the blood came from within his body. He knew, however, how the bitter cold bit his skin and the foul blood soured his senses inside the car ... didn't inspire confidence. *Must get out of car.* Somewhere behind him, he heard the little car's engine steam and hiss. *Either I'm weak, or I've a real problem.* The compressed driver's door proved more than he could manage. *Get out of the car, Victor.* Prodded by the voice in his head, his face contorting in agony, Victor tugged his legs free, inch by inch, from under the steering column. With what meager strength he still possessed, he grit his teeth and roared a string of vile words as he dragged his body through the wrecked window.

After he fell out of the little car in a heap, glass shards embedded in too many places for him to count, his pained eyes looked up to see the trunk of the tree he'd hit moments before. "Holy *shit*! How am I alive? Do I want to be?" Somehow Victor had escaped from the bisected car and crawled through icy, crunchy snow toward a house near the tree, desperate for aid. No one was home. "Not good." He knew the chances he'd find someone around were pretty slim in the vacation ski village. The conditions on the slopes were too good to be inside at home, despite the imminent stormy weather.

"Where's my phone?" He panted as he patted himself down gently. He turned to see the bloodied trail he'd left behind. Victor knew he was in trouble but still wondered what had happened to the truck that had hit him and ruined his new "baby."

"She's going to kill me," he muttered and sighed.

"I'll save her the hassle."

Victor looked startled to his right at the ponytailed man standing by the corner of the house, his clothes soaked, and a gun pointed at Victor. "You the driver? What the hell were you doing? Put that fucking thing down. Obviously, I'm not going to accost you, though I sure as hell have a right to." Victor coughed and began to shake, unable to ignite a normal fight-or-flight response.

The stranger didn't budge. He waited, frozen in place,

to confirm the man's identity. "Who are you?"

"Who am I? Who am I? I'm the driver you just hit, you son of a bitch. Who are *you*? I want your goddamned license and information ... after you call for help. I'm bleeding and freezing and—" Victor shivered harder, as shock insidiously took control of his tough guy act. *What the hell is going on?*

"Your name?" He took two steps closer, the gun still aimed at Victor.

"M-my n-n-name is in-in-injured, asshole. Put down the gun, man, a-a-and c-c-c-call for help, damn it." *What is this guy's problem?* Chills and nausea inundated Victor. He leaned over and vomited the lunch he'd eaten with Elena down the steps he'd managed to drag himself up. "N-n-not so g-g-g-good second time around." Victor lay back, exhausted. His ears rang. His vision blurred. He looked at the stranger. "If you won't help me, c-c-could you at least ca-call my wife, Elena, and let her ... kn-know I've been in an accident?" *This isn't good.*

The stranger lowered his gun and walked behind Victor. He bent over the dying man and spoke in a low, measured tone. "Victor."

The lawyer struggled but looked up at him, unable to focus. "How do you kn-know my nn-name?"

"Elena sent me to take care of you."

"D-d-don't understand. You know m-my wife? Just had l-l-lunch—"

"She wanted you to know there would be no more issues between you." The smoothtalking stranger answered and raised his weapon once again.

"Wait! Please ... don't ... understand."

"Do you think she's stupid? You continue to support Rachel, despite your wife's demands, and I quote, to let 'the gold-digging whore' go."

Violent shudders stormed through Victor's body. Despite the freezing cold, the sweat poured down his face and the pungent fear roiled up and down his broken body. He knew this stranger wasn't here by mistaken identity. "Tell Elena I've always l-l-l-loved her." He crumpled, prostrate on the steps, his breath shallowed.

"'Her' Elena or 'her' Rachel, to clarify?" tormented the stranger.

But Victor didn't reply.

"Perfect. Saved me another bullet."

Chapter 119

FINALLY

NO NUMBER OF years could wipe out the passion between them, though somehow, they'd never gone beyond kissing in high school. Now, as adults, they were acutely aware of an intense, undeniable attraction that bordered on palpable, erotic magic. "Like we'd been thwarted lovers in a past life."

An alarm in Dane's head alerted him for the need to go slow. *Tonight isn't about mere sex with this woman. No regrets this time. No interruptions.* He shifted off of Julie and offered his hand as he got off the floor. At first, she was confused. As she stood, however, he sunk to his knees in front of her, like a well-choreographed ballet. His hands skimmed her bare sides, took her pajama bottoms with them, and left her completely exposed to him. Julie's breath caught in her throat at the familiarity of his controlled moves, while her hands raked his disheveled hair back into place with her fingernails.

Spellbound by her powerful touch, he buried his senses where the pajama bottoms used to meet her hips. He inhaled her scent as he kissed her naked, creamy skin and moaned in ragged sighs. "Oh—my—God—"

"Oohhh … I know."

All I want to do is put your back against the wall, bury myself inside of you, and stay there for the rest of the night. Correction—for the rest of my life. "I'm sorry, I can't help it. Your skin is like perfumed satin." He knew their connection would be so extreme, he could lose his mind and forget what happened between them. Without realization, he froze at the thought. "What is it?"

"Decades of waiting, total access now." His voice husky, concerned, he gazed up at her with lustful, hooded eyes. "I somehow need to savor every moment." She sank to her knees to face him, their noses mere inches apart. Another moment in heavy silence, his restless fingers scorched her torso. "This isn't impulse or infatuation, some opportunity or mere convenience." Hands by their shaking sides, he kissed her deep, luxuriating in the taste of her. Intoxicated, he lingered and craved more. "I froze from fear ... of the possibility of going crazy, I mean ... like ... lose-my-mind crazy, forget-the-feeling-of-touching-you crazy."

He seems to so believe this, what do I say or do? His personal muse, she opted to play it straight—wide-eyed, but straight. "And your conclusion, Counselor?"

Dane consumed her in his embrace and ravaged her mouth until she couldn't breathe or think beyond his name. Her nipples, rigid against his chest, begged for his touch. "So be it."

She smiled and burst out in laughter. "I'm sorry! I don't mean to laugh. You've always been so serious, so I'm just relieved." Her whole body melted even more into his. "I had no idea two people could feel this way, either. Our skin, our chemistry ... decadent ... illegal."

Dane once again brought them to their feet and took a slight step back. As his desire tested the zipper's strength, he freed his jeans of the strain to take his wallet and room key out of the stiff pocket.

"This draw is … primal, an imprint. I've waited my entire life … for you, for this." Julie flushed, hungry for his touch as she watched his every move. "What you do to me. …"

"*You've* ensnared *me*, Mr. Michaels. I'm at your mercy." She watched his pants fall to the floor. Her lips parted as she lost her breath and hesitated to look up from his hands, stilled by his sides. Her head stayed down as her gaze travelled up to his. *I don't dare move. He's right. Memorize every sinewy movement.* "I mean, look at you. You're … you're … perfect." Her eyes grew wide as she realized she'd spoken aloud.

Dane's pupils dilated, almost in disbelief at her words. He kicked his clothes aside and clasped her face. As their lips no more than touched, he murmured on them, "Perfect for you."

She kissed him hard, no longer patient with her own longings. Julie hooked her thumbs into his brief's band, skimmed his low back with her extended fingertips, tugged downward in command, and escorted them to the floor. He groaned and watched as she sprung him free, grazed his rock-hard flesh with her lips as she rose, and whispered against his lips, gruff and dominating, "No more barriers between us."

"Holy shit!"

Their naked realization made them both greedy with need, their hands determined, bodies magnetized, hypersensitive. Undefined doubts and unanswered questions were cast aside like their clothes. So were their sudden, desperate fears as they gave in to each new touch between them.

At first, so absorbed in her, Dane mistook Julie's trembling as a green light. When her hands quieted, he tasted her familiar, salty tears in their kiss. He gathered her hands onto his bare chest and simply held her tight. Grateful for any reason to hold her, let alone naked against him, he felt her relax. Her sense of safety in his arms seemed to grant permission for more gentle tears to fall. *Just hold her*, he decided.

Julie looked up into Dane's eyes. Her tears slowed to a trickle. *What is she looking for?* As he thumbed off her tears, he just held her face, a thoughtful awareness.

The understanding of the gentle gesture and tenderness in his eyes further quieted her fears. *Is it conceivable he's here for more than tonight? This isn't merely a calculated conquest to distract me from what he's up to? IF he's even up to anything.* Again, unasked questions hovered. *Where will our choices lead us?*

Dimmed lights, cool hotel room, and sultry music staged the seduction. *Who's seducing whom?*

Dane felt her thoughts yield to some internal decision. Astute enough to know they may not see each other for a very long time—possibly ever again—they hesitated for just a moment more. Aware. The point of no return. A sensual bass rhythm hypnotized. Aware. When their lips met once more, there'd be no pulling them apart. Naked bodies vibrated. Aware. They accepted their fate without a word spoken. A tender kiss deepened.

Dane's lips sought to caress away Julie's fallen tears, first from her dampened cheeks, then down her soft, stained neck. Her involuntary shudder was his carnal cue. He gently worked his way to the back of her neck, sending chills over her inflamed skin. Brilliant stars mixed with the waxing moon to cast a luminous glow on her body. His skilled touch ignited her ... everywhere. "We've waited so long."

"We're so ready." Julie's hands stretched up behind her to find the back of Dane's neck, damp with restraint. She held him close and surrendered her achy flesh to his brazen, starved hands. He knew to be thoughtful, deliberate, with every move, every touch, every connection.

"Whatever I told you"—he murmured behind her ear and felt her body quiver in response—"about my noble intentions. ..." He then pressed his hard body into hers and tilted his hips into her back, nibbling her lower lobe. "God"—he rolled her sensitive tips in his fingers—"please forgive me. They've disappeared." His ragged confession in her ear begged, "Forgive me." As if in a dance, he moved her away from the window and pivoted her back to the adjacent wall to face him.

"I forgive you. I pray I can forgive myself." She kissed him ravenous, their tongues teased, desperate and deprived of decades.

Dane pulled her one knee over his hip. "You've nothing to forgive yourself for." He pressed his hardness against her opening, pinning her, and took her hands into his own, doing the same on either side of her head. "You've done everything you could to keep me at least at arm's length distance ... if not a continent's." His chuckle was soft. "I'm being a selfish bastard." Just his firm hands on her own, palm-to-palm, caused her knees to give. "Maybe this convinces you I'm here for the long haul. I'm not walking away ... again."

"The pinning me to the wall or your near pene—" She began to tease him.

Dane interrupted her. "Stay put," and he let go of her hands. *Oh my Lord, my palms ache without his touch.* Their hips still connected, he reached for his wallet and withdrew a familiar, small packet. "As much as I dislike these things and wish I'd had children with you, we don't need any further challenges right now. Agreed?"

Julie flinched at the mention of children, a flash of guilt in her eyes, but sighed in agreement. "Just to be clear, I'm no fan of condoms, either, but full disclosure, Counselor—I'm clean. You?"

"Yes." He looked her straight in the eyes and held them for a moment.

He ripped open the small pouch and enlisted her help in rolling on the thin sheath. It glistened in the room's soft lighting. Dane moaned when Julie's hands touched him. "That. Was. Insane. Hot." Dane bore into Julie's eyes. *Damn, I hope you feel about me as I do about you.* He began to kiss her again, at first gentle and dreamlike. But as their kiss intensified, almost devouring each other, he plunged into her in one full motion. The oxygen left their collective lungs. "Holy fucking hell—"

Julie shuddered. "My God—had no idea."

Dane shifted Julie's hands around his neck. "Hold on." Then he just lifted her other knee to wrap around him and, with the wall as leverage, pushed into her farther. She took all of him.

Neither dared move at first. Then he pulled almost all the way out and claimed her again, buried deep within her. "Where I've always fucking belonged," he said, his inhales harsh, uneven. "Any further questions?"

"None," she whimpered.

Connection fierce, nerve endings ignited, synapses fired. Dane slid out of Julie, then sank into her again and again. He anchored their bodies against the wall with his hands flanking her shoulders in an exquisite, unhurried rhythm. His breath hot against her ear, "Convinced?"

"Of what?"

He used his forehead as another anchor over her shoulder. "I'm not in you, in this, just for tonight." He paused inside her.

She couldn't resist her giggle. "Can't stay in me forever. Besides," she rasped, as she caught her breath, "if you tried to run away right now, I wouldn't be held liable for killing you. I'd be let off for your cruel and inhumane treatment, crime of passion."

"I'm serious. I'm—"

"So am I." Her clasp was firm on his damp neck. "Please," she begged, "don't stop." She turned over her shoulder to trail kisses on the inside of his forearm, then over her other shoulder to kiss his jawline. "You're not real."

"Surreal or real—from the start … you … this … feels …" His voice was hoarse with emotion. "Hang on tight." He snatched her dewy back from the wall and spun their connected bodies around to lay her on the bed, tender but single-minded. He moved in and out of her faster, deep within her.

Julie's shallow, erratic breaths signaled how close she was until Dane halted just outside of her wet heat. Her eyes flew open with a gasp. "Good." He fought for a breath. "Now keep your eyes … on me." Julie barely nodded, as he began a dizzying, relentless pace, their gazes unwavering, more resolute, with each thrust. She rose up to meet him, complete surrender as he plunged deeper, harder yet more sensual than the last. Eyes riveted, communication at their souls' levels, a synthesis they'd never experienced before.

"How can this be?" Julie begged in disbelief. *What's happening? I can't control this … like a … free fall.* Frightened by her overwhelm, she was compelled to break eye contact. Julie pulled Dane to her and kissed him, tasted him, their connection. A pulsing bass softened the harsh, clear electronic keyboards in an inviting, almost hypnotic mix in the background.

As his lips left hers and trailed from her jaw along her graceful neck, she accepted his lips and lifted her chin to the ceiling, eyes closed in ecstasy. "Open them. I want you to see me worship you."

"That scares me."

"To be worshipped?"

"Yes."

"Why?"

"Because it lets you in … close."

"And?"

Her shallow breathiness betrayed the professional tone she tried to use. "We have meetings in the morning." *None of which I care about right now. Please see through my fears.*

"I believe we're already talking mergers here." He pulled out of her with a sudden, fiery glint. "Look at me. I'm not boring you, am I?" He set his jaw.

Her head turn from side to side almost imperceptible, she couldn't banter and so chose raw honesty. "I'm afraid," she whispered.

Dane eased back into her, gliding upward, deeper. *I want this with you forever. When do I tell you?*

Julie's head rolled back as she pushed her aching body up to meet his, giving in to the rhythm, the emotional chaos, between them.

"Look at me, baby. Don't be afraid. Haven't you heard me? Together is where we've always belonged. Let's enjoy us for as long as possible." He felt her shiver and savored how close she was. Then he drove himself to her core. Her gaze flew open and once again locked onto his.

"Oh God—Dane!"

"I'm with you, baby—"

Finally, they surrendered to each other.

ACKNOWLEDGEMENTS

Ever wonder how a book "happens"? I promise you. It doesn't just happen.

I'm guided by Gem and a fleet of Guardian Angels in varied forms.

I'm loved, fed, and often just (barely) tolerated by my handsome and generous husband, Brandon, and our three terrific kids, Jessica, Alexandra, and Jack (now four including our new son-in-law, Drew). What a WILD, crazy, and amazing last 18 months!

Mom, Dad, Phyl, Steph, Niki Roosma for always asking "where is it?" or "how's it going?"

Daune Thompson for her relentless and unyielding support, encouragement, guidance, and love. I'm BEYOND grateful to you! Angel on a mission!

Cheri for her firm hand in pulling the story line out of me. Angel. Period.

Lois Lee for sane listening, tough organizing, sanity keeping, and still loving me. Angel with a tilted halo.

The following "angels" are mentioned in the order in which we met or alphabetically ... I think! Jonna Bournias (an eye for clean rooms); Phoenix Police Department's Community Engagement Team, especially Detective Joel Leavitt, for organizing my terrific experiences with the outstanding men and women who serve our community, and Officers Jeannie Leonard and Corynn Haggerty for allowing me to tag along and bug them with tons of questions, even now; Scottsdale Police Department for their guidance, especially Detective Derek Litchfield and Retired Officer Reggie Johnson, both men with humor-peppered patience; B2 (golden advice); Jerry Lee Sadler, who generously brainstormed forever ago with me; former neighbor Bud who knows cars; Zach Frangos for sharing colorful escapades; and Jill McMahon for her perspective about character psychology AND showing up at 5 a.m. OTF!

Joyce Mochrie, my copy editor and proofreader with an eagle eye for "One Last Look." Thanks for having my back, front, etc.

Kris Hetrick and Kerry Pellicane for sharing with their friends and starting a movement! Your support, friendship, and encouragement pushed my next steps.

Beta readers Lisa Berry, Andrew Hetrick, and Michele MacCollum, who answered the call to action with candor and kindness. Thank you! Thank you! Thank you!

Sisters in Crime/Desert Sleuths Chapter, wonderful, real people with great guidance and kind words. Damon Suede, who challenged my thinking at a Romance Writers of America/Desert Rose Chapter Workshop (another great group of people). Your resource *Activate* is exceptional! Thank you for listening at O-Dark Thirty on the way to the airport, then asking me those hard questions. Good luck in your new role! Darren and Georgia Hardy, Julie Ward-Glen, the A-Team, Insane Productivity, and the High-Performance Forum programs for teaching me how to leverage my laziness—SANELY.

Orange Theory Fitness Coach Joe for keeping Jill x 2 fit and engaged—even at 5 a.m.; Dr. Mike Mitchell, wife, Danette, Lloyd and wife, Kathy, for putting Humpty Dumpty back together again multiple times, then keeping her healthy; Dr. Robert Guyette and team, Kendis Browner, Sabree Loera, Trinity and the Desert Nail Spa peeps for keeping me fab; Katie Mathis for making me look good in photos; Carlos Avelenda for creating sensual cover art; Fred Hughes for keeping my website sultry and website freak-outs to a cool minimum; Lee Wilmeth for addressing computer glitches; Charles for reminding me when NaNoWriMo approaches and keeping books in order. Paul Salvette and BB team for layout and diligence.

Lastly, a shout out to Junipine Resort in beautiful Sedona, Arizona for a peaceful escape to finish hard-core editing.

See? Books don't just happen. WHAT a team effort!

ABOUT THE AUTHOR

R. Jill Maxwell, the author of two romantic suspense fiction novels, **G.A.S.P.** and **B.A.I.T.,** has been weaving stories since childhood. Married for 36 years, she is a proud parent to three young adults and one groovy grandchild. **Daily Parenting Reflections: A Journey Within** marks her first venture into non-fiction.